Beauty and the Rake

The Rookery Rogues
Book 3

Erica Monroe

Qullfire Publishing

BEAUTY AND THE RAKE

Copyright © 2015 by Erica Monroe

Excerpt from *Stealing the Rogue's Heart* copyright 2017 by Erica Monroe

Cover design by Teresa Spreckelmeyer/The Midnight Muse Designs

Cover photo by Kim Killion/Hot Damn Stock

Quillfire Publishing

ˋBN: 978-0990022978

ᶠormation, address Erica Monroe at http://www.ericamonroe.com.

To every girl who has ever felt lesser
You are very much more.

And to my grandmother
Who makes me believe I can catch the stars.

Chapter One

W *hitechapel, London*
October 1832

Red was everywhere.

Abigail Vautille shouldn't have been surprised. Since that fateful day when her left hand was forcibly rammed into a working loom, the color red had haunted her. Deep red scars from the punch card of the jacquard crisscrossed her skin. Pockets of exposed flesh remained, mangled red bubbles now crusted black. The bones had been reset to give her a range of movement, but she couldn't feel the brace of a cold wind on her flesh or the touch of a man's fingers against her skin.

If only she could staunch her emotions so effectively.

But, no, she was fated to face crimson. Scarlet was even the color of her once-friend Poppy Knight's hair. Poppy's investigation into their past employer had led to Abigail's torture.

Her stomach clenched at the shellacked ruby door of Cruikshank's gaming hell. A battered wreath hung in the center, the previously garnet holly berries shriveled and dead. No one bothered to use the carmine-rusted iron doorknocker. This was no longer a place that required a doorman.

Scoundrels came and went, invited by the new proprietor, Arthur Cruikshank. He was in league with Joaquin Mason, who ruled the rookeries from the back room of his main property in Shadwell, the King of Spades. With Mason's support, Cruikshank had turned this dank hole into a profitable gambling house.

Abigail knew the men here, their tells and their compulsions. Each battled a demon that only a hand of cards seemed to sate.

But familiarity didn't breed ease. The hollers of foxed men drifted from Cruikshank's, an unsettling cacophony. The building itself provided no comfort, constructed of crumbling gray stone. Gray like her constant mood. Auburn bricks made up the top floor, added after the original foundation.

Shivering in the frigid night air, Abigail drew her black cloak tighter around her to brace against the cold wind. With a glance upstairs, she brought the gloved fingers of her good hand to her lips to kiss for luck. She'd need all the help she could get in this godforsaken place.

After entering, she refused to give her cloak to the man who waited in the foyer. Cruikshank didn't employ him. When unsuspecting people presented him with their garments, he fled to sell them in the rag and bone shops. She couldn't help but admire his ingenuity.

Since she couldn't hold down honest employment any longer, she'd do best to follow his example.

Her eyes narrowed as she surveyed the crowd mingling in the lower rooms. Conversations drifted in and out, an indistinct hum. A sweet, pungent scent caught her attention from the open door to her right. Men reclined on dilapidated chaises in sleep or stupor, while two women blew into pipes, kindling the opium in their bowls until it glowed red.

"Mystery lady!" a man called, his unfixed gaze settling on her cloak. "Come back, mystery lady. Come play with me."

A lump formed in her throat. All these people, drowning their sorrows. Little she could do for them now. The longer she stayed, the higher chance she had of being a potential target for Cruikshank's less principled patrons.

She kept going, ignoring his summons, her skirts swishing against the dusty floor. Two staircases flanked the vast entrance hall. While the left staircase ended on a landing, the right staircase would take her up to the top floor where the faro and hazard tables were. The play was deep there.

She'd find her father at the back table. Inevitably, he'd be in the third chair, his hands shaking as he grasped his cards. There'd be a wrinkle where his thumb gripped too hard.

She reached down into the pocket in her cloak. No blunt. Not that she could pay the rest of her father's debts with a few coins. Settling the vowels for his last visit to Cruikshank's had taken the last of her savings. Years of hard shifts, aching knees, and pricked fingers, gone in an instant to the tables.

Now that she couldn't work in the factory, she had no way to earn back that money.

Three prostitutes lingered at the stairs, clothed in gaudy dresses with chemises peeking out of their stomachers. They roamed the halls in between their shifts in the cellar, which Cruikshank had converted into a whorehouse. He was always looking for willing lightskirts to fill the beds.

Abigail gulped as a flamboyant redhead with a gap-toothed grin caught her eye and waggled a brow.

Soon, she'd be one of them.

She mounted the stairs carefully, her uninjured hand grasping the railing for support. The hood of her cloak remained over her head, and she pretended it gave her a modicum of security. A shroud to hide behind, when it seemed everyone in Whitechapel knew her name and face.

People moved around her, passing her on the staircase and cursing her slowness. One foot in front of the other was never easy. Even before she'd lost the use of her hand, her unsteady gait had marked her as a cripple. As a child, she'd worked as a scavenger, sliding underneath the machinery to collect the broken bits of silk for reuse. The labor had distorted her body, and years of standing on her feet for fourteen hours, six days a week, had worsened her knock-knees.

Each step higher made her joints scream for relief. Her lungs, weak from the poorly ventilated conditions in the factories, burned with the effort.

But she persevered, for life had given her no other choice. Everyone she used to consider a friend had abandoned her. The sole kindness she'd known in the last six months was the whisper of a stranger when she'd been in the hospital.

Finally, she arrived at the top floor. A throng of people waited outside the faro room. Falling in line, Abigail peeked inside. Candles shimmered throughout, casting a golden glow. At least it was warmer than outside.

She'd already pawned the last of her books to pay for coal so that her little sister, Bess, wouldn't freeze in their flat. Her heart panged at the memory. Those books had been more precious to her than any other possession, but Bess had to be her first priority.

Come tomorrow when the coal ran out again, there'd be nothing left to sell.

Nothing except for herself.

She couldn't think of that now. If she did, her knees would sway, and her steps would falter. That would make her an easy mark. Already, she felt as though her movements were evaluated for signs of weakness. A chill skittered down her back. She shoved her battered hand into the pocket of her cloak and continued, trying to ignore the disconcerting sensation of being watched.

She was strong. She could survive anything.

The group behind her advanced, shoving her forward. She stumbled but managed to right herself before colliding with the man in front of her. The herd dispersed at the door, ambling to the various gaming tables. Abigail made her way toward the far corner of the room, pausing for a moment to lean against a post and catch her breath.

She scanned the crowd for her father, expecting to find him flanked on either side by intent players. Tonight, all the chairs were empty, except for three: the banker and two punters. A crowd of people watched the game proceed. The cards had split; the dealer took half of the bets on that rank. The onlookers let out a whoop of approval.

The mechanics of the game held little interest to her, for it'd always end the same: even if her father won, they'd still owe. Their debts were so high; they'd never dig out of this hole. She recognized her father: grizzly gray hair, the stoop of his shoulders, his threadbare green coat Bess had patched the week prior.

Across from him and facing her was a man Abigail did not recognize. As he purchased another check from the dealer, she swallowed back the dread that threatened to consume her. An unknown competitor meant her father might not receive leniency. Cruikshank had already told Papa that if he didn't start paying his vowels, he'd need to find a new place to gamble, or he'd have to face Cyrus. Known as an unhinged pugilist with a taste for blood, Cyrus Mason could make the injuries she'd incurred from the loom seem like papercuts.

And so, the cycle would begin again: another gaming hell and another night like this one. It didn't matter that she'd cut her meals in half for the past few months to ensure Bess had enough to eat. Or that they were three months behind on rent, and if they didn't pay up soon, they'd all be out on the bloody street.

Nothing mattered to her father except the game.

Abigail slowly steered her way through the crowd, minding her steps until she'd made it to the back table.

"'Ey now," one man complained as she accidentally bumped him. He turned, catching her eye. Even in the cloak, he recognized her. So much for anonymity.

He motioned for a few of his friends to step to the side to make room for her. "Move, mates."

Abigail nodded her gratitude, sliding into the vacated space. Her father hadn't noticed her arrival, so focused was he on the game layout.

"Come, Papa," she quietly bid. "Settle up your accounts and hope to God that this man lets you by with incremental payments."

She hated having to say those words. She hated the humiliation of having to stand there, while all the men leered at her as if she was the choicest bit of flesh they'd get all night. But if she was going to be a harlot, she might as well start expecting this treatment.

The unknown punter across from her father coughed. A cough meant to distract, to clear the air. She looked up to see who would be so polite in this den of iniquity. She focused on his features, and her stomach did a flip. A purely physical reaction, for what woman wouldn't have felt a surge of fancy for the way his linen shirt stretched over his broad shoulders. His oval face was classically handsome, chiseled with an impossibly straight nose.

The man's blue eyes narrowed. "He owes me two hundred pounds. You can't expect me to excuse so large a debt."

Two hundred pounds.

His voice rang in her ears, like the steady drum that signals a firing squad. Two hundred pounds. Each breath was harder. Her throat closed. Two hundred pounds.

The mob erupted with cheers at the announcement, eager for a potential conflict. Their hoots barely registered, for her heart pounded so hard, she feared it might burst free of her chest. The world spun around her, and she prayed the floor would swallow her up.

Yet nothing changed.

Around her, the horde grew impatient for a response. Whatever leniency they'd shown in allowing her into their midst had disappeared. Now she was a part of the spectacle, her pain on display for their enjoyment.

"'E don't got two hundred," one man jeered. "'E won't even pay me the two crowns 'e owes me."

"And 'e owes me twenty pounds!" another fellow added.

Oh, God. Her father had killed them all with the fifty-one cards of a faro game.

They were doomed. With vowels that large, surely, her father would be sent to debtor's prison. Hell, maybe they'd all be sent to Marshalsea. The thought of her little sister living in such squalor made Abigail's heart tighten. How would Bess survive?

"I can't pay you," her father mumbled as if he was just now realizing how much he'd lost. "Ain't got that."

"Then something will have to be done," his opponent announced.

Thoughts sped through her mind. Bess couldn't go to Marshalsea. It'd ruin her in a way Abigail couldn't countenance. Sorrow had seeped deep into Abigail's life, ripping apart all her hopes and dreams, but Bess deserved better.

What could Abigail offer this man? Their coffers were as

empty as their cabinets. The little blunt Bess brought in at the new textile factory already wasn't enough for the rent.

Abigail glanced down, taking in the plump curves of her breasts, her wide hips reputed to be perfect for grasping onto as a man tupped her hard. She was all the family had.

And if it were the last damn thing she did, she'd save Bess. This man knew Mason—perhaps a deal could be brokered to keep her father away from the hells too.

Abigail pushed back the hood to her cloak, revealing her blonde curls. Before her disfigurement, the factory boys had made it quite clear she stirred their attentions. But what was the price of her soul? Was she worth such an exorbitant sum?

"We can't pay you," she said, repeating her father's words. "But if you excuse my father's debts, I'll—"

The words wouldn't form. She gulped for air. A vision of Bess huddled in the corner of a filthy cell danced before her eyes. So, this was how her degradation would begin, not in a brothel, but in a hell. How could she go through with this? She'd be signing her soul away to the devil.

She couldn't think of another choice.

She needed to entice him. He wouldn't accept a single night for two hundred pounds—even as a virgin, she was not worth it. A man as good-looking as he was wouldn't pay that much for one lay with a working-class girl.

One month with her. She dismissed that idea immediately. A month away from Bess was too much. Two weeks instead. She'd start there.

"I'll spend two weeks with you. My virtue in exchange for two hundred pounds."

* * *

MICHAEL STRICKLAND SHOULDN'T have been at this hell. As a newly promoted inspector for the H-Division of the Metropolitan Police, he'd been forbidden from consorting with the criminal ilk.

But God, he was tired of following those rules. Tired of living in a holier-than-thou way, when he knew he was as much of a sinner as these cowards, shattered by the call of the tables and the song of gin.

As if that wasn't bad enough, he was going mad.

The woman swathed in a black cloak looked so much like the girl he'd visited in London Hospital six months prior that he almost rose from his seat and demanded her identity. That girl— Abigail Vautille, he'd never forget her name—had disappeared back into the rookeries upon release from the hospital without even a "thank you" to the two men who'd paid her bills.

The hollers of the gamers soothed him. He was at his best in a crowd, when he didn't have time to think. It was easier to brazen through his problems than engage in self-examination. Perhaps he'd seek out a new mistress, lose his pain in the tight fit of her quim against his cock. He'd do anything to keep him from thinking of Miss Vautille and his part in her torture.

But the woman pushed the cloak back from her face and revealed an angelic visage he knew all too well. Her azure eyes settled on him, frosty and deadened to the world. For a moment, he forgot how to speak.

He slid his hand down underneath the table, pinching his leg. A prick of pain answered, but he didn't wake. This couldn't be a dream, for in his dreams, she wore significantly less cloth- ing, and she was much more enamored with him.

The real Abigail Vautille stood before him. Not the healthy, happy version he'd created in his mind, but a woman who bore the mutilations of a maniac's torment.

She spoke. "If you excuse my father's debts, I'll spend two

weeks with you. My virtue in exchange for two hundred pounds."

Everything crackled back to life. Two weeks with Miss Vautille. Two weeks learning the curves of her body until they were like a second language to him. Two weeks riding her, tupping her, groaning his release, and then starting all over again. They'd bring to life every one of his nocturnal fantasies.

This was the best damn game of faro he'd ever played. Even if she wasn't a virgin—given she'd grown up in Whitechapel, he suspected that was likely—two hundred pounds was a fee he'd willingly have paid for her favors.

He knew she'd stopped working at the factory; weaving required the use of two strong hands. What other option did she have besides prostitution? He shouldn't be surprised, of course, but a twinge of sadness echoed somewhere deep within him.

What a bloody bag of moonshine. Why should he care if Miss Vautille was a ladybird? Hundreds of women, most likely even thousands, worked in the flesh trade in London alone. He'd never harbored any sentimental beliefs about sex. Bawdy houses existed because men wanted impersonal connections. Prostitution was a job like any other—even if it was supposedly illegal, the great majority of Met officers ignored those laws when presented with a sweet taste of paid cunny.

The miscreant on his right gave him a hard shove, almost sending Michael face-forward into the cards. "Ye gonna dip yer wick in her cunny, lad?"

"I bet she ain't even a virgin," said another man, sizing her up.

"*I* bet she likes the cock in 'er mouth. Look at dem lips. Ripe for my pecker," came another rejoinder.

Miss Vautille stood as immobile as the bolted-in table. Her chin rose high. She was proud—too proud for a brothel. Either the bullybacks would whip that out of her, or she'd have to find a new profession.

Unless Michael taught her how to appear biddable. He'd be doing her a favor, wouldn't he? A girl as pretty as she was could make good coin as a fen, far better than she made in her old factory job. If he reached out to some of the abbesses he knew, he could get her situated in a nicer bordello where she'd warrant higher socket money. Enough that she could get away from her gamester father.

"I'd say two weeks is a nice down payment," Michael mused, not wanting to sound too enthusiastic at first. If Miss Vautille knew she held him by the balls, there'd be no hope of negotiation.

The bastard who had spoken so giddily of his pecker reached out a hand to stroke Miss Vautille's rear. She cowered at first, but she didn't move away from his hand. Her chin raised a fraction more. Her gaze became detached as if she were miles away from here.

Michael lunged forward. She was *his*, damn it.

He caught the bastard's wrist, wrenching so hard to the right that the man let out a yelp of protest.

"The only reason I've not ripped your throat open is that I haven't claimed my due yet," Michael hissed. "But for the next fortnight, this girl is my property and *my* property alone, do you hear me?"

"Just a little touch," the man complained. "That's all I wanted."

Mr. Vautille let out a pained groan, trying to reach for them both, but falling short in his gin haze.

Michael twisted the imbecile's wrist again until the man's eyes bulged, and tears streamed from the pain. "If any of you touches even a hair on her head, I will bring the full force of the H-Division down upon you. We'll move so fast your strumpets will be left wondering who will pay for their tuppence cunny now that you've been hung at Tyburn."

Dropping the man's grimy wrist, Michael wiped his hands on his breeches.

"Best believe 'im," groused a spectator. "Bloody Peelers, the lot of 'em."

"Cruikshank shouldn't allow his sort," protested another man.

"I'm allowed here because Joaquin Mason has deigned it so." With this statement, he challenged each of them to take offense further. "I don't think I need to explain to any of you what Mason does to those who disagree with him."

One man audibly gulped, while another took a large step back from their table. Michael knew he'd hit the right note with this lot. An arrest might build up one's reputation on the street, so it wasn't an effective threat. Retaliation by criminal royalty like the Mason family, however, was enough to send most of these men running for shelter. In Mason's hells, unsanctioned violence didn't spread. Debts were paid on time. The proprietor always got his cut.

"Gotta be bringin' the Masons into it when we was just havin' some fun. Come, let's go. Better take it elsewhere, and all that." Uttering various protests, the throng drifted toward the other tables.

Michael was left alone with the Vautilles. Mr. Vautille crumpled before him.

Miss Vautille directed venomous gazes at her father and him. Her gloved hands clasped the table, using the edge to hold up her weight. "My virtue may be on the cutting block, sir, but I assure you I am *no one's* property."

Michael waggled a finger at her. "You won't become a successful courtesan with that attitude. Your job is to make men feel important, not impotent."

Mr. Vautille lifted his head up from the table, twisting around in his seat to face his daughter. "Abbie, please—"

"Silence," she ordered.

Mr. Vautille immediately closed his flapping lips. There was a dictatorial quality to his daughter's demands that only came from a childhood spent having to raise one's own parent. Michael knew that tone, having used the same on his mother during her too-short life.

"The arrangement will begin in two days' time," she declared, her voice so firm he couldn't help but admire her resolve. "I must be allowed to gather my things first, to say goodbye to my sis—" She stopped, her bottom lip quivering for a second before she composed herself.

He ought to say something, anything to keep her from dissolving into sobs. Probably a ploy to up the price—those tears at the corners of her eyes couldn't be genuine, could they? No woman who cared about her virginity would offer it up as an easily traded commodity. She'd exhibited such steely control he had no trouble believing she'd arranged everything to her benefit.

"Do you need more time?" That wasn't what he'd meant to say at all. He shook his head, reminding himself that this was all part of her strategy.

"I may be a virgin, sir, but I'm no schoolgirl," Miss Vautille snapped. "I'm well aware of how this works. You claim you dismiss our debt, but you'll take us into custody as soon as you no longer feel so generous. Those men back there, they said you were a Peeler, and so I trust you even less."

He felt her words as a slap across his face. Rarely did people point out his faults to his face, and never so bluntly. "I assure you; my word is good."

"Forgive me if I don't believe you," she said, rising to her full height, some heads shorter than he was. She still used the table to support her weight, but in his eyes, she was a raging tempest. "While my father may care so little about what happens to the rest of us, I won't see my family in Marshalsea."

"That's not going to happen," he said.

She remained unconvinced. "We're already in dun territory. You know Mason will have us thrown in there when he realizes his gruesome brother can't bleed the blunt out of us."

He shrugged. "I'll pay the two hundred pounds owed to Mason. That'll make it even." The hell owner cared little *who* paid the debt, as long as he received the money.

"Can't pay you," Vautille interjected suddenly as if he'd just woken up. He slumped back in his chair again, his bloodshot eyes barely focusing.

From the first round Michael had played, he'd marked Vautille as an easy target, and still, he'd continued playing.

Abigail glared at her father. "I'm taking care of it, Papa. Do you understand we're ruined now? All because you couldn't keep away from the bloody tables."

He expected to see some flash of hurt in Vautille's eyes at his daughter's callous words. The man remained impassive; his threadbare coat huddled around him; hands thrust in his penniless pockets. Vautille had given up, perhaps long ago.

Michael turned his gaze to Miss Vautille instead. To her ripe lips, perfect for kissing. To her haughty cerulean eyes. At the end of the two weeks, he'd have her panting for his touch.

"There's one more thing." Miss Vautille frowned at her father. "You said you were here because Joaquin Mason knows you. I'd like you to have Mason bar my father from ever entering another gaming hell."

Vautille groaned at this pronouncement, but he couldn't seem to muster up enough energy to protest. His head lolled back.

Michael stroked his chin with his thumb and index finger.

"That's a weighty request. I can certainly get him banned from Mason's own hells, but *all* of the hells in the surroundings areas will take some work."

She ran her tongue across her lips, slowly, provocatively. "I'll make it worth your while, I promise."

God's balls, he couldn't resist her siren call. He nodded swiftly. "I accept your terms. Shall we shake on it, as two gentleme...er, gentle*people* might?"

Extending his hand, he ignored Vautille's attempt to interject his approval. A man who had to depend on his daughter's help at the tables was no man at all. Debts were to be honored, or a man could not live with integrity.

Hell, Michael would pay the rest of his life for his sins, for his vowels wouldn't wipe away with the drop of a coin.

After a moment's hesitation, Miss Vautille raised her right hand. The cool press of her glove against his bare palm shot heat through him, startling him. He couldn't help but imagine those gloved fingers wrapped tight around his rod, the friction of silk against skin.

Once their palms parted, he reached into his pocket, drawing out a scrap of parchment. "If your father will meet me at Cruikshank's counter, I will add the terms of our agreement to the ledger book so that there is no question whether or not your debt has been paid." He hated having her name dragged into the public record, but it'd be common knowledge by the next day, regardless. Drunks had a horrid way of spilling secrets.

The vowels paid; they said their adieus. "In two days' time," he bid her, slipping her his address.

"Don't forget to talk to Mason." She turned, refusing her father's arm for support.

Chapter Two

Two days later, Michael headed to Wood Street early, hoping to get most of his work done before Abigail arrived that evening. He pushed open the doors to the station house, grimacing at the noisy lobby. His head throbbed mercilessly. He'd spent the night at Cruikshank's again, securing Joaquin Mason's promise to brand Vautille as *persona non grata*. If anyone allowed Vautille to place a bet, Mason would now consider it a special affront, whether or not it happened at one of his establishments.

The discussion with Mason had taken place over way too much blue ruin. Even Michael's vision was slightly blurry. Gin would be the death of him if he didn't perish between the shapely thighs of one of Covent Garden's finest doxies.

As he strode down the hall, the same sergeants that had once talked with him about the latest mill or their evening plans now passed him by with a nod of acknowledgment. Before, he was the one they'd crack jokes to, plot revenge with, or invite for a night trawling through London's worst public houses. But the instant he became an inspector, those men were no longer his friends.

He picked up his mail and went to his office. Pausing outside, he ran his thumb across the plaque on the door. "M. Strickland," making him the fourth in his lineage to hold rank in London's constabularies. Therein laid the entire reason he'd been promoted: not because he excelled at his job, but because of his last name. The superintendents wanted constancy, something to quiet the concerns over too much change in the past year. It didn't get any more consistent than the Strickland family.

After entering his office, he flopped down in his chair. Stacks of paperwork littered the desk. He pulled out from his mail a report on arrest rates for this quarter. While the statistics for the department were improving since Jonah Whiting's dismissal for corruption, the men weren't content. For the first time in their lives, the officers now had to report back immediately after their patrols. No more leniencies in filing the proper documentation. They were watched like hawks for signs of dishonesty.

But the numbers indicated that once the men adjusted to the new order, their productivity would show a pronounced improvement. Michael dipped his quill in ink and sketched out projections for the next quarter in the right margin.

He let the ink dry, pushing the paper off to the side of his desk. Returning to his mail, he sorted everything into piles without much thought, for the majority of it all was quite regular. An invitation to another dreadful party from his sister, Frances. The latest briefings on closed cases. Notice of the next departmental meeting.

A mud-covered square of parchment fell from the pages of another report, and he snatched it up. As he read, his heartbeat quickened. His palms were suddenly sweaty. He breathed in increments, jagged gasps that did nothing to calm him.

Scrawled across the foolscap in a deep-brown ink far too

close to blood was the following message: *I'm gonna make all of you regret arrestin me. I'm comin for you and the whore.*

Grabbing the note, he burst up from his chair and sprinted down the hall to Superintendent Bicknell's office. He tugged the door open and entered without knocking.

"Strickland, what in the blazes has possessed you?" Scowling, Thomas Bicknell readjusted his eyeglasses.

Michael didn't speak. He simply shoved the note at Bicknell.

Bicknell's expression transformed as he read. Gone was the irritation that Michael had barged into his office unannounced. He pushed the note from him as though the closeness of the parchment could summon the devil himself.

"Clowes," Michael demanded. "Where is Frank Clowes? The prisoner transfer was yesterday, wasn't it?"

Bicknell shifted in his chair.

"The transfer," Michael repeated. "Clowes was supposed to be on his way to the penal colony by now. Did anything happen?"

"Er, well." Bicknell stared at his desk with rapt fascination. He'd never been the type to accept responsibility for anything, and his diversion tactics increased in relation to the importance of the problem.

Which meant if he was avoiding Michael's gaze, something had gone terribly wrong.

"Clowes didn't make it to the ship, did he?" When Bicknell didn't answer, Michael leaned forward, his feet planted firmly on the ground, and his legs spread wide. "That man murdered two women and tortured another. When were you going to tell me? Or were you just going to wait until I was mauled on my way home?"

Clowes had been the main enforcer for the Larker gang. His cruelty was renowned in the H-Division.

"Now wait here, Strickland," Bicknell protested. "I just received word of it this morning. I was going to brief you."

Of course, you were. And I'm the bloody Duke of Cumberland.

Somewhere along the line, Michael's people—the fourteen sergeants that served beneath him—had bungled this. It was on *his* head if Clowes hurt someone else. If his men didn't catch the blackguard, all the progress the department had made in the past six months would be for naught.

"The math was sound." He'd run the numbers thrice. Transporting Clowes to a penal colony was the best option. It minimized his ability to harm British citizens and ultimately cost less than keeping him in gaol. Assuming Clowes didn't die on the god-awful voyage to Australia, once he arrived, the other convicts would make quick work of him.

Michael wracked his brain for something they might have missed. Three patrollers to escort the bastard to the docks. Seven seasoned guards on the ship.

"You and your damn equations," Bicknell grumbled. "If you weren't usually right, I'd take all your damn quills just so I never had to hear about your calculations again."

Usually right.

"It's not my mathematics that is the problem," he protested. "How did it happen?"

"The carriage was waylaid before they arrived at the docks." Bicknell sighed. "The driver turned the corner, and suddenly there were five armed men. One of our men is in hospital, while the other two received less critical injuries."

"Shit." He carded his fingers through his hair. "Was there any sign of where Clowes might have gone?"

"Men lost him in Ratcliffe. It's a bloody maze in these rookeries. Ought to level the whole damn place." Bicknell grimaced. "Note's probably our best bet."

Taking a seat across from Bicknell, Michael examined the note again. The resemblance of the ink to blood made his stomach slosh. Who had Clowes hurt to write this?

I'm gonna make all of you regret arrestin me. I'm comin for you and the whore.

"For the time being, let's ignore the blood. The letter is addressed directly to me." Michael pointed to the postmark on the other side of the parchment. "We can assume Clowes wants vengeance for my arresting him in the Larker case. But the 'all of you' indicates he'll go after anyone who was involved."

"Just what the department needs," Bicknell groaned. "Who's the whore he's referring to? The Moseley girl is dead."

Michael thought of a pair of sharp eyes, hair the color of spun gold, and a beatific face hiding the hellion beneath. *Abigail.* Of course, it'd be her.

The Larker case had brought Miss Vautille into his life in the first place. When Thaddeus Knight had demanded the department investigate the murder of a young factory girl, Michael had dismissed the case as nothing more than the common scuffle with a doxy over her fees. These crimes happened in the rookeries; it was unpleasant but routine.

But Knight kept digging, unearthing a criminal labyrinth that reached beyond the Spitalfields factory owned by Boz and Effie Larker. When the Larkers realized the police were investigating, they'd turned their suspicions onto one of their employees, who'd been found in the factory after hours.

By the time Knight located Miss Vautille, she was near death from Clowes's torture.

"Abigail Vautille," Michael said with certainty. "It was her affidavit that convinced the magistrate to deliver a harsher sentence to Clowes."

Bicknell's brows furrowed. "The girl with the scarred hand? I never expected to hear her name again."

I didn't either until last night.

He kept his expression blank so he wouldn't reveal his true connection to her. "I'd like to protect her personally."

Bicknell shook his head. "Impossible. Can't spare you."

"You can and you will," Michael ordered. If Bicknell wanted to make this harder, then he'd use Bicknell's worst nightmare against him: the press lampooning his precious reputation. "You saw what attention the Italian Boy got, and he was just a poor beggar. What do you think the newspapers will say when they learn we let a murderer escape?"

Bicknell gulped. He glanced from the note to Michael and back again. "It's going to be a bloodbath, isn't it?"

Michael nodded solemnly. "The East End already hates us. All it will take is one sketch of Miss Vautille, and the toffs of London will be won over by her beauty."

"All those papers," Bicknell lamented. His posture sagged. Even his mustache seemed to droop. "I'll give you one week."

"Two," Michael countered. "Two, and I'll tell everyone I'm on that holiday you told me to take when my father died."

"Claudius was a good man," Bicknell said automatically. "If ever there was a reason for a holiday, it'd be to commemorate his life."

Michael bit down the urge to inform him that Claudius Strickland was a sorry bastard who should have died long ago. "Yes, he was. So, we have an agreement. I take two weeks, keep Miss Vautille at my townhouse, and I want two patrollers guarding the grounds."

Bicknell deliberated. "Two weeks, two patrollers, and I never have to hear another one of your equations again."

"Done." Michael extended his palm, shaking Bicknell's hand. "I'll collect Miss Vautille shortly."

She'd arrive at his house later today, but Bicknell didn't need to know that.

And while he was withholding information, Abigail didn't need to know about Clowes either. He'd be able to keep watch on her in his townhouse. His men would keep him informed of any changes.

Women in peril were as bad as women in hysterics. He couldn't take the chance that Abigail would do something foolish like flee from his home. Best to keep her calm. Let her think this was all business as usual. He'd stick to the terms of their agreement. Bedding Abigail would distract her, which served his purposes well.

He rose and headed toward the door before he turned around. "Have you informed Knight yet?"

Bicknell blinked.

"He ought to know," Michael said. "If it weren't for Knight and his wife, Clowes would still be running loose. I'll tell him."

Bicknell's admonition followed him out. "Strickland? The next time you barge into my office without warning, I'll dock your wages, Claudius's son or not."

* * *

"It's only for two weeks," Abigail reminded Bess. "What with work at the factory, you won't even notice I'm gone."

The two girls sat in the last chairs left in their flat. Bess shivered, hugging her thin shawl tighter. Abigail stared at the crumbling, sooty brick of their fireless hearth and vowed that the first flesh money she got would go to buying coal.

Their mother had died giving birth to Bess, leaving Abigail to become more surrogate mother than sister. Though Abigail was ten years older than Bess, the two girls had spent almost every day in each other's company. Lord knew Papa had done nothing to raise Bess. He'd done nothing, nothing except bring trouble to their door.

Now Abigail would pay the price.

But she wouldn't expose Bess to the truth of their situation.

"I don't understand why you have to leave," Bess said, her voice a strange mix of childish petulance and an adult's weariness, despite her nine years of age.

"I told you I'm filling in for one of the flower girls," Abigail explained for the fifteenth time that day. "It is easier to stay with the rest of the girls than keep making the trek to Covent Garden every day."

"You're being very vague, you and Papa both." Bess peered up at Abigail, her blue eyes wary. "And I don't like staying with Mrs. Henderson."

"I know you don't, but it's better that you stay with her than be alone while Papa is out." Their neighbor had agreed to watch Bess while Abigail was gone.

On the way back from Cruikshank's hell, Abigail had made Papa promise to remain silent about the real reason she'd be away. If Bess knew what Abigail had done to save her, she'd claim she could help the family too. Take more shifts at the factory, or volunteer to work again as a piecer. Bess was getting too big to slide underneath the machinery to repair the broken threads in the silk. At most, Bess slept four hours a night—more shifts would mean even less rest.

She would become careless.

When people became careless around the machinery, they lost limbs. Or worse, their life.

She had only a few more hours here before the hack arrived to take her to Strickland's. Abigail tugged at her glove, making sure it fully covered her elbow. It fit her like a second skin. A long, jagged seam ran up the back of it, from where she'd had to patch the fabric after snagging it on an exposed nail in the Ten Bells public house. Her stitches were clumsy, but before the incident, she'd been the best embroiderer on Baker's Row.

"Something is not right," Bess continued. "I'm not a child, Abbie."

Abigail had never known anyone who could sniff out a lie faster than her sister could. That gave Abigail some hope at least; perhaps Bess wouldn't fall victim to a blackguard since her trust was as scant as the meat upon her brittle bones.

Abigail pursed her lips, fixing Bess with her best "Don't ask me any more questions" glare.

Bess rolled her eyes. "What's more, I fail to see how you're going to stand in the market for hours."

Abigail readjusted her full skirt so that the flowing material hid her ankles from view. "I'll have the cart to lean on." She didn't suppress the hurt that came from Bess's matter-of-fact indication of her knock-knees. The faster she stopped these questions, the better.

Bess grimaced. "I'm sorry, Abbie. I didn't mean any harm."

"I know." With her right hand, Abigail patted Bess's palm. "I'll be back before you know it, hopefully with enough blunt to get us a proper meal."

Hope shone in Bess's eager eyes. "Eel pies?"

"All the penny pies you'd like," Abigail promised, crossing her heart. If the flaky pastry sold down by the St. Katharine docks made Bess happy, Abigail would get her one.

With a mischievous grin, Bess ran her tongue over her lips, rubbing her belly at the same time. "I can almost taste them."

On any other day, Bess's melodramatic pantomime would have drawn a chuckle from her. Today, as Bess shoved half of her dirt-speckled fist into her mouth and pretended it was a pasty, Abigail felt the stifling weight of failure.

Again and again, she made promises she couldn't keep. Penny pies, coal, a chance at a better life. Before that fateful night, blind optimism had been her constant companion. She'd believed that eventually, good people received rewards for their pureness of heart and body.

The wool had been pulled from her eyes the moment Frank Clowes thrust her hand into that damn loom. Bad things happened to good people without rhyme or reason, and she couldn't guarantee Bess would be protected from the harsh realities of life.

She stood, smoothing the wrinkles out from her faded blue skirt. Just once, she wanted to make a promise she could keep.

"Would you like me to bring you back a flower?" A single flower should be easy enough to obtain. She'd cut through the toff neighborhoods on her way back from Cheapside. Someone would have a garden.

Bess nodded. "A rose. Could you bring me a rose?"

Abigail shook her head. "I doubt it, Bessieboo. Roses don't bloom in the winter."

Bess sighed, her lips pressed into a full pout. "Bloody winter. I'm cold, Abbie."

"I know, dear." Abigail pulled her own shawl from her shoulder, wrapping it around Bess's shoulders. "If I see a rose, you know I'll bring it to you, for you are the fairest of them all."

"You're exaggerating," Bess accused.

Abigail leaned forward, laying a kiss on top of her head. "I never exaggerate. You are clearly the prettiest lass in all of Spitalfields."

Bess let out a loud harrumph, but her smile told Abigail she'd hit the mark with the praise. "I'll miss you."

"Not as much as I'll miss you," Abigail said, drawing her sister into her arms. "When I return, I'll bring you all the chatter from the market."

And it'd all be lies.

* * *

A COLD WIND whipped through Michael as he continued toward his house, his boots crunching layers of dirty slush. Snowfall in London was only beautiful as it fell. Immediately upon hitting the ground, constant traffic pummeled the flakes. The farther he got into the rookery, the grimier the snow became, as animal dung mixed with sewage, mud, and the mold that hugged most surfaces.

He turned the corner, passing a beggar holding a sign that claimed he was a war veteran. His right arm appeared severed at the elbow. The mendicant drank what Michael guessed was gin out of a tin cup as he chatted with a slovenly woman leaning on the doorframe of a nearby dwelling. As the woman extended a rolled cigarette, the beggar unwound the ties on his sweater and grabbed the cigarette with his supposedly amputated arm.

At the sight of Michael in his blues, the man gasped and stumbled back. "Er, ah, guv, ye see—"

Michael shook his head. "I'm not interested in your scrounging for money, Jared, however dishonest it may be."

"How ye know my name?" the vagrant demanded.

"Everyone in Wood Street knows you, Kip Jared." He repeated the man's name for emphasis, appreciating the effect it had on the surly swindler. "You stand at the corner of Elm's Bakery and Ratchet's Pawn every day from six in the morning until two in the afternoon when you take a pint at the Ten Bells. Then you're back at it until seven in the evening."

Jared's jaw dropped. The woman he'd been chatting with looked from Jared to Michael and headed back into the house. The door slammed behind her.

Smart decision.

Michael tapped his truncheon against his leg. "There are many more things I know about you too, Jared, but at the moment, I've got bigger criminals to concern myself with. Lucky for you."

"Best be on my way then," Jared suggested hopefully.

Michael was about to wave him away, but an idea occurred to him. If he recalled correctly, Jared was in Knight's gigantic file as a possible witness to Anna Moseley's murder, as he'd shared a one-room flat with five other men on Wheeler Street in a collapsing lodging house. Wheeler was just a stone's throw from White Lion Street, where the textile factory was located. While Jared hadn't known anything about the Moseley's death or the Larkers, he might still be useful.

Michael pulled tuppence from his pocket and held it out to Jared. "How'd you like to earn some honest blunt?"

Jared shook his fist at him, the long string ties of his sweater waving in the wind. "'Ey now, I ain't no snitch. No rubbin' shoulders with Peelers 'ere." Still, the beggar stared at the coin with slack-jawed awe.

One more minute and Jared would agree. *As close to success as God's curse to a whore's ass.*

Michael palmed the coin, dropping his arm as he did so. Jared followed the movement, swallowing.

"It's a simple job, really," Michael began, careful to keep his voice flat to not alert Jared to how much importance he placed on this assignment. A man like Jared would leverage Miss Vautille's security for a larger payoff, possibly even to Clowes. But if the beggar thought he'd lucked into getting substantial coin for little work, he wouldn't risk upsetting Michael. "You remember a man named Frank Clowes?"

Jared sniffed. "Aye. That blighter got me 'auled in for questionin'."

"Terrible trouble that is, and for a man of your ilk," Michael agreed. "I bet that cost you at least a day's worth of blunt out here."

"So, it did," Jared grumbled. "I'da like to show 'im 'ow it feels."

27

Michael raised the coin again, making a grand show of admiring the way the sunlight flickered off the silver. "For the first time, Jared, it appears our interests are aligned. I want Frank Clowes too."

Jared scooted closer; his eyes fixated on the tuppence. "I ain't gonna testify," he muttered, his tone lacking the gusto it'd had before.

"I don't need you to testify," Michael replied. "What I need is much easier. You know the way of this neighborhood, probably better than anyone else."

Jared puffed up, looping his thumbs into the twine that held his saggy breeches from falling down his skinny hips. "'Course I do."

"Then you'll know if Clowes pops up in these parts," Michael said easily. "You see, I want to make sure Clowes gets what's coming to him. A man like that ought to pay for his sins."

Jared reached for the money. "Strange words from a Peeler."

Michael held the coin out of his reach, firmly grasped between his thumb and forefinger. "Peeler is my job. I'm an Anglican, same as you. God shall judge those who are lacking. I'm merely helping along His process."

Jared whistled in concordance. "That's what I been tellin' yer toff partners. I oughta get an award for partin' these fools from their blunt."

With a shrug, Michael extended the tuppence toward Jared. "So, you'll do it? I'd want word delivered to me at my townhouse if you see Clowes or hear about any of his associates coming to Whitechapel. There'd be a half-crown in it for you if your intelligence comes to fruition."

Seizing the coin, Jared stuffed it into his baggy breeches, faster than Michael could blink. "Ye got me word."

For whatever that's worth.

Presenting Jared with his card, Michael informed him that the townhouse was well guarded by the Met's finest, should the beggar get any ideas. Jared huffed at the very thought, but from the flash of disappointment in his eyes, Michael knew he'd already been plotting a heist. Toddling off down the street, Jared disappeared around the corner.

Michael had probably wasted the tuppence on the scrawny confidence man, but somehow, he was reassured. Jared reported to *him*, not the Met—it felt like ages since he'd sourced snitches from the general population. The Met was not keen on associating with the criminal ilk, whether or not their knowledge could be mined for better purposes.

After taking one last look at the alley, Michael continued toward the station. Cautiously, he picked his way around the rubbish, the broken bottles. The downed bodies of the vagrants sprawled out fast asleep in doorways. Despair everywhere. The master artist Hogarth hadn't exaggerated his Gin Lane piece, despite the claims of politicians.

How could anyone live like this? He remembered Knight saying that Abigail resided in a crumbling lodging house over by Drury Lane, one of the most depraved streets in Whitechapel. He'd explored his fair share of the rookeries during his time as a patroller, but every night he'd been glad to come home to his snug, clean bed.

In the past, he'd pushed any concern for the poor into the back of his mind. It'd been easier to pretend the denizens were all delinquents, since the crime rates for these areas were astronomical. The numbers had dulled him into believing the rookeries were a royal pain in his ass.

Abigail Vautille was not so simple to categorize. She was neither criminal nor entirely honest.

He reminded himself that nothing good had ever come from

unnecessary self-examination. The Clowes threat needed to be contained. He could do his civic duty as an inspector *and* enjoy the benefits of his bet with Miss Vautille. After the two weeks were over, he'd go back to his normal existence. It was a good plan. A solid plan.

Once a rake, always a rake.

Chapter Three

L ater that morning, Michael leaned back in his chair in his home office. Since he had a few minutes before Knight would arrive, he re-read the gaoler's report. Clowes's bellicose behavior had escalated after his arrest. The worst criminals behind Newgate's walls had nurtured his horrific tendencies. Aided and abetted by a few members of the Chapman Street Gang, Clowes had started a riot inside the prison. Only by the grace of God had the guards survived.

Clowes was the last one left of any importance in the old crew, after Effie Larker's death and Boz Larker's hanging. He'd been poised to take over the old operation, so the longer he was free, the better chance he had to get in touch with his old compatriots.

A knock sounded on his office door, followed by a familiar call. "Smithers let me in."

He glanced at the clock: noon. Never had he been so glad for Knight's dogmatic punctuality. "Come in."

The door opened, and in came not only Thaddeus Knight but his new wife as well. The smile on Michael's lips froze.

"Mrs. Knight," he said, dropping as formal of a bow as he

could manage in the little space between his desk and the back wall.

Poppy curtsied back to him. She was a dimber lass; he'd grant Knight that. Almost two heads shorter than the willowy Knight, she had startlingly red hair and a smattering of freckles that should've marred her features but somehow made her endearing.

Yet Poppy Knight perplexed him. No matter how much he complimented or teased her, she never responded favorably to his overtures as other women did. His flirtations were tried and true, honed by years of practice. He didn't want to seduce his friend's wife, of course, but he'd expected she'd at least find him amiable. After their twelfth meeting, he'd given up on winning her over.

She sat in the chair across from his desk. Knight took the other seat, his angular face a mask of imperturbability, as it always was. His posture was relaxed, his white linen shirt and gray waistcoat fitting his trim body far better than his blues ever had.

Knight wound Poppy's hand in his own with such ease that Michael found himself strangely envious of their connection.

Shaking off that maudlin feeling, he cleared his throat. "I didn't expect you to come, too, Mrs. Knight."

He should have known, of course. The two went every-where together now. But to a meeting on police matters? Really, Knight should control his woman better.

"Poppy," she corrected him, as she did every time they met. "And I'm sorry for the intrusion, but your missive said it had to do with the Larker case."

Michael arched a brow at Knight, silently questioning if his friend was sure he wanted to discuss dangerous business in front of his wife. Knight nodded. Poppy followed their quiet exchange with a frown.

Women these days. Can't live with them, can't be happy without shagging them.

No use beating around the proverbial bush any longer. He cut to the point. "Frank Clowes has escaped."

Poppy's face went ashen.

Knight's lips set into a firm line. "How is that possible? Last we spoke, he was bound for transportation."

There was a note of disapproval in Knight's tone that Michael didn't appreciate. As if he had already judged the management of the situation and found it lacking.

"People escape. You should know that Knight, given the family you married into." Michael directed a pointed glare toward Poppy.

"My brother was innocent," Poppy objected, her eyes narrowing. "If he hadn't escaped on the way to Newgate, they would've hung him for a crime he didn't commit. A crime *your* father arrested him for, need I remind you."

Knight patted her hand and murmured something under his breath that sounded vaguely like "There, there." It was comforting to know marriage hadn't made Knight any less awkward in his social interactions. Perhaps there was a god shining down upon Michael after all.

But when he glanced at Poppy again, he saw only love in her eyes. Women did not look at Michael that way. He was the recipient of seductive winks and salacious appeals to deities, not gentle, unbridled affection.

It was better this way. Knight was shackled to the same woman for the rest of his life, but Michael could have sex with any prime article he chose.

"My father made a lot of mistakes, including arresting your brother," Michael conceded. The worst of those mistakes had been driving his wife into an early grave, but Poppy didn't need to know that. "Rest assured, Mrs. Knight, I am not my father.

When I give you my word as a gentleman that we will catch Clowes, know that you can trust it."

He hadn't been a gentleman for years, but Poppy didn't need to know that either.

"Do you have any leads?" Knight asked, leaning forward. His eyes gleamed with the customary excitement of a new case.

"I shouldn't discuss this with you," Michael reminded him. "Since Whiting, the whole division is barred from sharing information with the public."

Knight winced. "Ah. Terribly sorry about that." If Knight hadn't put together the file on Whiting's involvement—with the help of the enterprising factory worker that was now his wife—none of this would have happened.

Frank Clowes would still be terrorizing the city, and Knight would still be with the H-Division.

Damn it all.

"I want you to be careful," Michael said. "Both of you. I'd like you to leave town until Clowes is found. In the course of investigating, we discovered Clowes is responsible for three other murders tied to the Larkers."

Poppy shuddered. "I can't believe I ever thought he was nice. The blackguard."

"He has a way about him," Knight stated. "He seems affable at first. But Effie Larker chose him as her hatchet man for a reason—he's as sick and twisted as she was."

Michael drummed his fingers on Clowes's file, open upon his desk. The twenty-year-old brute had grown up in Spitalfields as the son of false mendicants like Kip Jared. The elder Mr. Clowes still haunted a street corner in Bloomsbury, scars dyed into his skin with berries. From an early age, Frank Clowes had learned the only way to make money was to cheat.

Ignoring every dictate by the superintendents, Michael passed the file to Knight. "We received a note from him."

Knight opened the file. "What did it say?"

"That he was going to come after whoever helped put him in prison. That's why I wanted to meet with *you*." He stressed the "you," but Poppy took no notice of his exclusion.

Knight didn't look up from the file. "I'm glad you sent for us."

Michael resisted the urge to groan in frustration. "Of course."

Lost in thought, Knight flipped through the papers. After one read, the information would be cemented into his memory for life. While Knight discovered clues in patterns, Michael looked at the numbers, dealing in probabilities and variables. Together, they'd made one hell of a team.

Knight should've remained with the Met and helped them out. Then maybe they wouldn't have Clowes out on the damn street.

And Clowes would be Knight's problem instead of Michael's.

"Newgate was not kind to him while he awaited sentencing," Michael continued. "Apparently, the criminal lot doesn't like it when you kill young girls."

"Perhaps there is justice after all," Poppy muttered.

"Two girls murdered." Knight tilted his head to examine a particularly gruesome sketch from a different angle. "One fifteen, the other seventeen. I'd heard there was new evidence against him when the trial began. How did I miss this before?"

Michael sighed. His friend hadn't missed anything—there hadn't been any evidence to find before. Knight maintained his perfect record for accuracy in detection.

"Whiting buried it," he clarified. "The deaths were listed as suicides, and he made sure no one looked closer. When I was helping to clear out his office, I found some of his old files."

Poppy exchanged a glance with Knight, and he swiftly closed the file.

"You said he's targeting anyone who was involved in capturing him." Poppy's voice was barely above a whisper. "Has anyone heard from Abigail recently? It was because of her that we knew the true depth of Clowes's involvement."

Michael's gaze drifted to the promissory note, buried under a stack of files. Poppy didn't seem to notice, but Knight's eyes narrowed as he followed Michael's movement.

Knight's eyes narrowed. "Have you seen Abigail?"

"Actually, yes. I met her in Cruikshank's gaming hell." He didn't think Poppy would appreciate the details of his arrangement with Abigail, but there was nothing she could do about it now.

"In a hell?" Confusion flickered in Poppy's eyes until she remembered. "Ah. Retrieving her father, most likely."

"Indeed," Michael said. "Mr. Vautille had been at the faro table with me. By the end of the night, he owed me two hundred pounds."

"Two hundred pounds?" Poppy's mouth dropped open, then shut, then opened again, resembling a fish out of water. It'd be amusing if he didn't suspect she was going to shriek at him.

"I should hope you excused the debt," Knight said.

Michael waved his hand insouciantly. "Miss Vautille would not allow me to."

Knight's gaze narrowed in on the vowels. "Is that the note?"

Michael nodded. "Suffice to say, Miss Vautille and I have reached a mutually agreeable arrangement. You need not worry."

"May I see the note?" Poppy's voice left no room for disagreement.

This was why he didn't have long-term relationships. When women used that tone, it was because they were too used to getting their own way. And he, as every man before him, was powerless to disobey.

He passed the note deliberately to Knight. Poppy scooted closer, peering over his shoulder. When Poppy's face reddened and she pushed back her chair, fists planted on her hips, Michael knew he was a goner. She leaned over the desk, looking for something to hurl in his face. Knight grasped her arm, tugging her back to him.

"I'm sure it's not what it looks like, love," he murmured soothingly.

But Poppy was having none of his consolation this time. She pushed out of his hold, two quick steps bringing her right in front of Michael's desk. "You despicable, rotten, vile scoundrel!"

He opened his mouth to defend himself, but then thought twice of it. Why should he have to account for his actions? *If* Miss Vautille was a virgin, he was doing her a favor. Her first time with him would be far more pleasurable than with any of the other men she could expect to take on as a woman of the town.

He'd guard her for the next two weeks—whatever happened between them was no one else's business.

"I think you're overstating matters." He calmly pried the note from Knight's hands.

"Don't try and deny it. I see your signature on the note." Anger made Poppy's voice uneven. "You're no better than a whoremonger!"

He heaved a sigh. Knight was going to owe him at least three ales for this conversation.

"Mrs. Knight, plenty of women engage in the flesh trade. Are you objecting to the fact that your friend is now a lady of easy virtue, or to me being with her?" He held Poppy's gaze, refusing to be cowed. "Because if your objection is to me, you're quite right. I am a rogue. But it is my reputation that will ensure your friend greatly...enjoys, shall we say, her time with me."

When Poppy stammered in response, he continued, "But if it is her new occupation that bothers you, then you must consult *her,* not me. She proposed our arrangement, so I can only assume it was amenable to her."

"She has no money!" Poppy started toward him again.

He took a quick assessment of things in the room that she could throw at him and decided he'd best duck.

"Poppy," Knight tried again softly. "Do try and remember this is my friend you're talking to."

Michael's lips curled into a small smile. His friendship with Knight had transmuted from an office rivalry to geniality. He had sparring partners and lads he could call upon if he wanted a jolly good night of carousing, but Knight was the only real friend he had.

"Yes, he's an arse," Knight continued. "But I sense there's more to this story."

"Let's say for a moment I believe you're capable of honorable intentions," Poppy ventured, her lethal glance at him belying her words. "How are you going to watch over Abigail when you're at the station? I remember Thaddeus's long hours."

Michael shuffled through the papers on his desk, this time emerging triumphantly with a new sheet. "I've taken time off. I'll allow Miss Vautille to stay with me until Clowes is found, and then I'll send her back to her family with a full load of groceries."

Knight nodded. "That sounds vaguely acceptable if you sleep in separate beds."

He pasted a smile on his face that he hoped passed for acquiescence, and not questioning Knight's sanity. Clearly, Knight was too besotted with his wife to see Abigail's beauty.

Any man in his right mind would be a fool to refuse the chance to lay with her.

"You have to let me see her," Poppy charged. "She won't take my calls. I've stopped by a few times and talked with her younger sister, but Abigail refuses me. You've got to let me in."

"I will speak to Miss Vautille on your behalf," Michael promised. "But given the current situation, I think it's best if you leave town until Clowes is captured."

"We'll figure it out. We always do," Knight promised, putting his arm around Poppy. He glanced over at Michael. "And Michael will do his part."

Michael bristled. "Of course, I will."

Knight nodded swiftly, rising from his chair. "Thanks for letting us know about Clowes. I'll reach out to Dagobert Gottlieb too. He might have heard something."

Michael recoiled at the idea of involving Gottlieb. The fence had been one of Knight's informants during his time with the Met. When Michael had tried to convince Gottlieb to assist them again, Gottlieb insisted he only trusted "Herr Knight."

I can pick my own informants. I'm the inspector now, not you.

That line of thinking had put him in this mess in the first place. He hadn't reached out to Knight in months for anything relating to the job. If his team were to see him as good of an officer as Knight, he had to do this on his own. Though he'd continued to see Knight on a weekly basis, it had been for ales at the Ten Bells or sparring in the gymnasium.

Sketching a quick equation on foolscap, he calculated about a seventy percent chance that his officers would view him as incompetent for needing Knight's connections. On the other side, there was a thirty percent probability he'd appear magnanimous.

Feasible. He'd faced worse odds before.

"So, you'll talk to Gottlieb." He pushed the paper away from him. "And the other?"

Poppy feigned ignorance. Her association with London's greatest thief, Atlas Greer, was not widely known throughout the Met, but Michael was aware of her connections. The Gentleman Thief was her brother's best friend. People claimed he knew every illegal movement within the city boundaries and some that extended past London's borders.

Knight gave a swift nod. "I'll talk to him. And you needn't worry. I'll keep my girls out of harm's way—you just need to be concerned about Miss Vautille."

After they departed, Michael stared at the vowels, left on his desk by Poppy. Abigail Vautille would arrive in the next few hours, and he'd have to tame the hellcat into an amiable kitten that didn't want to claw out his eyes.

He'd already begun to regret this contract.

THE CARRIAGE WHEELS spun against the muck of the cobbled streets, a funeral dirge for the death of Abigail's innocence. Each turn of the spokes took her away from Baker's Row and the life she'd known.

She ran her good hand across her washed-out blue skirt, picking at the seam of the patch that Bess had sewn to disguise a tear in the fabric. Her once-spotless white sleeves were dingy, and without the horsehair pads that should have gone into the sleeves, the starched linen collapsed upon her bony shoulders. Her bright sapphire bodice was the only part of her outfit that did not bear some egregious offense to modern fashion.

"You don't have to do this." Papa sat next to her, leaning back against the squabs as if this carriage was theirs, and not some hired cab they'd been able to afford only because Strickland had slipped her the fare that night in the hell.

I don't want you to have to walk all the way to Cheapside. She heard Strickland's voice, low and gruff, yet somehow comforting. She'd lost her wits completely if she thought that bastard—who was going to strip her of the one thing she'd kept hers for these last nineteen years—had good in him.

It was only that he didn't want his product damaged.

"We'll find some other way," Papa continued, as though he hadn't irrevocably sealed her fate already. She refused to look at him, her chin raised high. Perhaps if she didn't turn her head, he wouldn't see the tears that dotted her eyes.

No more crying. He didn't deserve her tears any more than Inspector Strickland did.

She spoke through clenched teeth. "You didn't give me any choice, did you?"

"I could go in your place," Papa suggested. Now that he was sober, he was horrified by what he'd allowed her to agree to. His remorse was too little, too late.

"How would that work?" She sniffed. "I highly doubt Inspector Strickland fancies elderly cuckolds."

Papa coughed. But what began as a delicate cough to express his discontent of her characterization of him transformed into a shoulder-shaking, gut-twisting hollow croup. He yanked out a handkerchief, hacking up a chunk of blood and fluid into it.

She ought to feel some measure of pity. The rookeries had been hard on him too.

For a second, she was tempted to place her palm over his. She stared down at her glove, the stitches of the black silk as normal to her now as the shape of her nose, or the natural part in her hair.

"I'd give him my life," Papa rasped. "Let him take me to Marshalsea."

She stopped mid-reach, stopped because the idea was so damn tempting. God, what was wrong with her that she'd consider sending her own father to debtor's prison without remorse?

But he was her father, whether she liked it or not. Bess cared for him. How could she willingly send him to prison? She'd promised Bess they'd stay together as a family.

"And then Bess has no guardian," Abigail explained. "She already believes you care more about the tables than us. If you go to prison, there's no chance we'll be able to pay your way out."

"But you wouldn't have to do this." Papa patted her knee as if by touch alone, he could make it all better.

Abigail scooted down toward the window, drawing the curtains. They'd left Whitechapel, headed through Spitalfields, and now were on their way to Cheapside. The houses here had two or even three floors, none of which required a tumbledown set of stairs up the side of the building. There was little rubbish in the streets here, and several of the carriages passing them had coats of arms appliquéd to the sides.

Bess would have been beside herself to see this side of London. She probably would've demanded they stop every carriage to see if a duke was inside, even though Cheapside wasn't fashionable enough for those lofty peers. Cheapside was a neighborhood for barristers, rich merchants, and apparently policemen like Strickland.

Every clop of horse hooves on stone brought her further from the life she'd always known. She must remain strong, or she'd sink into the cushions of this carriage and never get back up. She thought of the man who'd visited her in the hospital—she couldn't remember his face. She wasn't even sure he'd been real. The laudanum prescribed to lessen the pain of her wounds had dulled her mind.

But whether he was a hallucination or a tangible person, she remembered his words. *You'll be fine, you hear me? You're a fighter. You're going to emerge from the other side stronger.*

She turned in her seat to face Papa. Once, he'd read her bedtime stories, taught her how to weave on the handloom, and brought her the last apple left from his cart so she could have a special treat for lunch. He'd disappeared inside himself after her mother's death. Been the reason she had to sell her beloved books.

Though he sat within arm's reach from her in this carriage, a chasm had opened between them.

As the scenery became steadily more residential, she drew herself up to her full height. "I'm no longer a little girl, Papa. You cannot pretend to be a hero any longer. I see you for who you really are."

She shouldn't have glanced over at him. Shouldn't have seen his face fall, as if she'd struck him in the stomach with her fist. His hand shook as it did during a particularly unsuccessful round of cards.

Because a stab of pain, his pain caused by her, sliced through the icy layers of her heart. She grabbed for his hand, wrapping her numb fingers around his lightly. She felt nothing. Yet somehow, this was right, to hold his hand in her damaged one and pretend that they still functioned as a normal family.

"Papa," she murmured, "I didn't mean it."

"We both know you did." His fingers squeezed around her hand, thumb running over the indent in her flesh that had never healed.

She didn't wince. Didn't pull away. If she could have, she would have gripped his hand tight enough that he'd know she wanted to believe he could be better. Now that he'd be banned from all the gambling dens, maybe there'd be a chance for him.

"I deserve it, Abbie-girl," he whispered. "I deserve your scorn. So, go on ahead and heap it on me, for all I been doin' is makin' you and Bess suffer for my mistakes."

"Perhaps that's not *all* you've done," Abigail dithered.

He let out a derisive snort.

"You've got a second chance now," she told him. "Don't enrage Mason by trying to go back to the hells. The second you step foot in that door, you'll be dragged off the premises."

"I give you my word," he replied, but the slight twitch to his brow made her doubt his words.

She sighed. At least Bess would be with their neighbor. Yesterday, she'd made sure that Mrs. Henderson knew the real circumstances behind her absence so that she wouldn't allow Bess to go along with any of Papa's wild schemes. Bess was to bring her week's pay to Mrs. Henderson, who would use it for the girl's upkeep.

Papa looked out the window. They sat in silence for the rest of the ride, hands clasped, united for the small space of this trip. She tried to focus on the memory of Strickland's broad shoulders filling out his superfine coat, his tanned skin, and muscular forearms. At least, she told herself, at least he had not the face of an ape. At least he was not twice her age, as so many of the men would be when she took to the streets.

She needed a plan.

Not just a plan for the next fortnight, but a plan for her future. Something that wouldn't involve her having to take charity from others. She'd earn her keep, damn it. Though she couldn't keep her virtue, at least she could keep her integrity.

She reflected upon her options. How could she keep Bess safe if she ended up as a case vrow? Not only did the idea of being owned by a brothel turn her stomach, but she'd also be expected to reside there. She wouldn't be able to watch over her sister. The money she made wouldn't be enough to secure any sort of future for Bess.

Abigail crossed off that class of prostitute from her mental list. If she were to become a woman of the town, she'd have to wait on the street corners for men to seek her out. That didn't seem particularly efficient, and she required blunt before the next month's rent came due. Otherwise, Bess wouldn't have a place to live.

She thought of how she'd learned to read. One letter at a time, then entire words, and finally full sentences. And when she'd realized her accent marked her as a factory girl, she had practiced every day to smooth out her natural dialect until she sounded perfectly bourgeoisie. She had been so very determined to become educated so that she'd be able to leave Whitechapel someday.

So that she could become something *more* than this.

An independent woman, free from the malice of poverty.

But fate had a cruel way of reminding her that she'd never become anything more than a broken, deformed weaver—now good for nothing but whoring.

Damn it all. If there were no future left for her, she'd make sure *Bess* still had a chance at a better life.

She watched as the traffic flashed by the hack window. If she'd taught herself how to read and speak without the stunted syllables of a born-and-bred rookery chit, then surely she could learn the art of debauchery. It couldn't be that difficult. What else was there to it besides lying on her back with her legs spread, pretending a man's rod was the best gift in the world? She suspected the men who visited prostitutes didn't expect genuine emotional investment in the copulation.

Tapping her fingers on the squabs, Abigail considered her options. Everyone knew that *skilled* lightskirts were in high demand amongst the rich, who married for money and not the suitability of their partners. A good courtesan could demand exorbitant fees. Enough that she'd be able to send Bess to school, and maybe even rent a house of her own.

The hack drew to a stop in front of a townhouse sandwiched between equally imposing properties. The house was two stories with pristine white paint over the stucco and brick, with well-tended flower boxes in each of the windows that blossomed even in this cold weather. Ivy covered the front of the house, a jungle in the middle of urban London.

Her breath caught in her throat as she peered out at the door. Red again. Red like the wine she'd need tonight to go through with this seduction.

The carriage door rolled back, and the driver stood at the side, waiting for them to disembark. Papa moved forward to help her down, but Abigail stopped him.

"I've got to do this on my own," she told him. If Papa came inside, he'd try to talk Strickland into throwing him into Marshalsea instead. Bess had already lost one parent. Though Papa was a shoddy influence, he was better than nothing.

Abigail took the hand of the driver, sliding down slowly so as not to jar her knees. She pressed the return fare into the man's hands, ordering him to take Papa back to their flat in Whitechapel. "By no means take him to a gaming hell, no matter what he says," she said sternly. The driver nodded.

The carriage rolled away. She stood on the street, surveying Strickland's massive townhouse. What did he do with all this space? Before her injury, all she'd needed in life had fit into one room: her books, enough food to survive, her three dresses and suitable appurtenances, and a sheet-covered pallet to sleep upon.

But according to the rumors around Cruikshank's, Strickland was prone to excess in all forms. He had some wealth, so he'd be an excellent start. Not high society, but respectable enough to command some attention. Her time with him would be a learning experience.

If she intended to become an accomplished ladybird, then she needed references. Men who could attest to how good of a lay she was. She swallowed down her dread, refusing to succumb to it. She'd done the only thing possible when entering into this agreement with Strickland, but she'd be damned if she didn't control *how* this whole affair was conducted. By the time two weeks were over, she'd have the skills needed to sell herself in the fashionable West End.

Nodding sharply, she set off down the walk to Strickland's townhouse. While traffic on the adjacent streets echoed, there was no sign of activity here. All the toffs must be inside, drinking tea from fancy cups until they had to dress for dinner. As she took another step forward, she heard the slap of boots on cobblestone. She turned around, expecting to see someone else in the walk.

But there was no one there.

Had she imagined the sound? She replayed it in her mind again. Maybe she was overreacting. Surely, lots of things made that noise.

The silent street felt cryptic. Too quiet. Prickles crept up her neck. All her senses roared to high alert. Something wasn't right.

"Is anyone there?" Her grip tightened on her valise.

There was no response. No one stepped out from a waiting carriage or emerged from the neighboring houses. She tried to tell herself this was nonsense. Why would anyone be following her? She hadn't told anyone else but Papa and Mrs. Henderson that she was coming here, and she highly doubted anyone reading the betting ledger at Cruikshank's would care enough to seek her out.

She couldn't shake the sensation that someone was watching. A shiver sliced through her, leaving goose pimples on her arms. She sped up, her half-boots pounding into the path. When she reached the door, she knocked as hard as she could, beating her knuckles into the wood. She glanced over her shoulder.

Her heart pulsated in her ears, but she was still the only person on the street. The fear made her mistrust everything. Her new plan, the fact that she'd let her father drive away, her own sanity.

She had a terrible feeling this was only the beginning of the danger she'd face in the next fourteen days.

Chapter Four

Michael didn't know what he'd thrown himself into this time. He'd been in over his head before—hell, his entire life could be summarized in that one state of being—but this time was the worst of it.

Women had never been difficult for him. He understood those in his acquaintance as primarily simple creatures, with needs and wants similar to his own. Pleasure, good food, good wine, and proper compensation for their efforts.

But one look at Abigail Vautille on his doorstep, her satin fist up to bang on his door again, and he was lost. He forgot about Clowes. He forgot about the scrutiny the division would face. Damnation, he forgot his own name.

Because standing there was the most beautiful woman he'd ever seen. In the dim light of the gaming hell, he'd considered her ethereal. She'd been a gothic beauty, that black cape and golden halo enticing his every fancy.

When he'd seen her in the hospital bed months prior, he hadn't been able to forget her. The nurses had patched her cuts, but her eye was still swollen shut then. The light sheen of perspiration upon her brow and the sick translucence to her almost-white skin had left him with the desire to rip Clowes's heart clean out of his chest for hurting her.

Even in her most downtrodden state, she'd been beautiful to him.

None of those experiences compared to now. Wisps of blonde escaped from her simple bun, framing her delicate face. Her skirt flared out around her hips; hips so rounded that visions of grasping onto her as he thrust into her hot wetness dotted before him. His throat grew impossibly dry. His gaze rested upon her plush lips, no longer pricked with dried blood as they had been in the hospital.

This was the best two hundred pounds he'd spent in his life.

"Inspector Strickland," she said, her crisp tones startling him back to reality. "Would you let me in, please?"

Was it his imagination, or did she sound a little too urgent? She probably didn't want to be seen by the neighbors. He jumped back from the door, holding it open for her.

She walked into the room, setting down the small, shabby portmanteau she carried onto the wooden floor of his entryway. Dust swirled up from the bag, winding around her skirt and clinging to the fabric.

She did not appear to notice it. Her blue eyes were wide and vibrant, fastened upon his face with an equal mix of trepidation and somehow...relief? Was she happy to be here with him? He quickly discarded that notion. Most likely, she was delighted she wouldn't have to spend two weeks upon his stoop while he gazed at her mutely.

What a nattering fool he was.

He shook his head. A clear mind, that's what he needed. The kind of clarity that only came with a hearty dinner. He tugged on the bell pull that hung in the hall, and the clang of a gong echoed through the house.

Miss Vautille jumped back at the sound, almost losing her

footing. He grabbed for her arm, holding her steady until she recovered.

"My butler will arrive shortly," he explained. "Smithers shall take your bag up to your room."

She blinked. "My room?"

"Yes." He'd decided it was better for her to have her own room. Less personal than if she spent all her time with him.

Her lips pressed into an adorable bow shape, but she didn't question him further. He rather liked that about her.

He halted mid-thought. When had he started to use words like adorable? Puppies and kittens were adorable. Women ought to be dimber or coquettish. Christ, this was how smart men like Knight ended up leg-shackled for the rest of their lives. He pushed his fingers through his hair, ruining a half hour of his servant's work.

Smithers appeared beside him. Though he was a large, hulking man, Smithers glided soundlessly, the product of many years spent first as a soldier and then in service. Michael gestured to the bag, and Smithers picked it up. His bushy gray-streaked brows creased.

Michael narrowed his eyes, signaling to Smithers not to inquire. Smithers tapped his finger to his bulbous nose and shrugged, his dark eyes twinkling as he set off toward Abigail's room.

He held out his arm to escort her. "I thought I'd show you around the house."

Her touch was light as she placed her hand on the crook of his arm. That touch sizzled through him, just as it had in the hell. Perhaps she felt it too, for her grip upon his arm tightened.

He sucked in one breath, then another, to quiet his wayward nerves. Clearly, the gin from the night before had come back to haunt him. This was a temporary madness.

He had things to teach her about seduction, not the other way around.

Striding down the hall, he slowed his gait to accommodate her staggering pace. He didn't mind the imposition. He had never understood how women could move swiftly in those cumbersome skirts. He preferred the freedom of movement that came with their nakedness, the removal of an absurd number of petticoats and outer trappings.

Yet Miss Vautille surprised him, for she matched his stride with a steadiness he had not accounted for. In not more than a minute, they had come to the third door on the right of the hallway.

He made a sweeping motion toward the bookshelves. "This is the library." Of course, she could see this was a library. "Should you wish to read, please, be my guest. What I have is yours while you are here."

She let go of his arm, proceeding into the room without further introduction. For a second, she stood in the center, her spine stiff and her hands outstretched. Then she was off, determinedly pacing toward the shelf of popular novels he'd collected over the years. He had not the sheer magnitude of Knight's library, but he still had a decent assortment of literature.

"I like this," Miss Vautille declared, her black-tipped finger running along the leather spines of the books. "What you have is beautiful, and I am..." She pursed her lips, turning to face him. "I am surprised to see it all."

"Did you not take me for a learned man?" He knew the answer already, for he took pains to appear a certain way to the ladies. Women weren't impressed that he'd begun his own moral statistics grid of London, using a choropleth map developed by Charles Dupin.

"I will confess I did not," she ventured, the slightest hint of pink cresting her cheeks.

Desire flashed within him. She was wrong. The library was not beautiful—she was.

"Fear not, Miss Vautille." He strolled toward her, coming to a stop behind her. "I don't fault you for misconceptions I actively cultivate."

Her hand paused on the volume of essays by Swift she'd been about to remove from the shelf. She tilted her head to meet his gaze. "We all live behind masks, don't we? Sometimes I think it is the only way to survive." As he'd done when he welcomed her inside, she gestured to the entirety of the room.

She let out a tinny laugh. "This world is harsh and barren, though I suppose you'd know little of that."

"I am aware of the plight of the less fortunate," he protested.

She scoffed. "What pretty language you use, Inspector. If you spent a day in the rookeries—one day truly in the stews, without this palace to come home to—I doubt you would describe us so."

At best, his townhouse was moderately respectable. Situated on the least fashionable street in Cheapside, his grandfather had won it in a game of cards. His neighbor on the left was a merchant, and on the right was a retired naval officer. Hardly the Upper Ten Thousand.

He surveyed Abigail curiously. "How should I describe you then?"

A sad smile twisted her lips. "We are creatures of malcontent, pressed further and further back into these dark corners until, eventually, we shall all smother each other."

Her speech—both the poetry of it and the smoothness of her accent—surprised him. She was cultured, much more than he'd expected. That intrigued him. He liked a puzzle, and she certainly was one.

"Miss Vautille, surely while you are here—" He wasn't sure

what he'd been about to suggest, but she'd have none of it regardless.

"While I am your fen, you'd prefer I not discuss such unseemly matters?"

At this rate, he'd rather her not talk at all. He frowned, biting back a response about how his father had always said women were better seen, not heard. Somehow, he doubted *that* would go over well.

Her face transformed, the combativeness fleeing from her eyes. She stepped closer to him, reaching out. Her outstretched palm flat upon his chest, she leaned into him, her voice dropping to a sensual whisper that caressed his mind. "I am sorry for not remembering my place, Strickland. Do you need to punish me, as you do to all your bed partners?"

The very idea had him hard in a matter of seconds. He added a check to his mental list of skills she'd need as a Cyprian.

"Saucy minx," he growled, his hand closing upon her wrist, wrenching her palm off of him. "If you continue to talk like that, I shan't be responsible for my actions."

"Men of your ilk never are," she remarked, the coolness of her eyes offset by the slow, seductive rise and fall of her chest. She leaned into him, the movement pushing her pert breasts up against the confines of her corset.

His breeches were tight against him, uncomfortably so. This woman, this bloody vixen, with her perfect body and her wild words. He'd always considered himself a man well equipped for vulgarity, as at home in Cruikshank's hell as he was in a drawing room. Skating on the edge of two social circles, an air of debauchery clung about him, enough that innocent misses were curious about him, and seasoned ladybirds sought him out in dark alcoves.

No woman had ever spoken to him the way Abigail Vautille did, frankly and without regard to his masculine pride.

He gripped her hand, his fingers closing around the thin planes of her wrist, guiding her closer to his lips.

"When I'm at work, I am the man in charge." He pressed a hard kiss against the silk of her glove, wishing that it was her bare skin. "When I come home, nothing changes."

"If you expect to be obeyed, you shan't find me worth the two hundred pounds you paid." She defied him, even when her eyes clouded with desire.

He knew arousal when he saw it, could sense the almost palpable shift in the air. Everything around them became new, possessed with a fledgling fire that, if stoked, would become a raging blaze.

"I'd consider you well worth the price," he told her, his voice already too thick for these minimal touches.

Her cheeks flushed as he continued up her wrist, kissing her open palm. Her lower lip quivered. He tasted silk on his tongue, bland yet tinged with the promise of more. This library, which had become a sanctuary to him in the past few months, swirled around him and faded into nothing.

There was only Miss Vautille.

"But maybe I should make you earn it." He took a chance, drunk off her reaction. Was there a bawdy harlot inside this chaste innocent? A woman who wanted taming as much as she longed to make him submit?

Her upper lip curved, playing skepticism like her ace. "You could try, but I doubt you'd be successful."

"I do so love a challenge." He grabbed for her waist, pulling her flush against him.

He acted on instinct, driven by the age-old need that influenced most of his decisions. He wanted her. He must have her. And so, he would, for he was a Corinthian and a rogue, and women could never resist these attributes combined in one man.

Dipping his head down, he brushed his lips over hers. A

teasing kiss meant to build up passion within her. He'd test the waters, judge how much practice she had. She'd claimed to be a virgin, but she was a Whitechapel lass, so surely, she'd have to know something...

But she didn't kiss like a girl who knew the strength of her wares. She fumbled against his lips, unable to find his rhythm. He pressed harder, and she backed off instead of picking up the pace. She lacked skill and finesse, but her innocence—and her eagerness when he began to nibble upon her lip in just the right way—intrigued him. Charmed him.

He slid his tongue out to dampen her lips. She didn't open her mouth to allow him entry. Her eyes popped open, and she froze in his hold. Soothing her worries, he went back to soft kisses, pressed along her jawline.

A breathy sigh escaped her lips; her head tilted back just slightly. Oh, this would be easier than he'd thought. The smallest sprig of hope budded within him.

Hope promptly crushed when she pulled away from him, escaping his hold upon her waist. Left him hot and bothered. His shaft was hard as granite.

One look at her was enough to cool that ardor. Dismay splashed across her face, in the sadness of those crystal-blue eyes. She might as well as have doused a bucket of cool spring water upon him.

"It is easier for you this way, isn't it?" Gone was the silky smoothness to her tone. She no longer met his eyes. "If I pretend to play the game."

He had not released her wrist. She remained in his hold. Her resignation disconcerted him. Did she not want this after all? Becoming a courtesan was a logical profession for her. Hell, if she were successful and landed a position as an aristocrat's mistress, she'd probably occupy a better social position than she had now.

"Miss Vautille—" The question was on his lips as he released her wrist.

"Yes?" She took a step back from him, her features schooled back into their usual detachment.

She was new at this. But that kiss had indicated she could play the game as well as any seasoned ladybird. An efficacious demimondaine was part-actress, part-seductress. With a bit more experience, she'd take the fast set by storm.

He proffered his arm again. "Shall we continue with the tour?"

* * *

STRICKLAND'S DINING ROOM table was by far the most mammoth piece of furniture Abigail had ever laid eyes upon. The not-so-good inspector lounged in his mahogany slotted back chair as if it was his throne.

She'd failed the first test earlier. When he'd tried to deepen their kiss, she should have accepted it. Acted as though she liked it. In truth, it wouldn't have taken that much pretending. Yearning for him had splashed giddily through her like the first downpour of spring. If he were someone else—if the circumstances were different—she would have responded to that kiss with equal passion.

His overtures had made her stomach flip precariously. She didn't have to work as hard as she'd expected to plaster a smile on her lips. When men were so openly vulgar around her, she usually hated it. But there was something about the ease of his manner—and the handsomeness of his face—that made her hope that sex with him wouldn't be as painful of an experience as she anticipated.

She swore she'd do better the next time. By the end of this arrangement, she'd be so damn tempting men would line up outside her door. She'd take their money, immoral though it was. It was the only way she could support her sister without assistance.

Gingerly, she readjusted her seat in the intricately carved mahogany chair with a red brocade cushion. She raised a polished silver fork to her mouth, feeling so out of place in all this richness. They sat at opposing heads of the table, as though they were indeed legal mistress and master of this great space. Uneasiness flipped through Abigail's stomach, and she lifted up a heavy glass goblet filled to the brim with Madeira.

So, she was common enough for him to buy her virginity, but apparently she still warranted being waited upon. Never mind that the butler was higher in class than she was. This had to be part of some elaborate charade. She was a status symbol to him, not a human being.

Draining a fourth of her goblet in one sip, she swallowed quickly to keep from gasping at the unexpected burst of flavor. She'd expected wine that tasted faintly of berries and mostly water, not drenched in sweetness and oak. Just another thing to add to her growing list of ways in which this place—and this man—disturbed her calm.

From across the room, Strickland's voice traveled to her. "Is the food to your liking?"

"Very much so." There was no denying she'd enjoyed the meal. A little too much, for in a matter of minutes, she'd cleared off a plate piled high with sweet rolls, partridge, fried artichoke bottoms, potatoes, sweet bread au jus, and carrots.

"Good." Strickland nodded his approval. "I want you to be happy here. This house is at your disposal."

She blinked. While she doubted that he was truly concerned about how she fared in these weeks, his words surprised her. "Thank you, sir."

His eyes locked on hers, and she was lost in his gaze. She

understood now how easily he was able to flip women's skirts. Hell, petticoats probably dissolved around him from the sheer heat of his stare. It was as if his eyes said "I'll make this the best damn night you've ever had," and his well-built body solidified that vow.

Very well then. She'd take the pleasure he promised and profit from it.

"It is the least I can do," he said. "Well, I suppose the very least I could have done was demand full payment, but that would've been rather rotten of me."

"Yes, it would have," she agreed, the sinking pit in her stomach expanding.

He shrugged. "I've been too long a man who does the very least. I know you don't maintain a high opinion of the Met, Miss Vautille, but contrary to popular belief, I do want to be able to look myself in the eye and not cringe at what I see."

He wanted to respect himself, but he had no problem with purchasing her to use at his whim. She bit back a harsh laugh. He cared only for the comeliness of her body. Her soul meant nothing to him.

What a pity he'd bought a broken ware. When he saw her scars, he might reconsider their agreement. Best that she keep the gloves on then.

She took another sip of wine. "If you can afford such a luxury as self-respect, then so be it."

If he'd caught the undercurrent to her remark, he didn't show it. He gestured to Smithers, who stood in the corner of the room, waiting for orders.

"More food for Miss Vautille," he commanded. "A woman should not be skin and bones."

Usually, she'd bristle at such an autocratic tone, but as Smithers dished out another serving from the spread on the table, her stomach rumbled. A grin broke out on Strickland's face at the sound. She blushed, eyes downcast, her fork poised in her hand.

"A healthy appetite is nothing to be ashamed of, especially if that appetite transfers to other proclivities," he teased.

The fabric of her dress was suddenly too heavy, for her body temperature had risen dramatically with his tempting tone. She bit into another currant bun and tried to compose herself. No, she wouldn't be affected by the great Strickland charisma. She had a plan, damn it, a good plan.

"Then your butler must be used to bringing you extra help-ings of everything," she said archly.

He laughed. "When it comes to good food and good company, I believe money shouldn't be an object."

His throaty chuckle sliced through her. She ought to thank him—this was just what she needed to harden her heart against him. No matter how bloody handsome he was, she couldn't fall for a man so oblivious to the problems of Whitechapel's poor.

For Strickland, this was all a game. He need not concern himself with the starving families on Baker's Row when he had more than enough food here.

"I've taken care of your other request," he said. "Your father won't be allowed to gamble anymore. Mason will make sure of that."

Relief flooded her until she remembered the other half of her promise. *I'll make it worth your while.* He'd expect her to keep her end of the bargain. Not only would she have to copu-late with him, now she'd have to submit to his other illicit desires.

She grabbed for the wine glass, swallowing the rest of the contents. Smithers came up behind her, immediately refilling her glass. She sucked down a quarter of that one too, in hopes it might help her to feel brave.

God had a sick sense of irony. It wasn't enough that she be

forced to whore, she must whore to the very man in charge of everything she loathed. She tugged her glove up higher on her left arm. How she hated these gloves! Hated what they stood for, hiding her scars from a world that refused to confront wickedness head-on. Cowards, from her father to the corrupt pigs of the Met.

When would the suffering end? How many pieces of her soul did she have to strip away until there was nothing left? No matter how judicious her plan was, she couldn't bring herself to relish her downfall.

She picked at the partridge. Meat that had been so succulent moments before tasted dry, composed of dust and dirt. Strickland knew nothing of her pain. He'd finished his plate too and moved on to a third glass of wine.

When his attention turned to spearing turnips onto his fork, she assessed him. He had sandy brown hair, rakishly unkempt from when he'd swept his hand through it. An athlete in every sense, he was muscle and sinews, wide-shouldered and toned. His shirt stretched over a well-defined abdomen she imagined would feel as stone did, hard and unyielding. His body was a machine, fit and ready for whatever life threw at him.

The only Met officer she'd met face-to-face had later married Poppy Corrigan, her old friend. Thaddeus Knight was tall and lean, with a boyish face and eyes that constantly calculated the world around him.

Michael Strickland was not like that. Everything about him bespoke arrogance. He did not walk; he swaggered. He did not smile; he smirked. And his long, oval face, with its wide forehead, strong chin, and straight nose, was better suited to a painting than a living, breathing man.

She hated him for his perfection. Hated him because no matter how much she resented him and all he stood for, she was attracted to him.

His eyes suddenly turned upon her. Studying her. She couldn't understand him. Why keep up this pretense of respectability between them when he'd already bought her? It was unnerving.

She'd not agreed to be friends with him. This was a business transaction. He'd take her body, but he'd never know her mind.

"If you have room for dessert, Cook has prepared a delightful trifle," he drawled, idly swirling the wine in his glass.

Four glasses he'd had. Anymore, and he'd either fall fast asleep as Papa did or slip into a belligerent rage like so many of the other drunkards she knew. Neither were appealing possibilities. If he slept, she'd have to go through this farce again tomorrow.

She wanted this over. Then she could begin to construct the proper walls around her heart, retreating within herself. She'd learned how to erect barriers in the past year, and no one had managed to slip past her cold reserves.

No one but the man who had held her hand in the hospital and told her it was all going to be fine.

"I'm afraid I've feasted so thoroughly I haven't any space left for trifle," she declared, proud of how level her voice sounded. This seduction would happen on *her* schedule. "I should like to retire for the night, Inspector. If you'd give me a few moments to prepare, you may then enter my room."

Chapter Five

Abigail did not light the candle. Twilight slatted in through the beveled panes of glass in the windows. This room was meant for a lady. Wallpaper painted with tiny pink roses adorned the walls. Dainty cherry furniture littered the space. One of the little chairs drawn up to the table by the window alone would have fetched three times her monthly wages at the pawnshop.

The bed was gargantuan, with a counterpane she assumed had to be down feathers from the softness. Sheets of satin, slick against her fingers as she ran her thumb across them, draped the mattress. She'd removed her gloves to undress, for it was hard to unfasten the hook and eye closure of her bodice with them on.

You're going to emerge from this stronger.

The phantom voice had been wrong. She wasn't stronger. She was breakable, and this act would shatter her into tiny pieces. No amount of money seemed worth this.

But Bess's future was. So, she'd summon up her last bit of resolve, and she'd pretend that she didn't think this would forever separate her from her old self.

The sheets were not red but purple. Purple like the bruises

ringing Abigail's eyes when Poppy had first come to her flat and forced her to go to the hospital. Purple like the violets her father used to sell in the market on Crispin Street. Abigail decided she loathed purple almost as much as she hated red, for purple was an in-between color, neither black nor blue, a mottled love child of both.

Purple was a color of beatings, of gasping for air, of drowning in rage.

She released the sheet, directing her attention to removing her bodice. Blue fabric, white sleeve puffs, the whole as dirty and tarnished as she was. Society didn't care that she'd kept herself pure. That she'd waited for marriage and love. Because love couldn't exist for a woman like her, cast out and deemed worthless.

Flinging the puffs on the floor, she slid down her skirt. The movement was not graceful. She hissed as her hand snagged on the twine cording of the petticoat underneath her skirt. Blood dotted her knuckles, the skin worn now from the twine. The outer layers of her skin were not substantial, feather thin as the stuffing of this counterpane. Her flesh blistered and bled, tore and twisted, each injury as immaterial as the next.

She was immaterial.

Her life meant nothing.

Her virtue meant nothing.

She pushed the petticoat from her legs until it balled around her. These heavy petticoats, these many layers of fabric, would not save her.

Stepping out from the skirt, she stood in her pantalettes, the last pair she owned. Perhaps she didn't even need to remove them, for they opened at the crotch, giving him access. Bile rose in her mouth, sharp and acidic.

Access. Entry. Words she'd deemed innocuous before, but which now showed their true obscenity.

Her corset was next. Boned busk in the middle, spiral laces in the back. A simple construction that held her upright when she wanted to stoop. She had no lady's maid—she wasn't even qualified to *be* a lady's maid—so she'd learned to lace up the back on her own. To fit the cord into each hole, locking into place this armor to ensure secrets remained impregnable.

In the past year, she'd traded three corsets back to the rag and bone shops before finding one that she could handle without heavy use of her left hand. In this corset, her breasts were plump. Shapely. She'd been proud of how she looked until she'd glanced down at her mangled hand. Then she'd remembered she was no better than a beast. She could have the trappings of the richest duchess, and still she'd be an animal.

Gone was the corset. Reluctantly, she pushed down the pantalettes, too, in case Strickland got rough. How was she to know his proclivities? In the library, he'd been frank about expecting obedience. Would he punish her if she were insolent? She'd teased him about it, but perhaps he truly would. She couldn't afford to replace the pantalettes, so she'd be practical in this. The undergarments came off.

Perhaps he would strike her. As she rolled her stockings down, she reasoned she'd already endured enough pain for three lifetimes. Anything he did would meet with emptiness from her.

Eventually, she'd become so dead inside that any attack would bounce off her. It'd be her solace as she rose in the demimondaine circles: she'd feel nothing.

She didn't fear the actual coupling in itself. No girl grew up in Whitechapel without intimate knowledge of sexual acts. In the one-room flat next door lived Molly McGee, who serviced men. From childhood on, Abigail had known exactly what the noises that filtered in through the walls were. Men were no better than rutting pigs for the groans and grunts they made.

In chatter, a few girls at the factory had claimed the losing of their virginity was the most agonizing thing they'd ever experienced. "Just for the first bit," one had said. "Then it gets better, but it's over so soon."

Abigail knew pain, and she highly doubted the push of Strickland's prick—however well-endowed he might think himself—could compare to the agony she'd already endured at the hands of the Larkers and Clowes.

She was unclothed. Bare. In shedding fabric, she chose to believe she'd discarded her old identity and become a new woman. No longer Abigail, but Beauty.

A properly sardonic name, for she wasn't beautiful. She was ugly to the core.

When she put those clothes back on, mayhap she'd become Abigail again. The sins of Beauty would fall away from her, and she'd emerge pure as new-fallen snow. She snagged her gloves from the bed, slid them back on.

He didn't get to see her scars.

A knock on the door broke through the quiet. She stepped toward it. Slow, dragging steps. For all that she'd claimed she wanted to finish this, in the moment, her throat clamped shut. This was it. There'd be no going back.

"Miss Vautille, I've brought you some peppermint tea," he called, leaving her to wonder if this was some weird ritual men insisted upon before fucking. Did she need to taste a certain way to make it good for him?

She tugged open the door. Stood there in her nakedness, too damn jumbled up to care what she looked like. "I only ask one thing: that you call me Beauty." Her voice shook, shook like her hand did, bracing the doorway for support. "Miss Vautille is no more."

* * *

CHRIST.

She was naked. Completely, irrevocably naked.

The tea tray slipped from his hand, crashed to the floor. Piping hot liquid spilled out over his shoe, but he shook his foot, for a ruined shoe was nothing in comparison to this sight. His brain sputtered. All blood flow had surely gone to his cock. He was hard and ready to possess her.

Immediately, the image of her burned into the darkest recesses of his mind: her body pink and pale, silhouetted by the dim light streaming in from the bedroom window. She wore nothing but the black gloves that reached up to her elbows. Those gloves were now emblems of carnal desire, soft satin he instantly wanted to be wrapped around his cock.

She said something about calling her Beauty. Her voice didn't land in his ears, but rather slid down his body as if it were honey. He'd call her anything she wanted if she'd only stay.

She reached out, her hand falling on his shoulder. Slowly, she massaged in a circle, her hands working out the kinks in his muscles caused by hunching over his desk for too long. God, he needed this. Needed her.

He didn't think to ask if she was certain, or even question why she'd chosen to present herself to him with only those damn gloves on. He wouldn't question this gift. Following her into the room, he closed the door behind him.

His eyes traveled downward to the indent of her hips. Hips wider than really was fashionable, but damnation, he loved a woman he could truly hold on to. That thatch of golden curls leading to her cunny had him thrumming with anticipation. How would she taste if he ran his tongue down those curls and dipped between her legs? She'd taste sweet, he guessed, better than any dessert he could devour.

He saw now the full extent of her knock-knees, what long hours in the factory as a child had wrought upon her body. But it was this imperfection that drew him to her, for it made her real. No longer was she the incorporeal spirit in his dreams, but a living woman.

God's teeth, God's hands, God's balls, and whatever other appendages of the deity that would help him get through this. She'd kill him before the night was over.

He was about to tell her just how much they were going to enjoy this when she ceased massaging him. Her hand shook. He reached for her, thinking that she was just scared. This must really be her first time. He could help her understand that after the first stab of pain, it'd all be pleasure.

Brushing his fingers along her chin, he kept his touch light. "I promise I'll make it good for you. There's no reason to be afraid." He leaned in, intending to kiss her.

As he met her gaze, a tear cascaded down her cheek. That one tear turned into two, three; then those tears became a full-fledged waterfall.

He jumped away from her. Craved distance as much as he'd craved closeness. His mind reeled. God's balls, he could track down the most elusive of thieves and interrogate a hardened criminal, but a crying woman sent him into a panic. What was he supposed to do with her now? He couldn't train her to be a Cyprian, not when she'd transformed from a seductress into a sniveling mess.

Damn her tears, damn his hopefulness, damn the night he'd gone to Cruikshank's.

Damn, damn, damn.

He fought the urge to run from the room, as he always wanted to when a woman cried. Somehow, he doubted his usual approach of leaving her alone until she sorted out her emotions would work here.

He coughed. It was half cough, half desperate intake of air. "I, ah, I did not, ah, naked."

She sniffled. He risked a glance at her. For the most part, she'd stopped crying. That was progress. He could handle snuffles. Hazarding a step toward her, he watched her judiciously for any signs of another outburst before he handed her a handkerchief from his pocket.

Accepting the cloth from him, she dabbed at her eyes. "I'm sorry. I thought I could handle this."

"The first time is hard," he said, with a vague wave of his hand.

"If you just give me a minute to compose myself, we can continue," she squeezed out between uneven breaths.

He took a step back from her. She must be mad if she thought he'd continue with her like this. "There's no way I'm tupping you tonight."

Or possibly ever. Her tears were now branded in his mind. He had wanted her to desire him—to feel the same attraction he felt for her. She didn't have to *like* him, but she did need to want him for him to have sex with her. He'd never take her unwilling. What kind of man did she think he was?

"You paid for this," she insisted. "I have a debt to honor."

"To hell with the debt." He cared little about the original parameters of their agreement now. She'd thrown that all to hell when she started weeping. "I may have paid for this, but I don't take sex from women without their consent. Christ, I'm not an absolute blackguard."

"That remains to be seen," she muttered. Her gloved hand fell to her hip, thrust out in a challenging pose. "What is the matter, Inspector? Do I not please you?"

He followed her hand to her hip with his eyes. There wasn't a single part of her that wasn't made for sin, but she wasn't for him.

He pulled his gaze back up to her face. Her tears had left salt tracks down her cheeks. The idea of sleeping with him had caused a complete emotional collapse in her. Damn it all. He'd never thought a naked woman could make him feel so ashamed.

Stuffing his hands in his pockets, he leaned back, resting his weight on the balls of his feet. "Your beauty isn't the issue. Put your damn clothes back on."

"This discussion isn't over." For all her defiance, she couldn't hide the relief that chased across her face. She spun around, the view of her backside nearly pulling a groan from him. She moved with the speed of a woman possessed, throwing her short-sleeved chemise on over her head without his approval. Skipping her stays, she had her dress back on before he could count to ten.

With her clothed, he could breathe again. Perhaps Knight was right: Michael thought too much with his cock. Or perhaps Knight could go sod off, since he'd found himself a wife that adored him while Michael traded barbs with a chit who reminded him of a feral feline, spitting and hissing whenever he neared.

"You bought me," she stated flatly. "You can have your servants wait on me all you want, but the truth remains you paid for my time. So, you should get what you paid for."

He gestured to the fall of his breeches, where his erection had dissipated almost completely. "I'm not the kind of man who finds pleasure in a woman's misery. I'm afraid the moment has passed, darling."

She watched him, her cat-like eyes flicking cagily from the door to him and back again. He didn't need to be a damn inspector to know she'd rather be anywhere but here.

Her disdain sliced through him. How addlepated he'd been to think she might remember him from his visit to the hospital. Perhaps it was better this way—that bond might have made things too personal between them.

He gulped for air, his earlier ardor doused by the red-hot ire splashed upon her face. The doxies he'd known coated their cheeks in thick rouge; Miss Vautille had enough emotion to paint her entire body cerise.

What made him so unsavory to her? Women had always raved about his attractiveness. He puffed himself up, trying to ignore the chink in his armor. Her opinion of him didn't matter, any more than the opinion of the fourteen sergeants that worked under him.

Damn it, he was Michael Strickland, and he didn't need anybody else. He certainly didn't need to create more complications by telling her he'd visited her in the hospital. He'd keep her away from Clowes, and then send her on her way home.

Her lips smashed into the thinnest line possible. "You can't have the two hundred pounds back. You purchased me. That was the deal."

He sunk into the chair by the door, elbows on his thighs, head resting on his outstretched palms. "I thought you *wanted* me to agree. I'm not usually propositioned by women who think sleeping with me would be vile."

"I had no choice," she mumbled.

"You always have a choice," he said. "And you should know I was quite willing to spend two hundred pounds on you, even if that's far above the going socket money."

Instead of preening as he'd expected, she snorted. "Am I supposed to be complimented by that?"

"Well, it isn't an insult," he barked. "Most women would be pleased."

"If you believe that, then I don't think you know women at all," she scoffed. "And I don't base my worth around my looks."

She picked at the patched seam of her glove. That tattered garment was a right hook to his gut: no wonder she didn't think she was stunning. Her scars were a permanent reminder of the blackest night of her life.

Either he could pile platitudes upon her about her beauty, or he could pretend he hadn't glanced inside her mind. Any emotional connection forged between them had a time limit. Better not to encourage attachment, when he'd only have to break her heart later.

"Regardless, I can afford to write off the two hundred pounds. Look around you. Does it look like I'm hurting for the blunt?" He waved to the room, still decorated the way it had been when the chambers had been his sister's. "I inherited this house outright when my father passed. Only good thing the bugger did in his whole bloody existence."

Her lip bent in a sardonic smile. If there was one concept she understood, it was a wretched father.

"And my job as an inspector pays well enough. Not enough that I'll be buying boots from Hoby's, mind you, but I'm doing fine on my own." He didn't tell her he made a good third of his income at the hells from drunks like her father.

"You can rest easy, Miss Vautille," he said. "Upon my blighted father's grave, for whatever that's worth, I promise you I won't expect anything more from you. For as long as you desire, your virtue will remain intact."

She opened her mouth to say something, but then stopped to consider. "You speak as though you suspect I'll change my mind."

He hesitated, wanting so badly to slide into the humor that was his defense. If he made her laugh, perhaps they could move on from this strange encounter. He might forget what she'd looked like, silhouetted in the dim twilight. He might forget her tears.

So, he let the lopsided smirk that had become his constant companion slip onto his lips, and with it, he was prepared for anything. "Most women find me irresistible."

"It must be this house," she suggested with a hint of a smile. "It couldn't be your abundance of charm."

"I'll have you know, I was called Sir Charm at Oxford," he retorted. "But that is neither here nor there."

Her nose scrunched up as she evaluated him. Apparently, she liked what she saw because she relaxed, taking a seat on the bed. "I meant to learn, you know."

"Pardon?"

"To be a courtesan." She let out a small sigh that affected him more than it ever should have.

His brows rose. "If that was your aim, I'd start with not crying when a man touches you."

A tiny trace of humor shined in her eyes. "Duly noted."

"If the concept of prostitution is so repellant to you, then why attempt it?" The question popped out before he could stop it. He knew the basic reasons, but for some reason, he wanted to hear her explain, her motivation.

She shrugged. "The money is good. Is there any other reason? I highly doubt women fall into vice because it sounds like a delightful way to pass the time. There's the risk of the French disease, the fact that your clients might be too rough on you, the likelihood of bedsores..."

She enumerated each possibility on her fingers until he held up his hand to stop her. If she continued, she'd make him want to swear off doxies forever. Life was much simpler when he didn't stop to examine *why* his bed partners had chosen their professions.

But he could make the best of their arrangement. As long as she *wanted* to bed him—whether in service of some higher goal or because she was attracted to him—he certainly wouldn't turn her away.

"Listen, if you want to excel as a ladybird, I'll help you," he offered. "Teach you the tricks of the trade."

She reflected upon this for a moment, a myriad of emotions splashing across her pretty face. Reluctance—that was her heart talking. Logic—her head. And finally shrewdness—her pocketbook.

She nodded. "We could perhaps start with the...less sexual aspects of seduction tomorrow. I suppose my acting could use some work."

He snorted. "You think?"

She ignored him. "Once I have that mastered, we can discuss sex."

He had a feeling he was going to regret this, but he'd do anything if it meant she wouldn't start crying again. "I think you should wait a few more days before deciding if you truly want to try this. We'll spend the first few days in conversation. Maybe it'll help if you get to know me."

"That sounds agreeable," she said. "Might I go home to visit my sister? I can come back in the morning."

Without the confines of their agreement, he had no reason to keep her here, so he'd have to reveal the threat to her life. His attempts at keeping her calm had already failed. She'd *cried*. Of all the things she could have done, sobbing was the worst.

He hated this. Not just because it was bloody inconvenient for him, but because her pain struck some part of him that he'd long locked away.

He wouldn't linger on the past. He'd make a clean breast of this, as a man should. "There is another reason I wanted you here."

Suspicion furrowed her brow. "And that reason is?"

"Frank Clowes has escaped."

Chapter Six

"**N**o."

That single word encompassed the total recoil of her mind at the very mention of Frank Clowes's name. *The bastard, the bounder, the blighter.* Every harsh word she could think of, she silently flung at the idea of him.

She didn't give voice to her revulsion, her fear, her doubts. She hadn't screamed that night when he'd tortured her, and she didn't now. She sat there on this bed in Strickland's house, and she said the simplest thing she could think of: that it couldn't be possible.

Frank Clowes was gone. He had to be. For all that Abigail had been subjected to in this past year, there could not truly be a God that hated her this much. There had to be some sort of good with the bad, and she had been short on good for so long she'd almost forgotten what luck felt like.

"I'm sorry, Miss Vautille." Strickland stood, his long strides churning the space between them. He was at her side in a moment; his hand extended as if he wanted to touch her shoulder, to give her comfort, but he dared not after all that had already passed. "I received a note from Clowes."

Her throat felt like it was closing. She fought to gasp out words. "What did it say?"

Strickland's voice lowered as if by being more placid, he could make this news less horrific. "He said he was coming for both of us. You can understand why I think it's best you stay here under guard."

While she was sheltered, what about Bess? What if Clowes came back to their flat looking for her and found Bess instead?

"My sister. You need to protect her," she told him. "She's staying with Mrs. Henderson next door."

He nodded. "We believe the threat to her is minimal, given she isn't in the age range that usually interests him. Nonetheless, I have assigned patrollers to the Baker's Row lodging houses. We're covering all the bases, I promise."

That was somewhat reassuring. "What if he comes at her on her way to work?"

"One of the patrollers will follow her, discreetly of course, at all times. We have placed a man inside the factory on White Lion Street as well, in case Clowes decides to revisit his old haunts."

"I still don't like it." She gnawed at her bottom lip, frowning. "Bess should be with me."

"Clowes wants you," he reminded her, his tone gentler than it had been before. "While he's still at large, I don't think it's a good idea for you to be near your family. You run the risk of them being used as pawns."

Abigail massaged her temples, trying to quiet her racing mind. She hated being away from her sister. But if Strickland's intelligence were right, she'd be risking Bess's life if she went home.

Strickland reached for her palm, patting it mildly. His touch consoled her, even as she told herself that he granted no respite from her pain.

Her vision faded, the lines of his hand becoming blurred spots. She saw her loom, an imposing mess of machinery, wood, and steel. And she felt Clowes's hands on her back, shoving her forward into the loom, holding her down no matter how she struggled. She let out a breath, then another; short, inconsequential breaths because she'd never be free from this. Never exist in a world where she didn't see Clowes as though he were in front of her.

"He was supposed to pay." She stared at Strickland's hand, so much larger than her own. At his fingers—robust fingers that weren't calloused as Clowes's had been. She shuddered. Hugged her dress tighter to her frame. It drooped around her without the shaping of her corset and petticoats.

Strickland watched her, his blue eyes flecked with concern. He must know very little about what had happened to her since he'd dropped the reappearance of her tormentor upon her with such little preparation.

She shifted upon the bed so that she sat directly across from him. Pulled her hand from his, no longer wanting the relief of his contact. Her voice became stronger from rage, gritty and tight. "Don't you see? He was supposed to pay. Your people were supposed to make him pay, and you couldn't even do that."

"I wish I had a better answer." He didn't look her in the eye. Rather, he stared at the ceiling as though it might deliver the easy answers to him.

She wondered if this was the first time Inspector Strickland had ever been at a loss for an easy solution. "Do you know what Frank Clowes did to me?"

"I am aware of the pertinent details, yes. Poppy Knight asked you to stand lookout for her while she went into Boz Larker's office after hours and retrieved damning paperwork."

Pertinent details. So official. She imagined she'd been nothing more than a name in a file to him. She was tired of being forgotten, pushed aside because her injury made her irrelevant.

"Poppy needed the paperwork to impress her sergeant paramour." She sneered. "She used me, you understand?"

"Both Knights are my friends," he countered. "I wasn't involved in the early investigation, but I guarantee you neither Poppy nor Thaddeus had impure motives. They are good people."

His earnestness clouded the room with untruths. How could she focus when his handsome face had scrunched up so in defense of the very villains she hated? She choked on her words. Failed to put her fury into competent sentences. She couldn't breathe, couldn't fight. She was mired in his wrong information.

He took her silence as agreement. "They wanted to catch a killer, a killer who was going to strike again in the factory. I don't know if you're aware of it, but there was corruption in my department." He had the grace to look properly chagrined at that, as if corruption in the Met was virtually unheard of instead of commonplace.

She found her voice. Watched him carefully, gauging how guarded she'd really be in this house. If he'd known about the Larkers from the start, yet done nothing to stop them, she wasn't so certain she'd be better off with him. "What was your exact participation in the case?"

"I came in after the fact." He didn't flinch at her question or appear as if he were obfuscating. He spoke neither too quickly nor too slowly, maintaining his natural speech rhythm. "Knight did all of the investigating, but Whiting dismissed him before the case was closed. I arrested Boz Larker and Frank Clowes and presented the evidence to the magistrate."

"I see." She knew all she needed to. The blame lay still on Knight and Poppy for involving her—Strickland had simply carried out what needed to be done.

She'd stay. The patrollers outside gave her some modicum of comfort. She'd never be truly secure while Clowes was alive, but Strickland provided her with a better sanctuary than she could get on her own.

Strickland ran a hand through his hair, ruffling his light-brown locks. "While Knight shouldn't have involved Poppy, he was fighting against a stacked deck. He was the one to find your friend Anna Moseley dead, and he wanted to avenge her."

The weight of his words whipped across her face. Her cheeks flamed.

"Not that anyone ever asks, but what *I* wanted," she ground out, "was not to be the plaything for a vicious bullyback. Your so-called friends escaped unscathed, but I bear the scars of their mistakes. Me, Inspector." She looped her thumb into the top of her right glove, giving it a yank.

He caught her hand before the glove could fully come off, alarm splashing across his attractive face. "I don't think that's necessary. I read the report."

Not so beautiful now was she? She was no fool. She'd seen his reaction before. Hell, anyone with eyes would've known how hard her nakedness made him. With this reminder of her imperfect physique, he no longer found her so striking. Would all men treat her like this? Emptiness sprawled out in her stomach, eclipsing any bit of feeling she'd had before. He watched her with idle curiosity, as men always did when they discovered she was no more than a traveling show aberration.

To hell with his curiosity. If he was so sure he knew exactly what happened to her, then this would all be mere recitation to him. But she suspected his little report hadn't properly informed him.

"When Effie Larker wanted information from me, she ordered Clowes to torture me. For hours until I fainted. Do you know what it feels like to have your blood stream down from your body, to watch it pool around your feet?" She leaned forward, her voice eerily calm. "Do you understand how a jacquard loom works?"

When he shook his head, she reached out, taking his hand in hers. She unfurled his fist, flattened his palm. "It's a system of cards advancing in a predetermined rhythm. That is how patterns are woven into the silk, you see. It's a revolutionary invention, cutting the work of the weaver by at least half. I watched for years as my friends were forced to find new employment because of this jacquard loom."

"I am sorry," he repeated, but she highly doubted that.

"But that's far from the worst of it, Inspector." She traced the lines of his palm, memorized the contours. "You see, the loom can be used as a brilliant torture device if you comprehend the interworking. Growing up around factories, Clowes certainly did. So, when Effie told him to make me talk, by any means necessary, he knew precisely what to do. First, he forced my hand beneath the frame, as though I were the silk to weave. Effie pumped the pedal, and the shuttle surged forward and caught on my hand. Dug into the skin. But that wasn't enough."

She began to tap her fingers against his palm repeatedly. "He wasn't pleased with the results. He had Boz hold me up so that I could reach the top of the loom where the jacquard attachment is. Up there, toward the back of the loom, there are approximately a hundred or so needles. When the pedal is pumped, the needles fall into position in accordance with the punch card, much as the shuttle flies forward too."

Strickland's face reddened. She held onto his palm. Somehow, his fury on her behalf made it easier.

"Imagine your hand being slammed on those sharp needles. Not just once, but many times. Because once Clowes figures out that he can make you scream out in pain, he's going to do it countless more times, until the flesh rips from your hand and bones are exposed. Until you feel your knees giving out from underneath you. Until you fall and you slam your head against the cast iron of the loom. Until you slip from consciousness. Until you're brought back by a bucket of fresh urine thrown on your face."

She felt Strickland become rigid against her hold. He reminded her of a coiled-up tiger, waiting for the right time to strike a gazelle. For a minute, at least, she'd allow herself the delusion he'd protect her.

"*That* is what people like Clowes do, Inspector. So, when you write your report, or whatever it is you worthless toffs do, you remember those 'pertinent details.' You remember my name." She pulled her hand from his, turned away.

"I have never forgotten your name, Abigail."

It was the first time he'd used her Christian name. She ought to tell him she hadn't granted him that liberty. But somehow, from him, it sounded right. Rhythmic. Beautiful.

"I don't know yours."

He sketched a bow to her. "Michael."

She didn't curtsy. Her knees bent at abnormal angles; curtsying had never been easy. She didn't want to expose herself to him again, though he had seen every curve of her body.

"I am more than an inspector, Abigail." The smoothness to his voice had returned. He was comfortable again, sliding into the role of a Peeler reassuring a scared witness. "I'm also a man who wants to protect you. Because I'm sorry how we handled the Larker case. Because—" He stopped, shaking his head. "Because I don't want Frank Clowes to hurt you again."

Somehow, she doubted that was what he'd been about to say originally. The stern set to his jaw, the stubborn press of his lips, told her not to question him. She'd catch him unaware later on, and she'd extract the information she needed.

He reached for her, his hand landing on her shoulder.

His firm grip, the weight of his palm against her knobby bones, was again oddly reassuring. She wouldn't think about that.

"Thank you, I think," she ventured. "But I suppose I'll see if your sentiment holds muster. If I am not dead by the end of this, then I suppose I'll owe you more than two hundred pounds."

"You don't owe me anything," he stated firmly. "And perish the thought of death. You are far too spirited, Abigail, to die so young. Only the good are taken from us too soon."

He winked, his devilish smirk back in full force. Her heart flip-flopped precariously. Oh, that wasn't good. That wouldn't do.

She focused on the threat. In demanding absolutes, she could form a plan of attack. "Tell me how Clowes escaped."

"He was bound for transport to Australia. One of the guards working was ill—he shouldn't have even been working, but you know what people are willing to do to make the rent." He frowned, his hand gripping her shoulder a little tighter. "The man was doubled over in pain. Clowes saw an opportunity. Somehow, he'd managed to craft a blade while in Newgate, and he had it on him. He stabbed the sick guard and managed to harm the other two."

She nodded. That sounded like Clowes. Quick thinking, cruel, and opportunistically violent.

"I take responsibility for this since it was my staff at work." He let go of her, taking a step back. "We failed you once more. The H-Division will be auditing all prisoner transport policies, on my watch. We will not let this happen again."

She knew she shouldn't believe him, but the fact that he'd admitted his failure comforted her. Before, when the Met had interviewed her, they hadn't acknowledged the department was partially to blame for her torment. They'd apologized, yes, but it'd been without meaning. "I'm sorry this happened to you" was not the same as "I'm sorry we failed you."

"You make a lot of promises, Michael," she said.

"Let me make one more. I solemnly promise to protect you from harm while you are under my charge." He crossed his heart, raising two fingers to his lips and kissing them.

He touched those two fingers to her brow, and she felt his touch as if he had really kissed her again. Heat burned through her, seared her.

She shook her head, trying to rid herself of the sensation. "Very well. I suppose there are worse things I could be doing for two weeks."

He grinned. "It's a grudging enthusiasm, but I'll accept it."

"Take what you can get," she retorted.

He strode toward the armoire next to the window and flung the doors open. She tilted her head quixotically. Several brightly colored garments hung from a metal rod at the top of the wardrobe. Women's dresses, from what she could tell, with a pair of black satin gloves much nicer than what she currently had.

"These are for you," he said. "I had my sister deliver them. She is about your size, I think."

"I can't possibly accept..." But oh, how the fabrics looked gorgeous. Expensive. Better than she'd ever had.

He shrugged sheepishly. "Don't get too excited. They are apparently all from two seasons ago. She was going to give them to her servants. I simply swooped in at the right time."

"Oh, but I can't take something from them—"

He cut her off. "Frances is a bored woman with little else to do but shop. I guarantee you those same servants receive ten other gowns in a year."

"Oh." She didn't have a reason to deny beyond that, other than the fact that she didn't want to be further indebted to him.

"I should like you to have clean clothes while you're here," he said. "Warm clothes. It is the least I can do."

There was that phrase again: the least he could do. She'd have to examine that later.

"I will wear them," she agreed.

She was tired of being respectful to everyone else. Tired of adhering to their picture of what a victim should be. No one ever remembered her plight, unless they wanted to prop up their position in society by giving charity to the less fortunate. Poppy had come to her shortly after the accident, accompanied by her new husband. She'd offered Abigail enough money to last her a few months, but that money had come with strings.

If Abigail had accepted that money, she would have had to forgive Poppy. To pretend that the one person she'd trusted above all else hadn't betrayed her.

And so, for tonight, she'd accept generosity from a relative stranger instead.

Chapter Seven

bigail awoke to birds chirping outside the window. Bloody *happy* birds, with their cheerful cheeps and their incessant singing. Resting her weight on her elbows, she rose up from the mountain of pillows Strickland's housekeeper had piled around her and glared at the offending avians outside, some ridiculously bright-yellow bird with wings spread wide, and another with mottled feathers.

How did anyone sleep in this environment? When Strickland left her room last night, it had been half past eleven. Yet not a sound echoed through his house until these damn birds. The mattress was too soft. The hot coals tucked in the warming pan underneath the sheets created a soothing lull of heat, sating the rancorous wind of winter.

Everything was too soft, too quiet, too gentle for a girl used to hardness and savagery. She couldn't breathe freely here.

Life in Whitechapel was a cacophony of clangs, bangs, and curses, each competing to be the loudest. At this time of morning back home, Mrs. Delgado would already have had three fights with her husband about blunt and one about the children being unruly. Her other neighbors would be preparing to work in the factories.

She never thought she'd miss the pleas of the false mendicants who haunted the corners, begging for pence so they could totter off to the dram houses. Never thought she'd miss the outraged shrieks of pedestrians when a hack driver took a turn too fast and almost ran them over. Whitechapel might be hell to the rich, but it was her home, and she'd fight tooth and nail to protect it.

Men like Clowes wanted to ruin Whitechapel with their cold-blooded cruelty. Before Clowes, she'd always felt comfortable. She knew the land, and she knew the people.

She burrowed deeper in the sheets, as though the yards of fabric could keep her protected.

Downstairs, the servants began to shuffle about, preparing the house for their master. In addition to Smithers, who served as Michael's butler, valet, and footman, there was also a housekeeper and a cook. The inspector was but one man—yet he needed a staff of three simply to exist. It was absurd. Yet it was modest compared to toffs.

The noise the servants made as they went about their duties was welcome, for it was a reminder that she was not alone in this vast house.

But the birds were another matter entirely. She groaned, covering her ears with a pillow. In the rookeries, the birds dared not make such outrageous hullabaloo, lest they become dinner to the urchins who couldn't afford a proper meal. Hell, Abigail herself had once served a carriage-crushed pigeon for dinner. Very little usable meat on the bones, barely worth the effort it had taken to pluck, but at least it had fed Bess for a night.

As if sensing the turn her thoughts had taken, the yellow bird outside her window opened its mouth and let out a loud shriek, his head tilted directly in Abigail's direction. Prying the pillow from her ears, she hurled it toward the window. "Curse you!"

The pillow hit the iron grate with a puff but promptly fell to the ground. The bird remained.

She swung her legs forward, sliding off the bed and onto the cold floor. Wincing, Abigail picked one foot up off the ground, alternating in an awkward dance. The fire had burnt out in her chamber overnight. The chill seeped into her bones, almost welcome, for the room she shared with Bess was always frigid.

That flat was small and old, with broken windows and a leaky roof, but it was home. It was where she'd first learned to read and write. Where, as a young girl, she'd sneaked in books stolen from the markets, burying the texts underneath the floorboards so her father wouldn't suspect what she'd done. When she'd filched the very last bits of the candles burning at the factory so she could pass the night poring over those same books as her father slept. Back when he'd been sober for most of the day, and he'd actually cared what she and Bess did.

She wasn't a particularly proficient thief, but those books had helped her through the roughest times. She'd stowed away every bit of knowledge in the hopes that someday she'd be able to escape Whitechapel. All those hours spent learning to mimic how civilized people spoke when now her argot would be naught more than faux pleasured moans designed to make her clients think she was enjoying herself.

She'd tried so, so *hard* to better herself.

She should have known better. No one left the rookeries alive. Those who were born poor remained poor. The wealthy profited from the underpaid factory workers, growing richer while their workers struggled and starved.

She'd been a fool to think she had a chance at escaping this life.

Sighing, Abigail made her way toward the wardrobe. A

knock on the door interrupted her, a hesitant tap-tap. Strickland's knocking had been an insistent summons, as bold and demanding as he was. Who was this then?

"Good morning. Miss Voughteel?" a feminine voice called.

Abigail grimaced as Strickland's housekeeper, Mrs. O'Neal, butchered her ordinary French Huguenot surname. Clearly, Mrs. O'Neal was not Spitalfields bred. It rankled her that Strickland couldn't be bothered to hire from within the community he was supposed to serve.

Calling for Mrs. O'Neal to enter, Abigail went to the wardrobe. She hadn't dared check it last night, thinking that if she did, the finery would disappear before her eyes. She had never worn anything so nice before.

But in the morning light, she refused to be conquered by such silly worries. She pulled open the doors. Five dresses hung in a silken kaleidoscope of vivid color from a wooden rod in the mahogany cabinet. She stroked the skirt of a green dress, pinching the fabric between her thumb and forefinger. She recognized this silk; had woven with it. Brocade, most likely made with the same type of loom that had scarred her, for the rose pattern expertly linked into the fabric with the precision only a jacquard offered.

"A rose. Could you bring me a rose?" Bess had asked.

When this tenure was over, she'd smuggle the dress back in her bags for Bess. Strickland had only mentioned that the dresses were hers for the time being. He hadn't given them to her permanently. For all she knew, his sister expected them back.

"'Tis nice, don't you think?" Mrs. O'Neal set down the tea tray on the vanity table tucked into the far left corner of the room. "Lady Elliot has exquisite fashion sense, for all her failings. I particularly like the pink one meself."

"They're lovely," Abigail replied, stepping closer to examine them.

Upon further inspection, the maroon "dress" was actually a cloak of heavy wool trimmed with white fur. She stared at it longingly, reminding herself not to become attached. Just because Strickland had said that he'd help her learn coquetry didn't mean he'd let her take the dresses with her. She could feasibly steal one of them, but not all.

But oh, the dresses would be perfect for her plans. She could truly appear like quality in them. Perhaps selling herself wouldn't feel so demoralizing if she at least *looked* like a Cyprian.

Besides the green brocade, there was the pink day dress Mrs. O'Neal had admired, a purple half-dress with a bow at the back, and a golden ball gown. Where did Strickland think she would wear that? Her stomach flipped at the idea of going to a party on his arm.

She took the steaming clay mug Mrs. O'Neal handed her and then reviewed the remaining contents of the tea tray. A small plate of sweet rolls from last night's dinner, the ones she'd loved so much. Three books. A jeweled comb for her hair.

Abigail barely resisted the urge to scoop the books up into her arms for further examination.

Mrs. O'Neal followed her gaze and immediately passed the books to her. "The master wanted me to bring you these."

Abigail glanced at the spines. The first two were novels she hadn't read, but the last one gave her pause. It was the Swift volume she'd wanted to inspect last night before their conversation had taken that damnably salacious turn. She'd forgotten all about the book after their kiss, yet he'd remembered. That was peculiar, but she wouldn't trouble over it. She set the books back down on the table and reached for the currant buns.

Mrs. O'Neal nodded approvingly. "You've got good taste,

and I said as much to the master when he had me bring the tray up. You liked them last night, he told me."

Abigail didn't know what disconcerted her more: how the kiss had left her flushed and fluttered from the top of her head to the tips of her toes, or how Strickland had noticed what she liked.

She chewed the square spiral-shaped bun, the lemon and cinnamon flavors perfectly complemented by the yeasty dough. Concerns about Strickland would have to wait until she was finished eating. Bread this good deserved her full attention.

"They are quite wonderful," she said. "The best I've ever had."

Mrs. O'Neal's face crinkled with delight. "Ah, yes, Miss, the very best. From the Bun-House near Sloane Square."

She would've taken smaller bites if she'd known the bloody rolls came from there! As a child, Abigail had heard stories of the former royal family visiting the Chelsea Bun-House every Sunday. She'd never been brave enough to go to the bakery on Pimlico Street, fearing they'd immediately know she couldn't afford their delicacies because of her ragged clothes. Now here she was, eating the famous Chelsea buns as though it was simply another day.

"That *is* impressive," she murmured, savoring the bread.

"The master likes the best when he can have it," Mrs. O'Neal said.

She wasn't the best. She needed to remember that. Whether or not he'd proven less atrocious than she'd originally anticipated, nothing between them had changed. He'd still bought her body and her time. When she saw him that afternoon, she'd tell him she was ready to become his pupil.

Mrs. O'Neal selected from the wardrobe the green dress, a fresh shift, stays, a new petticoat, and gray kid leather half-boots. "Well, come now, your bath shall be getting cold if we tarry longer. Finish your tea, Miss, and we'll be on our merry way."

Once she'd helped Abigail shrug into a wrapper, the housekeeper motioned for Abigail to follow her out the door.

"My bath?" Abigail queried, with a longing look at the remaining bun on the tray.

"Of course," Mrs. O'Neal replied. "The master would like you clean."

Abigail gulped, the roll now forgotten. Perhaps Strickland had reconsidered the few days of conversation first. Why else would he want to ensure that she was unsoiled? Did he intend for Mrs. O'Neal to check and see if she was still pure too?

Mrs. O'Neal didn't expand upon her thoughts. For a woman well in her fifties, the housekeeper had a spritely step. Down one corridor she went, and then another, until they'd reached the back portion of the townhouse. At the second room on the left, she stopped, thrust open the door, and motioned for Abigail to step inside.

A monstrous porcelain tub with gold-encrusted claw feet sat in the middle of the small room, no bigger than Abigail's bedroom in her flat. The sheer bulk of the tub eclipsed any relief she might have felt about this townhouse finally having a normal-sized room. The tub left little space on either side to move around the bathroom.

Mrs. O'Neal closed the door behind her, setting the bundle of clothes down on a stool. A stack of towels rested on the built-in shelf next to the stool. Stepping around Abigail, Mrs. O'Neal started to undo the back of her dress.

Abigail shoved the woman's hands away, spinning around. But with how crowded the room was, she ended up half on top of Mrs. O'Neal.

"Just what do you think you're doing?" Abigail demanded.

Mrs. O'Neal blinked at her, her mouth agape, as though

Abigail should be in a madhouse instead of this elegant townhouse. "Your bath, Miss. The water has already been run. I'm to wash you."

"I'm completely capable of washing myself." She skirted Mrs. O'Neal's attempt to reach for the back of her dress again. "If you want me to get in that damnable tub, you'll leave."

Mrs. O'Neal's muttered something underneath her breath that sounded like "heathen child," pushed a graying lock of hair back underneath her prim cap, and squared her legs. She placed her hand on Abigail's arm, fixing her to the spot. "I'm to help you undress, Miss, and that's what I intend to do."

Mrs. O'Neal's ruddy forehead creased with a few wrinkles, but none of the crushing weariness Abigail had come to expect from a woman her age. Her hands were soft, though her grip was firm.

For a few seconds, they stood there, facing off. The housekeeper's mouth tapered into a scowl. She showed no signs of relenting.

They'd be there for the rest of the morning at this rate. She wouldn't have time before dinner to read the Swift novel Strickland had set aside for her.

Abigail would have to undress. Mrs. O'Neal would see her scars, whether she liked it or not.

"Very well," Abigail sighed, turning around again.

Mrs. O'Neal made quick work of her dress. Abigail had not slept in her petticoat or stays. She stood in her shift, bare feet upon the tiled floor. When the housekeeper went to remove her gloves, Abigail flinched.

"Well, we can't be having those in the suds," Mrs. O'Neal scolded her lightly. "The silk's already worn. Bit of water would ruin it completely."

Abigail clenched her jaw. Mrs. O'Neal tutted. All right then, if the woman was going to insist...

The housekeeper worked the gloves down Abigail's arms, drawing in a terrified breath when she reached Abigail's left hand. Flinging Abigail's hand away from her, she backed away.

"What ha—happened to you, child?" Mrs. O'Neal gasped, her eyes wide. She couldn't look away from Abigail's marred flesh. "Did a beast claw you? Your hand..."

Abigail yanked the gloves the rest of the way off and tossed them on the ground. "You are mistaken, madam. I am the beast, and you should have left well enough alone."

"I—I'm sorry," Mrs. O'Neal stammered.

The mere sight of Abigail had reduced the competent woman to a stuttering mess. What would Strickland have said last night, if she'd shown him her scars? Would he still have suggested he assist her?

And why did she have a sinking feeling that her cares for his opinion ran deeper than what he could do for her?

"I require no assistance," Abigail stated. "And I don't enjoy your stares. So kindly take your rude gaping elsewhere, won't you?"

Mrs. O'Neal's jaw dropped several centimeters lower, her eyes rounding further.

"Now," Abigail hissed, pointing with her blistered finger.

Off Mrs. O'Neal went, the door slamming behind her. The smack of her shoes upon the wooden planked floor carried as she ran down the hallway.

"Great, Abbie, you've reduced the poor woman to running for her life," she muttered, sliding her shift over her head. She would have to grow thicker skin.

Stepping to the bath, she dipped a finger into the water. "Ow!" The water was scalding. Whatever washing she managed at home was done in a half-bath. She'd perch in the wide bucket as Bess poured the cold water over her head.

And the smell of this water—lavender and vanilla, so

fragrant that for a second she thought she'd been transported to a garden. Wouldn't it be lovely to smell as though she'd used the finest of French perfumes? To pretend that, for once, she was an earl's daughter clothed in the finest brocade?

She ought to use this time to plot her next move, not dream of things she could never have. Letting Michael teach her would be rational. It'd help her accomplish everything she should want.

Then why did the thought of becoming a courtesan make her stomach seize with dread? She needed to accept her fate. No matter how she felt, this was the best alternative. *Her* future might be bleak, but Bess's was still bright. Abigail would endure anything to make sure that possibility remained.

She surveyed the bath. Mrs. O'Neal wouldn't be daunted forever. If Abigail wanted any peace, she'd better bathe now. She clambered into the water, slipping and sliding against the soapy rim. Water sloshed from the tub, cascading onto the floor. She thought immediately of her new dress, but it was undamaged, placed as far away from the tub as possible.

Heat encircled her, at first sweltering, but as her body adjusted, she leaned back against the rim of the tub. Submerged in bubbles, she was a bloody princess, and this was her claw-footed throne. She ran the sponge against her skin, watching the layers of dirt dissolve into the water.

Truly, this was sinful, to be surrounded by such decadence.

She ducked her head under the water. Her straw-blonde curls flew out around her, encircling her in a web of gold. Holding her breath, she remained below the surface, enveloped by the quiet. Here, filth gone from her pink, scarred flesh, she was safe. Unable to be found by Clowes, for no one would think to look in this massive tub for the girl who'd escaped death.

Wouldn't it make more sense to stay down here? To let all her worries and cares drift away in the cleansing water? She was no use to anyone now, a withered husk of the woman she'd once been.

Her head throbbed. Her lungs fought for purchase. She couldn't hold her breath any longer. Without her command, her mouth opened, and water flooded her throat. As she was close to blacking out, she remembered Bess, remembered the whispered, "You're a fighter."

Bursting up from the water, she coughed and coughed until her body contracted in spasms. She sucked in one deep breath after another, her lungs grasping at the air.

Bess needed her. No matter how bad her life was, that fact didn't change. Abigail was the last remaining family Bess could count on, and she had a duty to protect her little sister. And so, she'd remain in this godforsaken town.

She was the girl who lived.

* * *

MICHAEL RECLINED WITH his feet propped up on his desk, and his hands folded behind his head. Untidy piles of paper littered the top of the desk. Once, the stacks had been a color-coordinated, tabbed, organized file on the Larkers. Thaddeus Knight had always been meticulous. Michael employed a more haphazard style: he shoved all the paperwork back into the file in whatever order it happened to be in his hand. When next he'd pull it out, the randomness of the contents would jar his memory. He'd see things in a different order.

Right now, he needed the lucidity that came from looking at a case from an entirely new angle.

Frank Clowes was one man in a town of hundreds upon thousands. One attractive, twenty-year-old man with a history of taking out his aggression on the weak and defenseless. Who lured women into his sick web of agony and derision.

Though he had not been directly the one to murder Anna Moseley in the Larker case, Clowes had seduced the fourteen-year-old girl. Earned her trust. And when she was no longer useful, he'd stood by and laughed as Boz Larker beat and stabbed her to death.

When Michael had originally captured him, Clowes hadn't just admitted to his involvement, he'd *announced* it. The pride in Clowes's voice made Michael's heart race, even now. Merciless bastard.

Michael hadn't been able to save Anna Moseley, and he hadn't been able to save the girl before her. Hell, he hadn't even cared about the damn case until Knight had been fired. Until he'd gone to the hospital and seen Abigail laid up. The memory had lingered long after he'd left. Her angelic face twisted in an anguished glower. The laudanum couldn't completely dull the ache of her injuries.

Michael stared up at the ceiling, silently counting to twenty. That didn't help either—he was no closer to locating Clowes. He'd dispatched foot patrollers to every place Clowes had frequented before his arrest, but no one had found him. If Clowes was going to hit up his old connections, he was certainly biding his time. The Met had known of his escape for three days.

Three days. Clowes could be all the way to bloody Shropshire by now.

He should have had more men watching Clowes. The strange hold Clowes had over people wasn't quantifiable in one of his equations, so he hadn't predicted the scenario properly. Knight would not have made this mistake.

Michael frowned at the documents. He pushed his chair back from the desk and stood, going to the liquor cart in the corner of his study. Selecting the decanter of gin, he sloshed some into a glass. At least those Clowes would most likely target were shielded. He'd dispatched foot patrollers to watch both Frances and Abigail's sister; Knight had taken Poppy and her daughter to one of the Gentleman Thief's secret houses; Abigail was watched by his own patrollers.

"Inspector Strickland?" Mrs. O'Neal called, her gentle knock barely sounding in his cavernous study.

"Come in," he called.

Mrs. O'Neal's portly figure filled the doorway. A short, stout woman who'd always insisted on wearing a dour black uniform and black mobcap—despite him informing her she wasn't attending a funeral and needn't dress so—Mrs. O'Neal was the very epitome of primness.

And she scared the bloody dickens out of him, had since he was a tot. But he was her boss now, damn it. If he wanted her respect, he couldn't show his fear.

He tapped his foot against the floor. "Yes?"

Mrs. O'Neal peered down her nose at him, her wire-rimmed spectacles slipping slightly, reminding him of when she'd scolded him as a child for sneaking another chocolate from the buffet table.

She arched her brows at his glass of gin. So, what if it was ten in the morning? He didn't need to be judged by his own servants, did he? He shrugged and motioned for her to continue.

"Miss Voughteel is ready for you." She puckered her lips, disapproval dripping from her like rain from the willow trees in his mother's old garden. "She is in the library."

"Ah, very good." He nodded. When his housekeeper made no move to depart, he regarded her skeptically. "Is there something else, Mrs. O'Neal?"

"Sir," Mrs. O'Neal began.

Oh, he was going to regret asking. Every time Mrs. O'Neal called him "sir," it was to shroud one of her notorious set-downs in the veneer of respectfulness.

"I hope your intentions are..." Her lips compacted so firmly he half wondered if she'd glued them shut. A full ten seconds went by as she struggled to find the right term. "Moral, sir. I hope your intentions are moral. She's just a young little thing."

He bristled, but he didn't let his irritation show. He affixed on a smile, keeping his tone cordial. "Your favorite person asked me to take care of Miss Vautille."

Mrs. O'Neal perked up at the thought. "Mr. Knight?"

Michael nodded. "Miss Vautille was friends with Knight's wife at one time. You know how sentimental he can be."

"I'll make sure she's taken care of," Mrs. O'Neal vowed. "Miss Voughteel was hurt. I think it's good then that you've brought her here."

"I'm pleased for your approval," Michael said, though in truth, he was more pleased he'd been able to head off one of Mrs. O'Neal's famous lectures. He still remembered how she'd hollered at him for placing a frog in his governess's bed.

"And you know if you were more like Mr. Knight, you wouldn't be without a wife," she added.

He suppressed a sigh, folding his hands together. "My intentions are not to wed her."

I'd like to bed her, but that's it. I'll teach her how to be a better lightskirt.

"You should really consider it further." Mrs. O'Neal turned on her heel, apparently considering her work done for the day.

"I don't *want* a wife," Michael ground out, but she was already gone. He drained the last bit of gin from the glass and headed toward the library.

Chapter Eight

Michael found Abigail sprawled out upon the ivory chaise, her legs extended in front of her, and her head resting on a plump pillow. For a minute, he stood behind one of the tall shelves, peeping out through a gap in the books. The last hints of afternoon sunlight streamed in through the big bay windows, casting golden glows across her pale skin.

For once, she appeared serene. Her flaxen locks were brushed up in some sort of intricate bun. He liked this look on her, liked the way it accentuated her ethereal features. He could almost imagine her as a fairy flitting through the forest.

He'd have to remember to thank Frances for donating her old gowns. Abigail had chosen the green dress, which had seafoam puffs of fabric on her upper arms, cascading into tight, long sleeves. Her wide emerald skirts hid an enticing view of her shapely legs—but he could just make out one ankle, encased in a creamy white stocking.

God, she was a temptress. Her every luscious curve was etched into his memory.

Mrs. O'Neal's voice rang in his mind. "I hope your intentions are moral."

Quickly, he raised his glance from that sensual ankle to her face. Her skin was rosy from the bath. The smudges of dirt were scrubbed away, and with them the last remaining vestiges of a woman hardened by the streets. She could have been any diamond of the first water.

Stepping out from behind the shelf, Michael rounded the corner. He took a seat in the chair across from her, not wanting to crowd her on the chaise. "Good morning."

"It is afternoon now," she noted. "The clock chimed twelve a few minutes ago."

He liked that she corrected him. Her defiant streak intrigued him. "Good afternoon then. What are you reading?"

She held up the book: *Candide*. His father's addition to the library, which meant it was the illustrated version and—

His eyes widened. Oh hell, this wasn't how he'd expected to introduce her to the joys of sex. He jumped up, reaching for the book. "That copy is not fit for a lady's eyes."

Her jaw set. She held fast to the book. "Ah, yes, the illustrations. Those were quite interesting. Thankfully, I'm not a lady. If I'm going to be a doxy, I should know what I'm dealing with."

He grabbed for the book again, but she removed it from his range in the nick of time. "There are far better ways to go about this."

"But none of them have Voltaire," she replied. "So, it's got bare asses and a few tits. Nothing I have not seen before. Just because I'm a virgin doesn't mean I'm completely ignorant."

Every muscle in his body screamed for him to climb atop her and demand she show him just how knowledgeable she was.

She flipped another page. A mischievous smile toyed with her lips.

If the pornographic pamphlet of *Candide* made her happy,

then so be it. Who was he to preach propriety? He settled back down in the chair, throwing his hands up to show defeat.

"It's not my book," he clarified because, for some reason, it mattered what she thought of him. "It belonged to my father."

"Then your father did two good things in his life," she replied. "Leaving you this townhouse and keeping this splendid edition."

He shook his head. "Can't agree with you there. Candide spends the whole book trying to be happy, only to decide he was happiest at the beginning with his mundane existence. It's bloody ridiculous."

"Spoken like a man of privilege." She grinned, the animosity from yesterday missing in her tone. "Of course, you wouldn't understand Candide's revelation, for you have been given all the creature comforts of life."

"I do work for a living," he reminded her. "And I derive pleasure from that work. Still, I'm hard-pressed to find any true meaning in that lewd work."

"I think you're a literary elitist." She grinned teasingly, and he leaned in closer, wishing he could capture those delicious lips with his own.

All in due time. She'd agree to bed him before the week was out.

"If you'll pardon me for asking, but how do you even know about *Candide*?" He gestured to the various shelves in his library. "I didn't think you had access to books like this in the factory. Every weaver I've ever had the misfortune of speaking to wants to tell me about silk."

He grimaced. Those were hours of his life he'd never get back.

"I didn't in the factories. But I'm resourceful. And I formed a lending library with my friends." She flinched as she said "resourceful." The movement was so slight he would have missed it if he hadn't been watching her closely. She wasn't telling him the whole truth.

"You mean you stole books," he observed.

She floundered for a second. Her mouth opened and shut. But soon, her customary control had returned, and she drew herself up, fixing him with a reproachful glare. "I prefer to think of it as *liberating* books."

He threw his head back, laughter booming out of him. Proud Abigail Vautille, with her radical speeches about class divide, was a thief! So much for her righteousness.

She sniffed. "I don't see what's so funny."

When he was finally able to breathe again, he struggled to assume an officious air. "You know I could arrest you for that."

Her face paled. "You wouldn't."

He let her flounder a bit longer before he smiled. "No, the image of you poring over a moldy old text while the rest of the neighborhood kids play ball is too delightful. Arresting you would take all the fun out of it."

She released an audible sigh of relief. As he'd suspected, she did not rush to thank him.

"So, tell me more about your book pilfering," he said slyly.

"That was when I was younger." Running her hand down her thigh, she effectively directed his attention back to her shapely curves.

Damn it. No. He had to remain focused.

"So, when you were a child, you read *Candide?*" Skepticism colored his voice.

"Oh, no, that was through the BRLLS." She spoke as though he ought to know exactly what she was referring to.

He racked his brain, but the acronym meant nothing to him. One more point for her. "I'm sorry, the what?"

"The Baker's Row Lending Library Society," she explained with pride. "I formed it with four of my friends when we were kids. Basically, whatever books we could nick, we brought to the club and we'd all trade."

He'd heard of child thieves working in tandem, but never had he heard of them stealing books. "There are so many other more profitable things you could have filched. Why books?"

"I should think it'd be obvious when you have a room like this." Her gaze traveled the length of the library and back to him. "It's not about the profit, but about the knowledge. I wanted to learn everything I could. Do you know how many girls born in Whitechapel get to move up in society?"

"Given the current census, I'd estimate one out of every hundred and fifty born," he guessed. "But that's a generous approximation."

"I wasn't going to be someone who worked in the factories forever." Her fingers traced the engravings on the leather cover of *Candide*, wistfulness sweeping across her features. "So, I read everything I could get my hands on. Greek philosophies, folklore, popular novels, even economic theories. "

He nodded toward the right section of the library. "I've got an entire bookcase on different mathematical concepts if you'd like to check those out."

She blanched. "I'm not much for numbers."

He placed his hand over his heart, gasping. "You are lucky, my lady, that I'm so compassionate. Otherwise, you'd have to listen to me lecture you for hours on the recent work of André-Michel Guerry to create a moral statistics map for crime."

Her hesitant smile affected him more than it should have. "I'd listen if it was important to you."

He gulped. His body suddenly felt warm. It must be the afternoon sun. It could not possibly be that devilish twinkle in her eye or the fact that she'd just volunteered to listen to him lecture on mathematics.

No one wanted to listen to him lecture. The professors at

Oxford hadn't even taken him seriously until he'd solved the equation one of them had been struggling with for years. "The fop has brains after all," they'd sneered.

They could all go to the devil. He was an inspector of the Metropolitan Police, and he had a beautiful woman hanging on his words. He'd save the discussion of mathematics for a later date. He didn't want to risk that she'd no longer be interested in what he had to say.

"While maths are fascinating, I won't bore you." He'd deflect her to another topic, one he found far less scintillating. "Why *Candide* then?"

"I believe that the world is fundamentally flawed," she said. "I'm a Whitechapel girl. Few people care about our existence. I used to think if I smoothed out my voice so that I sounded like the toffs, and read the proper books, I'd succeed."

Well, that explained her accent at least. He leaned forward, sensing she had more to say.

"But no matter what steps I took in the past to be something more, I've still ended up here. All that time—wasted. Perhaps you cannot circumvent fate by trying to find a better existence. Perhaps all that you are is exactly what's on the surface."

He doubted that when everything he learned about Abigail defied his previous assumptions. She was more than she appeared, more than he'd ever given her credit for in the past. The girl underneath the surface stunned him—her strength, her wisdom.

"I suppose so," he said weakly, for he did not want to dignify this new rush of feeling.

She shrugged. "Before, I tried so hard to reach beyond my station. I thought of what people expected a woman of culture to be, and I tried to become her. But it didn't help me. I have started to think that if I'm ever to survive, it will be because I focused on my own life—I cared for me and my own above the greater good."

"You will have learned to cultivate your garden," he offered wryly.

She nodded. "Precisely. There's no one else who will protect me, but me."

And me. He couldn't afford to make her any more promises —not now, not ever. Yes, she was here at present. Until his men caught Clowes, he'd take care of her. But that was all. He couldn't commit to her for longer than that.

He should leave her to her reading. Summon some foot patrollers to guard her while he went to the station house for an update on the search. Until she made her decision, she was effectively forbidden to him. He'd promised to respect her. Damn it, for the first time in his life, he was going to let a woman come to him.

Yet he was reluctant to part from her company. She intrigued him, with her strange taste in books and her fiery responses.

"You said you had a sister, correct?" he asked.

She looked up, suspicion splashed across her face. "Yes, why?"

He flagged her reaction as something to scrutinize later. Did she distrust him so much that a simple question into her family made her think he was up to no good? He pushed away his natural inclination to pry further into her motives. This was not an interrogation, and he needn't treat her as though she was across the table from him on Wood Street. He had not been with the Met so long that he couldn't have a simple conversation.

Or at least he hoped not.

"It is something we have in common," he said. "You already

know of my elder sister, Frances. She's thirty-two and convinced she knows best in every situation."

Abigail smiled. "My sister is nine and also convinced she has the way of the world figured out."

He leaned back in his chair, crossing one leg over the other. "Is she often right? Because Frances never is. She's a bloody badger, really, always prying into my business and judging me for how I live my life."

"I should not like to live with someone like that," Abigail mused. "Granted, my sister is far younger than yours, but she is the best friend I've got. I'd do anything for her."

Anything, including spending two weeks with you. She didn't say it, but the sentiment hung in the air between them, stifling their attempts at polite conversation.

Abigail clasped her hands together neatly, her gaze focused on her lap. "Bess is impossibly smart. I'd let her handle the household budget if I didn't think she'd turn half of the money over to Papa."

"Ah." He suspected she wouldn't appreciate his actual opinion on her spendthrift father, so he simply nodded. "When Frances married Lord Elliot, all I could think of was how happy I was to get her out of the house. When our father passed earlier this year, I thought Frances and I might go to war over his will."

Abigail pondered this. "There *is* such a thing as too much family togetherness. I imagine Lady Elliot was pleased to make such an advantageous marriage."

"Well, she better be, for how firmly on the shelf she was." He spoke without thinking, immediately regretting his assessment when Abigail's nose wrinkled. "Er, that is, let me explain something about my sister. She is, for all intents and purposes, a dreadful human being."

"But she's still your sister," Abigail pointed out.

"I don't believe that being family excuses one's bad behavior." He picked up *Candide* from the table, flicking through the pages absentmindedly. "My father was a rotter, my mother was mad, and my sister is a shrew. There you have the entire Strickland line."

Her mouth fell open. She'd shocked him earlier with her openness. It was only fair he did the same.

"Elliot is a baron, but you'd think he was the king for how he conducts himself," he continued. "I'll never understand what he saw in Frances. Perhaps he recognized a similar autocratic vein in her, or perhaps he simply realized she could make his servants just as despondent as he did."

"It was not a love match then, I see," Abigail said.

He shrugged, as nonchalant as she had been about the illustrations. "Money changed hands, as it usually does. Frances is happy in her own miserable way. I don't intend to marry, so the Strickland family name shall end with me."

"Now who is the pessimist?" she teased, the laughter not reaching her eyes as it had before.

She'd made it clear she didn't find him attractive. But she was a chit, and he'd never met a woman that didn't take a man's declaration of bachelorhood as an insult. He debated saying that if he were to marry, he'd want a woman like her. He pushed those thoughts aside, knowing they were foolish.

"My parents married for love," she recalled wistfully. "And for a while, I think they were very much enamored. When my mother died giving birth to Bess, my father died too. Not his physical form, mind you, but his spirit."

Impulsively, he stretched his hand across the table, taking her small palm in his and clasping it for a second. "I'm sorry that happened to you. It's hard enough to lose one parent, let alone two."

She did not speak. She held his hand. Timid at first, as if she was not sure she should be touching him at all, but then her grip became firm.

It was the simplest gesture. Their bare skin did not touch. Her glove was cool against his smooth palm. He had never been one for handholding, finding it too affectionate. It implied an intimate connection he neither felt nor desired to pantomime.

Rarely did he engage in any form of physical contact that did not have the result of sex; foreplay was admissible because it heightened the experience.

Yet something about this seemed right. He could not explain the sensation, for it had no logic to it. He did not push the connection further. He shouldn't even have reached for her hand.

All there was between them was a future of broken promises and complications. She deserved to be worshipped by a man who could commit to her. A man who'd want her for a wife, not a mistress, because he was steady and capable of seeing things in long-term relationships. Though he knew he could never be that man, for his life was a strange mix of bureaucracy and intrigue, he didn't break away from her.

He remained when he knew he should run because the grip had turned from the comfort of a second to something more unwieldy and harder to define. For a second—maybe a minute, he lost track of time as everything seemed to slow—they sat there like that, him leaning toward her, their hands joined over the coffee table.

ABIGAIL'S GAZE FLICKED to their united hands. She couldn't deny the tumbling of her stomach when he'd reached over the table and slid his palm on top of hers. Couldn't pretend that she was unaffected by the sweetness of it. His proposal to school her became more tempting, simply because it meant more time with him in this wonderful room.

She breathed in. This must be what heaven smelled like: musty books and leather furniture. A handsome man.

The old bookstalls in the Crispin Street markets paled in comparison to Michael's library. Floor-to-ceiling shelves of solid oak spanned most of the room. Each shelving unit created a separate haven for her to hide behind. A place to tryst. A fantasy.

She could live a million lives in the pages of these books, untouched by the cruelness of the outside world.

Her gaze darted to the copy of *Candide* on the table below their linked hands. At least three of those million lives she'd share with Michael. The circumstances would be different, of course. They'd be equals, partners forged in the fires of passion, and kept lit by their dueling intellects.

She ought to remember who she was. Tend to her own garden, instead of imagining pretend romances with a man she'd just met. She'd no use for fanciful notions. If she kept to her plan, she'd be able to earn enough money that Bess could have a secure future.

She dared to look at his face. His eyes were closed. Her gaze darted to his mouth, half-open, begging to be nipped. A boy at the factory had kissed her like that once, but she'd felt little apart from initial confusion.

With Michael though, she sensed it'd be marvelous—that he'd know what to do. Heat swarmed her body, unwelcome and unwanted, just from their connected hands. Dangerous, how he affected her. Dangerous and daunting.

She could no more pull her hand from his than she could deny the salacious turn to her thoughts. He was a hero to her now, giving her the gift of deciding when she'd tear out the last stitches of her old life and become the wicked Beauty.

The night before, if he'd chosen instead to take what she'd volunteered out of duty and desperation, would they still be sitting so calmly like this? Or would everything have become irreparably altered?

Michael hadn't moved. His breathing was even. While her heart flapped against her chest like the wings of the devilish birds that morning, he seemed perfectly happy to sit in silence with her.

She doubted he thought of her as anything more than a charity case. She ought to tell him now that she wanted only to learn from him. Nothing else. But instead, she lingered in this moment. Pretended that she had all the time in the world to decide that another course of action would appear before her.

His blue eyes opened. A lopsided smile cracked the perfect symmetry of his face. Slowly, as though he had all the time in the world to spend with her, he ran his thumb against the bridge of her forefinger.

She was—God help her—content.

His finger to her brow had scorched her skin before. But this, his thumb dragging against her palm in the softest glide, marked her. It said that she was his, for two weeks at least. He'd laid claim not to her body but to her soul.

This unspoken understanding between them, forged from their similarly irrational families, was far more treacherous than if he'd simply bedded her. She didn't want his comprehension. Didn't want him to see the parts of her she kept hidden from the world, for that would make her vulnerable.

She dragged her hand from his and moved so was she sitting upon her offending limbs. There, no more temptation. She ignored the answering pang within her.

She hadn't come here to fancy him. Any physical contact between them needed to be in line with her plans. She'd sell the illusion of love, not the real thing. In these close moments with

Michael, she feared it was all too genuine. She couldn't attempt to seduce him under these conditions.

Michael watched her, his brow arched. He did not speak. The silence closed in upon her. So, she fidgeted, hummed a little ditty. She did everything that would create noise because she could not bear the nearness that came with this quiet. The intimacy would leave too dark a stain upon her soul.

With Clowes loose, she needed to summon her strength. She'd hold fast to those dark places in her mind and allow the rage to encompass her as it had since that awful night. She'd been a victim then, weakened by her loyalty to Poppy. But now Abigail had no allegiance to anyone but Bess. Not to Strickland, not to her father, and certainly not to the bitch who had ruined her life by her insistence on poking her nose in places where it didn't belong.

Michael cleared his throat. He'd settled back against the cushions of his chair and now watched her for signs of acquiescence to their new friendship. She assumed the sourest expression she could manage. A deep-set scowl, lines rutted into her forehead. She was a warrior, damn it, and she wasn't so easily cajoled.

"When my mother died, I told myself I wouldn't believe in love," she said briskly. "Love is a foolish notion for poets. There is a fine line between madness and bliss, and I intend to stay on the right side of it."

A darkness passed over Michael's face, an oppressive melancholy that emanated off him in waves. He sat with his shoulders hunched, his hands gripping the armrests of the chair as though they were lifeboats in a troubled sea. The quickness of his transformation threw her, forcefulness in his expression when before there had been empathy.

"My father was a rotter; my mother was mad."

The memory of his words crashed into her. She'd meant to put up her own defenses, not strike an arrow into his heart.

She rubbed her thumb across her palm, tracing where he'd touched before, her mind racing. "Micha—Inspector Strickland?" She shouldn't use his name, not when she'd offended him.

His livid eyes set upon her, robbing her of breath for a second. How callous she'd been—how callous she'd continue to be if she didn't apologize. So surrounded by her own grief, she'd ignored his pain.

A part of her questioned why she should even care. Once the two weeks were done, he'd be gone from her life. The memories would be locked away in the recesses of her mind. She'd have to be coy, seductive, and able to convince wealthy men she wanted only them.

But for now, she could choose her own course. Abigail clasped her hands in her lap, drew herself up to her full height, and faced Michael's irate gaze.

"I'm sorry." The emotion in her voice rang out. "I spoke without thought, and in doing so, I cast a shade upon your mother's memory. I meant only to say that I wished my father had loved my own mother less, so that he might have taken her death better. Were his heart not so lost, I doubt I'd be here now."

His hands relaxed. Slowly, he flattened his palms. She watched him closely for any signs that he'd forgiven her heedlessness. His nostrils no longer flared. Yet the shadow across his features remained.

"What a pair we are," he remarked dryly. "Both victims of our families."

She didn't want to be a victim any longer. She wanted to live. But how could she be anything but broken? She'd forgotten how to exist normally.

"I'm sorry," she repeated, quieter this time. No longer was

she sure to whom she was apologizing: him, his mother's specter, Bess, Papa, or even herself.

"Nothing to be sorry for." He shrugged, the movement lacking his usual fluidity. "I am not some namby-pamby weakling, prone to fainting spells simply because you referenced my mother's malady."

"I didn't think you were, but I'd suppose it's difficult to speak of," she hedged, not buying his show of indifference.

"It is nothing," he insisted. "Why must you women always insist on examining your emotions? When you all retreat to the drawing room after dinner, I'm certain it is to flatter and braid each other's hair."

"I wouldn't know," she snapped, prickling at his inference. "I've never been to a formal dinner party."

"I assure you, you aren't missing anything," he said without remorse. "Four courses of the most uncomfortable conversations you'll ever have, all in the name of God, country, and that bastard etiquette."

She widened her eyes, blinking up at him innocently. "Why, if I wanted an uncomfortable conversation, I'd just spend the night with you."

He snorted. "The lady doth wound."

She smirked. "I speak the truth."

Trading barbs with him was easier than the tenderness they'd shared before. She knew the power of a backhanded compliment: the last ten years with Papa had taught her the effectiveness of manipulative passiveness.

"You called me Inspector before, and every time you address me like that, I feel four times my age. A man doesn't want to be professional in his own home." A sly grin toyed with his lips. "With an insult like that, my dear, I think we can now consider each other friends, or as friendly as two society wankers pretend to be."

"Very well, I'll make a concerted effort to think of you as Michael." He needn't know she'd already taken to doing so. His name felt *good* on her tongue, more than it should.

He scraped the pad of his thumb across the shadow of stubble on his chin, reminding her how he'd looked in the hell. So cocksure, certain he'd charm all he encountered.

She brushed at an imaginary wrinkle in the fabric of her borrowed skirt. God, he'd worked his magic on her, just as he did on everyone else. He'd enchanted her with books and sweet buns, and now his every word bespelled her.

He crossed one long leg over the other, his arm lackadaisically hanging over the edge of the chair. "You know, your sentiment was cruelly constructed but apt."

She blinked. "What?"

"I believe it was my father who drove my mother mad."

"There is no history in your family of mental incapacity?" She congratulated herself for that erudite turn of phrase. "Mental incapacity" sounded so much more polite than "as crazed as a syphilitic drab."

He barked out a hollow laugh. "When Father was alive, he loved to recount to a captive audience how my grandfather disguised my mother's madness with a particularly large dowry. Father swore Mother's lineage traced back to Anne Boleyn, and we all know she was mad as a March hare."

"At least you're related to a past queen?" She tried to look at the positive. Her own Huguenot ancestors had stowed away on a freighter and ended up as penniless weavers.

Michael rolled his eyes. "There's no truth to the Old Bastard's ranting. Mother was perfectly sane when she met my father. *He* destroyed her, through inattention and flagrant disregard for her feelings. I wasn't but four when I found him in bed with a Drury Lane vestal."

She recoiled, falling back against the cushions of the sofa. "Your poor mother! He was married."

"How old-fashioned of you, Abigail," he remarked drolly. "Men often take mistresses in marriage. It was not the infidelity that concerned my mother, but his lack of discretion in conducting his affairs."

Abigail frowned. "I don't imagine he was an easy person to live with." For all of Papa's sins, at least he had been faithful to her mother.

"Frances and I didn't call him the Old Bastard for nothing." Michael picked up *Candide,* holding the book sideways and eying the illustration. His smirk widened. "Fancy that pose."

She schooled her features into an expression of boredom, so he'd return to the point.

"Ah, yes," he said absently. "Father worked for the Night Watch. Thought he was doing the King's work, when in reality he was a prick with a billystick and a need for control."

She bit back a retort about how the new Met was no different from his description. She didn't want to insult him, not now. "Yet you still joined the Met."

His hand paused mid-flip of a page. His grin faltered. "It's just a job, Abigail, what I do. It pays the bills."

She'd touched a sensitive subject for him. "Still can't be easy to live in the shadow of your father."

"He was a scaly nigit. I don't care that he had affairs, but I resent the way he treated my mother."

"You truly don't care that he was unfaithful?"

"Of course not. I expected you to be a bit more open-minded in your ideals."

She narrowed her eyes. "Because of why I'm here?"

He shifted in the chair, not meeting her eyes. "No, I simply meant because of your past in the factories."

She hadn't expected such a judgment from him. Oh, she'd heard it all before: the religious fanatics reported that women who worked in factories not only took to drink quickly, but were also liberal with their affections. Until Clowes stripped her of her dignity, she'd prided herself on being different from that label.

Pushing herself up from the couch, she moved away from the table. Only when she was several paces away did she spin back around, facing him with her hands planted on her hips. "Has anyone ever told you that you're a royal arse, *Michael*?"

"Often, actually." His long strides brought him next to her.

She stiffened, preparing to flee in case he should try to touch her. But he simply loomed next to her, the woodsy scent of him flooding her nostrils.

He undid the buttons of his coat, winding his thumbs in the waistband of his trousers. "Perhaps we don't assume things about each other then. I've never enjoyed people categorizing me before making my acquaintance."

"What do you suggest?"

"I'd prefer for your impression of me to be formed by our experiences together and not the words of others." He extended his hand to her in a sweeping motion. "I promise only to allow my opinion of you to be colored by what you tell me if you'll do the same."

Damn him. Even his grovels were smooth. She retreated from him, setting back her shoulders.

She nodded briskly but did not take his hand. "To a blank slate."

Chapter Nine

Two days passed. It was the fifth day of Abigail's stay with him. He'd heard from one of his sergeants that Clowes had been located in St. Giles by an informant. His men were monitoring the area for further activity, but if Clowes was truly in West London, that was hopeful. The farther away he was from Abigail, the better.

He glanced at the clock. Twelve in the afternoon was at least a reasonable hour, unlike the early mornings he'd been keeping since Abigail arrived. He used to sleep through breakfast, for he usually went out to the hells after his shift with the Met. But with Abigail here, he awoke at nine to eat with her. She spent the afternoon in the library, while he went to his office to process the morning reports dropped off by his sergeants. They'd reconvene in the evening for dinner.

As he pulled on his greatcoat and did up the buttons, he marveled at the ease at which she'd slipped into his life. He should have found her company tiresome.

Yet the hours spent with her in the parlor after dinner passed in mere seconds. They talked about their mutually foolish families, the strange cases he'd investigated during his time as a sergeant, and the time she'd spent in the factory. He loved it most when she'd describe the books she read to him, for only then did her eyes sparkle. Her joy was infectious; he found himself smiling too, for no other reason than her happiness.

When the clock struck midnight each night, he was reluctant to part from her. He wanted one more smile, one more scathing remark, one more laugh from her.

Last night, he'd lingered too long with her hand in his. He'd kissed her gloved hand, as was customary, but he had not withdrawn his grip afterwards. The scant space between them had crackled with restless energy.

His gaze had centered on her bow-shaped mouth. Those plush, sweet lips he ached to draw between his teeth. Her tongue darted out to wet her lips. He'd edged closer to her. Just as he'd been about to kiss her, she'd dashed away.

He'd been left as cold as the snow falling outside on this frigid October day. As he scooted the curtain back from the window to survey the garden, he remembered another early snowstorm, when he'd been a lad of six years. At four years his senior, Frances had considered herself far too advanced to play with him. But on this day, she'd been in a rare good temperament, constructing a fort with him out of the snow.

Hopefully, the winter storm would bring forth similar agreeableness in Abigail. Michael tugged his hat onto his head and wound a wool scarf around his neck. Sheepskin-lined boots encased his feet. He had everything he needed for a walk out in the garden. Everything but her.

He'd invited her to come with him, but she was late.

Mrs. O'Neal and Smithers appeared, both looking too pleased with themselves. Michael mouthed a question, but they didn't answer. They parted to opposite sides of the hall. The door opened.

Now he understood why his servants were so smug. Silhouetted in the doorway, her maroon cloak adorned with white fur pulled up over her head, Abigail glowed.

He didn't move toward her. Rather, he waited by the window, watching as she came toward him. The cloak billowed out from her, showcasing the svelte lines of her rose-pink dress with the matching maroon bodice.

She must have felt his gaze upon her, for her cherubic cheeks pinked. God, her maidenly blush made his cock twitch to life. She stirred something primal in him. All he could think of was that he wanted to be the first—the *only*—to see that innocence alter into the lush crimson of a well-pleasured woman.

He blinked. Where had that possessive thought come from? He wanted to tup her, of course, but he had no right to claim her.

Abigail turned around to say something to Smithers. Damned if the old man didn't grin back at her.

A smart man might have admitted defeat when his servants had so clearly outplayed his hand. Michael had never been considered a smart man. He'd disappointed them so much in the past, they ought to know better.

He wouldn't become attached to Abigail, no matter how much they wanted him to. No matter how much *he* wanted to spend more time with her. She was here for two weeks, and then she'd leave. She'd forget about him as she moved on to a bigger conquest.

The servants wandered off under the auspicious claim they had work to do. Most likely, they'd end up at another window, spying on his walk with Abigail. Incurable sods.

"Ready?" he asked, extending his arm to her.

She nodded, resting her hand on his arm. "I'm not sure I understand why you want to spend the day out of doors."

He smiled at her quizzical expression as he opened the door

out into the garden. "Come now, Abigail, haven't you ever played in the snow?"

She held back. "Shouldn't we be concerned about Clowes?"

"My men have received intelligence that Clowes is in St. Giles," he said. "But I've got two patrollers guarding these grounds. In addition, Smithers is equipped with a pistol. He's a crack shot, though you'd never know by the way he comports himself."

"That old man?"

"That 'old man' used to be in the Army before he joined my family's staff."

Her brows rose. "Somehow, I cannot picture that."

"Smithers was a lieutenant," he said. "Served in the war against old Boney, but he got injured in battle, and the Army dismissed him."

She frowned. "Poor Smithers. Now he's in an entirely different type of service."

"I'm sure he'd greatly prefer facing a field of angry frogs than deal with me," he said dryly.

He stepped from the porch into the snow, motioning for her to follow. Cold smacked him in the face, alerting every one of his senses. This was what he loved about winter: no matter how deadened he felt inside, the raw frigidity always made him feel alive.

There was no wind today, only the constant chill. For now, at least, the snow had ceased falling. They stood at the edge of the garden, the brick path barely visible under a blanket of white. Icicles hung from the sagging branches of willow trees. His mother's rose bushes had frozen, the sharp thorns without bite. No one had been out yet. A yard of fresh snowfall stretched before them.

Abigail's hand tightened on his arm.

He urged her forward. "It's not so bad once you get used to it."

She cast him a disparaging glare. "I have been in snow before, you know."

Damnation, how he enjoyed every sneer from this prickly miss. Abigail Vautille had more piss and vinegar in her little body than half the sergeants he knew. If she'd been born male— and of surer footing—she would've made a damn good patroller.

He grinned as her scowl deepened. "It's harmless. Just a bit of fluff."

"I hate fluff," she muttered darkly. "And I don't act without purpose."

He grinned. "Haven't you ever done something for the fun of it? Because you want to know how it'll feel?"

She yanked the hood of her cloak tighter around her head. "I don't have time for fun." Her voice dripped with disdain he'd only ever heard from the working class. "If I don't bring in money, then my sister starves."

He made a mental note to send Smithers to London Bank. An anonymous transfer to the Vautilles of fifty pounds or so— not so substantial that she'd refuse, but large enough to keep her set up for a few months.

It'd be the best damn use of his father's money yet.

Patting her arm, he softened his smile. "Come now, love. You left Bess in good hands, didn't you?"

She tilted her head up, scrutinizing him with wide eyes. "You remember my sister's name."

Good. She wasn't immune to his charm. He had begun to doubt his prowess.

Hell, she made him doubt everything he knew.

"Of course, I remember. It was important to you." God bless his weird memory, which cataloged names and dates with unerring accuracy.

He led her down the path. Turning his head, he peered behind his shoulder at their footprints. The memorandums on his desk requiring action faded away. There was only the wild, reckless outdoors around him.

And her. He couldn't breathe without smelling the lavender of her soap. He couldn't proceed without hearing her footfall after him, irregular in step but somehow managing to keep pace with him. Though the air had begun to warm as the sun emerged from the clouds, he was certain that the heat flowing in his joints could be traced to the sight of her decked out in that velvet maroon cloak, which covered half of her bodice too.

"It's not a particularly large garden," he said apologetically. "I wish I could show you Vauxhall in the spring when everything is in bloom, and there are fireworks."

"This will do fine," she replied. "I don't imagine I'd fit in well at Vauxhall."

He tilted his head toward her, taking in her rich clothes and the gloves that covered scarred hands. Though he'd dressed her in finery and treated her like a queen, in her eyes, she'd always be the same gutter girl.

"That's the beauty of Vauxhall," he told her. "*Everyone* fits in there. There's something for you no matter what class you're from."

She stepped around a downed branch from one of the trees, holding her rosy skirts up with her right hand. "I suppose I'll have to revise my earlier view of it. But you still haven't told me the point of this outing."

He clucked his tongue. "Originally, I simply wanted to take a stroll in the fresh air. Now that you've admitted you don't know how to enjoy yourself, I have a new goal."

Eying him suspiciously, she dropped his arm and took a step back. "And what, pray tell, is that?"

He crossed his arms over his chest, leaning back on the balls of his feet. "To make you have fun. Why, I've lived my entire life seeking pleasure."

"Your reputation precedes you," she noted wryly.

"Ah, now, we said we wouldn't rely on the words of others." He waggled a finger at her. "*Tabula rasa* and all that, love."

"It's not that I don't know how to have fun," she clarified. "But rather that there's no point in it. The world is cruel. I see no reason to pretend otherwise anymore."

"Perhaps a wager then?"

"Absolutely not." The cloak slipped backward from her vigorous headshakes. "Gambling got us into this bloody mess to begin with."

"Not for blunt. For...something else entirely." He grinned wolfishly.

She retreated from him. "I haven't given you my answer yet."

Well, that settled it. Whatever desire he harbored for her, she certainly didn't share it. "You keep saying it like that, and my ego's going to get damaged."

She arched a brow at him. "Given how much you love yourself, I highly doubt that."

"I was merely going to say that if by the end of the afternoon, you're having fun, then I win. I'd like you to recite from a book of my choosing." He had a few volumes of particularly bawdy poetry that ought to bring a blush to her face.

"Ah. I suppose that'll do." She inched closer to him, her hand extended. "And if I win, I should like you to admit that *Candide* is a fabulous book in a three-paragraph essay with detailed drawings."

"Cheeky lass." He shook her hand. "It's a done deal."

"Now, for your first challenge..." He stooped down, intending to pack the loose snow up into a ball to fling at her.

But before he could launch his assault, something cold and

wet hit him. He straightened up, loose snow sliding down off his wool greatcoat. The larger part of her snowball clung to his coat, a veritable bull's-eye.

Mischievous wench.

Abigail stood back from him, her gloved hands slapping against her knee. Her laughter rang out, reminding him of church bells before Christmas mass. Her giggles claimed it was time for celebration, for a new dawn was upon them.

Bollocks. He didn't wax poetic. He was a man, damn it, and men kept stiff upper lips. Men weren't undone by golden-haired pixies, no matter how radiant her face was when she finally smiled.

He swept downwards, scooping up a handful of snow and packing it between his palms. While she remained doubled over, gasping for breath as she laughed, he aimed a snowball straight at her side.

Excellent aim, if I do say so myself.

She ceased laughing, wiping the snow off her coat. "I'll have you know I'm not responsible for any damage you do to your sister's garments."

He swallowed as warmth flooded through him. The damage he might do to that dress would be way worse than snow. With his bare hands, he'd rend that fabric in half—

Another snowball smacked him square in the jaw.

He swiped at the snow, his chin numbing from the cold. "Hey, now!"

She leveled her shoulders and narrowed her eyes. "I'm a damn good opponent. If you want a war, I'll give you a war."

From her outstretched palm, a third snowball flew, landing on his chest. When had she time to make the damned things? His coat would be drenched soon.

He dived for shelter behind the solid wood bench, but not soon enough. A snowball hit him in the thigh.

"Can't be beaten by a girl," he muttered, mocking his father's words every time Frances walloped him as a child. The Old Bastard had underestimated the sheer pugnaciousness of females, just as he had underestimated his son.

Balling up the snow in quick, solid handfuls, Michael created a small stockpile of snowballs. He darted to the side, scanning for a sight of Abigail. Her voluminous skirts peeped out from behind the trunk of a large oak tree down the path. She'd made good time, but with every purposeful stride, she left tiny footprints in two wide lines for him to follow.

He evaluated the garden as he'd once considered the paths he had to take as a foot patroller, judging on shortest distance, easiest route, and likely problems. If he remained huddled behind the bench, he'd likely be unaffected by her assaults. But he'd gain no tactical advantage, as his snowballs would smash to the ground before they reached her.

"Well, one must live dangerously," he declared, with a wistful glance at his bench haven. Smithers would decry his blatant disregard for his coat, but desperate times called for desperate measures.

He popped up the collar of his greatcoat so that it lined his neck, creating an extra layer of warmth atop his neckcloth. Scooping up as many snowballs as he could carry, he braced himself for an onslaught of cold. He half-wobbled, half-pushed up from the ground, and set off at a run down the path.

One, two, three snowballs slammed into his chest. Damnation, she had a wicked aim. Peals of laughter joined with the sound of slapping slush as she darted back behind the tree. How was she so speedy in that huge skirt, with her knock-knees and her injured hand?

He'd thought this would be an easy battle.

He should've known nothing with Abigail Vautille was ever easy.

Darting closer, he came within spitting distance of her tree. She skidded away, flinging a snowball at him as she did so. He bolted after her, sliding as the hard-packed snow underneath him became slippery. One snowball slipped from his hands, landing on his feet.

"So much for a worthy opponent," she teased, flashing him a grin that stopped him dead in his tracks.

Come now, man. Use your head. No, not that one. Your other head.

With fatal accuracy, he launched a snowball straight at her chest.

"Oh!" She jumped back as water splashed across her bodice. She brushed at her bosom with her gloved hand.

He gulped. He ought to look away. He ought to imagine anything but how her nipples must be pebbling from the cold—

Smack.

She struck him again.

"You're staring," she chided, but the satisfied flush to her cheeks bespoke her pleasure at his attentions.

He slid one hand behind his back, a giant snowball clenched in his fist. Sidling up to her, he ran a finger down the fur trim of her cloak with his free hand. "But why would I ever want to look away when you present such a delectable treat?"

She became more rigid but didn't step back. Blinking several times, she stood there slack-jawed.

He'd finally stunned her.

So, he reached out, flattening sleet against her bodice. She squealed, but he kept his hand on top of it, mushing the wet ball and sliding it around until it covered the entire front of her dress.

She jumped back from him. He followed her. Around and around the tree, they ran, chasing each other. He kept his strides short, his pace slower, so that he never quite caught up to her, the appeal of the game being in their giggling chase.

It was always the chase with him and women.

But he didn't want to chase anymore. Maybe he wanted her to come after him. Maybe he wanted something more: an equal exchange of bodies and minds.

He came to a grinding halt, leaning back against the tree. She paused next to him to catch her breath. Her cheeks flushed from exertion, and her nose was tipped red from the cold. He'd never seen her blue eyes shine so brilliantly.

"Are you enjoying yourself yet?" he asked.

She straightened up, making a show of smoothing her snow-coated cloak. Lifting her chin, she challenged him with her gaze. "Absolutely not."

"Then perhaps we ought to take a stroll down the path," he suggested, extending his arm to her. "Have you ever made snow angels?"

"I cannot think of any possible reason why 'snow' and 'angel' should be in the same sentence." Refusing his arm, she marched out into the snow, each step deliberate. After she'd proceeded halfway down the path, she turned around, hands on her hips. "Well? Are you coming?"

He hadn't been staring at her arse as she walked down the path. No, of course not, he'd been a complete gentleman, as befitted their newfound friendship. If she believed that...he had a share in London Bridge he'd sell her.

He shrugged, exaggerating the movement to take off focus from the fact that his face mostly assuredly appeared guilty. "You have never lived until you've made a snow angel, my dear Abigail."

"I highly doubt that." She motioned for him to follow her.

He trotted off after her, the cold slapping his face with every step. He was alive, invigorated, and utterly determined to win this bet. There were a few poems of John Wilmot's with her name on them.

Chapter Ten

She'd lost the bet.

Defeat ran through Abigail's body, undeniably forthright. The knowledge accosted her when she traversed the path, linked arm-in-arm with Strickland, his booted feet sinking into the snow with august grace she'd never possess. Her chest blazed with each breath. She'd pushed too hard, chasing him around. Once they parted ways, she'd fall into bed and not move for the next twelve hours. But for now, she forced herself forward, pretending that she wasn't exhausted.

She wouldn't let him see her weakness.

Devil take him! Even in her fatigue, she thrived out here. The garden had become a magical wonderland.

She'd expected to hate all of this. Winter was not a time to frolic outdoors; winter was a time to huddle by the fireplace until the very last ember died out. She now understood why aristocrats flocked to balls and Christmas parties in their comfortable carriages with their fur muffs and thick cloaks. They'd never experienced bone-chilling cold.

Clad in the fur-trimmed maroon cloak and the lush pink day dress, she was, for the first time in her life, warm after a snowstorm. Even the drips of snow that clung to her dress didn't affect her. And in the absence of cold, she knew she'd lost her sanity. Her body heated from the inside out, thanks to his damnably merry presence. His affable grin fired her heart, flushed her cheeks until she was sure the whole world must know her joy.

So, she painted a scowl upon her face and tried to summon back the ever-present darkness. She ought to be scared, for Clowes was out there, and in all her life, she'd never met anyone as evil as Clowes.

But as Michael tugged her along, she couldn't help but give in to glee. She felt safe here, safer than she'd ever been.

He led her down the winding path, past flower plots with shrubberies dividing the sections. Surely, he must need a gardener to tend to these plants—Smithers seemed to have to enough to do, though she still couldn't fathom how one man generated as much mess as Michael did. But for all the work Michael piled on the aging butler, Smithers still found time to ask about her day. She'd quickly come to look forward to their talks.

Michael claimed the garden was small, yet by her estima-tion, it was longer than the Larker factory and twice the width. She'd already counted two trellises that would be overflowing with ivy in warmer weather; four statutes constructed in marble and stone of random Grecian gods; three floral arches that led to alcoves with wooden chairs. A miniature man-made pond had been placed off to the right, set into a circular stone enclosure. Overlooking the pond was a hexagonal pavilion of smooth stone with intricate etched designs in an ancient alphabet—Greek, she guessed, since the *ton* was obsessed with classical architecture. Better to remain buried in lofty recreations of the past than confront the poverty in their own present.

Without any ado, Michael dropped to the ground in front of

the pavilion. He lay on his back, paying no attention to the wet white powder that now coated his coat and breeches.

Quizzically, she nudged him with her foot. "Should I be concerned for your mental well-being?"

He stretched in the snow, arms out, legs spread wide. "I told you I'd teach you how to make a snow angel. Come, lie down beside me."

Her gaze flicked from the ostentatious pavilion to his recumbent form. "You must be bamming me."

"I assure you, I am the image of solemnity." His sly smile did nothing to convince her.

"If this is an attempt to get me closer to you—oof!"

His hand crept forward, wrapped around her ankle. He tugged, and she tumbled to the ground, landing on her back an arm's length from him. Snow soaked her cloak. Sank in through her skirt to wet her petticoats.

"You can go to the devil," she muttered, turning her head to glare at him.

He didn't even try to hide his smug grin. "Such foul language from a pretty lady."

Pretty. No man had ever called her pretty once he knew of her scars. Suddenly the snow soaking her clothes didn't feel so cold.

"If it is foul language you want..." She began playfully. "You're a bloody, wanking rotter, Michael Strickland, a bastard better fit for poxed parasitic hog grubbers and ark ruffians. Have you lost every shred of decency in your wastrel, distended mind?"

"Oh, Abigail," Michael mock sighed. "Have a bit of fun. It shan't kill you."

She flinched. The last time she'd viewed life with such flippancy, she'd paid dearly. But she wouldn't let his words trouble her. She'd consider this another opportunity to practice her theatric skills.

"I'll be the judge of that." She shook her arm, snow scattering off her cloak. "I hope you're composing your essay as we loiter, for I expect it in full as soon as we return."

"*Au contraire,*" he objected. "I've already won the bet. I saw you smile earlier."

"I smile because your idiocy amuses me," she quipped, a chortle escaping from her throat before she could stop it. He was so comical, sprawled out in the snow like a lazy cat in a sunbeam.

His booming laughter resonated through the empty garden. The sound engulfed her, bringing forth more chuckles of her own until, for the second time that day, her shoulders shook, her sides ached, and her breath came in uneven pants.

She couldn't remember the last time she'd laughed like this, an all-consuming tide of merriment that deafened her doubts.

Damn him. Damn her inability to stay mad at him. Damn how in a week it all wouldn't matter anymore.

Her laughter died out in a strangled gulp of sorrow. What little bliss she'd found here would be ripped from her soon. There'd be no one like Michael to care for her then. She almost wished she'd never spent time with him—never known him—because in an unrelenting cycle of drudgery, she'd accepted pain as the new normal.

His strong hand gripped her arm, fingers curling into the fabric of her cloak. "Abigail," he murmured as if he feared to break into her reverie. His tone was respectful, containing none of the teasing notes of before.

Somehow that made this harder. Not just being here with him, but all those in-between details. If she ever again wore fine dresses or had porridge with a jam that didn't taste of grit and grime, it wouldn't be with him. She'd be with some other man, hopefully with a fat enough purse that she could afford to send Bess to school.

The past few days had spoiled her. Left her wanting this, to live in this dream world for longer than two weeks. Maybe it would have been better never to have come here. She'd forgotten what happiness felt like. How could she go on to a brothel after this?

Lying in the snow—the stupid, cold snow—next to Michael made her feel sheltered. Wasn't that the greatest lie of them all? There'd be no shelter, no security, for a woman like her.

She ought to know better.

She did know better.

Abigail drew back. She was about to push herself up from the ground, to end this false start. There could be nothing between them. Not now, not ever.

Michael patted her arm. "Where'd you go, Abigail?"

She blinked. "I've not gone anywhere. I've been here with you in this blasted snow, though it defies every bit of logic."

He shook his head. "That's not what I mean, and you know it. All was fine—you were laughing, you looked happy. Then you went quiet. Something's bothering you, little lamb, and I'd like to know what."

She ran a hand down her skirt, brushing off more snow. She didn't meet his eyes. She couldn't bear his compassion, any more than she could bear his charity.

Propping herself up, she rested her weight on her elbows and dug her boots into the snow. "It is nothing."

Please, please, believe me.

"Nothing is what you chits say when you're plotting something," he noted. "And nothing is what you claim when you want a gent to back off. But unfortunately for you, I'm not a gentleman."

She remembered their kiss in the library. No, he most

certainly was not. But maybe she didn't need a gentleman in her life—maybe she needed a rogue.

"I'm a crass inspector whose ties to any part of good society vanished in the dirt of the rookeries. I find out secrets for a living. So, tell me." He slid closer, circling his arm around her waist and pulling her toward him. "Or I could tickle it out of you."

The brush of his fingers against her side sent a thrilling jolt through her, while the frigidness of the ground warred with her quickly heating body. He spread out his hand, his fingertips feathering across her rib cage.

She shook her head.

He scraped his fingertips across her side. Dug in, not too harsh, but in that exact spot between her waist and hip that made her squirm. Oh, how his touch cut through her! Her nerves were raw. She slapped at his hand, trying to get away from him. He held her to him, the strokes of his fingers unrelenting.

She couldn't help it. He had her under his control. The prickles were so fierce they stole her breath. She laughed until her throat was raw, and she gasped for air.

"Very well, I'll tell you!" she shrieked, with another smack to his hand.

"Good. I knew you'd see reason." He released her, and she tumbled out of his grip.

"You and reason have no business being in the same sentence." She sniffed, sitting up. She pushed down on her right hand, balancing herself awkwardly as she lifted herself up. Once standing, she readjusted her hat so that it fitted properly and brushed the snow off her gloves. "I'm going inside, Michael. A hot cup of tea and a biscuit would do me wonders."

"What about the snow angels?" he protested with a frown, as though he was a boy, and she'd taken away the prospect of pudding. "We can't do it here since we've mucked up the snow thoroughly." He stood, coming to join her.

When she rubbed her arms up and down her sleeves for warmth, he came up behind her, enfolding his arms around her.

She leaned back into him. For warmth reasons, of course. It was not because of how his breath against her neck sent private tickles up her spine, or because the whisper of his rough voice against her ear made her long to be wanton.

To her surprise, he pulled from her, undoing the buttons of his coat. Then he came back, enveloping her in a clinch. The folds of fabric fell around her. The sun had come out, and for a few seconds, she forgot she was outdoors in the middle of winter.

"There, that's better." He ceased rubbing his hands up and down her arms. "Sometimes, all you need is proximity to fight the cold."

That certainly wasn't sensible. She didn't need his presence. Not this man she'd known for five days, despite the way he'd anticipated her wishes and quelled her anxious spirit.

As if he sensed her thoughts, he spun her around. Somehow, he managed it so that she was still wrapped in his coat but was now facing him. "Now, tell me what concerns you."

She flinched. "I was thinking..."

He smiled the sly smile that'd become so familiar to her. "I could smell the smoke."

The corners of her lips twisted in an answering smile to her discontent. "I suppose I've earned that, with my earlier remarks. But I was thinking about how lovely it is here."

"Told you, I won the bet," he crowed. "You *do* like the snow. The Earl of Rochester awaits, my dear."

"Wait, that's not what I meant." She tunneled her hands into the pockets of her cloak; half wishing the ground might swallow her up and end this uncomfortable conversation. "Well, I suppose it is somewhat, but there's more."

"With women, there always is," he drawled.

"You're incorrigible." She rolled her eyes. "Before, I was thinking that I'll be sad to say goodbye to this place. I miss my sister, yes, but there's something...almost soothing about your home. Smithers treats me as some high society woman—when I'm below him—and you let me be myself."

"Abigail, you know you're welcome here." The giddiness faded from Michael's features. Tucking her closer to him, he rested his chin upon the top of her head.

She fingered the shiny silver lapels of his waistcoat, holding tight to him as if she could anchor him here forever. The strapping planes of his chest turned her insides into the worst of jellies.

Nice women didn't allow men to hold them so close, and certainly not outdoors where anyone might see them. Society had forgotten her when she couldn't contribute any longer, so why the devil should Abigail be a nice woman? She needed to learn to tup a man. Better to learn from Michael, who'd make sure it was pleasurable.

"You said I'd keep my virtue until I see fit." She stumbled over the whispered words, rubbing the silk of his waistcoat between her gloved thumb and forefinger. "I want to become a Cyprian. But maybe I want to create memories with you before I do."

"Abigail, we don't have to do that." His voice came out strained, his eyes darkening with desire.

His coat dropped away from her shoulders at the movement, but she no longer cared about the frigid weather. She'd face a blizzard if it meant they could stay like this.

"I am not a good man." His eyes were unsettling dark cobalt, while his voice held an edge that flipped her stomach. "I'm a scoundrel."

"You know my story," she reminded him. "A fairy tale happily ever after isn't in my cards. I don't care that you're wicked, or that you can't give me more than this."

"But you *should* care," he countered. "And I bloody can't believe I'm saying this, but you shouldn't want me, Abigail."

"I'm damn tired of people telling me what my emotions should be." Her expression hardened. Once her time ended here, every desire she had would be secondary to the wants of whoever owned her. She'd never again have an independent thought.

If that were what she needed to do to give Bess a better life, then she'd do it. But she still had a few more days left with him. Days she could spend in his arms, pretending that this bond between them was real.

He released her hands but remained with her, close enough that she could ascertain every thread of his starched linen shirt. "I've used any number of tricks to get women into bed. I ought to regret this, of course, but I don't. I have rules. Never take an innocent, and never take a woman who isn't willing. But the rest I've left up to chance."

I'm willing. I want you to make the pain go away.

She met his gaze. She wouldn't look away. Wouldn't hide behind the walls she'd created. She was damn tired of being ashamed. Every day, she paid the price for another's mistakes. Maybe, just maybe, she deserved peace too.

"Is it wrong to want one good memory before I'm a moll?"

His face twisted, seized by a sudden onslaught of sadness. "Balls, woman, not every moll leads an unhappy life. Think of the wealth you might have someday."

She gulped down the panic welling in her throat. "There's

no point in pretending I'm not going to have to whore, is there? I ought to commit fully to the effort."

"You could do that," he said. "Or you could live out your remaining days here simply enjoying yourself. Plenty of people live their lives in delusions. Hell, half my childhood was spent helping my mother have tea parties with her imaginary friends."

She shuddered. Michael had an even worse childhood than she did.

"Look, if you don't want to become a courtesan, we'll figure something out," he said. "Surely, there's another job out there for you. Something that will make you happy."

She broke free of his embrace, taking three steps back from him.

He tracked her movements, but not with the cool, calculated reasoning of an inspector. The flare of his nostrils and the break in his tone all indicated he was influenced by her emotion.

"I can't weave any longer, nor can I trundle a cart. I've no formal education and no references. No one would allow a cripple in service." She turned from him, starting down the path. There was no point to this winter excursion anymore. She'd marred the calm with her foolhardy impulse to make this into something more than a friendly walk.

"I'll make it better," he promised. "I can protect you."

She didn't stop. Didn't turn around. His words fell on deaf ears, for she knew damn well there was no hope.

"Abigail, come back here," he pleaded, a note of appeal in his voice she'd never heard before.

Still, she walked.

He jogged after her, intercepting her as she crossed under a trellis. Coming up behind her, he grabbed her arm, spinning her around to face him. For a second, she stood there, flush against him, her breath bated. She didn't recognize this side of him, the storm of emotions flashing across his face. Longing, desperation, sadness...and something she knew immediately as burning desire.

He cupped her chin in his hands, pulling her head up. And then he kissed her, devouring her lips with his own. Their kiss before had been about two combatants gauging one another's weaknesses. But this was so much more—fierce and vulnerable. Her body responded instantaneously in a whirl of tightened muscles and tingling toes.

In that instant, she thought of nothing else but the glide of their joined lips and the perfect way he enveloped her. Kissing Michael became like learning to walk. Slow at first, but she grew more adventurous as the kiss continued. He traced the curvature of her lips with his tongue, memorized the shape of her mouth.

She kissed him back, following his rhythm. A groan tore from him, an eager, salacious noise that she'd caused. He tasted her bottom lip, making those little bird wings in her stomach flap so frantically she wondered if her body was truly airborne.

To hell with reading Wilmot, she was *living* Wilmot! Her fingers tangled in his hair as he angled her chin with one hand to deepen their kiss. Her knees went weak, but his other hand pushed into the small of her back, supporting her.

He released her mouth to travel his kisses down her chin, his tongue tickling her delicate skin. He nipped her, his teeth grazing her collarbone. The combination of pleasure and pain brought her higher. She was spiraling, spiraling as his hands found her breasts, cupping the already tender buds with his leather gloves. He caressed her with equal parts rhythm and gentleness, bringing forth the most salacious of moans.

In these long moments, she did not breathe; she loved. She did not think; she felt. In his arms, she was no longer broken, but a willing, wanting woman.

She never wanted it to end.

But like every other happy moment in Abigail Vautille's short life, the kiss concluded. He released her. She stumbled back without the balustrade of his arms. Raising a finger to her lips, she touched where his kiss had been.

Neither spoke. She couldn't read his face. He seemed as shaken as she was. She tried to formulate something intelligent to say, but as she remained gaping, he strode off to the house.

The kiss had surprised him too.

She watched him go, not one word said. The door to the garden slammed shut behind him, and it was just her, alone in this no longer so peaceful winter fairyland.

Chapter Eleven

Michael spent the next two days sequestered in his office, where he had a stack of reports waiting from his patrollers. He'd read through more paperwork in the last forty-eight hours than he had in his first few months as inspector. But until his team caught Clowes, he couldn't be lax about anything.

That morning, Smithers had delivered a breakfast plate to his office. Between different meetings with the sergeants assigned to tracking down Clowes and his regular work, he had little time to think, let alone eat a leisurely meal in the dining room.

As he ate his eggs and toast, he sorted the files into three piles: other cases, information on Clowes, and administrative issues. He'd clear off the clerical matters first, for those memorandums only required him to sign his approval. The standard casework could wait until that evening.

An hour passed. He'd completed the first round of meeting notices and budget summaries in record time. The reports detailing Clowes's whereabouts took more time. Abigail's well-being depended on his thoroughness, so he re-read each report twice and then plotted Clowes's travels on his map.

He pushed away from the completed pile of dispatches and surveyed the remaining paperwork. The clock chimed ten. At half past nine, Sergeant Marcus Hume was supposed to brief him on any progress in the Clowes case. As usual, Hume was late.

If the man weren't such a damn good investigator, Michael would have dismissed him for his constant tardiness. Hume didn't have Knight's analytical skills, but he was highly proficient at reading people.

He frowned. This was not the day for Hume to be late. Not only did this throw his schedule to hell, but it left him time to examine what had happened with Abigail. Rarely did he encounter a situation where he couldn't immediately ascertain a course of action. But this—whatever *this* was with her—completely perplexed him.

The absurdity of his situation didn't escape him. He was a grown man flummoxed by a pixie no taller than his shoulders. What in God's name was he supposed to say to Abigail after that kiss? He'd intended to seduce her and go about his merry way. Instead, after just a week in his home, she'd blown his world apart.

Every part of his house now reminded him of her. In the dining room, he remembered breakfasts with her and four-course dinners where she ate with a gusto that amused him. In the parlor, he recalled nights spent in quiet contemplation with her. He'd work on paperwork while she read by the fire. And in the library—the blasted library—he could not take in a breath without wondering which book she'd read next, or how he might arrange the furniture to suit her needs better.

The townhouse no longer simply belonged to him. In the

span of seven days, Abigail had somehow managed to transition from houseguest to beloved resident. Cook delighted in making Abigail's favorites dishes. Smithers regaled her with tales from his early Army service until he was hoarse. Mrs. O'Neal smiled now.

Clearly, his staff expected that he'd extend a proposal of marriage to the lovely Miss Vautille, if for no other reason than it would please them.

He crossed to the window. His office faced the back of his house with a view of the grounds. As he stared out the window, he didn't see the snow-capped foliage laid out in a picturesque English garden. In its place, he imagined sooty, decrepit Whitechapel. Women huddled with their babies in threadbare coats, toes poking out from holes in their shoes. Men with bedraggled beards and sacks slung over their shoulders trudged home from the factories in the snow.

Prior to Abigail, he'd never considered the poor outside of the crimes they committed. He frequented their hells and their dram palaces, but he'd always assumed he was a notch above them. He resided in good society. Not the high echelon of the Upper Ten Thousand, obviously, but as an inspector with the Metropolitan Police, his name carried weight. On the surface, he was respectable.

Respectable men didn't kiss women whose hearts they'd break.

Hell, he hadn't just kissed her, he'd *groped* her too. Virtue was the one thing Abigail had left to recommend her to a callous society that saw women solely in what purity they might contribute, a society that didn't value her heart, her spirit, or her innovation.

Abigail might be able to perform as a ladybird, but it wasn't what her heart desired. The joy in her voice when she discussed books was similar to his enthusiasm for his moral statistics map. She'd be happiest with a man who admired her for her intellect, not her body.

Yet he'd kissed her without regard to that, without promises made to secure her position, without thought for the future.

Michael had taken leave of his senses. Not that he ever had much sense to begin with, as his supposed friends would be quick to point out. Any attachment to Abigail would only end in sorrow. He was a man made for short affairs, not love.

Pushing back his chair, he stood up from the desk. On the wall opposite were portraits of the last three Strickland men, all in their Night Watch uniforms.

When the Met formed three years ago, he'd wasted no time in joining. He received a salary, ladybirds liked him in his blues, and family dinners were less awkward.

"Boy, you might make me proud after all," the Old Bastard had quipped one night with too much port in him. "But I doubt that."

A week ago, he would have said ascending the ranks in the Met was his ultimate goal. Now, he hadn't the foggiest idea. He couldn't let his men know that he had any doubts whatsoever about his purpose. They'd prey upon any show of insecurity. Use it as a reason to be mutinous. No, if he wanted them to believe he was in command, he had to appear wholly sure of himself.

Abigail Vautille had clouded his judgment. Clasping his hands behind his head, he leaned back on the balls of his feet. He remembered one night when he'd finally succumbed to Frances's request to attend one of her bizarre occult séances. This mainly consisted of a circle of ninnyhammer women gripping a triangular contraption to channel the spirits of the dead. Michael had taken great joy in informing Frances afterward that her "spiritualism miracle" was no more than him nudging the planchette.

He didn't need a talking predictor board to know he was doomed to repeat his father's mistakes. How could he not? He'd never known any different.

He'd shared countless kisses in his twenty-eight years, but none of those experiences had ever been like this. When he kissed Abigail, it was more than the sum of two lips pressing together. During his most poetic moments—damn it all, since when did he have poetic moments?—he'd describe kissing Abigail as a tidal wave. Surging through and leaving him both rapturous and devastated.

Smithers knocked, opening the door. "Marcus Hume, sir."

Michael motioned for Hume to enter. Smithers closed the door after him.

"Good morning, *sir.*" Hume placed an ironic lilt on the title of respect.

Michael appraised the older sergeant slowly, taking no pains to hide his critical eye. Hume had been with the Met since its establishment three years ago, and the Watch for seven years prior to that. Because of Hume's lower-class background—father was a butcher from the Highlands and mother had Huguenot lines, if Michael's memory served—his promotions had come at a slower interval. He had no family history of policing, and his half-Scottish ancestry did him no favors with the superiors.

And he was a pompous ass.

Hume returned his scrutiny, brow arched and posture relaxed. His short, wavy hair was streaked with early gray, though he was only ten years Michael's senior. Ashen scruff flecked his upper lip and his chin.

Michael's customary smirk slid onto his lips. "Well, what is it? Out with it, old man."

Hume's eyes flashed. "It's about the girl, sir. But if you'd prefer to spend your time tupping her in the comforts of your home—"

"I would watch your tone, Sergeant." Michael's voice crackled with barely suppressed fury, surprising even him. He smoothed his hands across his breeches, composing his expression. "The girl is protected here."

Leaning back against the door, Hume stuffed his hands into the pockets of his coat, his elbows out. "Highly convenient for you."

One of these days, Michael was going to throttle him.

"Nothing about this is *convenient*. Miss Vautille was tortured for information because we didn't act fast enough," Michael retorted. "Or do you need a reminder of how you told Knight he was a bloody fool for investigating the Larkers in the first place?"

"We all thought it," Hume jeered. "And you'd do better to forget Knight. He's not coming back. Got that new wife of his."

"I'm well aware of Knight's state of marital bliss." Michael moved back to his desk. "What have you found that involves Abigail Vautille?"

Hume pulled out the chair across from him and sat. Reaching into his pocket, he brought out an all-too-familiar tattered paper and passed it to Michael. "You're going to want to read this."

"Another note?" Michael gulped down his tension, determined to appear unaffected in front of Hume. He took the paper. His hand remained steady, though his breath came in irregular pants.

The note read, *"You're never gonna stop me. I'll always win."* At least this time it didn't appear to be written in blood. The ink was black and crackled in places. He studied the words for a minute. Wherever Clowes was, he didn't have access to well-mixed ink or decent stationery. He could still be in the East End.

God's balls, could nothing in his bloody life go right?

"So, he's planning to make a move." Michael brought his index fingers and thumbs together in a steeple. "We should double security around the house."

Hume pulled from his coat several folded papers and handed them over. "I don't know about that. Boys got a tip that he's been spotted in the West End. Down by the Rat's Castle."

"That certainly doesn't fit with the theory that Clowes is coming after both Miss Vautille and me." Michael flipped through Hume's report. Going off the initial account, several of the patrollers were now monitoring the various areas Clowes might go in St. Giles.

"Perhaps he's sending the notes to distract us," Hume suggested. "If we're busy wondering what he's doing, we won't see the real attack coming."

Michael nodded. "It fits his character. We'll have to cover all the bases then. This report is a good start, but it's not enough. We need solid leads. I want teams in both St. Giles and Whitechapel."

"The superintendents aren't going to like that," Hume said.

Michael tapped the memorandum on top of one of the many piles on his desk. "Bicknell approved moving any available men to the operation. He wants this solved as quickly as possible, and *I* want him off my back."

"Bicknell's a tosser." Hume grinned, catching Michael off guard.

Michael could count the number of times Hume had ever smiled on one hand. Apparently, all he'd needed to do was find someone Hume hated more than him.

"Our informants said his men have been inquiring about travel to Ireland." Hume leaned over, turning the pages in the report until he got to an outline of plans Clowes's men had made. "Heard he reached out to some of the rebels who think the Irish Reform Act didn't go far enough in liberation. He's going to take the best of his men with him and join forces."

He'd factored Clowes leaving England into his equation, but it hadn't rated highest amongst the possibilities. Perhaps he'd been wrong. He'd certainly made enough mistakes lately.

"The last thing England needs is that bastard working with the bloody extremists," Michael groaned. "Have any of our men seen Clowes?"

"Jeffries did," Hume replied. "Evidently, he hasn't gone farther than a stone throw from Madame Massle's brothel."

"I know the place," Michael said.

"'Course you do." Hume winked. "Redhead with tits the size of melons, I think you said."

Somehow, his description sounded coarser when Hume said it.

"If Clowes is in Little Ireland, that'll work in our favor," Michael mused.

"How you figure? St. Giles is prime thieving territory." Hume scrutinized his face, searching for clues.

"Oh, I just meant we might stumble upon a few extra arrests," Michael replied, hoping the lie was convincing enough. He'd been thinking of Atlas Greer, who held court at the Rat's Castle. As soon as Hume left, he'd pen a note to Knight and ask him to alert the Gentleman Thief. Greer was friends with Poppy.

"Suppose you're right." Hume didn't sound convinced.

"He won't be exposed for long," Michael noted. "We have to act fast."

"Jeffries reported Clowes has been gathering what's left of Larker's men. Must think we don't have snitches that far back in St. Giles."

Michael stifled a groan. The more power Clowes amassed, the harder he'd be to catch. But there was still hope.

"We should be able to take him at Massle's before he leaves the country," he said. "Dispatch a team as soon as possible, and I want you to lead the efforts, Hume. Clowes is a sick bastard, and we can't let him get away."

Hume nodded. "I've already sent three men to keep watch. Was just waiting for your signal."

He remembered why he tolerated Hume: while the sergeant was an arse, his actions were swift and efficient. "We need Clowes. Those guards' deaths at the college are on our heads too."

"You don't have to remind me." Hume's fists clenched against the arms of his chair. "One of those guards was a friend of mine."

Michael frowned. "Too many have been hurt by this bleeder. Go get him. Get him hard, Sergeant."

"With pleasure." Hume rose from the chair, extending his hand to Michael. They shook hands as partners on the same mission: to rain down the fire of retribution on a man who'd destroyed the people they both loved.

He blinked, his eyes barely centering on Hume. Did he love Abigail? Of course not.

Caring what happened to Abigail was not the same as loving her. He liked spending time with her. She amused him, and he found their discussions oddly invigorating. They were friends. It didn't matter that he dreamt of riding her like a green-broke filly, or that her kiss made his heart gallop. If they were to have sex, it'd be a purely physical connection. It'd have to be.

She'd be happiest with a man who could commit to her. He couldn't give her what she wanted. He was made for short affairs, not love.

As soon as Hume left, Michael pulled back out his chair. He

went over the reports and cross-checked his map. While he had hope for Hume's success in St. Giles, he wanted to be certain there wasn't anything he overlooked. Hume's report was detailed and contained information from four different informants, all of whom the Met trusted.

Numbers don't lie; people do. If only he could convince himself that separating from her was in their best interests.

Chapter Twelve

Though Abigail didn't have much experience in the matter, she was reasonably confident it wasn't proper to ignore a woman for three days after kissing her. It was the eighth day of her stay at his townhouse, and she hadn't seen Michael since their outing in the garden.

She'd corned Smithers the night before. At first, he'd seemed so dour to Abigail: a mammoth of a man, with shoulders spanning the length of her arm and tufts of gray hair that stuck out at the tops of his ears. Now, she knew behind his gruff exterior was a man who cared deeply for Michael. A man who'd befriended her without reservations. Thanks to Smithers and Mrs. O'Neal, she now felt like she had friends again. They'd shown her kindness and made her feel wanted.

So, when Smithers claimed police work had consumed Michael, she wanted to believe him. Knowing that Michael was working hard to protect her from Clowes made her feel invulnerable.

But he still could have sent her a message. They were in the same house, for God's sake. It would have taken him five minutes to seek her out. He must know where she was, given she always came to the library in the afternoon.

She scowled at her dainty china cup. The pattern was not faded, indicating the set was most likely purchased within the last decade. It was newer than anything she'd ever drunk out of before. Abigail frowned as she hefted the sterling silver teapot and refilled her cup.

If only the china had been cracked.

Everything in this house was far too nice for a girl like her.

Had Michael not come to her because he was giving her time to decide what she wanted? What *did* she want?

Before he'd kissed her—before he'd spun her entire world on its axis with his lips upon hers and his hands scorching her body as though her clothing was made of the thinnest silk—he'd told her she shouldn't want him. That she ought to want better.

Better than him!

As though she were a lady of Polite Society instead of a crippled weaver with a lifetime of tarting ahead of her. He was the cruelest blackguard to tease her so. She knew her place. This house might be an oasis away from reality, but it wouldn't last forever.

Michael had made that all too clear these last few days.

She was a fool to think he would return her feelings. It had been easier to ignore her desire when she could pretend that he was, at most, a teacher to her.

Abigail sighed. That kiss in the snow had been different. Real. She could no longer deny that every touch, every laugh shared with him, affected her. She'd learned nothing from him, but how to become attached to a man she couldn't have. He was the first thought in her mind in the morning, and the last when she went to sleep. With him, she felt alive again, as she had before the accident, but somehow better because she could share new moments with him.

She'd read enough novels in her short life to recognize the quiver of fancy. Though she knew it was a fool's exercise, she'd fallen asleep to thoughts of him the past few nights, imagining what their life could be like together. There could be no future for them, of course, but in those quiet moments with him, she'd allowed herself to believe their social standings shouldn't matter.

Michael had made her feel in those moments that she was truly worthy of a man like him.

She wasn't.

She ought to follow his example and spend the remaining days until Clowes was caught hunkered down in her room. Abigail sipped her tea, surveying the room.

She'd told herself when she sat down on the ivory chaise that she'd chosen this part of the library because it was the most comfortable. The lounge was directly in front of the fireplace, with two armchairs at either side of it, blocking off a small space.

But in reality, she'd come to this section because it had been where she'd first felt close to Michael. Perched on this couch across from him, he'd spoken of his family's sordid history, and for the first time in ages, she hadn't felt so alone.

It was the little things he did that touched her far more than they should. The stack of books on the table in front of her. Voltaire's *Treatise on Tolerance*, a few more novels she'd always wanted to read, and one mathematics book where he'd tabbed the pages that had to do with his moral statistics map. Since she'd taken to coming in here in the afternoons, Michael made sure that there was always a blaze roaring in the grate.

But those could all be gestures of friendship. It did not indicate he felt anything for her, outside of carnal desire.

Enough of this. Abigail waved her hand dismissively. She was a smart, resourceful woman who didn't need the love of a man. In her new life, men would be a means to an end. To use until a superior bid came along, and again she'd begin the process.

She'd survive on her own. She always had.

Depositing her teacup on the low table in front of the chaise, she stood up. The girls of the BRLLS would have loved this library. If she could bring them here, maybe they'd forget about Poppy. Maybe they'd remember *her* instead.

Poppy always had the best books. The Gentleman Thief considered her family, so whenever he acquired a book he'd already read, he gifted it to Poppy. The girls had been so delighted to have Poppy in the society that they'd elected her president, a position Abigail had always held.

And when Abigail had asked the girls not to ask Poppy to any future meetings, they'd ignored her request. Instead, Abigail never received another invitation. They'd uninvited her from the society she had formed, the society she'd depended on to make her something more than just another Whitechapel gel. Without the BRLLS, she'd felt so damn empty. So alone.

Poppy got *everything*. The dashing husband, a new life outside of the factory, a library rumored to have more books than Abigail could count.

Abigail was left to fend for herself.

Navigating her way through the bookshelves, she passed the volumes of serialized novels that had kept her interest for most of the last week. Today she needed something different, for she'd been reminded that nothing lasted forever.

Slowly, she ran her black-gloved hand across the full skirt of her violet day dress. While the rest of the dresses in the wardrobe had been of fine muslin, this one was of the softest, shiniest silk. Woven on a jacquard, she guessed.

She headed past the reading alcoves with plush chairs scattered throughout, the grouping of tables for research. Even beyond the circular cutout in the shelving for the staircase that led to the second level of the library.

She walked until her knees began to throb, and then she walked some more, welcoming the ache. Pain was a language she understood. Pain spoke in stops and starts, in the sudden unexpected stab, in the unnatural twist of a joint. Pain did not make false promises nor give false hope. In its unpredictable, selfish nature, pain became a friend she could trust. There was no use making plans. Pain would creep in at the slightest provocation, without warning or due course.

To win against pain, she simply must exist. Every waking moment was a victory.

She'd reached the farthest corner of the library. One lamp shone over the unkempt section. Such disarray must sting Smithers dreadfully. She was surprised he hadn't insisted on giving the area a thorough cleaning. Unless Michael had specifically forbidden the butler from tidying up... What did Michael keep back here that he didn't want Smithers to see? The servants had seemed aware of their master's roguish reputation.

Surely, these books must be exceedingly salacious if he needed to hide them.

Abigail ran her finger along the closest shelf, dust covering the tip of her black glove in a white sheen. Cobwebs clung to the tallest shelves. She'd start with the shelves at eye level and move on from there.

Heavy leather-bound volumes in a rainbow of colors lined the wood shelves. Leaning forward, she squinted at the titles. The light was so faint. She saw a few names in a vernacular she didn't recognize. She hoped the rest weren't in a foreign language—if so, this investigation would be an exercise in futility.

As she blew out a giant puff of air, the dust scattered, coating her hair, her dress, permeating her mouth and throat.

Coughing, she swatted at the dust on her dress, willing it not to stick to the expensive fabric.

"No, no, no." She groaned. Another swipe to her bodice. The dust shook off from the dress and onto the floor. She breathed a sigh of relief. The dress wasn't ruined. Assuming Michael didn't demand it back, she'd still have it for her plans.

Once her eyes cleared, she settled in to examine the two cleared-off shelves, which held several titles in English. She studied the spine of one in particular: *Sodom, or the Quintessence of Debauchery,* attributed to John Wilmot, Earl of Rochester.

"The Earl of Rochester awaits, my dear," Michael had said.

This must be the very book he'd intended to have her read aloud. She knew of Wilmot's reputation and had assumed anything the poet wrote would be salacious. She shouldn't look at it—it wasn't proper, and Michael seemed to have forgotten about the bet.

Still, he might remember it later. Better to be prepared, so that she could read the whole passage without blushing or stammering. How shocked he'd be, and it'd bloody serve him right, the rogue. In addition, the ability to recite bawdy poetry would probably be useful in the bordello.

Pulling the book down from the shelf, Abigail flipped it open. Her eyes widened as she stared down at the page. One dirty couplet after another told the story of a king who'd decided to legalize sodomy for his subjects. She read a few more pages, ultimately putting the book back on the shelf. The play was outrageous, yes, but it lost something in the translation. Perhaps if she were to see it on stage, she'd feel less indifferent.

Abigail searched the next shelf for a book she might be able to read. Amongst the texts were sketchbooks, bound together by cords of leather. Grabbing several of the pads, she set them on the ground. She carefully cleared off the dust from the opposite bookcase and sat down on the ground. Snug in this long-forgotten corner, she huddled against the bookcase, rearranging her skirts so that her ankles didn't peek out from beneath her capacious petticoats.

She flipped the first volume open.

Her brows arched as she examined the pages. The drawings started out somewhat tame. A portrait of a nude woman sprawled out on a chaise longue, a silk sheet suggestively wrapped around her body and trailing along the floor. Another woman, soap bubbles over her most intimate parts, her hand raised to her mouth in coquettish surprise. The rest of the top two books were largely the same: a singular woman with less and less clothing.

While some of the pieces were cruder in nature, several of the tomes contained paintings that she would have deemed as museum-worthy, were it not for the graphic nature of their subjects. In those pictures, she'd started to believe that the human body was the most beautiful thing alive.

She pulled out the middle book from the pile.

Suddenly she understood why Michael had kept this area of the library off-limits from his servants. This last book was far, far more scandalous.

"Well, devil take me," she murmured, running her finger over the inked page.

Abigail paused at an illustration of a man and woman in the throes of passion. The woman lay upside down on the bed with her feet propped up on the man's shoulders. He held firmly onto her hips, keeping her centered upon him as he drove into her. How did the woman bend that way?

For God's sake, Abigail wasn't an acrobat! She had a hard enough time getting around, what with her knock-knees. But maybe Michael knew enough that she'd be fine.

Pulling off her right glove, she ran her bare finger down the

Erica Monroe

page, tracing the solid contours of the male physique so attractively inked. A prickling started in the base of her spine, dragging throughout her body. Her breasts felt fuller, heavier, straining against the confines of her corset. She flipped the pages again, and the sensations...the sensations got stronger, more untamed, sweeping through her body at an entirely inappropriate pace. Her cheeks burned; her skin must be flushed bright-red.

No one knew she was in this area of the library. No one would come to find her here. What was the harm in looking? In *feeling?* Soon, she'd be in a world where there was no romanticized view of sex: the slam of a man's rod into her quim, whether or not she was bodily ready for him.

She deserved this moment of pleasure.

So, she turned another page. Squeezed her legs together tightly. Quickly, she pulled off her boots, sitting with her stocking-clad feet gathered up underneath her. She allowed herself to imagine what it'd be like to be the woman in the painting. What it'd be like to have a man on top of her, the weight of him comforting instead of frightening. What it'd be like to have sex with Michael.

Slowly, she moved the heel of her foot against her core. Nudged it against her warm, tender flesh. This desire—this burgeoning *need* within her—blossomed into an untenable force, on the cusp of something greater. She continued to stroke, her body pulsing. She was so close. A readjustment here, a slower touch...but then the feeling was gone, leaving frustration in its wake.

She shouldn't feel unfulfilled. What she'd been doing was positively sinful.

She *ought* to throw the book far from her. Or she should faint. That was what virginal maidens did after all.

But she didn't. She finished that edition and reached for

another. She looked at the provocative pages until her eyes were itchy and scratchy from the dry heat of the library. And when she finished the sketchbooks, she went back for more, only to find that was the end of them. A novel rested on the shelf, tucked in amongst a few dull books on cartography.

Memoirs of Fanny Hill by John Cleland.

Abigail recognized it instantly. Heat stung her cheeks. A few years ago, two of the factory boys had stolen a pornographic illustration from the book out of a secondhand shop. They'd proceeded to spend the next four days evaluating the girls by how they'd look with their "ruby mouths around a fat cock." Though they'd cornered Abigail during lunch, she kneed one in the genitals and ran off.

So had been the end of the perusal of *Fanny Hill*.

She'd always wondered what else could possibly be in a text that warranted such a graphic plate. Her curiosity was purely scientific, of course. She was an avid reader.

In the interest of becoming further educated, Abigail situated herself back down on the floor. She opened the book to a random page, reading a bit of the text: *her sturdy stallion had now unbuttoned, and produced naked, stiff and erect, that wonderful machine...*

She gulped.

Those blissful flickers of heat licked at her insides again. She kept reading, shifting her weight so that her delicate core might rub against her pantalettes. It was good—but not enough. She couldn't get close enough.

She wanted Michael to be with her. Wanted *him* to be the one touching her.

Why were men so confoundedly idiotic? Why couldn't he see that she made him happy? He could be here right now, giving her pleasure. If he'd just talk to her—touch her—they'd both find relief.

Instead, he'd locked himself in his office, leaving them both unsatisfied. So, she flipped the page to farther back in the book, coming to an image of a man fully dressed. His breeches were unclasped. He stood at the foot of the bed, between the thighs of a woman. Her skirts were pushed up around her; she wore no petticoats. Her legs and bottom were bare for all to see. She was angled to impale directly upon his member.

Abigail shifted again. Squeezed her inner muscles tight, and with the illustrations still in her sights, she breathed in ragged gasps. What would it be like to lie like that, exposed for Michael? What would it be like to be entirely his? When she'd stood naked before him in the doorway of her room, she hadn't wanted to be with him.

Hadn't loved him.

Damnation.

She loved him.

She didn't *want* to love him. Every reasonable bone in her body rebelled against the idea. In the beginning, he'd treated her as though she was just an instrument for copulating. She understood now that behavior had been an act, as much as her feigned philandering. But the more time she'd spent with him, the more he'd come to regard her as an equal. A partner. He'd arranged things in the library for her convenience.

No one had ever done anything to make her life easier.

She might be able to dismiss his efforts as mere kindness if it hadn't been for that kiss in the snow. That kiss had shattered everything she'd ever known. She couldn't go on as she had in the past. She loved him, even if it'd tear her in two.

Need for him seized her, tore her breath from her lungs, and clasped her heart. She envisioned being with him like in the illustration, peering up into his eyes and seeing equal longing, so possessed with desire that they hadn't managed to remove the rest of their clothes before coupling.

If she closed her eyes, she felt his hands on her, sliding down her hips, to her thighs, and then her calves as he wrapped her legs around him. With quick, decisive movements, she undid the buttons that connected her skirt to her bodice, pretending it was Michael's fingers sliding down the gap. Michael's fingers finding the slit in her pantalettes.

She grasped her bud between two fingers, toying with the nub. Pleasure flooded through her. Sinking into that feeling, she glided her fingers across the damp folds, pressing harder, desperate for that release, which lingered on the corners of her horizon. Her index finger nudged into her long channel, and she worked that finger in time to stroking her center, moaning in delight.

"Oh, *Michael*," she breathed, as the waves of pleasure rocked her. She collapsed back against the bookcase, still pressing her aching nub. Just when she'd reached the breaking point and couldn't take anymore, lips brushed against her own.

For a second, she believed him to be part of her fantasy, and she kissed him back, draining every bit of passion she felt into that kiss. She opened her mouth and his warm tongue thrust inside. Then it hit her.

He was real.

Her eyes sprang open. Her fingers stilled.

Michael leaned over top of her. They sat nose-to-nose, so close she could smell the earthy scent of his cologne, see every bristle of his unshaven chin.

Oh, God. Oh, God. He'd seen her. He'd heard her.

He'd kissed her.

Again.

Chapter Thirteen

This woman was going to be the death of him.

He hadn't meant to spy upon Abigail. He'd only wanted to *talk* to her. Smithers had informed him that she was in the library, but at first, he couldn't find her. When he was about to leave, he heard paper rustling, followed by a long, husky moan. There could be no mistaking the noise of a well-pleasured woman. He paused at the doorway, wondering if he'd manifested his dreams—for every night since he'd kissed her in the snow, he'd replayed that sound.

Until he heard her cry out, her voice breaking on the highest note, tapering off into an indiscernible whimper. Blast it all. That was Abigail, nestled back in amongst his father's dirty book collection. Who was she with? He didn't stop to think of the fact that his house was guarded, for his blood boiled so at the thought of someone else touching her. Of someone else pleasuring her.

She was *his*.

He rushed toward the back of the library. The bastard better be ready to name his second because with God as his witness, he'd draw pistols at dawn with her despoiler. If anyone was going to be deflowering her, it ought to be him.

His ire changed to something else entirely when he found her. Alone. Her skirts flung about her, her hand most definitely down her petticoat. He gulped for air, blood pounding in his ears.

Fuck, fuck, fuck, she was going to kill him.

Then she said his name, and all bets were off.

The kiss was inevitable. Whether it was fate or God's work or some devil in control, she was in his bloodstream. He dropped down to his knees and leaned in to kiss her before he even realized he was doing so. He needed her so badly it replaced all other thoughts.

His long list of past paramours faded into nothing. He sucked upon her bottom lip, licking at the seams, and when she opened to him, he slid into her wet, ready mouth. There was only Abigail. Her lips upon his brought beautiful chaos to his life. Nothing he'd done before her mattered anymore. He'd been lost, and she'd found him.

"Abigail," he murmured, not daring to draw back from her. He couldn't leave her.

She blinked up at him, long lashes fluttering against flushed cheeks. "How long were you there?"

"Long enough." Roughness tinted his voice.

The pink of her cheeks darkened. He fought for air, for he'd never seen her so beautiful. Her pleasure had left a glow, a staid contentment that her mortification could not shake. He loved to see her happy, and even more to know that he'd brought about her happiness. At that moment, he counted making Abigail Vautille sigh with satisfaction the biggest achievement in his life.

She squirmed in his arms. He gathered her up, ignoring how

her skirt bunched up at odd angles. Strands of golden hair cascaded from her chignon, framing her face in wayward curls.

"You're embarrassed." He tucked a stray lock behind her ear, his fingers lingering on the edge of her cheek. The sharp angle of her chin enticed him. He wanted to place kisses across the line of her jaw, but that could wait. The strength of his desire must be splashed across his face, to say nothing of his unyielding erection.

"Of course, I am." Again, she didn't meet his gaze. "Women are never supposed to do what you saw me doing—"

He interrupted her with the touch of his thumb to her lips. "Those rules don't apply in my house, you hear? You've as much right as any man to seek your pleasure. Anyone who tells you otherwise is wrong."

"An entire society cannot be wrong," she told him, looking away from him.

"It most certainly can." Earnestness possessed him, in the vigor to his claims and the hastiness in which he cupped her chin in his hands and tilted her face up toward his. "A real man would *want* you to enjoy sex. He'd spend the rest of his days trying to think of ways to make you come because you screaming out his name would be the ultimate satisfaction."

She peered up at him, her wide eyes full of doubt. "I've heard men crow about how hard they tupped a woman, not how loudly she screamed their name."

He readjusted her in his lap, one hand on her hip to hold her closer to him. He'd been that man before, considering the women he slept with as conquests. He'd only cared about his partner's enjoyment if it added to his own.

He'd been wrong, so very wrong. Abigail's pleasure was important. It was everything.

With his other hand, he pushed her hair back from the nape of her neck. He pressed light kisses upon her creamy skin. She shivered against him, and he traced the svelte line of her chin to her ear with his tongue. God, she smelled of lavender from the perfumed bathwater, but underneath that was a scent purely her own. Wonder and fire, hope and pride.

Lowering his head, he brushed his lips against her earlobe and whispered, "Then you've been meeting the wrong sort of men."

"I suppose that's possible." Her voice was half squeak, half whimper and he knew he had her.

"Oh, it's very possible." During their first meeting in this library, he'd promised her she'd want him to take her virtue, and he was right. He felt no sense of victory in his success.

She'd changed the rules on him. Hell, she'd obliterated the whole damn game. Every step he would have taken in the past toward a swift and sinful conclusion no longer applied. He didn't just want to tup her once; he wanted to hold her in his arms until the morning came, and then he wanted to share breakfast with her in his bed.

Christ, where did these thoughts keep coming from? He didn't stay the night. Women appreciated that about him. He wouldn't darken their doorstep with expectations of watching the fireworks at Vauxhall or taking carriage rides in Hyde Park. Those typical courtship rituals usually sent him running.

He wasn't fleeing now. Though sound rationality dictated he should set her dress to rights and ignore this fiery attraction, he didn't.

He held her tight in his arms and breathed in the softness of her hair. Running his fingers down her arm, he memorized the lushness of her skin and praised the Lord for modern fashion. Her purple dress had cap-sleeves, baring her forearms to him.

He ached to remove her ever-present gloves, but he feared her response. Instead, he allowed his gaze to drift downwards, to take in the round plumpness of her breasts, pushed up gloriously high by her boned corset. Though he'd deny it if anyone asked, he pretended that this closeness between them could last forever.

"Michael?" She scooted back in his lap.

"Fuck, Abigail," he groaned. Her taut bottom hit his cock at just the right point as if she'd been made to fit him. "That feels so good. Like this." He moved her against him to show her the correct placement. "Is that good?"

"Yes," she stammered, tilting her head to look up at him. "Really good. Like before, when you saw me...but almost better." Her cheeks flushed again at the mention of him watching her.

Almost. That would never do.

"I'll have to work harder then," he murmured, nipping at her earlobe. Out of the corner of his eye, he spotted the book she'd been reading before he'd interrupted her. He started to reach for it, and she stopped him, shaking her head. He snaked it out of her grip, flipping it open to his personal favorite section. It wasn't Wilmot, but it'd work.

Passing the book back to her, he pointed to the section he wanted her to focus on. "You still owe me a reading, remember?"

She groaned. "Haven't I been humiliated enough for one day?"

His grip tightened around her waist, giving her a reassuring squeeze. "What you did is *not* humiliating. Of course, I would have preferred you sought your pleasure with me, but watching you is a second best I'll gladly take..."

"Michael!" Her scolding had little effect with her rounded bottom snug against his cock. She'd shifted to get closer to him.

If bawdy words aroused his wicked minx, *Fanny Hill* would do just the trick. He tapped the paper in her hands, clearing his throat.

She rolled her eyes at him. "Very well then. You're as sore a winner as I suspect you are a loser."

She gave another little wiggle of her rear, and he intended to tell her that his winning streak wasn't the only thing that was sore. Then she started to read, her breaths coming faster with every sentence, her skin flushed and damp.

"Here was no room either to sit or lie but making me stand with my back towards the door, she lifted up my petticoats, and with her busy fingers fell to visit and explore that part of me." She faltered, her grip on the book loosening. It would have slipped from her hands entirely had he not caught it in time, steadying her hold. She readjusted herself in his arms so that she could face him. "You can't expect me to read this. This is beyond the realm of decency—"

He placed a finger over her lips, quieting her. "I do not live in the usual realm of decency, as you put it. In addition, who decides what's forbidden? The very society you've been railing against."

She considered that for a moment. "But it's Sapphic. Do you really find that erotic?"

He winked at her. "Most men do, darling."

She frowned, reading out the next line deliberately as if she was proving a point to him. *"With her busy fingers fell to visit and explore that part of me where I was perfectly sick and ready to die with desire.* See? Men aren't instrumental to their pleasure. You'd have no place in this scenario."

Her confusion, and subsequent triumph over what she thought to be an adequately made conclusion, brought forth a throaty chuckle from him. "Men are not sensible creatures. We are all convinced that if we wandered into that scene, Fanny and Phoebe would want *us* to do all the touching."

She regarded him skeptically. "I doubt that, because the

next line is *the bare touch of her finger, in that critical place, had the effect of a fire to a train.* And oh!"

He'd allowed his hand to drift, cupping her breast in his palm.

"*Her hand had instantly made her sensible to what a pitch I was wound up,*" she continued, no longer trying to find the logic in it. She leaned into his touch, coaxing him on when he grasped her nipple between his thumb and forefinger and rolled it. "*And melted by the sight...*"

She couldn't read any longer. Flinging the book back, she fell into his arms, and their kiss left them both breathless. When they finally broke apart, he resolved to show her exactly how *he* would have orchestrated that scene.

Sliding his hands under her bottom, he scooped her up and laid her onto the rug next to him. She opened her mouth to protest, but he was already on his knees in front of her, pushing her skirts up around her. The long, corded petticoat would have to go. In a flash, he removed that from her and deposited it beside them. He let his fingers run up her thighs, tracing the seams of her pantalettes, reveling in their simplicity. She was too unique for lace. Somehow, the white cotton with no trimmings suited her.

"What are you doing?" She watched him suspiciously.

"What does it look like?"

She rolled her eyes. "I mean, I know *what* you're doing. I've heard about it before, and in those sketches..."

He supposed he ought to be thankful for his father's obscene collection.

"But I cannot again so soon. You saw me before." She'd turned crimson, and he had to fight not to kiss her again. She was so bloody adorable.

"Miracles of the female body." He whipped her pantalettes off her legs.

"Someone could see us," she gasped. Yet she didn't move away.

"You didn't worry about that before, did you?" He grinned wickedly, nestled between her legs.

"I wasn't naked before—"

"Settle, my dear." He dragged his fingers up her palm, his light touch causing her to shiver. "Smithers won't come within a yard of this library, and he'll tell Mrs. O'Neal not to enter either. They are aware I've come to find you." He let his gaze rove down her frame, devouring the sight of her. Exposed before him, she was pink and perfect. "Do you trust me?"

She gulped, nodding her assent.

"Then know that what I'm about to do will bring you pleasure." He dared to slip a finger across her already wet core, every touch hardening him.

Her thighs were as ravishing as he remembered from that night, but this... He'd not prepared for the sheer magnificence of her. Finding her bud, he ran his roughened thumb against it.

Her breathy sigh let him know she was enjoying this greatly. She leaned her head back against the bookshelf, closing her eyes. Oh, she'd watch him when he feasted on her, but for now, he'd allow her this moment to catch her breath. He slid his thumb across her bud, slowly. She was warm and tight around him, and he ached to be inside her.

He would wait. This night was about her, he reminded himself. His own needs came secondary. There were other ways to bring a woman to pleasure without taking her maidenhead.

He felt the changes in her body as well as saw the effects, for she shuddered in his arms, her breaths coming in jagged pants that blended with his until the very air around them felt passion soaked.

He positioned himself flat on the ground before her, spreading her legs to allow him access. Lightly at first, he touched his tongue to her center. The taste of her alone was almost enough to send him over the edge, but he'd not rush her. He flicked his tongue against her, his strokes soft and slow. She shuddered against him, and he grew bolder, grasping her bud between his teeth and nibbling lightly.

"Oh, devil take—" She couldn't finish the sentence, for he'd returned to licking her, now at a more rapid pace. Her hands fell to grasp his head, holding him to that spot.

"Abigail." He paused, her scent still heavy in his nostrils, begging for him to finish. "Look at me."

She shook her head.

"Look at me, or I shan't continue." He had no intention of carrying out that threat, but she seemed convinced, for she opened her eyes. "Much better."

He returned to her, working her until she shook from the effort to stay still in his touch. He clasped one hand in hers, the other still positioned on her hip to guide her. Sparks scattered up and down his spine, eating at his resolve. He'd told himself he'd take it slow with her. But at this pace, she'd make him come like a green youth, and he hadn't felt her touch on him or had his cock in her.

She gave another push with her hips, growing more frantic. "Oh, God," she cried, her hand tightening against his.

Her cry spurred him on. To hell with slow, to hell with pretending to be a gentleman. He'd never been one anyway.

It was poetically apt she'd want pleasure that didn't hold back. His Abigail lived hard. She slammed against the shelves as he licked her, books spilling around them. A sketchbook thwacked him on the head, but the pain made it better. He'd found that elusive spot between coherent thought and reality, where he existed solely in this moment with her.

Then she was spiraling, her euphoric moan piercing his soul.

* * *

THE NEXT DAY, Michael breakfasted with Abigail. They hadn't spoken about the event in the library. "Event" wasn't the right word. What else could he call it? Nothing polite. Nothing properly worthy of the world-shaking sensations that clutched him, forcing him to question his previously held stances on sex.

This had been lovemaking. He didn't make love, he fucked.

"I quite enjoy the chocolate." Abigail took a dainty sip, cupping the mug in both her hands. "The pound cake is also delightful. Very fluffy."

Michael nodded, half listening to her chatter on about the various treats spread out on the sideboard. Once he'd observed her sneaking an extra slice of cake at dinner, he'd switched his normal breakfast of eggs and leftover meat from dinner to include pound cake, those Chelsea rolls she adored, and a selection of fruit preserves. Watching her gobble up delicacies she'd never been able to afford in Whitechapel had quickly become the favorite part of his day.

She paused, mid-lift of the cup to her mouth. Her saucer remained on the table. She didn't know to lift the saucer with her cup.

"You haven't eaten any of your eggs." She gestured toward his still-full plate. "In fact, you've barely touched your food. Is something troubling you?"

"No, nothing at all," he lied. Curse her ability to puzzle out the differences in his temperament. Rarely did anyone look past his smirk, and when they did, he could dissuade them with a quip or compliment.

Abigail saw beyond the surface. He felt human in the light of her gaze, for she witnessed the worst sides of him, and she didn't run. She stayed, damn her. Stayed through the breaking of his resolve, stayed so he could drink up every drip of the pleasure he wrought from her body, stayed while he pretended it had never happened.

He piled his fork high with eggs and meat to convince her that this was a day like any other for him. She observed him, the slight tilt of her head indicating he'd have better luck fooling the charlatans he interrogated than her.

He swallowed. The eggs tasted rotten, the meat leaden.

"I may have some good news." Another partial truth, for while the news was good for her, it was not for him.

"Oh?" She set her cup down. Chocolate sloshed over the rim, splashing onto the saucer. Instead of coloring with embarrassment as his sister would have, she blotted at the mess with a serviette, her attention focused on his announcement.

"I met with one of my sergeants two days ago," he said. "They received a tip that Clowes has been spotted preparing to leave the country. Currently, he's in St. Giles."

Her fist clenched on the side of the table. "So, he'll be gone soon."

"That's one theory." He'd expected her to be jubilant. If Clowes was in the West End instead of Whitechapel, he wasn't concerned with harming her. "However, I did receive another note from him. This time, he said we'd never stop him—that he'd win."

Her forehead scrunched. "What could that mean?"

"I'm leaning toward believing that he's gloating about his preparations to leave. My men are keeping a watch on St. Giles, and I've also got a team surveying Whitechapel. But it's cause for hope, my dear. There'd been no sign of him before, and now we've got leads."

Abigail regarded him skeptically. "If you say so."

He reached across the table, patting her hand. The minor contact was a mistake, for he craved going to her to massage out the knots in her shoulders. He held back, reminding himself that she'd be gone soon.

"I know you don't have much faith in the Met, but have faith in me. I've got my finest men on the job."

Her eyes fastened on him, shining with more adoration than he'd ever deserved. "I *do* have faith in you."

She saw all his faults, and she hadn't deemed him less. How could she care for him so?

Michael drained his mug of coffee, not minding that it was too hot. The burn gave him something else to focus on, besides her sweet body encased in another of Frances's dresses, the pink one again with the scooping bodice that nearly drove him mad.

The dining room erupted in a flurry of activity. He'd wished too fervently for a distraction.

Smithers rushed in, with Mrs. O'Neal nearly stepping on his heels. Something crashed in the kitchen, and Cook's cursing resounded through the open door.

"What in God's name?" The question was scarcely out of his mouth before the source of the disruption sailed in, brandishing her closed parasol as a weapon against Smithers's efforts to keep her back from the dining room.

"I'm sorry, Master, but Lady Elliot insisted." Smithers jumped out of the way of Frances's sweeping parasol just in time.

At Smithers's imploring glance, Michael nodded, dismissing him. Mrs. O'Neal stayed put, her feet squared, arms crossed over her midsection. She angled herself toward Abigail, as though preparing to leap over the table and protect the woman she'd adopted as her new chatelaine.

"What is it that couldn't wait for a letter?" he asked, making no attempt to veil his irritation. He'd lost count of the number of times Frances had barged into his house and judged how he lived his own damn life. "The Post longs for your service. In

173

fact, they may be the only organization that *wants* to hear what you have to say."

Abigail's eyes widened at his brusque tone. She looked into her cup, shrinking back in her chair. The small movement drew Frances's attention.

"That's why you wanted my old clothes? I thought you were going to give them to the street urchins, not bring the urchin home." A scowl set deep into Frances's angular face, sharpening the already hard curves of her features. "When you dress your latest mistress like she's quality, it's insulting to those of us who actually have class."

The accusation stung him as the slash of a whip. He *had* purchased Abigail's time. Until Frances had pointed it out so maliciously, he'd not realized how horrid it sounded.

He'd be damned if his sister shamed Abigail. Her beauty transcended sheer aesthetics. She was the best damn person he'd ever met.

No one would make Abigail feel lesser in his house. This was a battle Frances wouldn't win.

He caught Mrs. O'Neal's eye. The housekeeper gave him an almost imperceptible nod and left the room. He'd take care of Abigail.

"I'll leave you to your discussion," Abigail said, setting her serviette down on the table. She stood. Her gloved hand brushed against the fabric of her borrowed dress, and she jolted back, as though burned by the touch.

"Stay, Miss Vautille," he commanded, his fingers fisted on the edge of the table. "Lady Elliot should be the one to leave."

"I'm not going anywhere," Frances insisted.

Abigail sat down, glancing between Frances and him, her discomfort clear on her face. As if she believed his sister was right, for Frances had wealth and societal prestige.

Frances wasn't right, nor was this the first time he'd found himself on warring sides with his sister. They'd fought over anything and everything over the years, from trivial matters like jam being better than marmalade to whether or not he should join the Met. If he was ever pleased with something, Frances made it her mission to crush that pride.

He plopped back into the chair and reached for his coffee with a bored sigh. "If you must stay, do not insult my guest, Frances. It's unbecoming and shows what little class *you* truly have."

"Your guest you feed at our father's table," Frances retorted. The bright-red feather in her hat flapped with her every movement.

"*My* table," he amended. "The Old Bastard passed it on to me entirely. Hazards of being a lady, sister dear."

Abigail straightened in her chair, frowning at him. "Strickland, I do not think—"

Frances interrupted her. "I wish you wouldn't continue to call Papa that. He didn't mean to be the way he was. He was... troubled."

Michael shook his head. "He was a royal arse. It's not my fault you decided to believe him in his last few months. He knew he was going to Hell, Franny—he would've said anything to get into Heaven."

"That's not true," Frances protested. "He loved us. He would've told you so, if you'd visited him."

"Forgive me for not wanting to exchange pleasantries with the bastard who drove our mother into Bedlam." He took one breath, then another, focusing on regulating his breathing. He remembered his mother behind the iron bars of her tiny cell at the sanatorium, her fingernails digging into her skull until her scalp bled. "And you *let* him. You did nothing to stop him."

Frances softened her voice. "She was mad, Michael. It was the best place for her."

"It was the most convenient place for you to shove her away, you mean," he countered.

Frances sent a pointed look to Abigail. "Must we discuss this now?"

He didn't care about etiquette. Abigail belonged in his home —Frances did not. "Why are you here then?"

"I didn't come to fight with you," she sniffled, pulling a handkerchief from her reticule and dabbing at her eyes, though no tears glistened. "I was concerned because you hadn't responded to any of my letters. You never write to me anymore. It's as if you don't care at all."

He hadn't cared about her since they were children, when he'd been naive enough to believe they could have a bond simply because of their blood tie. But after the years of her caring only about how she appeared in society—and ignoring him unless he served her greater purpose—he couldn't bring himself to be hurt by her again.

Dropping her hurt façade, Frances faced him with the stage presence of a grand actress about to deliver her best line. "I had to find out about your *activities* with this..." Her nose turned up, but at his glare, she withheld the insult she'd probably been about to deliver. "This girl from Hume."

"Hume?" Michael slapped his serviette onto his plate and stood up. "You've been talking to my sergeant? How the hell did you even meet Hume?"

Frances's spindly fingers toyed with the red-corded balls that adorned her black redingote. "Papa was in the Watch with him."

"You hated Father's job." He narrowed his eyes. Somehow, the urge to throttle Frances lessened when he could only see her part of her face. "When I joined the Met, you told me I was wasting my life. You called my cohorts 'cod-headed meat packers.'"

"I did no such thing," Frances protested, yet there was no longer spring in her righteous indignation. She'd taken too long to respond. She looked away for a split second, giving him the advantage.

Frances *never* conceded a fight she knew she could win. She was happiest when she could draw blood.

She moved back from the table. With forced nonchalance, she patted her brunette curls, done up so neatly underneath her fashionable black hat.

An idea formed in his mind, drawn from the tremor in her voice and the flush to her cheeks.

Michael was a man of probabilities. Frances hated her husband. Hume was about her age, and he wouldn't be looking for a long-term relationship. He'd be the perfect man for a fling —discreet and cynical enough that he wouldn't care if she were married.

Damnation. He'd thought he couldn't dislike Hume any more than he already did, but playing cicisbeo to his sister was a whole new level of low.

"Frances." The crispness to his tone snapped her attention back to him. "Exactly how *personal* is your relationship with Sergeant Hume?"

"How dare you ask me that?" Frances's voice, usually so full of vitriol, had become brittle.

Maybe he'd been wrong; maybe there was more to this affair. Maybe Frances actually had feelings for Hume.

He took a step toward her. Could he forgive her for all her previous criticisms of his life? Tell her he understood her actions, even if they cast a societal stain upon their family? He ought to do something. Maybe trapped behind walls of steel was a sister he could come to love.

He hazarded a look toward Abigail. She nodded, encouraging him to go to the sister she knew he loathed. Maybe this would start a new era for them.

The moment severed. Before he could get to her, Frances rounded the breakfast table, her parasol slapping against her leg. She stood rod straight in an attempt to force imperiousness into her reedy frame.

All he saw was frigidity, in the tilt of her chin, the cold cut to her eyes, and the twist of her rouged lips into a cruel sneer. He braced himself for a verbal assault.

"How dare you ask me those questions," she repeated, "in front of your *whore?*"

A deadening quiet descended upon the room; it sliced his throat with a razor, leaving him dripping, bleeding, and defenseless. Until this moment, he hadn't fully comprehended what it meant to be a harlot. He'd thought of the money Abigail could earn, and the lifestyle she'd have if she were popular.

None of that mattered if she didn't have her integrity.

"That's enough," he roared. Crossing to stand by Abigail's chair in a visual show of support, he held Frances's spiteful glare. "You will apologize to Miss Vautille, or you will leave my house, do you understand?"

"It's fine," Abigail protested quietly, pushing back her chair. "I should be the one to leave. Lady Elliot can speak to you in private then."

"See, your kept bird understands her place." Preening, Frances pulled out the head chair that Michael had vacated and settled in it. She waved toward the door, expecting Abigail to exit.

He hated to see Abigail without her fire. This couldn't continue. "No. It's not fine, and *Lady Elliot* should damn well know how to conduct herself better." He strode toward the door, opening it. "Out. Now."

"Well, I never," she huffed, but something in his demeanor

must have convinced her he meant business. She stalked out, halting in the doorway.

Fixing her lethal glare on Abigail, her sapphire eyes darkened with malice. "You think he's going to make this a *mésalliance*, trollop? You're as common as a barber's chair. He'll use you and toss you back to the gutter he found you in as soon as he sees fit. And he *will* see fit. They always do."

Chapter Fourteen

"She's right." Abigail sat primly on the settee in the parlor, where Michael had insisted on following her when she'd fled the dining room. "You shouldn't have dismissed your sister. She didn't say anything that I won't hear many more times in the future."

Lady Elliot had only pointed out the obvious: she should not keep pretending her relationship with Michael was anything but that of a strumpet and her whoremonger.

Abigail straightened out the folds of her skirt so that it hid her ankles from view. She needn't have bothered. He'd already seen her with her skirts hiked up around her waist, and her pantalettes clean off, her skin bare and exposed to his greedy eyes.

He followed her motion closely. Since Lady Elliot had departed, he hadn't left her side, no matter how much she'd assured him she was fine. His compassion affected her, sinking into the depths of her being.

His sharp voice echoed in her ears. "Frances isn't right."

She wanted to believe him. She wanted to linger in this make-believe world forever, passing as his. If she couldn't be with him as his affianced, she'd accept the illusion of being his.

After all, once she left here, her life would become one great deception.

"On one hand, I can recall the number of times Frances has been right in her thirty-two years." He held up three fingers. "The first time was when she predicted our father would never approve of me." Down went his ring finger, leaving his middle and index still upright. "The second time was when she said Mama would never be sane again."

"Michael—" Abigail tried to stop him. He'd already done so much for her. He needn't dredge up old wounds for her benefit.

He dropped his middle finger too, ignoring her attempt. "And the third was when she said I don't write to her anymore. Frances is many things—vain, prideful, bitter—but insightful is not one of them."

Abigail pinched the bridge of her nose, closing her eyes. When she could not see him, it was easier to refute him. "As much as I appreciate your support, you can't deny that she sees things the way the rest of the world will. When I leave here, my reputation is ruined for sure. Instead of people suspecting I'm a whore, they'll have definitive evidence in Cruikshank's betting book."

She opened her eyes. He was by her side in an instant, kneeling beside her chair so that he could take her hands in his. She'd remember this when she was in the arms of another man. She'd pretend it was Michael she lay with.

"It's a bloody cruel world out there," he whispered. "And if I could, I'd fight every single one of those blackguards who dared besmirch your name."

"It's a lovely thought." She allowed a small smile to curl her lips, for his thoughts were always lovely. What he lacked in follow-through, he made up in earnestness. "But what good is a reputation? It can't stock our larder or put a roof over my sister's head."

"I can't claim to understand the challenges you face," he admitted. "If my old mates saw you, I'd be deaf from their shouts of approval at my conquest."

"I highly doubt that," she replied deprecatingly.

His lopsided grin tugged at her heart. "You have no idea how stunning you are, do you?"

When he'd told her before that she was beautiful, it'd been with a matter-of-factness born from years of dissolution. It hadn't mattered then.

But now he'd glimpsed into her mind. Her soul. For a second, she allowed herself to think that she was gorgeous—*all* of her. He'd never seen her scars, but maybe he wouldn't judge her. Maybe he'd understand.

"I have been thinking." His thumb stroked hers, the gentle glide soothing her worries more than any physical connection ever had.

"I thought I smelled smoke," she teased, forcing a light tone, though a quick stab of pain cut through her. Their time in the snow felt like years ago, not days.

"Cheeky chit." He chuckled. "But I think you will like my plan."

He released her hands, standing up.

"Mind you, I haven't worked out all the details, but I doubt there will be any problems." As he spoke, he paced back and forth, weaving a steady path until she thought the carpet would bear tread marks. "I have made a significant amount from the gaming tables, and Father's death left me with a decent sum."

"What are you talking about?" She held up a hand to stop him, for his constant back-and-forth made her dizzy. "Start from the beginning. You said you had a plan. A plan for what, precisely?"

He drew up beside her, flopping into the chair to the right of the chaise. "For you."

"A plan for me?"

He leaned forward, and without thought, she did too. A shiver spun down her spine. She'd go along with anything he proposed when he looked at her as if she were the only woman who mattered.

God, how she wanted to matter. She'd been forgotten for ages, pushed aside after the incident. She wanted to be seen to be important. But most of all, she wanted him.

"I told you that I'd make things right for you," he said. "Once Clowes is found, I'm going to meet with my account manager and make a withdrawal. I want you and your sister to be solvent, Abigail. I don't want you to be—to have to do this anymore."

She recoiled into the far edge of her chair. "You want me to accept your charity."

"No, I want you to accept my help." He crossed his arms over his chest, drawing her attention to the way his simple linen shirt strained over his muscles. He was strong and able-bodied, while she was reduced to accepting donations.

She met his gaze, her head held high. "*Helping* was paying my father's debt. You were to receive something in return."

He frowned. "It isn't a sign of failure to accept my assistance. Everyone has hard times—the trick is how you cope with that adversity. Or do you actually want to have to sell yourself to the highest bidder?"

Silence squeezed her throat. She'd dealt with adversity. Lord, she'd dealt with it, and she'd always come out on top, until six months ago. She looked down at her fingers, clad in the black satin gloves he'd provided, swirls of jet that in the right light shined full of hope and promises.

The light was not right today. Nothing was right when he

pitied her. She'd sworn that when she had to sell herself, she'd do it with pride. She'd know that she contributed to her family, and she would earn her keep. If she accepted his money, she'd be free from worry until the money ran out, but she wouldn't have her pride.

She shook her head. "You wouldn't understand."

Hurt warped his face. "Why? Because I'm more affluent than you?"

"Yes." She couldn't lie to him. Their lives had been so markedly different that it was as if a chasm stood between them, forcing them to shout at each other from opposing sides.

He rubbed the back of his neck in a circular motion, the same rhythm he'd used featherlight against her most intimate parts, stroking her until she crested. "I cannot change how I've been raised."

"I wouldn't want you to." She traced a circle upon her thigh, her fingers mimicking his motions. "You were given a chance at greatness."

"And I squandered every opportunity," he spat. "The Met promoted me because they wanted another Strickland in office. I've never had a relationship that lasted longer than four nights. I'm nothing but a depraved scoundrel."

"That's not what I see when I look at you." She drank him in, noting the lines of his face as though she was meeting him for the first time. Strong jaw, curved but not overly pointed. Broad forehead, currently wrinkled with doubt.

A man she could love.

A man she *already* loved.

"When I look at you, I see your compassion." Her gaze traveled from his face down to his robust shoulders, his well-built chest, and his damnably good-intentioned but misguided heart. "I see a man who is scared of how people will perceive him. So, he hides behind a roguish veneer, pretending that if he doesn't care for anyone, he'll never be hurt."

"It worked before," he noted.

Her praise had calmed him. He was the type of man who needed accolades. She understood that now. It did not make him less, any less than her desire for independence did.

"It worked until I met you." That vow fled from his lips, so swift she almost missed it. "I care about you, Abigail. If that makes me guilty of giving you charity in your eyes, then so be it. I won't stop caring for you."

His words were as soothing as his fond caresses, leveling away some of the ache. While his intentions did not completely negate the effect, he had not meant to wound her.

He cared about her. Someday, could he love her? Maybe her hopes were not so fruitless after all. But she didn't know if she could survive it if he was fickle, and he forgot her like the rest of society. What if her heart broke into so many pieces she couldn't repair it? Or what if, instead of pain, there was only happiness?

The voice from the hospital echoed in her mind. "You're a fighter." She'd doubted those words so many times in these last six months. Yet during these nine days in his house, where no one had known her before the incident, she had become self-assured.

"You want to 'save' me, Michael, but I don't need to be saved." As her voice rang out clearly, she realized she was telling the truth: she was no one's victim.

He propped his elbows on his knees, chin between his outstretched palms. "The money I'd give you would make it so you could find a better home for you and Bess."

Didn't he know she wanted *him*, not his money? His townhouse had been a wonderful respite, but if she couldn't have him, she'd rather stay in the rookeries. At least she'd drown her sorrows in the same haunts she'd frequented all her life.

"A home being more costly doesn't make it a better home. Violence happens everywhere." She imagined her flat, the brick spotted with her own blood. Before the incident, that house had felt like the most unassailable place in London. "Growing up, I felt more protected in a neighborhood where people have the threat of accountability. Even Clowes served some time in prison."

"We're going to get him, Abigail. I swear to you with all I have, I'm going to catch that bastard." The urgency behind his words built up her assurance and made her feel sheltered.

"I have every belief you'll achieve that goal." She had to believe he would. The prospect of Clowes finding her again was too frightening.

His voice was softer than normal. "Your confidence in me matters."

She wanted to matter.

"Some of the people in Whitechapel are good, and some are very, very bad." She tugged on her glove, readjusting it, the proof of their vileness carved into her skin. "But before I came here, it was the only place I'd ever known."

And now your house has become my second home. Do you wish I could stay as much as I do?

He smiled, a gentler smile than she'd grown accustomed to, one tinged with pride for her, and maybe even approbation of her logic. "Then I won't worry so much for you. But I still wish you were close by."

"I'll be only a hack ride away." Even she didn't buy her faux optimism.

Their gazes locked. The moment transformed. The tenderness became more charged, almost palpable. She dared not move, talk, or even breathe, for fear this precious bond between them would shatter.

His words became a confession of closely held secrets. "I'd rather have you in Cheapside."

"And I'd rather be here with you," she murmured.

A notion percolated in the back of her mind. Perhaps it was mad. If he didn't accept her bid, then she'd truly have no other option but the brothels. But when he smiled at her like that, she couldn't help but risk it all in hopes the return would be greater. She now understood the lure of gaming.

"There might be another way you could help me," she began, uncertainly at first, then the words all in a rush. "You could make me your mistress."

His jaw dropped.

She continued on, her stomach tumbling. "You'd take the money you intended to give me and use it toward my upkeep, and my sister's, here. It wouldn't be charity because I'd be doing something to earn it."

"By 'doing something,' you mean fucking me."

"That's not quite the terminology I'd use, but yes."

"That's what you want?" He blinked at her, jaw still slack. "To be a prostitute after all? Despite everything you've told me?"

"I'd be your *mistress*," she clarified. "You said you'd school me if I wanted, and I accept your proposition. Either I work in a brothel or a protector hires me exclusively. Why shouldn't it be you, Michael?"

"But you'd still be a courtesan," he insisted. "You said you were only going to do that for money, and if I can give you the money outright, you've got no need to sell yourself."

She clasped her hands together to keep from fidgeting. "That was before I knew you."

Before I loved you.

He had not looked away from her. His eyes, darkened with desire even in his angst, seared through the last of her will. If a fall from grace meant she kept him in her life, she'd gladly succumb to it.

"It's because you know me that you shouldn't submit to this." The anguish in his voice gave her pause. How low must he believe himself, if *she* of all people was not worthy of him? "You deserve so much more."

She couldn't bear the thought of him hating himself. "Michael, you've given me everything. Free run of your house. A library beyond my wildest dreams. Friends, for Mrs. O'Neal and Smithers are true gems."

He stood up. Took a step toward her, then another, until he was in front of her chair. His hand darted out toward her shoulder, but he did not close the gap between them. "It's the least I can do."

"No, the least you could have done was demanded payment. Either in full from my father, or my virginity. You didn't do that." She grabbed hold of his hand, interlocking her fingers in his. "You accepted me, and that is the greatest gift of all."

His grip closed around hers firmly. As though he'd never let go. As if she only had to say the word and he'd stay forever.

"You gave me no choice." A smile creased his lips, but it didn't reach his eyes. "You come storming into a room, Abigail. You've got a ready retort for any situation. I could stand naked outside with a bloody pineapple on my head, and you'd probably bring out a shaved ice to serve with it."

She laughed at the image, but then her laughter died out at the sorrow on his face. "If I'm prepared for everything as you say, then I'm prepared for being your mistress."

"I have no doubt you'd make the finest mistress in all of England," he said.

"Then what's stopping you? Is it the money?" She pressed his hand, wishing she could extract from the contact what troubled him. "That's a mere formality, in place because I'd want Bess to stay here too. I know that's unconventional—"

He cut her off. "Your sister isn't my objection."

"Then it's me?" She dropped his hand, pushing herself up from the chair. Put as much distance between them as she could. "You don't want me."

He let out a sound halfway between a groan and a sigh. "You know that's not true."

"Why did you kiss me?" She whirled around, facing him. "Not just in the snow, but the library. You touched me, *kissed* me, where no man has ever touched me. Was it a game for you? To make me feel for you?"

"Christ, Abigail." He'd never sounded so anguished before. "Everything between us has been real. If what happened in the library didn't indicate to you how badly I want you, then I don't know what will."

"And I want *you*. Can't you see that I love you?"

She'd said it. Oh God, she'd said it. She flung her hands up to cover her mouth in hopes she could push those words back in, but it was too late.

The words lingered in the air, soaking up every bit of space between them until there was just this declaration smothering them both.

"I shouldn't have said that." Her throat tightened, making her sound choked. "Please, please forget that I ever said anything."

"I will do no such thing," he declared, holding her gaze steadily. "I won't forget what you said because I love you too."

He loved her.

He *loved* her.

He loved *her*.

In the next second, she was in his arms, pressed against his chest, the beat of his heart in her ears. He'd taken her tarnished soul and polished it until it shined new and bright. "I will be the best mistress you'll ever find. I swear to it."

He pulled back, turning away from her. "I haven't agreed to any arrangement."

She watched him dumbly. "But...you love me, and I love you."

"It's never so simple." His posture became rigid, poised to head off into war, not profess his adoration. "I love you so much, it bloody terrifies me. I'm a Strickland. Time and time again, the men in my family have hurt the women they claimed to love. You'll come to hate me."

"I could never hate you." Coming up next to him, she rested her hand on his arm. His tense muscles relaxed under her touch.

He leaned into her hold. They stood in front of the window, staring out at a street that might not hold any potential for them, yet they were unable to look away. "I'm sure my mother never thought she'd hate my father, and she died in the asylum he sent her to."

She peered up at him, wishing he'd see she believed in him. "What happened to your mother is horrible, but it doesn't determine your future. If anything, that has made you a better man. You will never do to me what your father did to her."

"I don't want to hurt you." He clasped her palm tighter as if their joined hands could anchor him. "The very idea of hurting you makes me want to choke something."

"You said yourself, I'm horridly irrepressible." The tiniest smile toyed with her lips, despite the somberness of his words. "If you hurt me, I'll recover. We are both fallible creatures. I'm sure that I shall not always be a delight to live with."

"Do you really think I could be better?" He brought his hand up, covering her palm with his. "I want that. I've ruined so many things, Abigail, and I'd understand if you don't trust me—"

"I *do* trust you." She cut him off. With each statement, he'd grown more impassioned. "I meant what I said in the library. I trust you. More than I do anyone else."

He released her hand, going back to the chaise and sitting down. She followed him. Her steps were slow, her rhythm irregular from her knock-knees, but she walked with a purpose. She wouldn't be ashamed of her disadvantages, not with him, not now. Carefully, she dropped to the ground in front of his chair, assuming the same position he'd taken earlier.

"Let me make *you* a promise then." Taking his hands in hers, she rested her elbows on his knees. "I'll stay by your side. You've reminded me that I'm strong enough to wage my own wars, but I'd like you by my side when I'm fighting. I'm ready to be your mistress."

Squeezing his hands, she released him and rose. She left him sitting in his sterile parlor, hoping that he'd allow his life to clutter with the chaos of their feelings.

Chapter Fifteen

She loved him.

Michael shouldn't be overjoyed at this. Love wasn't practical. Emotions led to heartbreak, and he'd been a bachelor for so long he didn't know if he'd be able to change. Before Abigail, he'd considered his life complete. He worked cases, he produced statistically definable results, and when he needed to unwind, he knew what bit o' muslins to call upon for dalliances.

So why did he feel so damn elated? Loving Abigail was a complication he didn't need. When he'd first seen her in the hospital, he'd been dumbstruck by her. She'd seemed so delicate, his waiflike beauty. Now that he knew her, his initial impression rang false. She didn't need help from anyone, least of all him.

But he loved her.

Try as he might, he couldn't ignore that fact any longer. Over the course of ten days, she'd bewitched him, the devilish minx, with her bright smile and her rebellious social philosophies and her sinful curves. She was not perfect—she was incredibly stubborn, and she always thought she was right—and for that, he loved her even more. Around her, he could be himself, flaws and all.

He'd sneaked into Abigail's room earlier that day when he'd known she was out in the garden with Smithers and slipped twenty pounds into the pocket of the apron she'd worn the day she arrived at his house. It wasn't as much as he'd wanted to settle on her, but at least it was something to start.

He drummed a jaunty beat against the top of his desk. Earlier that day, Smithers had caught him *singing*. He hadn't sung in years! The only positive part was that Smithers had missed his dance with his truncheon.

Michael leaned back against the leather headrest of his chair. Swished the gin in his glass. Glowered at the dancing flame of the one candle lighting his otherwise dim office. In that golden flame, he saw Abigail's flaxen hair, her reddened lips from his kisses, the flush to her cheeks when he'd spread her thighs apart and licked her delicate bud.

This was a definite problem.

She wouldn't be the first mistress he'd kept. In his early twenties, he'd entertained a succession of women before deciding it was worth neither the effort nor the expense. He preferred the spontaneity of one-night encounters.

Abigail was spontaneous. He remembered her tucked away in the back of his library with *Fanny Hill* stretched out on her lap. Her fingers down the waistband of her skirt. Her head thrown back as she cried his name...

His cock twitched to life at the memory. How did the very thought of her make him hard? Bloody, bloody hell. At the beginning of last week, he would have readily agreed to the idea of her being his mistress. She was beautiful—the most beautiful woman he'd ever seen—and through protecting her, he'd assuage his guilt over her torture.

Now, the notion revolted him. He couldn't fathom his bold,

spirited Abigail beholden to him. To *anyone*. She ought to be an equal participant in whatever relationship she entered.

With her, he could no longer imagine reducing passion down to a business arrangement. She deserved a man who'd do right by her, who'd honor her in both his thoughts and his actions.

She deserved marriage.

Could he give her that? Earlier that morning, he'd drawn up a budget for what it'd be like to have Abigail and her sister live with him. From a fiscal standpoint, he could afford it. But *should* he take Abigail as his wife? He knew the answer to that without hesitation. No.

He was not a man who remained steadfast. The thought of growing old together and raising a brood of children usually was enough to make his blood curdle. He enjoyed his unattached life, and it suited him well, regardless of whatever his servants claimed.

But numbers didn't lie—people did. And he was no exception.

The numbers said he ought to make Abigail his wife, that it was the best scenario for all involved. But could he doom Abigail to a life of unhappiness when their relationship no longer fulfilled her?

As he drummed his fingers against the table, he imagined what waking up every morning next to Abigail would be like. He didn't recoil. He wanted to run, yes, but not way from her—to her bedroom.

Fear gripped his throat and wet his palms, choking him in a way none of the dangers he'd faced as a policeman ever had.

He loved her, but his feelings were inconsequential. For no matter how she felt toward him currently—her admission of love yesterday constantly replayed in his mind and yet he still couldn't believe the words—he couldn't believe that it'd last. She might become homesick for Whitechapel, or after being accustomed to increased privilege, she'd start to find life as dissatisfying as Frances did. Or else he would, and he'd make her hate him.

He'd never seen a marriage that lasted. Even Knight's great love with Poppy would lead to disaster. He knew this with the unyielding certainty he used to have in his own skills as a foot patroller. There, he'd learned to trust his instincts. In his role as Inspector, he couldn't rely on simply presentiment—he needed facts and indisputable evidence too. Too many people's lives depended on him.

His men had sent word that they intended to raid Madame Massle's tonight. With any luck, by morning, they'd capture Clowes before he left the country.

Michael frowned into his glass. He couldn't shake the niggling doubt. Something didn't feel right about this operation. Sightings of Clowes had been confirmed by multiple witnesses in the West End, and Jared hadn't come back with anything new.

He missed consulting with Knight, back when his friend's success didn't equate to his failure. Grabbing a blank piece of paper, he drew out a model in the right corner of the map. Given the movements of his henchmen and the last known location, as well as the data from previous cases, he could triangulate Clowes's basic location. He plotted each point on the map, as he'd done multiple times in the last week. The repetition soothed his mind.

When they'd first convicted Clowes, Michael had tried a buffer formula on his factory crimes, and the outcome had been sound. Clowes's house was within walking distance yet gave him enough distance that the police wouldn't have thought of him without the testimony of the Knights.

He frowned at the map. A man like Clowes would have

established a bigger buffer, an area where he wouldn't commit crimes because he'd fear leading the police straight to him. All the points on the map from recent events were too close to Madame Massle's.

It didn't make sense. He made a note on the paper to contact Hume tomorrow.

Pushing back his chair, Michael ambled toward the door, stopping to grab the decanter of gin. No point in taking the glass with him. He intended to drink himself into an oblivion that didn't consist of Clowes's blasted escape tactics or Abigail's tempting mouth.

He blew out the candle and proceeded down the hall, the gin sloshing in time to his steps. Gin would fix everything, at least for the night. In the morning, hopefully, he'd know just what to say to Abigail. A man could hope, couldn't he?

Lost in his own thoughts, he almost didn't register the noise. A high-pitched keening sound, echoing from one of the bedrooms. Quickly, he counted the doors. Third door on the left, the blue room—oh, fuck.

Abigail. No, not Abigail. Anyone but Abigail...

He flung the decanter onto the ground. His hand flew to the small pistol holstered at his waist, cocking the weapon in seconds. He stood with his feet a comfortable distance apart, positioning the three lower fingers of his right hand on the pistol grip, thumb resting on the back of the gun. As he crept down the hall, his mind spun through various scenarios at a rapid-fire pace.

If it was Clowes, then the bastard had subdued his two patrollers outside. Clowes must be armed because there was no way Smithers would have conceded without a fight. How had Clowes figured out what room Abigail was in? Process of elimination, most likely.

His heart pounded in his ears, while his breath came out in

erratic puffs. The pistol remained steady, the weight in his hand reassuring. He knew the gun, knew the accuracy.

The cry came again, louder this time, followed by a woman's voice. "No, no!"

To hell with sneaking up on Clowes. Speed was his best advantage. He burst forward, boots slamming onto the Oriental rug, running faster than he ever had as a patroller. Those chases had been about the job. This was about pursuing the villain who'd harmed Abigail.

He slid his index finger onto the trigger. With his other hand, he flung the door open, ready to shoot if the situation should require it.

There was no one in the room.

No one but Abigail.

He'd anticipated his eyes adjusting to the darkness of her room, but the fire in the hearth had not burnt out yet. The embers gave off a glow that cast across the room, highlighting her bed. He approached with his finger still on the trigger, fearing the danger that hid in the shadows.

A part of him couldn't believe that she was unscathed and truly alone in this room.

Her cheeks streaked with tear marks, and the sheets twisted about her, showed she'd spent a large part of the night tossing and turning. Had she been dreaming when she'd cried? God, he hoped it was something as simple as that.

She stirred in the bed, her eyes opening slowly. "Michael?" She recognized him, her gaze on his face, then dropping down, taking in the pistol in his hands. Her eyes widened. "Why are you here?"

"Checking." He stalked past the bed to the drapery and the bay windows. He drew each drape back, verifying that no one hid behind them. He then tackled the wardrobe, pushing the dresses aside.

"What in God's name are you doing?" she demanded, braver as drowsiness fled.

Satisfied that no one had entered the room unknown, he uncocked the gun and set it on the table. Spinning on his heel, he nodded stiffly. "It seems you had a nightmare."

She blinked, shaking her head as if that could clear out the cobwebs in her mind. "Yes, I suppose that's true," she murmured. "But that doesn't explain why you burst in here as though wild dogs bit at your heels."

He shifted his weight from one foot to the other sheepishly. With her severe gaze on the pistol, he felt silly—no matter how real the peril could have been. "You were crying. I thought you might be in danger."

"Oh." She sighed. "I'm sorry. I'd hoped the nightmares were gone."

Advancing toward her, he gently sat on the edge of the bed. He should leave. Being with her created more unneeded obstacles. He couldn't look at her silhouetted in the firelight without remembering how her skin had slid so smoothly against his or the lush sashay of her lips upon his own.

"I'm fine now," she said, lifting her chin in a valiant—but ultimately fruitless—attempt at convincing him. "You can go back to bed. I'm sorry I interrupted your night."

The second apology in as many minutes. Where was the girl who'd declared so glibly that she was a worthy opponent to him? He compressed his lips, deliberating.

She'd been raised to be dutiful, his Abigail, to ignore her own wants and desires for the good of her family. He remembered how she'd appeared standing nude at the door to this very room, although this time he recalled it with an air of clinical detachment. He suspected she'd once been buxom in the areas where she was now too thin, too pinched from months of poor nutrition. He followed the tracts of spilled tears upon her cheeks and felt his failures anew.

He still wasn't certain he could be the man she needed, but at least he could grant her the space to be honest. She ought to have someone caring for her as she did everyone else.

"I'm not going anywhere." The words tasted strange upon his tongue, a promise he had not intended to make.

But that was the trouble with her. Everything with Abigail became a promise in its own right, a hint at something more.

Chapter Sixteen

Michael observed her with the same levelness he used in interrogations. A mask to hide the frantic beating of his heart, the desperate desire to be by her side until he was certain she was fine. "This is a regular occurrence, the nightmares?"

She rearranged the sheet up around her, hiding her night-dress from his view. He swallowed a sigh of relief, for it was one less enticing reminder of when he'd dipped his head between her legs and tasted her cunny.

Closing her eyes, she took a deep breath. "Since the incident." She raised a gloved hand to her face, sweeping a stray golden curl from her face.

She wore the gloves to sleep.

He was struck by how deep her scars ran; to cope, she couldn't look at her injuries, even when no one else was around to see her. The decanter of gin outside in the hall was evidence enough of how he'd learned to deal with his own demons over the years.

"Tell me about the dreams," he urged, maintaining the

distance between them, even though he ached to pull her into his arms and soothe away her hurt.

Raising her gaze to his face, she assessed him for a second, the slightest wobble to her lower lip the only indication that she was not in complete control.

"I'm back in the factory. Clowes is there; that part never changes. There are times when Effie Larker is with him, and she's shrieking at him to finish the job, to make it neat and pretty because he's already ruined one of the finest silks with the bucket of urine he poured upon me."

His stomach sloshed. He'd tried to forget that detail. What had happened to her was inhumane and sick.

Wounds that wretched needed stripping away in the same darkness that created them. So tonight, he'd stay by her side until she quieted, and he'd listen to her confession.

She needn't be scared anymore.

"You know we will find him," he vowed to her as much as himself. "My men are going tonight."

She sagged back against the bed pillows, letting out a sigh of something that sounded almost like relief. As if she believed him.

"Can't you see that I love you?" she'd said.

He did not deserve her love, yet she'd given it to him freely.

"And when we do find him, I will personally make damned sure he pays for what he did to you." He wished it were Clowes's throat that he wrung between his hands, not her counterpane. "Clowes will know what it's like to be tormented by someone with the power to make him wish for death. I'll torture him until he begs for mercy, and when he asks for mercy, I'll kick him in the stones."

A small smile curved the edges of her lips. "I should like very much to see that."

She loosened her grip on the sheet, and his eyes tracked the slow descent of the fabric. Her night rail was white, innocent as she was, but flimsy where she was flinty. He should divert his attention elsewhere.

But he wouldn't look away—*couldn't* look away.

He needed her to know that he saw her, every part of her, and he didn't want to run. Her strengths and faults combined to make this total picture. He loved her with every bone in his body, even though he knew he shouldn't, even though he knew it'd all turn to rot. He loved her, and he'd die to protect her.

So, he reached for her, gripping her smaller hand in his rough larger palm. The cool slide of silk against his skin was not as enticing as it had once been, for it hid who she was, and he wanted no illusions between them. He held her gaze, her cerulean eyes reminding him of turbulent waters on jagged rocks. Every problem that arose, she'd beaten down with her strength of will.

"Sometimes I dream Poppy's there too," Abigail whispered. She stared down at their merged hands, her irregular breathing steadying. "Instead of Clowes being the one to shove my hand in the loom, it's her. She helps him torture me. And you know what? She has this gruesome smile on her face, the same one she had when she found those damned papers in Larker's office. And I know she'd do it all again if given a choice."

"You can't truly believe that." He thought of Knight's wife, her impassioned face almost as red as her hair from defending Abigail's honor. The two women had been close, but he didn't think he'd entirely grasped how much Poppy's friendship had meant to Abigail until now.

Abigail sneered. She didn't pull her hand from his, but she settled back against the pillows, farther away from him.

"I believe it because it is the truth." Her tone dared him to contradict her. "Why should Poppy have regrets? She got everything she wanted out of the deal."

He squeezed Abigail's hand, wishing he could will away her hatred with his touch. "You know she regrets you being hurt. But Poppy didn't torment you, Clowes did."

"So, you side with them." She slumped on the bed, defeat running through her. "But you said you loved me."

She tried to tug her hand from his, but he held firm.

"I *do* love you," he confessed, for though he'd said it before, it had been in the heat of the moment. Now in the quiet of her bedroom, it felt as though he was revealing a truth long kept secret. "And it's because I love you that I can't allow you to continue down this path. You think you're hurting the people who did this to you, but you're only hurting yourself."

She squirmed on the bed, directing hellfire glares at him. "I don't want to talk about this any longer."

He pulled her to him, his arms surrounding her. She'd cling to the darkness, his wildcat, but eventually, this wrath would eat her alive. "Abigail, please." His voice was as low as the spark of flames in the hearth. "Do you know what I did after my father died?"

She stiffened against his hold. "No."

"I threw myself into work," he explained. "Every case I got, I finished in half the normal time because I refused to sleep more than two hours a night. I existed upon gin, boiled potatoes, and overdone mutton because that was all the coster in front of the station house had."

Her nose wrinkled. "I've had worse."

He nodded, recalling how she'd ravenously fallen upon her dinner that first night. "It wasn't until two months after the funeral that Knight forced me to take a night off. We went to one of my sister's god-awful soirees. The music was akin to the wails of a dying cat, and the food was only a hair better than gutter rubbish, but I realized something."

"That the rich are never satisfied?" she suggested acerbically.

"Bloody woman, can't you tell I'm trying to discuss my feelings with you here?" he grouched, releasing his ironclad grip on her. "I thought women were supposed to like displays of emotion. Hell of a lot of good it does me with you."

Soon she sat beside him, her legs flung over the side of the bed, feet dangling in the air. "I'm sorry. Please, tell me what you realized. I'll listen this time."

He let out a loud harrumph. Just this once, he'd like her to react the way normal women did. "Not that it will have the grand dramatic effect I planned originally, but I learned that if I didn't deal with my grief, I was going to combust."

"I'm not grieving," she objected. "And that makes a fourth time Frances was right since the soiree helped you."

He peered at her skeptically. "Fine. Four times, though I believe this was really Knight's achievement, since he snatched up the invitation and demanded we attend."

She arched a brow at him. "Mere semantics."

"But it doesn't change the fact that you, my dear lass, are most certainly grieving," he declared. "I haven't seen such blatant sorrow since the king died."

"King George was a bounder," she scoffed. "Why anyone mourned his passing is beyond me."

"You little libertine." He wanted to laugh and agree with her pronouncement because the fourth King George had indeed been a bounder. But his position as an inspector sobered him. "Be careful who you express such opinions to, or you're liable to be hauled into gaol as a traitor."

She flashed a wicked smile at him, piercing his heart. "Ah, but Michael, aren't I safe with you? You'll never tell anyone what I say."

Safe.

"Yes, you're safe." With everything he had in him, he'd make sure that was true. "No one's going to hurt you here."

Not even me.

Scooting closer to him, she laid her head down upon his shoulder. "I know."

He rested his chin atop her head, relishing the closeness of her. "I think you need to forgive Poppy and Knight for what they did. Place the blame where it lies and nowhere else."

She rubbed at her eyes with the back of her palm. "They betrayed me."

Hadn't he, in a sense, betrayed her too? By refusing to look into the Larkers when Knight had come to him? He tried to remember what he'd told her about his part in the inquiry, but the details were hazy.

Better that he not make a full breast of it now. She needed someone to believe in and, damn it all, he'd be that person. Abigail had been battered and bruised so many times, but that was the past. He was determined the future would be much brighter for her.

"So, you say they did." He draped an arm around her shoulder. "When I told them about you coming here, Poppy almost jumped down my throat. She begged to see you. She was so bloody worried about our wager."

With good reason.

He squeezed Abigail's shoulder and prayed he wouldn't end up doing more damage to her. "Poppy cares about you, and so does Knight. You can continue to push them away, hurting not only them but also yourself. Or you can accept their help."

Disguising her sniffle with a well-placed cough, Abigail leaned into his touch. "I don't need anyone's aid."

"You do, and you should bloody well take it," he informed her. "There's no shame in you asking for help. You've been dealt a bad draw, and you need some new cards to get back your winning streak."

"It would all come back to a hand of cards," she noted with an ironic smile. "I hope you realize this applies to you as well."

He blinked. "What does?"

She linked her hand in his, toying with his thumb. "Accepting help. You're hurting over your father's death. If you want to talk about it..."

He'd rather be punched in the eye than examine all the reasons he hated the Old Bastard, and he wouldn't have to look far for somebody willing to do just that to him.

"I'm here for the next few days, at least," she murmured.

God, he longed for her to be in his house—in his life—for longer than just four more days. But could he make this commitment? Trepidation bubbled in his gut, the fear not just that he'd fail himself, but that he'd fail her.

"I'll be fine, love. Few sparring sessions at the gymnasium will fix me right up. You needn't worry about me." He released her hand, rising from the bed. He let his eyes travel down her insubstantial night rail one last time, the mere sight of her enough to heat his blood. "I ought to be going. Ladies must get their beauty sleep after all."

She stopped him with a hand on his hip, her delicate touch sizzling through the band of his trousers. "Do you think you might stay the night with me? It is a large bed. There is plenty of room for us both."

His body went rock hard at the suggestion. As her gaze fell to his growing erection, obvious even in the firelight, her round cheeks pinked.

It was nearly enough to undo him. That flush, so innocent, so unworldly. She knew little about pleasure. Only what he'd taught her. He was many things: scoundrel, rogue, hedonist. But he'd be more for her. He'd honor her needs.

"That is, to sleep," she hazarded, the breathiness of her voice creating an entirely different notion. "I'm not saying that you have to give me an answer to my plan now."

For one minute, then another, they stared at each other. Neither dared speak. He waited for her to retract the proposition, to realize her foolishness not only in giving herself to him but in saying she loved him. But she didn't.

She drew in an unsteady breath, her saucer eyes fixated upon him. He let his eyes roam down her heart-shaped face, from her pert nose to the sharp angularity of her chin, as strong as she was. She'd slept so violently that her blonde curls were finally, finally unrestrained. Waves of champagne cascaded down her shoulders, ending just above her breasts.

As if he needed a reminder—as if her naked body wasn't seared into his mind—her white night rail left little to the imagination. He simultaneously thanked and cursed the makers of modern millinery. God's balls, he could see the darkened skin of her areola, her nipples firm and erect under his scalding gaze.

Slowly—so slowly, he wasn't certain his eyes could be trusted at first—she licked her lips, pink tongue dipping out to caress the upper edge. Oh, God. God and Heaven and Hell and devils because devils *had* to be involved. He couldn't staunch the groan that ripped through his chest. His breeches were so tight against him from that one damn seductive movement.

He knew it then: resistance, when it came to Abigail Vautille, would always prove futile. The need to touch her was deep in his bones. He'd fought valiantly to allow her a more suitable man than him, but in the end, she was his.

"I'll stay," he ventured. "But you and I both know there won't be any sleeping."

Chapter Seventeen

S *tay the night with me.*

She'd lost her mind. Everything about this house struck her with madness: the sheer opulence of bourgeoisie existence, the servants that were neither French Huguenots nor London-bred, the library with its obscene collection of pornographic pictures. Michael was everywhere. Even when he was not with her, this house was his. These things were his. This style of living was his.

She was his.

And therein lay the crux of her madness. Technically, if she were to be specific, the crux *sat* on the bed beside her. Silently Michael observed her, sans his coat and neckcloth, his powder-blue waistcoat unbuttoned. The rolled-up sleeves of his white linen shirt revealed his way-too-muscular forearms.

He was a bronzed god in the low light of the fire, while she was a monster.

The idea that he'd want her seemed unbelievable. But he'd said he loved her, and she knew he would not lie about something as important as that. In fact, she couldn't think of a time when he had lied to her.

Always, he'd treated her with blunt forthrightness that she valued far more than the kid gloves everyone else wanted to use around her since the incident. His honesty was the most important thing to her.

To him, she was not broken beyond repair. There was still hope for her.

"Think hard about what you're asking," he murmured, his eyes never leaving her face.

He saw her. Not the beast she'd come to believe she was, but a girl who was beautiful, independent, and smart. He saw the girl she'd been before. Perhaps even a better version, for she'd triumphed over adversity and emerged like a phoenix.

"I have thought about it," she told him. "Did you think I'd ask to be your mistress if I didn't want this?"

"It is possible you might have considered me the lesser of two evils." A flash of doubt, sneaking past his cocksure exterior before he promptly snuffed it out with his typical smirk. "I suppose when compared to life on the streets, I am quite desirable."

"It is indeed possible," she agreed, reaching for his hand and tugging him closer to her. "But unlikely."

"I'll still look out for you, you know that. I meant what I said about settling a sum on you and your sister." He didn't bridge the gap between them. "You don't have to do this to win my support."

"For a reputed rogue, you're damnably hard to seduce." She rolled her shoulders, letting her head fall back so that her breasts lifted higher in the thin night rail. The motion had the desired effect: his eyes darkened, his focus centering entirely on her bosom.

He gulped, and she knew it was not for lack of want that he'd been unsure, but rather out of respect for her.

"Abigail—" He swallowed, his hand fisting around the coun-

209

terpane. "I'm trying to save you from a foolish decision. Once you give away your virginity, you can't get it back."

"I am aware of that, yes," she replied acerbically. "Did you mean it when you told me you loved me?"

"You know I did." He sounded pained that she'd question his affections. "I love you."

No matter how many times he said it, she'd never grow tired of hearing it. "Then why would I ever want anyone but you?"

He released the counterpane. Grabbing for her hand instead, his fingers closed over hers, clutching her so tightly that she dared to think he might never let go. This could be permanent between them. Maybe her fate wasn't sealed in the first turn of the bar onto the next flat, perforated punch card. She could be a woman of bold decision and even bolder desire. A woman who fought for what she wanted.

And what she wanted was him. She'd wanted him since the moment he defended her to a table of unruly men at Cruikshank's when he'd claimed her as his.

"Are you sure?" His voice didn't reach above a whisper. The words hung in the air between them, the only sound in the room.

The change in him struck her. Gone was the scoundrel who smiled and flirted at the drop of a hat. He awaited her response with bated breath, his gaze hot with desire but his movements surprisingly shy. She squeezed her fingers against his reassuringly.

She nodded. "I'm surer than I've ever been in my life."

With his hand still in hers, he shifted on the bed, his thigh rubbing against hers as he scooted closer. He cupped his hand underneath her jaw, lightly bringing her chin up so that her eyes met his. His lips brushed hers in the gentlest of kisses—so soft, her heart sang.

There'd been an edge to their other kisses; a war played with their lips on opposing sides. But this was real, raw, and perfect because she knew his true feelings.

She kissed him back, certain of her own prowess. Kissing him was a lexicon in which she was now proficient.

Her stomach flipped as he grazed her lower lip, again his touch so light it was almost torturous. She wanted more. She wanted to be so wrapped up in him that she forgot where she began, and he ended, assuaging all her fears this was temporary. If this were the only time she had with him, if he didn't agree to her scandalous proposal, then she'd cement this night into her memory.

She'd experience it all.

She had half a mind to tell him she didn't want him to hold back when the urgency of the moment changed. Perhaps it was the way she drew his bottom lip in between her teeth, slipping her tongue into his mouth to fence with his. His growl reverberated through her, sending a shiver down her spine. His hand slid from underneath her chin to the back of her neck, and as his fingers dug into her tender flesh, he deepened the kiss.

What had been sweet became wild, all-consuming.

Still kissing her, he pressed her down upon the bed. Their eyes met for a second: his questioning, hers full of want. She inclined her head, and on her consent, he kissed her again, then broke away from her. He pulled back the sheets, revealing her bare legs and feet to him. Instinctively, she went to grab for the sheets, but he stopped her, locking one hand in hers. The other stroked the pad of her foot, sliding up to her ankle, then her calf.

Frissons of heat fired within her. The urge to cover herself began to fade, for with his hand sneaking up toward her knee, she felt deliciously reckless. If she was going to be ruined, then she'd enjoy it, basking in the wantonness.

"You're beautiful." He leaned down, placing a kiss along the back ridge of her knee. "When you were naked before, I couldn't stop thinking about how damn beautiful you are."

Her cheeks grew warm from his words. Hell, her entire body was warm. She didn't care that the fire had burnt out, and a chill had settled in the room, for his touch heated her thoroughly. His hand traveled farther up, meeting with her thigh.

She smiled saucily. "I remember your reaction was quite pronounced."

He moved their entwined hands to the waistband of his pants, then lower until she palmed his erection. It was not new—she'd seen evidence of it before—but this time with the proof of his desire in her palm, she was awestruck. She investigated the shape of him, cupping his balls, then moving on to the hardness of his shaft.

"It is so big," she said, partly because she'd heard the strumpets who went to the Ten Bells say that this type of compliment never went astray with men, and partly because she'd always believed the pictures were exaggerating the girth of a man.

He laughed, the hearty sound echoing. "You always know just what to say, don't you?"

She lowered her eyes demurely. "I don't know what you mean. How will that big, big rod ever possibly fit inside of little me?"

"Oh, it'll fit," he growled, sweeping her up in his arms. "It'll fit like it was made for you."

She was crushed up against his solid frame as he kissed her hard, ravishing her mouth. Sparks collided. Fires started. All from his lips upon hers, the give and take of their kisses and the devastatingly sensual slide of his hand across her body.

He took hold of the hem of her night rail, pushing the light fabric up, up, up her thigh until the sweet part between her legs was visible to him, as she'd been in the library. Leaning back, he surveyed her for a moment, making a noise of approval before he came back to her, enveloping her in a deep kiss. Her hands slid behind her, beneath the pillow, grabbing the hem to tether herself to this world while his kisses drove her toward bliss. His upper body pressed against hers, chest to chest, the rub of his shirt buttons against her pert nipples creating such tempting tension. His hand braced her side, fingers splayed across her rib cage, and she thought that for the first time in her life, she had everything she needed.

He trailed kisses down her neck, along the line of her jaw, in the hollow of her collarbone. Her breasts felt heavy. *More,* she told him with her body, tilting her head back to give him better access.

"Cheeky chit," he praised, rewarding her by cupping her breasts, running his thumb across her nipple appreciatively. Somehow, he'd managed to tug the neckline of her night rail down without her realizing it. He ducked his head down and then his lips were on her nipple, sucking, licking, devouring.

God, he was good. He'd earned every damn rumor about him, but she wouldn't think about the other women he'd been with before this. She'd think only of how he'd moved to her other breast, biting at her nipple and drawing from her a salacious moan.

"Ah, so you like that?" He grinned against her flesh, chuckling. "Do you know what *I'd* like?"

She mumbled inarticulately. If he expected her to form complete sentences during this, he was sadly mistaken. But since he was probably expecting a response, she shrugged.

He laid her hands on the row of closures on his shirt, and she went to work unbuttoning. The task was cumbersome, as the buttons kept sliding against the silk of her gloves, but he kept her well occupied with his kisses. His hand was on her inner thigh, dangerously close. Even the rustic scent of him was a distraction, clouding her senses.

When the shirt was undone, she slid it off his shoulders, marveling in the expanse of tanned muscle before her. Experimentally, she let her finger glide down his chest, watching as he shivered from her explorations. His moan echoed through her as she toyed with his nipple, as he'd done to her. So he liked that, too, she noted, securing that information away for future use. She continued her course of study, following the line of fair hair that peeked out from his breeches.

"Not just yet," he told her, nudging her back down on the bed. "Not until you're thoroughly ready. I want your cunny to be so wet my cock slips right into you."

Her body felt as though it was in an inferno already. How much more ready could she get? But then his mouth was on hers again, and his kisses were pulling her further and further away from her grip on reality. She lost rational thought. Instead, she threw herself into this new world where she was desirable.

Michael would bring her endless pleasure, and she'd reciprocate, until the end of time.

When he pulled back from her to catch his breath, a roguish grin curved his lips. "Every part of you is alluring, did you know that? You steal my breath away."

She came crashing back to reality. Dread sank in her stomach, twisting her organs. He thought she was lovely now, but he hadn't seen the horror of her hand. The curvature of knock-knees could be excused, for they were common in areas where factory work was the main occupation.

Her hand was revolting. He couldn't look on the scarred, blackened skin and not be revolted. She could barely handle seeing it, and it was a part of her now.

She gulped down her panic. Tried to focus on his weight between her thighs. He laid a kiss upon her neck, and she worked her gloved fingers through his hair, wishing she could feel his sandy locks upon her fingers but not brave enough to strip off the last vestiges of her hidden self. With the gloves on, at least she could pass as normal.

His body went stiff against her. Everything stopped for a second as he sat upright, confusion flickering in his eyes where before there had been only unbridled longing. "Abigail," he said, almost sternly.

"Did I do something wrong?" She reached for his arousal, thinking that she should have been tending to him instead of letting him bring her pleasure.

"God, no." He shook his head, his breath coming out in pants. "But this isn't right."

"I told you I want this—"

"No, no, that's not what I mean." He captured her hand, his thumb looping in the seam of her right glove. "I want to see you. All of you. Won't you let me?"

"You've seen all of me," she reminded him, snatching back her hand from him. She tugged her glove back up. "This isn't necessary. It'll only disgust you."

"Nothing about you could disgust me." He fastened his smoldering gaze on her, and again she wanted to believe him, even if she knew he was lying. No one had ever viewed her scars without recoiling in horror.

She'd be changed forever in his mind, and not for the better. But when he looked at her like that, she wanted to let him.

Swiftly, she swept off her right glove, dropping it over the side of the bed. "There," she said, hoping he'd forget his foolish request and get back to kissing her.

"I know it's difficult," he said, as though he could understand her pain when she knew damn well he couldn't. No one could. "Well, I don't *know* it is, but I imagine you might feel scared to show me. But love, I've stripped my soul naked for you. I've told you things about my family that I've never told anyone else. I won't judge you, Abigail. I need you to know that."

"Please, Michael," she pleaded, squeezing her legs tight against him. She ought to yank her nightdress back up. She ought to run from the room, go back to her family, even if it'd mean she'd be penniless. At least then, her last memory with him wouldn't be his revulsion.

He leaned down, effectively keeping her from leaving. He whispered in her ear, his breath tickling her sensitive neck. "I'll make you a wager."

"Another wager?" She felt herself relaxing back into the pillows, his weight over her reassuring. He was physically strong when she wasn't, powerful enough to defend her against the bastards that had hurt her before. But he'd let her get in the first punch, and that meant something.

"The first one worked pretty damn well for us," he murmured.

As he placed another kiss along the column of her neck, she couldn't help but agree with him. "Go on."

"If you let me see your scars, I'll take you as my mistress." Another kiss, another touch that sent her mind spinning.

She managed to summon up the power of speech. "And if I don't?"

"Then we'll have one night together." He hovered over her, his lips so close to hers, but not broaching the distance. "Abigail, if you're going to live with me...I want to know you, all of you. The good and the bad. It's only fair because I can guarantee you I'll be a royal pain in your arse most of the time."

She laughed in spite of herself. Michael was egotistical and dogged, but then she was just as stubborn and hardheaded. While she certainly didn't relish this idea, if showing him meant she had more of a chance to stay in this bubble of bliss, she'd do

216

it. She'd close her eyes and pretend he wasn't looking at her. "If that's your terms, then…"

He started to remove her glove, slow and seductive, but she batted his hands away. There was nothing sensual about this reveal. She tore the glove from her fingers and dropped her palm on the bed, making sure she wasn't touching him with her disfigured flesh. She expected he'd retreat, but he simply examined her hand from a distance, a contemplative expression on his face.

"May I?"

She nodded.

Gingerly, he lifted her left hand, inspecting the damage. He ran his thumb over the besmirched skin, tracing the contours of the scar tissue that had formed over her muscles. She couldn't feel his touch there; the nerves had long ago been deadened.

But she *saw* his touch. She couldn't close her eyes. She couldn't pull away from him. She was stuck at this moment, watching him as he watched her. His hand on hers, his perfect flesh against her repulsive wounds.

"Must have hurt like the dickens." He stated the obvious, and she gave him a look that implied such. Somehow, his casual statement lifted her concerns, and she began to relax. There was no pity in his eyes, only the dawn of understanding.

He feathered a kiss on her knuckles. Her heart sped up impossibly, tight in her chest. Had he been anyone else, she would have suspected him of setting her up for ridicule. But he simply shrugged and placed her hand on his chest.

"Touch me," he bid her, his tone allowing no room for argument. "With your hands. I've been dying to feel your hands on me, woman, instead of those damned gloves."

She hesitated, but the feel of his strapping chest against her good hand was too much to resist. She ran her palm across the planes of his shoulders, down his rib cage, pressing softly with her fingers to reassure herself that this was real. She dared to trace the muscles of his abdomen with her scarred fingers. The sensations in her uninjured hand seemed to amplify, compensating for her deprived nerves.

She was touching Michael, and he didn't flinch. He didn't tell her she was a beast, fit for nothing but tupping hard with the candles burnt out. The moonlight streamed through the windows, casting a glow on them.

Growing impatient, he guided her down to the waistband of his breeches.

She laughed. "Ready now? I ought to make you wait, as punishment for before."

"You'll be the death of me, minx," he rasped.

He let out a ragged breath, his eyes heavy with desire. Her fingers slid inside the fall of his breeches. When he let out a groan, she decided to relieve him of his ache. Unfastening his breeches with her right hand, she worked them down his hips. In a quick maneuver, he shucked his breeches and small clothes.

No illustration could have prepared her for this. If she'd thought him imposing with clothes on, then naked, he was enough to strike her breath from her completely. Her gaze roved down his frame hungrily, drinking in every centimeter of his body.

"Like what you see?" He grinned at her, and for once, she felt that his habitual smirk had relayed a secret between them.

He was hers tonight, hers alone.

But she didn't get a chance to tell him that, for he'd gone for her night rail, heaving the hem of it up and over her head. He deposited it on the ground unceremoniously. Propping up her knees, he pushed her legs apart, settling between her thighs, her feet resting on his shoulders.

He took in the sight of her, a low growl escaping his throat. "God, you kill me. I want so badly to be inside of you."

"I want you to be," she told him. "I want to feel what I felt in the library, but more."

"And so you shall," he agreed. "But we have all the time in the world for that."

Michael touched her, touched her as he had before, but this time it was so much better. He'd seen her scars, and he still wanted her. His thumb against her center was enough to rush pulses down her body, even more so when he began to rub her nub in a circular motion. She squirmed against him, and he held her steady. When his head dipped between her legs, she was certain she couldn't possibly take any more.

Yet he kept teasing her with the hot flicks of his wet tongue, the rhythmic nibbles of his teeth. He slipped a finger inside her, testing her readiness. She'd tell him she was ready—oh so ready—if she could form sentences. He took advantage of her inability to speak, thrusting that finger, hitting an elusive spot within her that made her keen with pleasure.

His mouth, that finger, everything combined until she was reeling, she was falling, she was spinning out of control. Screaming her release, she came crashing back down.

"Taste yourself on my lips." He kissed her, thrusting his tongue into the depths of her mouth, pantomiming what he'd do to her soon. "You taste so good, you know that? I could lick you all day."

She was limp in his arms, given up to pleasure. It made her reckless, willing to be bawdy. "Then maybe you should."

"Ah, but then I wouldn't get to fuck you, and I have been waiting a *very* long time to do that." He dropped his grip on her to move over the top of her completely, carefully keeping his weight off of her. His hard member was against her entrance now, and that mere bit of contact was so divine she couldn't wait to have him in her.

"You're sure?" he asked through gritted teeth, straining to hold himself back.

In response, she reached down with her right hand, taking hold of his shaft and guiding him in her. For a second, they remained like this, him at the very cusp of her entrance, not moving, while she became accustomed to him.

"I need to move," he cautioned her. "I swear it'll only hurt this one time."

With one long stroke, he surged into her, and the pain ripped through her, a sharp stab that made her eyes water. She welcomed it. For the first time, this was pain she'd chosen, pain she'd asked for, pain that would change her irrevocably in a positive way.

He'd gone still above her, his muscles taut, his face awash in concentration. "I'm sorry, love," he whispered, kissing her throat. "I'm so sorry."

Life had tried to break her, but she'd emerged fiercer. She wanted this—wanted *him*.

She gave a tentative push of her hips to show him just how strong she was. Michael let out the breath he'd been holding as she arched her back, giving herself up to being filled by him, joined with him. He started to thrust again, the rhythm slow, just enough to strike a match within her again. The pain faded, replaced only by the building pleasure his movements wrought.

"You like that?" The husky quality to his voice would have been enough to make her answer yes, regardless.

She nodded.

"Then tell me," he ordered. "Tell me exactly what you want, or I won't do it. This night is about you, Abigail."

She gulped. He'd seen her touch herself. She could tell him exactly what she wanted. "I want you to move," she whispered. "I want you to tup me."

"Tup you, *how?*" He grinned, beginning to slide into her again.

"Just—like—that," she gasped, for he'd found the best rhythm. Stars began to dot her eyes. They moved together, she a step behind him until she grasped the pace, and then they were two in tandem. Two became one as he filled her, and one became two again as he pulled out, over and over again, until she was shaking from the pleasure.

There was only him, only goodness and light. The past wound around her, but it no longer touched her.

Reaching for her injured hand, he curled his fingers in hers, holding on to her as he thrust deep within her. That stroke was as black powder poured upon her lit fire, for she exploded all at once, her ears roaring and white light flashing before her eyes. He wrenched from her at the last moment, spilling his seed on the floor. He collapsed next to her, thoroughly spent. They lay there, hands entwined, breaths ragged, as they each tried to regain their senses.

She had become Beauty, but she was still very much Abigail. Now she saw she could be both.

Chapter Eighteen

ichael watched Abigail sleep, marveling at the calm that settled across her sprite features. Her beauty struck him as it always did, but more so now when she was tucked away in his embrace. She slept peacefully, free of the ravages of nightmares. He wondered if he'd had something to do with that, if she truly did feel at ease with him.

He saw her in his mind's eye as she'd been in the throes of passion, her eyes closed, and her freshly kissed lips moaning out his name. He replayed this memory, again and again, convincing himself that this had happened, and the woman next to him was not a phantom he'd conjured up in feverish need.

Her fair curls splayed across his pillow. Her lavender scent clung to everything in the room, soft and delicate like her body, mixing with the smoke from the fire he'd rebuilt before crawling back into bed with her. She'd smiled at him, patting the spot next to her. When he'd joined her, she'd laid her head down on his shoulder.

"Do you have any regrets?" he'd asked her, praying to God that she'd lie to him if she did so that he could have this one night with her without the hard truths crashing in upon them.

But she'd shaken her head. "I was with you."

She'd stated it so simply, as if that one sentiment summed up her existence. *I was with you.* She'd turned in his arms, propping herself up on her elbows and planting a kiss on his lips. That small kiss had escalated into a torrent of passion, as he'd come to expect with her. One kiss was never enough. One touch wouldn't satisfy him. He must have her again. Even as she rested in his arms, he wanted her, wanted to brand her body with his love, wanted to be the only one in her mind for the rest of eternity.

He couldn't change positions without fearing he'd wake her. With any other woman, he would have felt trapped, but with Abigail, he held her tight. He'd lie here with her forever if it meant she wouldn't leave. If he could continue to hear her laughter at one of Smithers's bad puns, see her merry smile when she'd found another objectionable book in his library.

Her steady breaths lulled him into a sense of repose he hadn't felt in years. He let his fingers trail up her arm, barely brushing her skin until he came to the lacerations on her left hand. His stomach lurched.

She'd expected that the wounds would disgust him. Feared it. But he could not look at her crushed hand and be reviled. How could he, when it was partially his fault she was disfigured?

If he'd only listened to Knight—if he'd been willing to put his arse on the line and go against Whiting before the evidence became staggeringly clear—maybe Abigail would still be at the factory. Maybe she'd have met a nice boy and fallen in love with him. His head filled up with maybes until his chest was tight. He hugged Abigail tighter to him, his eyes never leaving her scars.

She was the combination of her past and her present, and whatever future they'd have together would include these moments. He loved her, loved her so much that it seized his breath and staggered his mind, for he'd never been a man who gave credence to deep emotions. His feelings for Abigail were vast in a way he could not quite comprehend yet. He only understood that she was his, and he hers.

Damn him to the fieriest depths of hell, for he couldn't bring himself to wish he could undo the past events. Abigail had come to him because of her wretched past. Now, as he breathed in the scent of her hair and traced the curve of her knees with his foot, he knew he wouldn't part with her for anything.

And he knew, with the same soul-searing truth as when he'd figured out his mother had tumbled so deeply into madness that sanity was impossible, he'd die for Abigail. When she was in his arms, he understood for the first time in his life what it meant to have someone to shield above all else.

He'd been her first.

This bond between them was irreversible. Even if she realized she could do so much better than him, he'd still be linked to her. He pressed a kiss to her brow and watched as her eyelids quivered.

She shifted slightly in his arms. Her fingers peeked out, curling around the covers, just as she'd held his hand before. "Can't you see I love you?" she'd asked him, and he heard her voice in his ears all over again.

He did see. He saw her as she was presently, her bare body tangled up in his. He saw her in the gaming hell, her lower lip trembling, but her chin rising fiercely. He saw her as she'd been in London Hospital, frail and weak. And he saw her as she'd been in the parlor before, proposing to be his mistress.

It was not enough. The furthest thing from his mind when she'd arrived on his doorstep had been taking a wife, but now he found himself desperate for her acceptance.

He'd only encountered a few circumstances in life where he

hadn't sailed through with ease: when his mother had been committed to Bedlam, when Knight had quit the Met, and that night he'd found Abigail waiting for him naked. He'd hurt her then with his thoughtlessness, and though she'd forgiven him, as he lay beside her, his sins still stung.

As the fire crackled in the grate, it occurred to him that the struggles in his life had always been with the people who mattered most to him. His mother had slipped from his life without so much as a cry for him, so gone was she to the plague in her mind, and the loss of her had broken something inside of him. Something he hadn't been willing to recognize until Abigail had sauntered into his life with her sassy quips and her equally broken heart.

He didn't know how this union between them would turn out. A part of him still firmly believed it would end in sadness.

But he had to proceed. For years, he'd been a scoundrel. He was through with that, through with the dissipation, the hubris. He was no longer the most important person in his own life.

That role belonged to Abigail, and devil take him, he'd spend every damn moment of his ne'er-do-well life making her happy. He'd taken her virginity, effectively ruining her. Honor dictated that he ask for her hand, whether or not she'd accept simply being his mistress.

He'd never given a damn about honor before, but now it seemed crucial to his very existence.

The scraps of a plan came to him like wisps of a dream. How she'd mentioned that she'd never been to a dance. The gown Frances had given him—before she'd realized who Abigail was—because she found it amusing that a less fortunate would show up to a society event in her cast-offs. This would be the last time Abigail would wear clothes picked out by someone else. As with everything else under the sun she'd managed to espouse views upon, he assumed she had a definite opinion on fashion.

He stretched, careful not to wake her. Listening to her breathing again, he let the sound steady him. This was how it was supposed to be between them: this easy state of being, her in his bed, her leg draped over his, and her arm slung over his shoulder. If his luck held, he'd have many more years just like this.

* * *

"GOOD MORNING."

Abigail awoke to the rub of Michael's whiskers against her cheek, his dulcet whisper in her ear. They were naked in bed, her back nestled to his front. His arm draped over her, one hand linked in hers and the other cupping her bare breast. Somehow, she'd managed to sleep with her legs in between his.

For a moment, confusion flashed in her mind until she awoke enough to put the pieces together. He hadn't left. She didn't know what to think of a man who stayed. Most of her old friends in the BRLLS claimed their respective partners scurried off after taking their pleasure, leaving empty arms and cold beds.

But not Michael.

"You stayed," she murmured, tilting her head so that she could look up at him. "Thank you for that."

"It is my house," he said with a grin.

"Oh." She fought the urge to pull the sheet up tighter around, hiding her body from his hungry eyes. He'd loved how she looked the night before, but that had been in the dim light of the fire. In the morning sun, when he could see her scars without the damper of darkness, would he still feel the same toward her?

"I'm quizzing you." He placed a kiss onto her cheek, and her pulse quickened in response. "Where would I be if not with you? You didn't honestly think I'd leave, did you?"

She squeezed his hand, the pressure reassuring her. "I don't know."

He palmed her breast with his other hand. "If you'd think I'd leave this delectable view, you're mad, my love."

My love. He'd never called her that before. Love, dear, chit, yes. All those were terms of endearment men used interchangeably with women. But to be his love was something different entirely. He'd branded her—not just her body, but her mind too.

"Forgive me for ever thinking you'd be typical." She relaxed into his touch, letting out a moan of approval as he pinched her nipple.

"Ah, my wench enjoys that." He didn't wait for a response. Releasing her hand, he propped himself up on one elbow, giving her an appreciative once-over. Any desire she'd had to cover up disappeared as he dragged his fingers across her chest, the slight touch sending thrills through her body. "I love you, Abigail. Never doubt that."

She stretched, winding an arm around his midsection so that she could bring him down on top of her. He obliged eagerly, greeting her with a long kiss. When he finally pulled back, he made a move as if to get out of bed, but she draped her arms around him, holding him close to her.

"Not so fast." She darted a quick kiss on his lips. "Did you really think I'd let you leave so soon? After a night like last night, you must know I'd want to do it again."

He chuckled at her enthusiasm, tweaking her nose. "As much as I'd like that, I don't think it'd be wise. You'll be sore today."

Shifting, she felt the answering ache between her legs. She wrinkled her nose. "You may be right. How unpleasant."

Concern crossed his face. "But well worth it?"

"Of course." She smiled, kissing him again to assuage his worries. "I wouldn't change a single thing about last night."

"Good." He caressed her cheek, the rough pads of his fingers against her skin drawing forth the most exquisite sensations. But all too quickly, he was out of bed and reaching her for night rail, hung on the bedpost. He passed it to her and set about collecting his own scattered clothes.

She watched him, her core tightening at his tanned, brawny frame and that firm, bare arse. As he pulled on his breeches, she sat up straight, not bothering to hold the sheet up to her breasts. "Why don't you come back over here?"

He turned around, pausing in buttoning his shirt. His mouth fell slightly open at her appearance. He swallowed, readjusting his breeches to accommodate the evident stirrings of an erection.

"Abigail," he ground out, his voice strangled. "I am trying very hard not to make it public knowledge that I compromised you last night. But if you continue to look like that—"

She leaned back in the bed, her arm propped up behind her head, while her other hand had disappeared suggestively beneath the covers. "I don't know what you mean. How do I look, exactly?"

His head snapped up. He prowled to the side of the bed and leaned in. "You look so damnably beddable, it's killing me not to throw you over my shoulder and fuck you against your bedroom wall until the entire household knows exactly whose cock is buried in your cunny."

Sliding her hand slowly up his arm, she ran her tongue over her mouth, tasting him on her lips. His reaction made her feel bold.

She seized upon that wantonness, a devious smile twisting her lips. "So do it. Make me come, you big, bad rogue."

"Woman, you'll drive me mad," he growled, grabbing for her. With his arm around her middle, he hoisted her into his arms as though she weighed next to nothing.

She had no time to think. In a moment, he'd crossed the width of the room. Backing her up against the wall—no, it was her bedroom window, for those were curtains behind her back—he spread her legs.

She followed his direction, hooking her knees around him, so that she balanced with her spine against the cloth curtains, the coldness of the winter morning permeating her skin. Michael's neighbors, if they stared at this window for any length of time, might conclude he was fucking a new mistress.

Her window overlooked the main drag. If by some chance they happened to put together that the woman in the window was the factory worker who'd been staying with the inspector, she'd be rightly and truly ruined.

Even if she weren't identified, if the curtains moved the slightest bit, anyone in the street below would see her arse cheeks smashed up against the wood frames. They'd see as Michael bit at her breasts and nipped her neck. They'd see as he came hard and fast, his body ramming into hers. Oh, God, *everyone would know.*

That thought should have been enough to make her beg him to put her down. Instead, she held tighter to him, her fingernails raking his back. He held her up with one hand, while the other opened his breeches and slid the fabric down his legs. Heat surged through her body until she was certain she was on fire from the inside out.

Everyone would know. They'd see her dirty little secret, and there'd be no denying what she'd done here.

She couldn't hold back. The silk of the curtains decadently glided along her backside. Wetness slicked her center, and her stomach tightened with every pulse of desire. Throwing her head back against the window, she let out a long moan, the sound of her own desire only heightening her pleasure.

She *wanted* society to watch.

"That's it, darling," he coaxed, his kisses to her neck like assaults to her sanity.

While the night before had been about softness, sweetness, this time between them was hard and fast. He pushed himself inside her with no apology for her soreness, no wait for her to grow accustomed to his girth. He drove into her, one long stroke after another. Slammed into her with a pace that bordered on frenzied.

It was devastatingly wonderful. "Oh, Michael," she whimpered as his fingers dug into her arse to steady her.

"That's right," he praised, biting down on the pressure point of her neck. "Say my name. Tell everyone who's making you come."

She cried again as he plowed into her, his wicked rod hitting that exact point she needed. How could he make her feel this way? Last night had been good, so good, but this, this was everything. She grabbed hold of the curtains, bracing herself against him. Until he stopped.

Her eyes sprang open. "What? Why are you..." She couldn't put together a coherent sentence.

"Say my name," he ground out. "Or I won't let you come."

Later, she'd make him pay for that demanding tone, but now she only knew that it made her hotter and wetter. "*Michael.*"

He smacked her arse, resuming his earlier tempo. With each pound into her, he brought her higher, faster than she'd ever come before.

"I'm going to—I'm going to—" She couldn't crest until he did. She ought to wait for him; she ought to slow...

But as she thought this, there was a bang in the hallway. A serving plate perhaps. *Everyone knew.* She couldn't hold back any longer. She came crashing, milking every last drop of her release from him.

*   *   *

"Night rail, now." His voice ragged, Michael gave a final pop to her rear and then carried Abigail over to the bed.

As she pulled the cloth over her head, he grabbed the washcloth left by the basin of water on her nightstand. He kept his back turned as Abigail redressed, focusing on cleaning up the mess they'd made. He'd barely been able to pull from her in time, spilling on the damn floor.

This couldn't continue. He'd meant to leave before the servants figured out he was here. He had an entire plan laid out. He'd change the sheets, erasing any trace of his having been there. In the eyes of his servants, she'd still be pure.

When he asked to marry her, it would appear that her virtue was intact. Why he bothered with the illusion when at every turn Abigail had defied his expectations of what a traditional miss would do, he didn't know.

But it seemed important to give her this dignity and to avoid any uncomfortable questions from his overly delighted staff, who all wanted her as their new mistress.

Mistress.

There was that damned word again. He made the mistake of turning around just as her night rail slid slowly down her body. His cock twitched in response, already anticipating their next go-around. Already, the dirtiest words for what he'd like to do to her were forming in his mouth. He bit down on his tongue to keep from spewing a filthy sonnet to her body.

Christ, was he to have a permanent erection around her? No woman had affected him like this before. No one—not even the most adventurous of courtesans—had made him so hard, so fast.

"That was fun," Abigail said, tossing him his breeches. "While I loved last night, this...this was better, I think."

For a second, he simply stared at her. His jaw had fallen open again. This kept happening around her. She liked it *more* this time around? When he'd plowed into her so fiercely, the entire bloody room had shaken from the force of their coupling? When he'd not tampered down on his basest desires, but had given in entirely to the unbridled passion that she stirred within him?

"You—ah—you liked that." He carded his hand through his hair, blinking at her. "You like my hard cock in your wet cunny?"

Damn it to hell. He couldn't help himself around her.

She tilted her head. "Should I not have? I thought it was particularly erotic. I was under the impression I am allowed to enjoy what we do. Sex is what a mistress does after all."

Her words were the slap he needed to get control of his randiness. He'd intended to propose to her, not have sex with her against the window with nothing settled between them.

He pulled his breeches on and then set to buttoning his shirt, not responding to her until he was fully dressed again. Once she was his, properly his, they could tup against any window in this damn house, and he'd see to it that their next times were as rough as she wanted.

He ignored her watching him appreciatively. Ignored the swing of her seductive hips as she went to the water basin and scrubbed her face.

"I have a surprise for you tonight." He didn't answer her earlier question, deciding this was a better course of action.

She turned around with the rag in her hand. "What kind of surprise?"

He wouldn't go to her, no matter how that night rail hugged her curves and displayed them in the most tempting fashion. No. He'd stay the course and get the hell out of this room. He strode toward the door, not acknowledging that she followed him. Only when his hand was on the doorknob did he turn around.

"If I told you, it wouldn't be a surprise." He leaned in, allowing himself the quickest kiss to her forehead. That at least was a more innocuous part of her anatomy than her lips. "Mrs. O'Neal will be in soon. I was going to suggest changing the sheets so she wouldn't know I'd been here, but I suppose that's pointless now." He blanched. "I'm sorry. I meant to keep your reputation intact in the eyes of the staff..."

She shrugged. "Let them judge."

He hadn't heard her right. "Pardon?"

"I said, *let them judge*." She gave another shrug. "For the past six months, all I've cared about is what people think of me. But last night, you looked at my scars, and you didn't flinch. Michael, you acted as though it was no big matter. As if I'd just been scratched."

"I didn't mean to make light of your injuries," he apologized.

"No, that's not what I mean at all." She was quick to correct him, smiling. "I mean that for the first time, my past didn't define me. So if your servants want to talk about what happened between us, then let them, because I'm finished caring what others think. I won't feel ashamed about being with you. I love you, and I don't need anyone's damn approval for that."

He couldn't hold back the grin that formed at her audacious declaration. He laughed as he had when he was a boy, one loud whoop of delight after the next, for this woman made him feel alive. He gathered her in his arms once more, kissing her hair, her cheeks, her nose, her lips, anything he could touch. "Christ, I'm glad to hear you say that."

But as the kisses grew more passionate, he parted from her, though it took everything within him to do so. "Mrs. O'Neal will come by before dinner to ready you for the surprise. I've got some work to do in the office until then, so I'll bid you adieu now."

She reached for him, but he wagged his finger at her. "Enough, my wanton lass. If I don't leave now, I never will, and then where would your surprise be?" With one last wink, he hurried out the door.

Chapter Nineteen

When Mrs. O'Neal came to prepare her for dinner, Abigail had been ready for hours. She'd started the day in the library, but she couldn't focus on any of the books. Finally, after a half hour of pretending to read the same page, she'd given up and retreated to her room. She'd taken *Northanger Abbey* with her in case by some miracle, she was able to think straight, but it had sat unread on her bedside table.

She'd managed to fix the curtains so that there was no sign of what they'd done that morning. But all the tidying up in the world wouldn't obliterate the memory. Would Mrs. O'Neal treat her differently now? Servants, especially those in the Strickland townhouse, were probably used to scandal. Though she'd meant what she'd said to Michael about not wanting to care about anyone else's opinion, she didn't want the kind old housekeeper to *dislike* her. Mrs. O'Neal and Smithers had been so welcoming to her. She'd come to regard them as friends.

Last month, she would have stated unequivocally that she'd never have friends again. Friends were a liability. Yet as she opened the door to Mrs. O'Neal, Abigail couldn't deny the fact that she'd missed having companions. She'd thought she'd never trust another person again as she'd trusted Poppy, but Michael had proved her wrong on that too.

"Come along, dear, we've got a lot of work to do," Mrs. O'Neal bid her, gesturing toward the dressing table in the corner of the room.

Abigail followed her, sitting down on the stool. "Do you have any idea what surprise Michael is planning for me?"

In the mirror, she saw Mrs. O'Neal's lips start to turn up in a smile, but then her expression resumed its characteristic flatness. "If you think I'm going to go against the master's instructions, you've learned nothing about me."

"Just a little hint," Abigail wheedled, as Mrs. O'Neal picked up a brush and began to tackle her unruly curls.

"Absolutely not," Mrs. O'Neal stated. "What in the world did you do to your hair to make it so tangled, child?"

Abigail blushed, looking down at her hands. Was Mrs. O'Neal hard of hearing? Or perhaps this was the housekeeper's way of telling Abigail that she'd ignore any signs of her activities with Michael.

Mrs. O'Neal stopped, brush poised in the air. "Oh. I see." There was that hint of a smile again, gone so quickly Abigail wasn't certain she'd really seen it. "Well, we shall have you cleaned up in two shakes of a hog's tail."

"Did you know that in Whitechapel, hogs wander the streets?" Abigail blurted, first to change the subject and second because she wanted to see how the prim Mrs. O'Neal would react to such knowledge.

Mrs. O'Neal's nose wrinkled as she spun the stool around. "That's quite unseemly."

"That's life," Abigail stated. "When you don't know any different, it doesn't seem so strange."

"I suppose that's true," Mrs. O'Neal agreed, helping her up from the stool. "Now, off to the bath with you."

After her bath, Abigail returned to her room, clothed in a dressing gown. Mrs. O'Neal went to the armoire, selecting from the bottom drawer a pair of gold gloves with tiny roses embroidered at the cuffs. Before Abigail could ask her why she'd need such fine ornaments, Mrs. O'Neal set the gloves aside. Next, she pulled from the wardrobe the extravagant golden ball gown that Abigail had assumed wasn't meant to be in Lady Elliot's gifted dresses. She'd half-expected Lady Elliot to demand it back when she'd visited.

Mrs. O'Neal placed the frock on the bed, along with the requisite petticoats.

Now it was Abigail's turn to raise her brows. "Are you sure this is what he wants me to wear?"

Mrs. O'Neal gave her a look that said precisely what she thought of Abigail's second-guessing. "I'm to dress you and do your hair before you go downstairs."

"Is Michael taking me somewhere?"

Mrs. O'Neal started to fix Abigail's hair, ignoring her question.

"He said not to leave until Clowes was caught," Abigail mused, more to herself now than the other woman. "So whatever he's planning must be somewhere in this house. But that gown is far too nice for a simple dinner."

She considered the possibilities while Mrs. O'Neal tended to her appearance.

Under the housekeeper's skilled hands, her rambunctious hair was schooled into submission. Her ratty curls became luxurious locks, somehow spun from Rumpelstiltskin's prized thread. Abigail's tresses had been coiffed so that the top swept upward, but the rest loosely cascaded around her shoulders. Simple golden balls adorned her ears. She wore no necklace.

Mrs. O'Neal applied pink stain to her lips and rouge to her cheeks. After affixing a crown to her partial up-do, Mrs. O'Neal stood back to survey her handiwork. "Magnificent."

Abigail had to agree. "I look like a princess."

"A princess needs a proper dress," Mrs. O'Neal said, collecting the ball gown from the bed. She helped Abigail shrug off her wrapper and then assisted her with the full petticoats that made the dress fluff out properly.

When it came time to step into the dress, Abigail hesitated. She'd never worn anything as elegant as this.

Mrs. O'Neal did not care if Abigail faltered. She slipped the dress over Abigail's head and tugged it down, cinching up the duskier bodice. The cap sleeves were filmy, different from the usual horsehair puffed sleeves Abigail was used to. The insubstantial fabric lined her bodice, too, coming together in a vee above her breasts.

"There," Mrs. O'Neal said with satisfaction. "A true princess if I ever saw one."

Abigail stared at herself in the mirror. The wide skirt flared out in shiny waves of gilt. Darker half-moons in the same color as her gloves accented the dress. She gave a tug to her gloves, swallowing down her trepidation.

In a dress like this, she could be anyone. She might not come from the expected aristocratic roots, but she was just as worthy as the other women who wore clothing like this.

I love you, Abigail. Never doubt that.

She had Michael's love. If ever in her life she'd felt like a princess, it was now.

* * *

HE WAITED FOR her at the top of the stairs, his tall frame outfitted in a royal-blue coat, a yellow waistcoat, and a starched white shirt with a mustard neckcloth. While she remained uneasy in this extravagant dress, he stood with his shoulders back, his head held high, every bit the confident man she knew. He belonged in these accoutrements as much as he belonged in his blues.

She had not before, but with him, she believed she could belong anywhere.

As she stepped toward him, the train trailed behind her across the floor, and though she had viewed this part of the gown as impractical at first, she now understood why women insisted upon it. She felt as though she were walking on clouds. For the first time since she'd been here, she didn't exhibit the staggered drag that was her natural gait. She simply floated.

But as she neared him, she no longer thought of the trappings of finery that adorned her. His eyes fixed on her, love shining in his brilliant blue gaze. Everything else faded away as she returned his smile.

She took the arm he extended, and together they descended to the main hall. When they reached the ground floor, instead of ushering her out the door, he led her down the hall and into a wing she hadn't visited since the initial tour of his house. If her memory served, this space had been his mother's conservatory, built onto the back of the house and facing the garden. The heavy curtains were drawn back from the floor-to-ceiling windows to let in the moonlight. Candles glimmered in every wall sconce, splashing the room in bright light. All the furniture had been cleared from the room, except for a long table off to the side brimming with delicious-smelling food.

Music began to play. She startled at the noise, but Michael turned her toward the right corner. Smithers sat at the pianoforte. Next to him, Mrs. O'Neal stood regally, a tin whistle in her hands.

Abigail dropped his hand, surveying him quizzically. "I don't understand."

"You said you'd never been to a ball," he answered. "So I brought the ball to you, or at least the best parts of it. No mandatory idle chatter with ninnyhammers at dinner. No forced partner switches, and certainly no ridiculous rules about the number of times I'm permitted to dance with you. Just you and me, my love."

He'd remembered. Not only had he remembered, but he'd also gone out of his way to arrange this dinner and dance. Tears sprung at the corner of her eyelids at his thoughtfulness, and she touched her glove to her eyes to staunch the flow. "I love it," she breathed, hugging him. "It's wonderful."

He retook her arm and led her to the dinner table, where Cook had been drafted into serving since Smithers was otherwise employed. "It's a bit unconventional, yes, but I thought that fit us nicely."

"We've never done things the standard way," she agreed, as the cook placed a sumptuous rack of lamb on her plate, along with roasted potatoes, gravy, and carrots.

"Ah, but that's the best part about us," he teased. "Why be ordinary when you can be extraordinary?"

So the rest of the dinner went, with him making jokes and her laughing. Conversation with him was easy—words ebbed and flowed, and when they'd run out of things to say, they sat in comfortable silence. Perhaps that was what she appreciated most about him. She need not be anyone but herself.

When they'd finished the last of the chocolate cake, Michael pushed his chair back and then helped her up from hers. "May I have this dance, my lady?"

She nodded, not trusting herself to say anything that wouldn't come out like a gleeful shriek.

Mrs. O'Neal started the song, high-pitched, breathy notes

pouring from her tin whistle. On any other night, Abigail would have called the tune melancholy, but as soon as Smithers joined in on the pianoforte, she thought she'd never heard such beautiful music before. The two instruments blended in perfect harmony, discordant on the surface, but melodic when paired the right way.

Just like her and Michael.

He escorted her out into the middle of the room, his hand joined in hers. As the music swelled around them, he placed his hand on her waist and waited for her to assume the proper position.

"I've never waltzed before," she confessed. "Somehow, I don't think the dance halls the costers host is what you have in mind."

He pulled her close to him, placing her hand on his shoulder. He then lifted their joined hands so that he could lead her. "I'll let you in on a secret," he said as they began to glide across the floor. "You just follow my steps. And if that doesn't work? You teach me how to dance like a coster."

She beamed up at him, her anxiety soothed. "I think that could be arranged."

Michael's firm hands steadied her. Her skirts swirled about the floor after him in a filmy tempest. Soon she was able to follow the steps to the waltz without having to exert a great amount of effort.

She could focus instead on the nearness of him. The way his hand at her waist made her all sorts of tingly, though he'd touched her far more intimately before. But it was this—the gentlest of touches—that nearly undid her. His scent filled her nostrils. Pine, cigar smoke, and something undeniably male. She couldn't breathe without smelling him, without feeling him, without looking into his eyes.

It was intoxicating. Could she be drunk on love? Doubts

hummed in her mind, but she ignored them. So what if Michael hadn't formally acknowledged her as his new mistress? He'd planned this beautiful evening for her and admitted his love for her.

A wave of giddiness swept over her. As he twirled her around the room, quizzing her about this and that, she laughed until her breath was short and she was dizzy from the many spins. She hardly recognized the passage of time. All that mattered was that she was in Michael's arms. She felt loved.

When her back wasn't to the servants, he caught her eye, winking at her as his hand slid down from her waist and cupped her bottom. He ducked his head to whisper into her ear. "All I can think about is stripping that bloody gown off of you."

His breath against her neck and the heat of his palm on her rump brought a flush to her cheeks. She'd thought he would tire of her after the first two times, but he was still as randy as a young buck.

He twirled her around, his hand still on her rear, even though she faced his staff now. His wicked grin was enough to forestall any objection from her. She'd wanted sex against the window, and she wanted this too.

"You're a little exhibitionist," he murmured. "I like that about you."

Her brows furrowed. "It doesn't make you think I'm tawdry?"

"It makes me think you're honest." He spun her around and brought her back to him. "I never want you to question yourself when I'm around. I like that you're open about your desires. It makes it easier for me to fulfill them."

"Ah, you're so certain you can satisfy me," she jested.

"I haven't had any complaints yet." Smoothly, he turned her again, the grace of his movements reminding her just how skilled he was in bed. He laughed, apparently sensing the shift in her thoughts, for his smile was smug.

Last week, she might have tried to deny her attraction to him so that he wouldn't get the upper hand. Now, there was no point. He held her well within his grasp.

She leaned into him, resting her head on his shoulder as they swayed in time. "This is an amazing surprise."

He held her closer. Mischievous mirth sparkled in his eyes. "It's not over yet."

She drew back from him skeptically. "There's more?"

Releasing her, he waved to Smithers. The butler ceased playing. The sound of Mrs. O'Neal's tin whistle filled the air, sweet and harmonious. Michael dropped down on one knee before her, pulling out from the pocket of his coat a square box.

He couldn't be proposing. She must squash the hope that desperately cloyed within her. Their difference in social standing eliminated all possibilities of equality.

"Abigail Vautille, you have entranced me since the first moment I saw you." He opened the box, revealing a gold necklace with a tiny amethyst heart on it.

So this was a formal acknowledgment of her position as a mistress. She should nod. She should thank him. She should kiss him.

She should do anything but fervently wish he'd ask for her hand in marriage.

But he continued, and all certainty about what *should* exist between them vanished. "Will you do me the honor of becoming my wife?"

Chapter Twenty

A terrible silence filled the conservatory. One, four, then twelve seconds ticked by, until Michael was convinced the time had stopped between when he'd asked the hardest question of his life and this moment, as he awaited Abigail's response.

Abigail stood above him, an impenetrable fortress of woman, while he remained on this damnable floor, beseeching her to accept him. He was more vulnerable than he'd ever been. His knee ached from bearing the weight of his body.

He never begged.

But she was worth it.

Say something, please.

Her words came out in a fit of jerks and halts, the trepidation in her voice killing him. "Are—are you jesting me?"

"What?" He couldn't fathom her response. "Do you really think I'd play such a cruel trick?"

"No, but—"

"Christ, woman, I'm on bended knee!" He gestured to his current position, waving the box with the necklace in it so wildly it almost upended. "I've told you I love you. I've told you

I want more from you than a mistress. How could you not know that I'm serious?"

"Oh." She reached, not for the box but for his hand. Pressing his palm between both hands, she helped him up from the floor. In a flash, she was in his arms, nestled on the blue fabric of his coat, her warm body snug against him. "Then yes, of course, I'll marry you!"

Over in the corner, Smithers struck up a jaunty tune. Mrs. O'Neal followed him on the tin whistle. As the music played, Michael clasped Abigail to him, consumed by her sweet floral scent, by the joy in her reply. Happiness washed over him in a torrential downpour. Every reservation he'd had disappeared because she'd said yes, and she was to be his forever.

Tilting her chin up to meet his, he enveloped her lips in a kiss. She melded to him almost immediately, giving and taking what he offered with her own brand of passion. His heart beat against his chest while his blood thrummed to the sound of her sighs.

He could have kissed her forever.

Abigail pulled back from him, her pretty lips puckered. "But what about Lady Elliot? She'll never speak to—"

He silenced her with another kiss. "You let me worry about Frances. If she can't accept us, then it is her problem, not ours. I can't say that I'll lament the loss of her letters and godawful party invites."

"Family is important, Michael," Abigail scolded him, her face paling as a new thought struck her. "Oh, God, my family. If we marry, you could be held responsible for all my father's debts."

He shrugged, no longer caring about his damn budgets. It didn't matter, as long as he had Abigail. "So, I'll pay them."

"You have no idea how much he's gambled." She grimaced.

"The sum sickens me. At least you ensured he's not able to gamble any longer."

"Abigail, all I care about is that *you* are happy." He tweaked her nose, delighted when she smiled back at him. He had a lifetime to soothe her worries. Damnation, it felt good. "And your sister, for she matters to you."

Abigail's cheeriness had returned. When she smiled at him, she positively glowed. "Bess will be delighted."

Tugging her closer to him, he kissed the nape of her neck, his tongue caressing her skin. "She's not the only one who's delighted. I'm the luckiest man alive."

Abigail laughed, playfully smacking his chest. "Haven't we given your poor staff enough of a show?"

"You're right," he agreed. "There are some activities much more suited to the privacy of a bedroom."

LATER THAT NIGHT, when they rested intertwined in the sheets, both well sated and fatigued, he wove his fingers in hers and kissed the top of her head. The amethyst necklace he'd sent Mrs. O'Neal to buy for her hung around her neck, long enough that the charm fell in between her breasts.

She wore no gloves. He'd insisted she remove them, unwilling to sacrifice the ecstasy that was her bare hands stroking down his body, encircling his cock. He felt the stirrings of arousal in him at the memory of it.

She rubbed her thumb up and down the length of his index finger. "If this is a dream, please don't wake me."

He nipped her ear. "No dream. Just the beginning of a new life."

She sighed, stretching out against him. "I keep thinking if I blink, it'll all go away."

"You won't get rid of me that easily." He draped his arm across her side, a niggling feeling in the back of his mind. He'd been about to tell her something in the ballroom before they'd kissed...

She burrowed closer to him. "If Clowes has his say, we might not be here for long at all."

"Devil take my brain," he cursed under his breath, remembering what he'd meant to say. Of course, Clowes. In the rush of his yearning for her, the bastard had slipped his mind. "The Met would have my head for being so damn distracted."

"I don't understand."

"I received a message tonight," he explained. "I expected that my top sergeant would tell me Clowes had been caught."

She clutched his hand tighter, her nails digging into his palm. "And has he been?"

"No." He felt her body tense against him and strove to reassure her. "But we have evidence that Clowes booked a ticket on a steamer to Ireland. My men questioned Madame Massle and found the receipt in Clowes's room at her brothel."

She relaxed marginally. "Did anyone see him get on board?"

"Sergeant Hume saw the back of his head as the ferry pulled away from the dock. Clowes was about to go into the cabin. Hume dived into the water after the ship, but ultimately the ferry was too fast." Though he'd certainly have preferred to catch Clowes, he couldn't help but snicker at the image of Hume soaking wet.

"Will anyone be waiting for the ship when it docks?" she asked.

"We've contacted some of our assets in Ireland." He wasn't entirely confident they'd be able to retake Clowes, for the Met had little foothold outside of London. Still, having Clowes in Ireland was preferable to him being in the City.

"I hope you catch him." She drew her foot up against his leg, the touch so casual it made his heart swell.

He'd spend the rest of their lives making sure she was always as comfortable around him as she was in this bedroom. Abigail with her guard down was beautiful. He felt privileged to be the one she trusted.

Her foot trailed a bit higher up his calf. "Do you trust Hume's judgment?"

"Hume is a good officer, despite his abysmal personality and whatever history he has with my sister." Michael groaned inwardly at that thought. As soon as things settled down, he'd have to order Hume away from his sister, as much for Hume's own good as for Frances.

Abigail shifted to meet his gaze, the faint light of hope shining in her eyes. She dragged her fingers up his arm, her touch as faltering as her words. "Are you sure? Is he *really* gone?"

He nodded. All of the evidence pointed to the jackanape having left town. "I also had my patrollers search his room, and all of his belongings were gone. In Clowes's second note, he said we'd never stop him. I think he was referring to his departure from England."

Her lips split into a wide smile. "Then we're finally free of him?"

"Yes, my love." He laid a kiss on top of her head and linked his fingers in hers. "We are finally free. You're going to be mine for a long, long time."

He held Abigail closer to him, calmed by the feel of her beside him. Their nightmare was over. Their new life had begun.

Abigail settled against him, her eyes drifting closed. He couldn't remember the last time he'd felt as tranquil as when he was with her. Nothing else was as important as she was.

Michael thought of the day when Knight had told him he was leaving the Met. "You're giving in to the whims of a chit?" he'd asked, thinking Knight was weak for succumbing. Now, he saw the bond Knight had with Poppy was too crucial to risk. No matter what, he'd fight to keep what he had with Abigail. Nothing would come between them.

He was glad he'd told the Knights about Abigail from the beginning. He wanted to tell them of the love he'd found with Abigail, but he wasn't so sure she'd support this idea. After all, she and Poppy were still at odds.

"There's something I've meant to ask you," he murmured, choosing his words carefully.

Abigail slanted her chin upward so she could see him. "Another question?"

"Of significantly less momentous proportions," he assured her. "I'd like to tell Knight and Poppy of our engagement, but I know how you feel about them. Perhaps you'll think it's none of their business."

Her face scrunched up. "Is it important to you?"

He nodded. Knight was the one colleague who hadn't abandoned him after his promotion. "He is my friend, and once she was yours. Don't you want that friendship back?"

She stilled in his arms. Shook her head. "I...I don't know. Possibly? I miss the closeness we had, the feeling that we'd always be there for each other. I miss being able to talk to her about anything." The admission came out heavily as if she'd held it back for a long time.

He remembered Poppy's face, crumpled by the loss of her friend. "I know she misses you. And if she could, she'd change what happened in an instant. Love, we were all so damned foolish, not taking the Larkers seriously."

Abigail sat up suddenly, as though she were a marionette whose strings had just been pulled. "What do you mean *we*?"

He stiffened, her razor-sharp tone telling him he ought to be careful with what he said. "When Knight presented Anna Moseley's murder, we all wrote it off. Everyone in our division. A girl dying in the rookeries is sad, yes, but it doesn't indicate a conspiracy."

Her icy-blue gaze connected with his, and the air crackled with her anger. "You were mistaken. Anna Moseley was murdered, and I paid the price because your department didn't look into it sooner."

He struggled to remember what he'd told her when she'd asked about his involvement in the case. *I came in after the fact.* Shit. It was not exactly a lie, as he'd completed the investigation, but technically... Michael had withheld the complete truth about Knight coming to him with the case before he was dismissed.

He'd believed it was the best thing for Abigail to believe he'd had little involvement with the investigation. Who was he fooling? It'd been the simplest way to ensure she wouldn't hate him. His earlier justifications for his actions dissipated, leaving only his mistake.

God, he was the worst of bastards. How could he have botched this so badly? He should have told her. He should've been honest. Instead, he'd acted as though her thoughts didn't matter, as if she didn't have a right to hate him. All because, at first, he'd wanted to bed her casually. Then, as he'd begun to fancy her, he'd kept silent because he wanted her to stay with him.

Hadn't he learned anything from the Old Bastard's errors? He'd treated Abigail with cavalier disregard, as his father had done to his mother.

"That's in the past." He ran his hand down her back, trying to soothe her concerns. He had to get her back to him. One second, they'd been content in each other's arms, and the next, she was pulling away from him. "What we have now is amazing —why waste more time going over what happened six months ago? I thought we'd moved beyond this."

As soon as he'd said the words, he knew he'd chosen wrong, for she moved off of him, settling on the other pillow.

"Is that what you thought?" Her fingers toyed with the chain around her neck, almost as if she was ready to tear it from her neck. "Well, *I* thought you understood."

"I do understand." He tried to reach for her, but she slipped from his grip. "I was a coward, a bloody, bloody coward. I didn't want to be dismissed. Didn't want to hear the Old Bastard crow over how he always knew I'd amount to nothing. I regret every day that I didn't get involved when Knight originally came to me."

She tumbled from the bed in her haste to get away from him. "You *knew*? You told me you came in after the investigation was over."

When he started to go after her, she snatched up the sheet from the bed and wrapped it around her. As if him seeing her naked appalled her. How had they shifted from sex up against the window to this?

Excuses raced through his mind. Lies. More promises. Anything that would bring back the love in her eyes, replace the revulsion and fury. Damnation, it used to be so easy with other women.

But with her, he couldn't smooth over her ire with a well-placed line. She was worth more than that. She was the best damn thing that'd ever happened to him, and he'd risked it all by not telling her the whole truth.

"Whatever you want to know, I'll tell you," he avowed. "I'm going to make this right."

"When?" she whispered. Her question was so quiet he

almost missed it. "When did you know Anna's death wasn't random?"

He got out of the bed, not bothering to grab a blanket to cover up. He would not be ashamed in front of her, not when he had the sinking notion that everything between them depended on this one bloody conversation. "Knight had suspicions from the start. But that's all they were. Suspicions. I didn't know for sure until Knight was dismissed, so Whiting could cover up any involvement he ever had."

He went toward her, intending to take her in his arms. If he could just reach her—touch her—maybe she'd remember that they were good together. This bond between them mattered more than bygone sins.

She stepped back, holding her hand out to stop him from coming to her. "Don't touch me. Don't you dare touch me, not now."

"Abigail, I'm sorry, I'm so sorry." He couldn't go to her, couldn't force her to believe him, so he pushed all his emotions into those words. "Please, please, believe me, if I'd known what they were going to do to you, I never would have ignored the signs."

Holding her hand up to him, she advanced closer, until he could've stretched out his arm and touched her. But the pale white of her face and the coldness that emanated from her stopped him in his tracks. He saw the defacement of her hand, and bile rose in his throat. Though he had not slammed her limb in that loom, he'd contributed to her torture. The Met had a duty to protect the innocent. He'd shirked that duty in favor of his own career advancement. Now he stood as a newly promoted inspector, wealthy and powerful, while she'd lost everything.

She didn't close the distance between them, denying him the relief of touching her. As if she was no longer his. Her face had become a cold mask, as she'd looked that first night at Cruik-shank's.

"The signs, as you so put it, cost me the life I knew." She no longer spoke to him with any sort of affection. "My ability to work. My sense of self. I bear those signs every damn day, and I can't ignore them. All this time, I've been so angry at Poppy, but at least she did something! At least she tried to get justice for Anna. My scars aren't Poppy's fault. They aren't Knight's." Her words were like bullets slicing through his heart, leaving nothing but shattered organs. "It's *your* fault."

Chapter Twenty-One

She should've known better.

That one thought kept echoing through Abigail's mind. She thought it when Michael got up from the bed, his bronzed body bare, calling to her in the most primal way. She thought it as she approached him, her hand outstretched so he could not ignore her scars. She thought it as he acknowledged his true involvement and asked for her forgiveness.

She should've known better.

She was a Vautille, and to be a Vautille meant to live alone. There'd be no happiness for her. In the months since the incident, she'd prayed her life wouldn't worsen. Surely, she'd received her share of bad luck. The play must alter sometime. How foolish she'd been to think anything could change.

To think *he* could change.

He was nothing but a self-centered reprobate. In the end, he'd do whatever it took to get what he wanted, and he'd wanted her in his bed. A few lies meant nothing to him. Why had she believed she could alter him?

She should've known better.

"Abigail." He made her name into a desperate plea, and her traitorous heart wanted so badly to crawl back into his embrace. "Before I met you, I was lost, don't you see? I didn't know what it meant to care about anyone else."

Her hand slipped back down. She didn't have the strength to face him so openly. Where were her gloves? She scanned the area, locating them on the armchair by the door. They'd undressed so quickly upon entering her room last night she hadn't time to put them away.

She crossed the room, grabbing up her gloves and sliding them on. She'd hide behind her armor, pretending that he hadn't seen inside her soul, for it was the only way she knew to survive.

Turning to face him, she drew in a breath. Snapped her gaze back up to his face. "Put on some damn clothes, would you? The sight of you sickens me."

Hurt spanned his face, setting his jaw. For a second, she thought he'd refuse. But he strode over to his breeches and put them on. She breathed easier once he was clothed, yet each gasp for air still sliced away at the softest parts of her. Those weak, wretched bits that loved him still.

She tried to quiet her pounding heart. "You don't know how to care. If you did, you wouldn't have lied to me about this."

His face crumpled at her harsh reply. "You were so angry about what Clowes had done to you. If earlier I said that Knight had come to me and I ignored his deductions, would you have stayed? No. You might have run from me, and I wouldn't be able to protect you. I thought it'd be easier this way."

"Easier for *you*," she spat, pointing a finger at him. "I trusted you! I thought for the first time, here's a Peeler who won't lie to me. Here's one who acknowledges his prejudice against the rookeries and wants to do better. Here's one who accepts responsibility for his mistakes."

"I was wrong. I failed you. I failed that poor murdered girl. I'm a smug son of a bitch who cared more about tupping you than your feelings." He strode toward her. His expression was properly abashed—devil take her, how she wanted to believe he was sorry. "But I'm *not* that man now. I want you to know the truth. I love you, Abigail. I love you so much it's ripped away those narcissistic, foul parts of me."

She backed away from him, retreating until she was almost on top of the chair. She couldn't get any farther away from him. Her mind jumbled when he was this near, and all she could think of was that she didn't want to be the object of his pity. "How do I know it's really love and not your guilt?"

He brushed a hand through his hair, tugging at the ends in frustration. "Because you know damn well I'm not the type of man who'd propose marriage because he feels guilty."

"No, you'll just settle money on me," she retorted. "That's why you wanted to help, isn't it?"

"Part of the reason why," he admitted. "But not the only reason. I wanted to protect you. Because I love you."

"You lied once. Any promises you make from here on out are colored by deception." Her bottom lip trembled. She drew it between her two front teeth to stop the quaking. "When I told you I loved you, you said nothing about this. You allowed me to believe everything was real between us. I lay with you, Michael! Not because of our deal, but because I felt for you."

Tears burned the back of her eyes. She'd rather die than let them fall. She wouldn't allow him to see her pain.

He reached for her, lowering his hand before he even walked toward her as if he knew it was now futile. "I hoped you'd understand I was going to spend the rest of my life making amends. I know the cards you've been dealt are bad."

She wanted to tell him that he knew nothing, but that was a lie too. She'd bared her soul to him, but he hadn't thought to reward her with the same honesty. He knew *everything*. Her hopes. Her fears. Her most intimate desires.

His voice was but a whisper. "And anyone else would have broken under these circumstances, but you didn't. When I saw you in hospital, you looked so frail, but there was still this fighting spirit to you. I remember leaning down and whispering in your ear that you'd come out the other side stronger than before."

"That was *you*?" She hated the way her voice trembled. The slide of a single tear down her cheek, no matter how hard she clenched her fists or told herself she wouldn't give in.

"I went to see you." He mistook her devastation for relief, crossing the room to her. "I couldn't stop thinking about you. Knight had said you were hurt badly, but you were making an impressive recovery. You're a fighter."

You're a fighter. Why hadn't she recognized his voice? She'd replayed his words so many times in her mind. The sound had lost any semblance of reality, but she still felt reassured when she remembered it.

The throb of her heartbeat echoed in her ears, so loud she could barely stand it. She was suffocating here. Every lie she'd believed in the past two weeks lined up to crush her, shiny lies designed to delude her.

She had nothing to hang onto now. The voice—the one kindness she'd known before him—no longer rang true. When she'd wanted to end it all, that voice had shored her. The compassion of a stranger had reminded her that there was still good in this world. She'd asked the nurses who had come to see her, but none of them could remember. Eventually, she'd concluded it was better this way. That one moment had meant so much to her. She hadn't wanted to take the chance that meeting the visitor would sully her memory.

But all along, it'd been him. She had nothing of her own now, nothing that wasn't tainted by his betrayal.

She couldn't move from this spot. Couldn't gather up her things and run from him. She could only shake. Her nails dug into the fabric of the sheet she had wrapped around herself, and she cared not if she snagged his expensive linen. Let him pay for the damage she'd done. It was the least he could do.

The least he could do. How many times had he said that? The memories spun around her like weft threads, waiting to be woven into the saddest tapestry. He'd made a life out of contributing the least amount he could to society, and still, he'd succeeded. She'd worked hard since she was six years old, and she'd gained nothing.

His voice tore her from her thoughts. Soft, yet with a hint of gruffness, his words reverberated within her. He mollified her even while she strained against the situation. His grip on her was too potent.

"When I saw you again at Cruikshank's, it felt like fate," he murmured. His hands might as well have been on her for how personal his words were.

"It wasn't fate." Another tear fell down her cheek, so she swiped it away with her battered hand. "It was dumb, stupid luck."

"I don't believe that," he said. "Abigail, I am not a perfect man. But around you, I become something more. Someone I can look in the mirror and not loathe."

She threw her head back, a bitter laugh shaking her shoulders. The sound of that laugh steadied her. Made her feel powerful.

"How funny, considering that when I'm around you, I hate myself." She'd thought she was finally gaining strength to fight the past, but now she wasn't even sure who she was.

He didn't deserve to know how he'd built her up. How everything felt empty now, lies piled up on top of lies.

"You can't mean that," he protested, yet his tone gave every indication he believed her claim. Then he knew her little if he hadn't marked the change in her this past fortnight.

It had all been false. She clenched her fists together, finding solace in anger because the urge to burn everything around them was familiar. Ignoring him as he implored her, she fixated on the rage.

Before her eyes, she saw red. A blinding, consuming red that inflamed everything in its wake. She'd believe in that red if it meant she might come from this with her integrity intact. She wouldn't be pitied by any man.

She went to the wardrobe, her rapid, gangly steps displaying her deformity. One more reminder she'd never have been a good society wife. From the bottom shelf of the wardrobe, she tugged out the dress she'd worn when she first came to his house.

"Turn around," she demanded. "You don't get to see me now."

"Is this really necessary?"

She didn't dignify that with an answer. This distance was absolutely necessary. She needed it. Without it, she'd break in front of him, and she'd never get that part of herself back.

She'd given him everything. Her heart. Her virginity. Her very soul.

He sighed, but he finally turned around. She put on her old clothes. The worn blue muslin scratched against her brittle skin, grown too used to the finer dresses he'd provided for her.

She ignored the ache. Reminded herself that this clothing was the last thing she had left of herself before she'd succumbed to his charms. Before she'd become another one of his ladybirds.

She started toward the door. He came after her, getting there first, blocking it with his broad frame. Though she railed at him, punched him square in the chest, he wouldn't move. He crossed his arms over his midsection and looked down at her. At least she'd managed to wipe that smug smirk off his lips.

"Please don't leave," he pleaded. "I meant everything I said. I want you to be my wife."

When he reached for her, she didn't have time to react. She was enveloped by him, back in his arms, her head smashed against his white linen shirt, pine in her nostrils, and heat streaming through her body. Despite everything that was wrong, his embrace felt right. She was home.

The red fury galloped away from her, a wild horse tamed by his saddle. She was tired, so tired. Her head swum with allegations and misconceptions until she could not pick the right reality. No longer was there a possibility in front of her that wouldn't involve hurt. He held her to him, yet he did not restrain her. She could leave if she desired to do so.

She stayed. Those tears she'd tried so valiantly to hold back streamed freely down her cheeks, soaking his shirt, leaving an imprint of her failure. She'd believed him, always.

Abigail knew nothing except that his presence pacified her, defying logic. She leaned against him as a split woman, no longer Beauty, but not quite her former self either. While he murmured apologies and comfort, these warring impulses gripped her. She both longed to be his wife and to bury him in the darkest corner of Whitechapel where no one would find his corpse. He'd neglected to investigate Clowes, and she'd been hurt. He'd lied to her. He'd broken her one source of strength.

He'd changed everything, and she didn't know what to believe.

Finally, he withdrew. Dipped his head and pressed his lips to hers. For a second—a sweet second—she responded. His kiss tasted of broken promises, of wishes unfulfilled, and the tantalizing lure of what could never be. She broke from him, readjusted the fall of her dress, and pretended she hadn't been affected when they both knew damn well she had been.

"Stay," he bid. "Stay with me, and we'll work through this."

It was a tempting offer. So tempting that she almost agreed. Her world spun before her, full of missed opportunities and choices she'd never have because of that one night in the factory. She couldn't think of the despair in his eyes. Of how her throat closed at the thought of leaving him. She must remember what had been taken from her.

"I need time." She gave a hasty nod because that much she was sure of. "You cannot expect me to sort this all out immediately. Of all the people I know, I didn't expect that you would have failed me. I need to go home."

"You are home," he replied.

"To *my* home," she corrected. "I need to see Bess and my father."

He looked as though he hadn't thought of them in days. She stiffened. Perhaps all his promises about giving her sister a home were for naught too.

"I'll give you a week," he vowed. "After a week, I'm coming for you. I won't lose you, Abigail."

"A week," she agreed, partially because it was the only way she'd be able to leave without him objecting, and partially because having a date set in stone when she'd see him again calmed the clamor in her head.

She departed the house without a goodbye to Mrs. O'Neal and Smithers, unable to muster the words to thank them for their kindness, and afraid they'd persuade her to remain within these walls. With Clowes off to Ireland, she was secure in returning to Whitechapel. She slipped through the garden and out onto the street, stopping to pluck the frozen remains of a rose from one of the bushes.

Bess would have her rose.

Chapter Twenty-Two

T hree days passed. Three days in which Abigail did not return to him. He hadn't received so much as a letter from her. He'd hoped, God he'd hoped, that when she had time to think about their fight, she'd realize they had too much to lose to remain apart.

He'd been wrong about that, just as he'd been wrong to not tell her immediately of his participation in the case. If he'd been forthright with her, would she still be here? Would he be planning a wedding instead of poring over these reports on Clowes's departure to loosen the knot in his gut?

He didn't have answers.

He didn't have anything without her.

Pushing his plate away from him, Michael glared at the breakfast dishes piled high upon the buffet. Cook hadn't adjusted to cooking for one again. He remembered the way Abigail had set upon dinner the first night, the color finally returning to her wan cheeks.

He'd enlist Smithers to take the remaining food out to Drury Lane for whoever wanted it. When he'd walked to work yesterday, he'd crossed through the rookeries. He'd seen it all anew. During the last few years, he'd wandered these streets numb to the pain of these people, thinking of his job and his problems. He'd seen these people for the trouble they caused him in his prior position of sergeant, then the investigations and paperwork they created for him as an inspector.

Abigail didn't see them as lawbreakers. She'd grown up here. She lived in a grouping of tumbling-down tenements he hadn't visited yet but knew from Knight were on their last legs.

It had never hit him so completely how different their worlds were until now. While he'd been raised to view Spital-fields as an open sore, festering and infecting the good, hard-working people of nearby Cheapside, Abigail saw this place as home.

Abigail had trusted him to keep her from harm. He'd forsaken that trust before he ever met her by choosing his career over his duty to protect those who couldn't defend themselves. Because of men like him, criminals prospered, believing they were invincible.

The system was broken. No longer could he ignore the corruption in the Met. While Whiting's treachery had made it palpable, Michael had postulated long before then that the Met was following the same path as the Night Watch before them.

It didn't matter that he'd changed, or that the department had overhauled procedures. Abigail was still hurt. He'd still wronged her. Nothing could erase that.

He took a sip of coffee, wrinkling his nose. Abigail had made him see the world outside of his insularity, but if she wasn't around, what was the point?

Most of his life, he'd refused to examine any of his shortcom-ings. He'd blustered on, believing that if he simply *acted* confi-dent, he'd be infallible. Now, with all of his iniquities laid out before him, he couldn't ignore it.

Shoving the coffee across the table, he glowered at the last report from Hume.

No signs of Clowes or his top men. Ireland contacts haven't reported back. Case should remain open until they do.

–MH

Signs. For the rest of his life, he'd hate that word, for he'd remember the way Abigail had flung it at him like a lethal threat. And if that was not bad enough, there are Hume's assumption that he could determine which cases remained active. On a normal day, such presumptuous behavior would have grated on Michael's nerves.

Today, he'd gladly punch Hume in the throat.

Gathering up the reports, Michael pushed his chair back. He'd already sent a letter to Knight to inform him of Clowes's likely departure. At least Knight's family would have the freedom to walk about London again.

Once he located Smithers, and the remains of his breakfast were off to the rookeries, he'd feel somewhat restored. It'd be his way to honor Abigail, even if she'd never know what he'd done.

As he entered the main hall, he nearly ran smack into Smithers. He slid to a stop in the nick of time, almost tripping over the edge of the Oriental rug.

"Sir," Smithers gasped out. "Please excuse me."

"It's no matter." Michael took a closer look at the butler. Smithers's imperturbable mien was marred by a creased brow and a grimace. "Have you been running? I know you wanted to be prepared in case anything happened with Clowes, but I hardly think sprinting in the house is the right way to go about it."

Smithers smoothed his hand over his impeccable attire. "There is a man here to see you."

"Ah." Michael started to follow Smithers toward the parlor but paused halfway there. "People come to see me all the time without it causing you consternation. In fact, visitors usually overjoy you. I think it makes you feel important."

Smithers directed a withering glare at Michael. "This man is not like the others. He is..." The butler frowned, at a loss for a polite expression. "Sir, he smells as though he bathed in horse urine."

Michael wrinkled his nose. "Perhaps you'd better show him out. Can't have the whole bloody house stinking like piss."

"I tried," Smithers countered. "He claims you ordered him to come here. Even produced your card."

The only man Michael had given his card to was Kip Jared, and that had been in case he had news of Clowes.

"Damnation, why didn't you say so?" Michael hurried to the parlor, Smithers following at a more sedate pace.

As soon as Michael entered the room, Jared raised his fingerless-gloved hand to his head in a mock salute. "Mornin', Inspector. Told ye 'e'd want to see me, old man." The beggar waved his hand at Smithers. He hadn't bothered to tie up his arm.

He must be going to the gin joint after, not pandering on the streets. If Jared expected to receive payment from this visit, then he must have information on Clowes.

"What news do you have?" Michael sat down on the settee, ignoring the twist of his stomach. Whatever bad tidings the mendicant brought, he'd handle it.

"What's the rush, mate?" Jared yawned, sprawling out in the armchair. "Can't we stay awhile? Take some tea? My belly's been rumblin'. It's 'ard work out there."

Smithers snorted. "The only work you've ever done—"

Rolling his eyes, Michael held up a hand to stop Smithers from arguing. The last thing he needed was for Jared to whine for the next hour about ill-treatment by the police.

"One cup of tea. We'll talk while Smithers brews it." He

gestured to the door and ignored Smithers's exaggerated sigh as the butler exited the room.

"Bit uppity for a servant, ain't 'e?" Jared crossed one stained leg over the other, his sludge-encrusted boots sinking into the ornate rug.

Oh, you have no idea.

Michael tapped his foot impatiently. "If you don't start talking soon, I'd be delighted to have my 'uppity servant' toss you out into the street."

"Now, now, we don't need none of that." Jared shook his head emphatically. "I 'ear things, remember? And like ye said, I been listenin' to the men talkin' at the factory on White Lion."

"The old Larker place, yes," Michael said. Abigail's sister still worked there. "The new owners are supposedly legitimate."

"I ain't got no idea of that." Jared shrugged. "But I been watchin' this one cub, Randal Russell. A real up-and-comer, they say, takin' over where them Larkers left off. That's just gibber—there's always been somebody wantin' that damn territory—but I 'eard 'im say somethin' 'bout yer Clowes."

Michael leaned forward. "What did he say?"

Jared cocked his head to the side, stroking his scratchy chin as if trying to remember. "Can't recall. Maybe a biscuit would unlock me mind. Man gets famished, ye know."

Michael clenched his fists to refrain from throttling him. While Jared wasted his time, Clowes could be wreaking havoc upon London. "I swear to God if you don't tell me, Jared, I'm going to make sure you're hanged."

"Fine, fine, no biscuit," Jared grumbled. "I remember it now. I was at Ten Bells, and I 'ad a wee nip too much, so I ended up back in the alley spewin' me guts. Young Randy was there too, with a bunch of his mates. They been cast out for bein' too noisy."

Michael stifled a groan. Of course, his entire case would hinge on a false beggar vomiting in the back of an alley. Christ, could his luck get any worse?

"So, they don't notice me," Jared continued. "Ye'd be surprised what a man can get away with when everybody thinks 'e's just some dumb old codger." Jared winked, and again Michael had the feeling the beggar was far smarter than he'd originally assumed. "Randy says, 'e's goin' on 'oliday, paid for by Clowes."

He remembered Clowes's note: *You're never gonna stop me. I'll always win.* God, he'd hoped the threat meant Clowes was out of the country. Yet the phrasing of the words could just easily indicate the bastard was taunting them before he made his attack.

The sinking feeling in Michael's stomach now equated to a steel anchor. "Did he say where he was going?"

Please don't say Ireland.

"Land o' the Paddies." Jared's nose turned up. "Can't fancy why meself. Bloody bunch of bogtrotters. Who'd wanna go there?"

Michael gripped the arm of the chair, his nails digging into the fabric. "You're certain?"

Jared appeared insulted. "I might've been foxed, but I got me good ears. Cub said Ireland, and I don't mean the tiny land by way of St. Giles."

"Son of a bitch." Releasing his grip on the chair, he massaged the pressure points on the side of his head. He needed to remain calm. Detached. Logical. "What does Randy look like?"

Smithers entered with the tea, effectively ending the conversation. Jared blustered through Smithers serving his tea, demanding four lumps of sugar.

"Enough," Michael demanded as Jared gestured for his sixth splash of cream. "Your bloody tea isn't even tea anymore. Tell me what Randy looks like. Could he pass for Clowes?"

Jared settled back in the chair, sipping his tea delicately. The bounder might as well have his pinkie up in the damn air.

"Now." Michael's tone was so lethal even Smithers snapped to attention.

Hastily, Jared swallowed his drink. "Suppose so, yes. 'Bout the same weight and both of 'em be tall. Hair's the same too, I'd say."

"God's balls," Michael ground out. "The bastard's loose on the damn world, and we got fooled. Again."

"That's luck for ye." Jared shrugged. "I still get my blunt, right? I got bills to pay."

"As if you would actually pay your debts," Smithers retorted.

"I could 'ave paid some of 'em," Jared argued. "I could 'ave some real vowels. Ye don't know what I 'ave."

As they bickered beside him, Michael's whole world whirled on its axis. He didn't need quill and paper to recognize that Randall Russell had taken Clowes's place on the steamer to Ireland.

Damn it all! He shouldn't have let Abigail leave. His calculations had indicated that Clowes wouldn't leave the country without tying up loose ends—namely him, Knight and his wife, and Abigail. It was simply a matter of probabilities.

Michael swore under his breath. Just like when Knight had first come to him with the Larker case, he'd brushed aside his experience in favor of the easier answer.

You're never gonna stop me.

But he would stop Clowes. He had no choice. When it came to Abigail's welfare, he'd protect her at all costs, even if it meant his own life. He'd promised her he'd guard her, and instead, he'd allowed her to flee—maybe straight into the arms of a murderer.

He had to find her.

Springing up from his chair, he interrupted Smithers mid-rejoinder. "I've got to get to Abigail. She could be in trouble."

That was all Smithers needed to forget the argument with Jared. "I'll get my gun." He scurried from the room.

"So, me blunt?" Jared asked, holding out his hand.

Michael threw some coins into the man's hand. When Jared went to sit back down in the chair and finish his tea, Michael grabbed his elbow, towing the beggar from the room with him. He sprinted with Smithers to the hack station, arriving just as a cab pulled up. Bounding into the cab, he ordered the driver to Whitechapel, with an extra fare to come if he made it quick.

Abigail would not pay the price for his failure again.

NOTHING FELT RIGHT anymore. Not the flat where she'd grown up, not the Ten Bells where she'd had her first sip of gin at three years old, not the path she used to travel to the factory. No matter where Abigail went in Whitechapel, the falseness of her own existence struck her.

She belonged in neither the gritty rookeries nor the respectable Cheapside.

Even time with her sister was strained now. Too many lies lay between them. She'd managed to field Bess's inquiries on her whereabouts so far. Eventually, she'd run out of easy answers or get trapped in a falsehood.

While the frozen rose had pleased her, Bess sensed something was strange about Abigail's behavior since her return. The night before, she'd fetched Abigail a bowl of broth warmed on the hearth and said she hoped it took away the chill. Abigail had thanked her, preferring Bess to think she felt ill—it was a less upsetting story than the truth.

With Bess in mind, Abigail set out for the market. It was Tuesday afternoon, so the majority of vendors would be looking to unload their less palatable food before it soured. She'd be able to bargain with the merchants she knew personally. If Abigail brought Bess a penny pie, she might be convinced that everything was back to normal.

She passed the Infirmary for Asthma, Consumption, and Other Diseases of the Chest, waving at one of the nurses as she continued up Paternoster Road to the southern entrance of the market on Crispin Street. Weaving around the carts and benches set up outside the walls, she arrived inside.

The cruciform market-house stood in the center of the square, framed by four L-shaped buildings with individual courtyards. Houses faced either the surrounding streets or the inner market-place. Though the market-house was but a single story with an added attic, Abigail had always found it ominous, for the four wings had no windows, plain sides, and a domed roof. The clock face built into a rectangular turret ticked mercilessly, counting down the minutes until she'd have to face Michael again.

Four more days. He'd said he'd come for her in four more days.

How could she possibly come to grips with everything that had passed between them in such a short amount of time? She couldn't.

Surveying the busy market, she decided to start with the closest building, where her father's friend Smythe leased a fruit stall. She hobbled into the chaos, expertly navigating through the stalls packed to the brim with merchandise. The market noise was deafening, but to Abigail, this was a second home. Neighbors gabbed with a butcher while frolicking children almost upset the balance of a girl with a bushel of flowers in her arms. With her cloak billowing, her black gloves back on her hands, Abigail could vanish in this market.

No one would be the wiser. That anonymity had appealed to her after the incident.

Then she remembered the intensity of Michael's gaze. The knowledge that finally, after a lifetime of being inconspicuous, someone had seen her for who she really was.

Suddenly obscurity wasn't so attractive.

"Abigail?" A woman's voice startled her from her reverie. "Abigail, is that you?"

Abigail turned as the woman touched her shoulder. *Poppy.* If only she'd kept walking! Too late now. Not only was Poppy affirmed of her identity, but the child holding her hand reached for Abigail.

"I was on my way out," Abigail insisted lamely. "Places to be, you know."

"Abigail, please," Poppy implored, her suppliant eyes never leaving Abigail's face.

God, how Abigail hated Poppy's eyes. The color of sparkling emeralds, Poppy's gaze captivated her, made her want to comply with whatever Poppy asked. Even if it meant going against everything Abigail held dear.

So she stood still. The noise of the crowd became a dull roar, replaced by the sound of Poppy's voice. The previous six months faded. She was flung back into the past, skipping home from the factory with Poppy's one-year-old daughter, Moira, clinging to her hand. Bess had always walked with Poppy, prattling on about her day.

"I've missed you," Poppy said.

"So have I," Abigail blurted, regretting the words when Poppy's face lit up. "It doesn't change anything."

Poppy's grin disappeared. "How long are you going to stay angry with me, Abbie?"

Abigail glanced pointedly at her injured hand. "As long as I bear these scars, so I'd say for eternity."

Poppy let out a frustrated sigh, whatever she'd been about to say forgotten as Moira tore free of her mother's hold.

Moira flung herself at Abigail. "Abbie!"

Reflexively, Abigail bent to embrace the girl as she had so many times before. When she went to pull away, Moira clutched at the back of Abigail's dress, keeping her captive. For a second, Abigail considered prying her tiny fingers loose but then discounted the idea.

Of all of them, only Moira was innocent in this ordeal. She was but a child—she couldn't understand why Abigail had disappeared from her life. Carding a hand through Moira's red hair, Abigail held the girl close to her. Moira chattered on, unaware this embrace would be their last.

Uneasiness flittered across Poppy's fair face as she watched them. "I can't apologize to you anymore, Abigail."

Poppy's firm but low voice, with its Surrey lilt and the cadence of her Irish relatives, affected something in Abigail's heart. Whether or not Abigail wanted to admit it, she'd always admired Poppy's quiet grace. Her smooth gait was unmarred by the factories, for Poppy had grown up on a farm in Surrey. While she was hampered by bitterness and sorrow, Poppy had braved troubled waters and been rewarded with Knight's love.

Abigail would never have that same happiness with Michael. Regardless of how much she missed him, the dissonance between them couldn't be repaired.

She rose, patting Moira's back. "I wouldn't accept your apology anyhow."

"Oh, Abbie, I wish you wouldn't speak so. In the beginning, I thought I deserved your wrath. I did." Sadness dripped from Poppy's tone. "I was willing to let you rant and rave about how I'd caused this. I thought that was what I deserved for emerging untouched while you were scarred."

"It *is* what you deserve," Abigail interrupted, though she'd started to question the veracity since the night she'd poured her heart out to Michael.

His words came back to her. *Place the blame where it lies and nowhere else.*

Looping her hand in Moira's, Poppy gave her a gentle tug. Moira released Abigail's dress, toddling back to Poppy. Mother and daughter stood side by side, mirror images that haunted Abigail.

"I know you're angry at the world," Poppy said. "But I tried to get justice for Anna. Our friend. I wanted her family to know her killer had been punished. I don't deserve your continued hatred for that. I want us to be friends again."

"You should have left the case to the Peelers," Abigail said. She turned her back on Poppy and retreated, narrowly missing a stall full of potatoes.

Moira babbled after her, but Abigail tried to block out the sound.

"I should have." Poppy's voice carried. Just like no matter how far she ran, memories of Poppy would always follow her. "And if I could go back in time and change that, I would, but I can't. I made a mistake. But I wasn't the one who tortured you. It wasn't me, Abbie."

Abigail spun around, insults ready on her tongue. Yet as she locked eyes with Poppy, she couldn't form the words. She was so tired of clinging to her hatred. So tired of living in the dark.

"No matter what you want to believe, I did not shove your hand in that loom." Poppy stepped closer to her, her own

273

perfect hand outstretched. "All I've wanted these past six months is to be your friend again."

Abigail looked from Poppy to Moira and back again. She thought of the dreams she'd had, where Poppy was the one brutalizing her. Dreams did not make a reality. When she wished for things to be different between her and Michael, they did not magically become so.

Clowes had left the country. He could not hurt her again.

Michael had shown her light before he'd betrayed her trust. A new life, if only Abigail could break the chains of this one. But could she forgive Poppy? Could she pardon Michael?

People hurried by, directing glares and curses at them for clogging the aisle. Still, they lingered, within arm's reach of each other, yet so far from the easy carefreeness they'd had before. Maybe they could never get back their old friendship.

"I want to move on," Abigail murmured. "I want so badly to forgive."

Tentatively, Poppy bridged the distance between them. Abigail held out her hand, and Poppy took it, squeezing tight. They stood there in silence, not daring to speak until Moira let out a giddy shriek. Latching onto the hem of her apron, Moira cleaved to Abigail's side. Laughing, Abigail squatted, lifting Moira up into her arms.

"You've grown so big," Abigail marveled, shifting the toddler so that she was squarely on her hip.

"Growing like a weed, Thaddeus says." Poppy smiled. "I was going to visit Petticoat Lane after this and pick through the clothing stalls. She's too big for most of her clothes."

Abigail bounced Moira up and down, grinning at the girl's squeals of joy. What would it be like to have a child with Michael? She imagined walking the market hand-in-hand with a tot Moira's age, with Michael's eyes and his infuriatingly symmetrical face. He'd be a good father, determined not to perpetuate the cycle the Old Bastard had started.

"Can I ask you something?" When Poppy nodded, she continued, "How did you know Thaddeus was the right man for you?"

"Because he saw the real me," Poppy said without hesitation. "He was kind and generous, and he didn't care about my past."

Abigail considered this. Michael had viewed her scars and didn't think she was marred by them. He'd arranged that ball simply because she'd said she'd never been to one. Repeatedly, he'd gone out of his way to make sure she had everything she needed.

He'd given her a choice. Leave the darkness behind and stay with him or surrender to the hurts of the past. He'd made a mistake in ignoring the Larker case, but *he* hadn't been the one to torture her. If she detached herself entirely from the case—if she closed her eyes so she couldn't see her hand—she could even understand why he hadn't taken the case.

That didn't make what he'd done right.

Neither of them could change the past. He shouldn't have lied to her about when he'd become involved in the investigation. That hurt her, perhaps more than his initial ignorance, because when he'd lied, it had been to her face. She'd been there before him, real and broken, and he'd fed her an uncomplicated answer.

But he regretted his actions. She didn't doubt that. She recalled the anguish splashed across his face, how his voice had broken when he'd asked her to stay with him. In the course of their two weeks together, they'd both changed. The man he'd been when she first met him—the man so concerned with his own desires—had transformed before her.

I love you, Abigail. I am not a perfect man. But around you, I become something more.

They were both at fault. She'd stewed over the hurt for the last six months, lashing out at anyone who tried to reach her. Yet he made her want to be better, just as he claimed she'd done with him.

If they were willing to make mistakes, to stay with each other even when they were not at their best, wouldn't that be the true test of love? She could accept that he was flawed, and he'd endeavor to make amends for his past errors. In accepting him, she'd gain that same level of empathy from him. She didn't have to be perfect around him. She only needed to be herself.

Just as she used to feel she was understood by Poppy. God, she missed their friendship.

"I think I've found that man," Abigail said. "I've been in hiding with Inspector Strickland."

"Because of Clowes," Poppy supplied, as though that were the only reason, when Abigail was reasonably sure Michael had told her about the debt.

Abigail smiled gratefully. "These past two weeks have been the best of my life."

Poppy let out a happy squeal so high-pitched, Moira wasted no time echoing it. "Oh, Abigail, I'm so glad to hear that." She paused, her forehead crinkling. "Then what are you doing here? Why aren't you in Cheapside?"

Abigail took a deep breath. "I ran. I...I'm not sure how to put the past behind me. How can I be with him if he knew about the Larkers? And then he didn't tell me about his real participation in the case."

Moira tugged on the hem of her dress, babbling happily. Abigail placed her gloved hand in the little girl's much smaller palm. When Moira was around, she had a hard time remembering why she was upset about anything—the child's enthusiasm was catching.

Poppy watched them with a wide smile. "I'm not saying what he did was right, but if he'd told you originally, would you have felt at ease in his home?"

"Of course not," Abigail replied. "I'd have hated him just like the rest of the bloody Peelers."

"Then I'm guessing that's why he didn't tell you." Poppy's nose wrinkled as she thought. "Knowing Strickland, he probably figured he'd never see you again after these two weeks. He's never been the most..." She endeavored to find the right phrasing. "Committed to the long-term."

"He asked me to marry him," Abigail told her. "And I had accepted."

"To *marry* him?" Poppy squeaked. She rushed forward, wrapping both Moira and Abigail in a giant embrace. "Oh, Abigail! I never thought I'd see the day Michael Strickland married. But it's you, so I shouldn't be surprised. Obviously, he sees how special you are.'"

Abigail blushed as Poppy pulled back from the clinch. She'd forgotten how much Poppy believed in her. She set Moira down. "You've always been convinced I'm something grand."

"Because you are," Poppy said with absolute conviction.

Abigail tugged on her glove, remembering how it felt to be without the silk. How loved she'd felt in Michael's arms. How content she'd been. "I want to forgive him. I do. But..."

Poppy nodded. "It's going to be hard. Yet if you don't go to him, won't you regret it?"

She would. She'd regret it every damn day of her life. Losing Poppy and Moira had hurt, but losing Michael would sever her heart in two. Without him, everything dimmed. The things she'd enjoyed were no longer quite so fulfilling because he wasn't there to talk about it with her.

"Go to him now," Poppy urged. "Let no time waste. You deserve to be happy, Abbie."

"You're right," Abigail said. Poppy had been right all along—she'd just been in too much damn pain to see it. Thanking her, she gave Poppy a quick hug and Moira a kiss and then hurried from the stall.

It would take some time to feel completely comfortable with Poppy again, but hopefully, she'd be able to make things right with Michael. He'd promised not to give up on her.

She prayed that he still felt that way.

Chapter Twenty-Three

Michael hadn't been able to find Abigail. She wasn't at home, at the Ten Bells, or waiting around the factory to walk her sister home. He'd gone with Smithers to the Knights to warn them of Clowes's deception. Knight had set out immediately to retrieve Poppy and Moira from the market.

But that didn't help Michael. Unfortunately, Knight hadn't seen Abigail for some time either.

Their last stop had been to Wood Street. His sergeants were back on high alert, and Michael had requested that Hume and Jeffries come to his townhouse to set in place further security. Once he found Abigail, he intended to move her back in here, whether or not she agreed. This was home territory. He'd have the advantage.

Smithers smacked his hands together as they entered and went into the parlor. A frown darkened his weathered face. "I'll go put on the kettle. Least you'll be warm as you tear Whitechapel apart looking for Miss Vautille."

Michael nodded his thanks, pulling off his gloves and tossing them onto the table. Crossing to the window, he pushed back the blinds to survey the street. The only sight he wanted to see was a hack pulling up with Abigail inside of it. With all other options exhausted, he figured he'd camp on Abigail's stoop until she eventually came home.

If she came home.

He wouldn't blame her if she left Whitechapel. With the money he'd stuck in her apron pocket, she could flee with Bess. She could finally have something worthy of her.

How could he have been so damn blind? He should have told her from the start how he'd visited her in the hospital. Instead of being mad at him, she might have appreciated him coming to see her. With Abigail, nothing went as expected—he liked that about her. She challenged him. She was proud, vivacious, and so utterly full of life. She reminded him of the easy delight he'd felt as a foot patroller, content to be out in the elements, free of the classroom. Somewhere during his rise in the Met, he'd forgotten the simple joy of life. Of being understood by another person. Of no longer hiding behind a roguish veneer.

The world had been theirs to change, if only she'd stayed.

Smithers's yell echoed through the house. "Oh, God, no. Strickland, come outside quickly!"

Mrs. O'Neal and Cook met him in the hall, but he ordered them to stay inside the house. Following Smithers's voice, Michael bolted toward the garden. He found the butler squatted in the snow, the back door flung open. Sprawled out before Smithers was the prone form of a man dressed in blue, the bronze buttons on his uniform splattered with crimson.

Michael knelt down beside the corpse. One of the foot patrollers assigned to the house, though the man's face had been disfigured so brutally he could only hazard a guess as to the patroller's identity.

"Christ." Bile seized Michael's throat. He swallowed it back down, composing himself.

The gaping wound in the man's stomach was probably what had killed him. He'd been disemboweled. Michael held a handkerchief to his nose to staunch the sickening stench of the man's intestines, pulled out from his body.

Blood streamed from the man's broken nose, crusted his cheeks, his split lips. Michael surmised that his face had been bashed in with a blunt weapon repeatedly, some of the wounds possibly delivered postmortem, fitting with the personality profile Knight had drawn up for Clowes. The killing wasn't enough for Frank Clowes—he viewed his victim's corpses as a canvas, and his mutilations were art.

"Bastard," Smithers cursed, scuffing his feet in the snow. He'd turned around, clutching his coat to him, as though he could ward off the evils of the world if he were properly outfitted.

Michael pushed himself up from the ground. He often witnessed death in his line of work, but that didn't make it easier. This patroller had perished, senselessly, needlessly, protecting *his* home.

Nodding at Smithers, Michael cast his gaze to the sky, mumbling a short prayer.

"That ain't gonna save his almighty soul, Sergeant."

Dread stopped Michael's heart. His hand flew to the truncheon sheathed at his side. In one fluid movement, he had the billystick in hand.

Frank Clowes emerged from a shaded alcove. The youth with the eager eyes he'd arrested was gone, replaced by the hardened brute who'd knifed his way through Newgate's worst factions.

Beside him, Smithers spun around. He gripped his flintlock rifle like a club. The gun wouldn't be accurate in close quarters, but Smithers's years in the Army had made him a skilled hand-to-hand combatant.

Michael was glad they'd fight together, for three burly men flanked Clowes. While he was skilled enough to fight multiple opponents, Clowes was highly unpredictable. His men were also armed. One had a lead pipe, while another smacked a cudgel against his palm.

Clowes advanced upon them. The silver dagger in his hand glinted in the dying sunlight. Dried blood coated the tip. "Inspector now, I'd forgot. 'Cuse me for not payin' you the respect you ain't deservin'."

Michael assessed Clowes coolly, buying time to plan an attack. "You didn't have to kill him. I would've come to you."

Clowes smirked, malevolent glee twisting his handsome features. "I'm not one for wasted opportunities. I'm free, you see? With the Larkers, I'd rules to follow. Ain't nobody to chain me now."

"You're your own man," Michael mused. He shifted his weight from one foot to the other, the movement bringing him almost imperceptibly closer to Smithers. "You could go anywhere. Hell, even if you'd taken that steamer to Ireland, we wouldn't have followed you. Not enough men for a full-scale pursuit."

"Why would I do that?" Clowes traced the jagged scar across his cheek with the knife. He gestured to the man at his side. "Everything I been wantin' is here. Right, Hittles?"

Clowes's man nodded eagerly.

Out of the corner of his eye, Michael saw Smithers brace for attack. He inclined his head, tapping two fingers to his leg. Smithers would take the two men on the right, leaving Clowes and his associate for Michael.

"What is it you want?" Michael asked, keeping the conversation flowing.

If they attacked first, they'd have the advantage.

"I want to bring pain." Clowes dug the tip of the knife into his own flesh, just enough that blood pebbled at the surface, causing the mark to turn white. "You're weak, Inspector. I'll harden you. Craft you into somethin' more."

Another droplet of cerise slid down his face. "Then I'm gonna finish my work on that dirty drab. You took her from me, you and Effie Larker, and I ain't *finished* yet." He caught the blood on his tongue, grinning.

Michael surged forward. Smithers was a step behind him. The men on the right took off farther into the garden. Smithers ran off after them. Left on his own with Clowes and Hittles, Michael felt the change in the air. This fight had been inevitable, from the moment Clowes had chosen Abigail as his next victim.

Swinging out with his truncheon, Michael connected with Clowes's side. Clowes stumbled but did not go down. The knife fell out of his hands, and Michael kicked it away from him before parrying an attack from Hittles.

He bounced on the balls of his feet. A moving target was harder to hit. He couldn't stay in one place, couldn't let his back get exposed to the other men.

Fending off jabs, Michael thrust out with the truncheon, connecting with flesh—of which man, he was no longer sure. Hittles advanced, but Michael held him off with a fist to the jaw. He blocked a wild haymaker punch from Clowes with his elbow, swinging around to smack the truncheon into the man's knees. Instead of hurting Clowes, the hit only invigorated him.

Clowes's fists came down upon Michael, beating into his chest, his arms, anywhere that he could direct a blow. Pain shot through his body, blistering, agonizing pain. He heard Clowes caw with triumph, the very sound shattering any hesitation he might have had about this fight to the death. There was no Met to defend him here. He'd hurt, he'd bleed, and he'd die unless he fought dirty. His mind homed in one instinct: survival.

He let Clowes think he was beaten, all the while waiting for the perfect shot.

"Everybody before was so scared of Boz Larker. They never saw me comin'. Do you know what that's like? That power of bein' unexpected?" He motioned for Hittles to stay back, advancing upon Michael. "You went and took that from me, but I remade myself."

Clowes swung out. Michael sidestepped. At last, he was in position. He slammed the truncheon into Clowes's gut as hard as he could. Stunned, Clowes doubled over, clutching his stomach. Michael brought the truncheon soundly down onto his head, dropping the blackguard to the ground. Stepping over his prone body, Michael turned, confronting Hittles.

While Clowes had been trained on the streets of Whitechapel, Hittles lacked the impassioned cruelty of his master. His punches were a moment too slow. Michael easily avoided them. Hittles was a big man, not light on his feet; he intimidated but did not know how to parry. Dancing around him, Michael landed another solid crack to his legs and deflected the returning facer.

By God, he could actually win this! He stopped considering the angles and allowed himself to enjoy the fight. This was another round in the gymnasium, fighting against a newcomer. A smile slid on his lips as he jammed his elbow into Hittles's nose. Blood cascaded down his face. Yelling, Hittles cradled his nose in his open palms, trying to staunch the flow of blood.

Michael didn't see Clowes behind him until it was too late.

* * *

No one answered the door at Michael's house. The parlor curtains were drawn apart, so Abigail peered inside. Michael's gloves were on the table, and a fire burned in the hearth. She tried the door, but it was locked. Had he gone out? Maybe he was in the courtyard with Smithers. She circled around the house, coming to the back gate. She'd expected to find it closed. Instead, the door was wide open.

When Abigail stepped inside the garden, she'd hoped that Michael was here. That he'd forgive her. That he'd say they could be wed after all.

She hadn't expected to see Frank Clowes on the ground.

He was supposed to be in Ireland.

She was supposed to be *safe*.

But with Clowes on the ground, the threat lessened. Perhaps he was dead. Oh God, she hoped so, even if it made her wicked to wish for another man's demise. Please, Lord, let the suffering be over.

Transfixed, she watched as two men fought near Clowes's body. She didn't recognize the larger man, with his patched overcoat and striped scarf. His opponent was pummeling him. There was a crack, and blood poured from his nose.

The fighters shifted. The taller man now faced her direction. And she knew, even from this distance, that it was Michael. Knew it with every fiber of her being, for though she couldn't see his face clearly, his body was imprinted on her mind. She stayed where she was, not calling for him, afraid she'd disturb him, and he'd lose the advantage he had on his opponent.

Clowes shifted in the sludge. So slightly, she was not sure she'd seen it at first. As if her fear was bringing him back to life. But suddenly he stood, knife outstretched, and he sneaked toward Michael's back.

He would hurt Michael.

"Michael!" She screamed out his name, her tongue leaden in her mouth. But her voice wasn't strong enough. He didn't turn around, didn't acknowledge her.

She had to get to him. Holding her skirts up with one hand, Abigail sprinted forward, her half-boots sinking into the snow. She couldn't find easy footing; the continued cold temperatures had turned the slushy terrain into a treacherous mix of ice and hard snow. Yet still, she ran, tripping and pulling herself back up. She ignored the ache in her shins, the creak of her knees.

Clowes lunged.

"Michael, look behind you! Please, Michael!" She kept screaming, her breaths uneven, her heart drumming in her ears.

As she rounded the corner, she saw him turn his head. His jaw dropped. Clowes stabbed. For a second, she couldn't tell if the knife had sliced into Michael. But there was blood, spewing blood, gushing blood, drowning out everything. He stood, his hand sliding up to the gash.

Michael's knees gave out, and he slunk to the ground, landing in a sodden heap. She ran toward him, bounding over an overturned tree branch. Her screams had alerted Smithers, who dashed to her from the other side of the garden, another man trailing him.

She didn't care about Clowes, about the danger to her. All she cared about was Michael. Saving him, loving him, protecting him. Let everything else go to hell, as long as Michael was alive. Falling to the ground beside him, she cradled his head in her lap.

He did not stir. His eyes remained closed.

"Please, no, you can't die," she cried. "I love you, Michael. I love you so much."

He breathed. The shallowest of breaths. He was alive, but she couldn't be sure for how long. He needed medical attention. She wrenched her gloves off, pressed them to the wound to try and lessen the blood loss. The stench of it stung her nostrils, sweet yet acidic, bringing her back to the two days she'd spent alone in her flat, bathed in her own blood, after Clowes had tortured her.

Out of the corner of her eye, she tracked Smithers's movements as he took on the remaining two of Clowes's men. The drumbeat of her heart had become cannon fire, the harbinger of war. As she reached for Michael's truncheon to face Clowes, his maniacal laughter filled the air.

She was taken back to that night. Being lifted up to the jacquard attachment at the top of the loom. The slam of her hand against those needles. The prick, the splice, the blood cascading. Blood was everywhere. It stung her.

His laughter echoed in her ears. While she'd suffered through these past six months as a shell of her old self, he hadn't changed. He was the same attractive bastard, pushing a lock of wavy hair out of his eyes. He had the same arrogant sneer.

"I've come back for you." He advanced upon her with the same carefree stride. "I'm gonna finish what I started, Abigail, and this time there's nobody interruptin' us. We'll do this nice and slow."

Michael's blood dripped onto the ground, but still, Clowes was not satisfied. He'd keep coming for them until they were dead, and even then, he'd probably dig up their damn corpses so he could torture them all over again. She'd feared facing him again, feared it more than anything else, but now that he was in front of her, she lost control.

The red overtook her. Mindless, bloody red. Every moment before had prepared her for this fury, this pounding red. She leaned her weight on the truncheon, pushing herself up from the ground.

She moved with speed she'd never known she had. She was no longer Beauty, no longer Abigail, but a demon of an entirely new nature. Brandishing the truncheon, she delivered a swift, strong smack to his chest. When he didn't flinch, she smacked him again.

He didn't fight back. He smiled.

"That's it," he coaxed her. "I'll teach you to embrace the pain."

"There is nothing you could show me," she grunted, slamming the truncheon into his shoulder. "I already know everything there is to know about pain. My life *is* pain."

He caught the truncheon in his hand, jerking it back. Leaning in, he dropped his voice to a whisper. "You know I've killed him. It's what you deserve, you little bunter, thinkin' you could escape me before I finished with you."

In the blink of an eye, he had his hand on the truncheon. His grip was more powerful than hers. He gave a great push, and the billystick crashed against her midsection. Her breath knocked from her. Her eyes watered. She couldn't focus.

"No one gets away from me," he hissed. "I've been makin' plans for you. You'll be my finest creation. If you thought before was bad, you ain't seen me now."

Wresting the truncheon from her, he threw it to the ground. She dove for it, but he was too fast. He scooped her up, planting her back on her feet. He held her against him, her backside to his front, the knife pinned to her throat. He leaned against a stonewall.

Thrashing, she fought him. Tried to free herself from his hold. But his iron grip was too tight. He'd trapped her again. The realization crashed down upon her, stripping every other instinct away until she was overcome with helplessness.

With the point of the knife, he nicked her sensitive flesh, and then dragged the knife along her skin. "I could slit your throat here," he murmured. "You'd be such a pretty little thing.

You remind me of Anna Moseley. Did you know when Boz cut her, she begged for her life?"

"You sick bastard," she spat, even as the cold steel of the knife pressed into her. "She was just a girl."

"No one is just anythin', Abigail." He tutted her. He turned her slightly so that she faced Michael. "You see what I done there? He looks better, I think. Like he oughta been that way all along."

She couldn't tell if Michael was still breathing. Oh God, she didn't know if he was alive. Her shoulders shook with the effort to suppress her cries. She couldn't function.

Then came the pain. Clowes dug in the knife. She felt her blood trickling down her throat. Tears rained down her cheeks, the salt mixing with blood. Red, red, red. She'd forgotten how other colors looked. The world swam before her, and she wanted to fall, to give in to the agony because, at the end, she'd be nothing. In death, she'd find release.

His breath was hot, vile against her ear. "You're always gonna be my victim, Abigail."

Victim.

Over and over again, she'd been his victim. She'd torn apart her friendships, given up her one greatest love because of what he'd done to her. Even in gaol, Clowes had held her captive. Michael was possibly dead now, all because he'd tried to protect her. Smithers was off fighting two men, all to save her.

No more.

She was done being a victim.

With one great push backward, she rammed her elbows into Clowes's gut, shoving him back against the stonewall. His head smacked against the stone, startling him enough that he released her. She tore from his arms, sweeping up the abandoned truncheon in her uninjured hand. She swung with wild, reckless abandon at his head.

The clap of wood meeting bone resonated. Clowes slumped to the ground, broken and useless. But she didn't give him the chance to get up. She clobbered him repeatedly, tears flowing down her face, blurring her vision. Still, she slammed the truncheon down on his chest. Screams tore from her throat, indecipherable screams, raw rage coiled up so tight and finally released.

Strong arms encased her. She lashed out against the hold, but it was Smithers, calm, resolute Smithers, telling her the bounder was out of commission, and she needn't flog him further.

Sagging in his arms, Abigail let the truncheon slip from her fingers.

Chapter Twenty-Four

As soon as Smithers released her, Abigail ran back to Michael, settling in the snow beside him, careful not to upset him. Smithers was saying something—that the other assailant had turned tail and ran when he'd seen her pummeling Clowes—but none of that mattered because Michael's eyes were open. His breathing had stabilized.

"Oh my God, Michael," she gasped, seizing his hand in hers. He blinked up at her. "Abigail? I thought I saw you."

"I'm here. I love you. I was so wrong, Michael, so bloody wrong." She feathered kisses upon his knuckles, needing to touch him and reassure herself that he was truly alive. "I never should have left. It was stupid and bitter, and I'd understand if you don't forgive me, but God, I hope you do."

He reached for her, wincing in discomfort. She shook her head, telling him he should stay still.

Instead, he brushed his hand across her jaw. "I love you, too, you silly lass. You're all I've thought about. I'm a miserable sod without you."

She leaned down, kissing him. He tasted of blood and

combat. She'd never get enough of him. Never want to be anything but his.

"All I want is to be your wife," she whispered, drawing back from him. "To love you forever, no matter what bloody bad luck we might have. We're in this together until the end."

He pressed his hand to her good hand. "And I'll hold you close, no matter what. We've fought against a maniac. What more could happen?"

She smiled, squeezing his hand back. "Knowing us, nothing ordinary."

He winked, the mischievous rogue, flirtatious even in his darkest hour. "Mrs. Strickland, you shall be. It's about time we had some pretty in our line of lunatics."

Smithers coughed, pointing to the garden gates. Two Peelers raced across the snow, truncheons slapping against their legs and top hats bobbing. "Charming as this all is, sir, perhaps we ought to delay until your officers get their report? While Miss Vautille's glove was a nice field dressing, you'll need proper care."

"Of course," Michael agreed. He squeezed Abigail's hand. "We'll have plenty of time together, my love."

Abigail's heart filled at his words. They had the rest of their lives ahead of them. Together, they'd build new identities, each bolstering the other in times of sadness. She looked down at her injured hand, wrapped up in Michael's larger palm. Michael had seen her tattered soul, but he had not flinched. He cared not that she was part beast, part beauty. Instead, he understood that her scars were a part of her now, as much as her flaxen hair or her love of literature.

She could not change the past—and maybe she no longer wanted to, for that act of violence had brought her to Michael. It had made her stronger. Forced her to see that she could withstand anything.

She'd never be alone again.

* * *

ONCE MICHAEL WAS treated and dismissed from London Hospital, he went with Abigail to her flat. The driver let them off on the outskirts of Whitechapel, for the roads were too narrow to permit the hack. With her hand lightly placed on his arm, Abigail led him through back alleys, picking carefully around the piles of rubbish. Her pace never slowed, even as she wove around a man and his dog, both passed out in the middle of the pathway. Whenever they came upon someone she knew, she greeted them with a cheery smile and an inquiry about their family.

He'd loved her in his townhouse, exploring a whole new world, but he loved her even more in her natural surroundings. He imagined this was how she'd looked before the attack, confident and at ease. She directed him around one corner and into the street, expertly pulling him between two stopped carriages. A coster's cart had tipped over, making the road impassable. Two men hurriedly scooped up the fruit, depositing it back into the cart.

She grinned. "You've got to move quickly around here."

He winked at her. "I like to take my time when it comes to you."

Laughing, she took his hands in hers and tugged him down another thin path. They reached Baker's Row. A three-story tenement building flanked a crumbling courtyard with weeds poking out from the fragmented stones. The tenements divided into four sections, each with individual staircases.

A few children chased each other around, while others played in the dirt, as though this was an impressive garden and not a shambling ground better fit for demolition. He shoved his hands deep into the pockets of his coat, resisting the urge to look away. This was Abigail's home, and she loved it. He'd see the good in this place.

She took the stairs to the middle flat, sliding her key into the lock and opening the door. He hesitated at the entrance, but she hauled him inside with her.

"Bess? Bess, are you here?" she called, undoing the strings to her bonnet.

"Abbie!" A young girl burst into the room, flinging herself immediately at Abigail.

He'd know the girl as Abigail's sister in an instant, even without an introduction. She was the spitting image of Abigail, except for the fact that her hair was ginger. She had the same apple blossom cheeks, the same sparkling blue eyes, even the same defiant stance.

"Bess, I want you to meet someone." Abigail drew back from the embrace, reaching for his hand again. "This is Inspector Michael Strickland."

"Hello there." He bowed to her, giving her his most winning smile. If ever he'd wanted to make a good first impression, it was with Abigail's sister.

"A *Peeler*," Bess pronounced with absolute contempt. "Why are you bringing a pig into our home?"

Apparently, the Vautille women were destined to dislike him on sight.

"I'm not just a Peeler," he protested, not entirely sure how to react to a nine-year-old's disdain.

"When I went away, I met him." Abigail squeezed his hand, reassuring him that she wanted him here. "And I'm bringing him here because I wanted you to know we're betrothed."

Bess's eyes narrowed as she looked from her sister to Michael and back again. For a moment, neither she nor Abigail spoke. He observed their silent exchange curiously. Bess raised her eyebrows, and Abigail smiled in response.

"Are you happy?" Bess asked finally.

Abigail let out a chuckle, dropping Michael's hand to ruffle Bess's hair. "The happiest, Bessieboo. You don't have to worry about me anymore."

Bess pulled back, eying him with open skepticism, but her posture relaxed. "I'll be watching you," she told him solemnly. "Don't hurt my sister."

"I wouldn't dream of it," he told her, matching her serious tone.

"You two will do just fine. You're both bloody stubborn," Abigail declared. "Where is Papa?"

"In his room," Bess answered.

Abigail knocked on his door, entering after he answered. Bess followed her after, and Michael hung back in the doorway. Vautille sprawled on the bed, staring up at the ceiling. A toppled tin cup rested on a chest of drawers by his bedside, next to a plate with crumbs.

Vautille pushed himself up when they opened the door, swinging his legs around. His eyes were as red as they'd been in the gaming hell, but his hands did not shake as he gripped the side of the bed.

"Abbie, did you see the—" He stopped, catching sight of Michael. "What in the blazes are you doing here, Peeler?"

Bess opened her mouth to speak, but Abigail nudged her and pointed toward the door.

"Just a few minutes, I promise," Abigail said. "Then we'll talk more."

Bess departed. Michael stepped into the room, shutting the door behind him.

"Michael has asked me to marry him, and I've accepted,"

Abigail told her father. "It's done with, Papa. Clowes is gone. I'm happy."

Vautille blinked. He glanced up at the ceiling, as though it'd provide all the information he needed. But as in Cruikshank's, no easy answers came to him.

He centered on the second matter. "The bastard is gone?"

"I can personally attest to that," Michael said. "My team has him in custody. He's set to be executed next week."

"Praise the Lord," Vautille muttered. "Newgate was too good for him."

Abigail explained the events of the last two weeks to her father, glossing over the more sexual parts of her time with Michael. When she'd finished the story, Vautille stood. He held onto the bed for support, his body trembling. Abigail came forward, letting Vautille hug her.

"I'm so sorry," he murmured. "I should never have let you go."

Abigail drew back from Vautille, a flicker of sadness in her eyes as she surveyed him. "It worked out well, Papa. *This* time. I love Michael. But if the same were to happen again, and it was Bess on the line..."

"Never," Vautille vowed vehemently. "I would never."

Abigail shook her head. "I don't want to take that chance. I'd like Bess to come live with Michael and me. She'll get a chance to go to school."

Vautille eased himself back onto the bed. He reached for the tin cup, frowning when he found it empty. "You'll let me visit?"

Michael traded a glance with Abigail. She nodded.

"Of course," he said. "You're welcome in my home always."

Vautille sighed. "She should be with you."

"Thank you," Abigail said, pressing his hand in hers. She hurried out of the room, likely to talk with Bess. The girl would probably have a million questions, given Abigail's earlier descriptions of her inquisitive nature.

Forcing his fingers through his grimy gray hair, Vautille hunched on the bed. For a second, Michael considered following Abigail. He'd never been good in these situations— never known what to say. But this was Abigail's family, and though her father had failed her once, it had not been through outright malice. Vautille was sick. Not in the same way his own mother had been, but still ailing.

"I'll take care of them," he promised, knowing it was one promise he'd keep for the rest of his life. "I love your daughter, and I'm going to make damn sure she's happy. Bess, too, for she's my family now as well."

Vautille raised his head, locking eyes with Michael, his hazy glance focusing for a second. He did not speak. But he nodded. A swift, decisive nod. Michael turned and left the room, going to rejoin Abigail. Michael couldn't save Vautille from himself, any more than Abigail could, but at least he'd given him some solace.

Later that night, as Abigail slept beside him, he laid his arm over her and held her close to him. She was everything he'd never known he wanted, and now the very idea of being without her sent him reeling. Somehow, she'd filled up the darkest spaces within him with her brightness.

He'd be with one woman for the rest of his life, and that was exactly how he wanted it.

Always a rake, but now *her* rake.

* * *

ON THEIR WEDDING day, red was everywhere.

Abigail's dress was constructed from crimson and purple silk, found in a stall on Petticoat Lane, and remade by Poppy

297

into something beautiful and daring. She held a bouquet of red roses. Even the carpet she walked to the altar was red, a crushed velvet soft underfoot.

Red had become her liberation. She'd faced pain and suffering, and she'd come out on top. As she stood up in front of the priest, she sent up a silent prayer of thanks to the heavens. Michael, glorious Michael, held her hand—her hands free of gloves, for she had nothing left to hide from him.

It was a small service, with the only attendees being her sister, the Knights, and her father. Frances had declined their invitation. While Abigail was sad for Michael, he'd shrugged and said eventually she'd come around.

They said their vows without hesitation. His steadfast faith in their union strengthened her. Whatever obstacles they'd face in their married life, they'd face them together. These words were a formality, a public expression of the bond they'd already formed. Their real vows, the ones stamped upon her heart, were those they'd uttered in his garden. To cherish each other forever; to be there in times of fortune and ill luck.

No matter what their hand of cards revealed, they'd play the game until they won.

Epilogue

C*heapside, London*
December 12, 1837

Michael bounced his son in his arms, grinning when the little boy let out a loud giggle. Shifting Hugh so that the babe sat more on his hip, Michael pushed back the parlor room curtain and peered out. "What do you see outside? Is that a carriage?"

The babe, too young to know more than a few words, simply stared outside with wide eyes. Michael dropped a kiss on his crown, letting his cheek rest against the top of Hugh's head.

Abigail entered the room, a cup of tea in her good hand. Over the years, she'd been able to increase her strength in her left hand, but she still felt more confident carrying things with her right. She never wore gloves anymore. He didn't lament the loss of them, especially not when they retired to their bedroom for the night.

"Any sign of her yet?" Abigail called from the doorway.

"A carriage just arrived," he said, nodding toward the hack

that had pulled up. "But it's unmarked. Could be her or could be one of the neighbors."

"Hopefully, she'll get here soon. Poppy and Thaddeus will arrive in an hour." She made her way to him. Sipping the tea, she leaned over his shoulder to look out the window. "Come on now, open the door. What's taking the driver so long?"

Just as the driver bounded from his stand onto the street, a child's shriek resounded through the house. "Momma!"

As usual, they heard their four-year-old daughter before they could see her. They both turned back around. Lily sprinted into the room, one foot clad in a black patent leather shoe, and the other still wearing only a stocking. Smithers trailed behind her, fruitlessly waving her right shoe.

"I tried, Mrs. Strickland," Smithers explained, extending the shoe to Abigail. "But Miss Lily has a mind of her own."

Abigail set her cup of tea down on the table and took the shoe. "Why don't you want to wear your shoes, Lily?"

"I don't like them," Lily announced, giving Smithers an arch look. "I can't run in them."

"Lil, you know you're not supposed to run in the house," Michael reminded her, as he stifled a laugh from Smithers's harassed expression. The old butler acted annoyed, but everyone knew he loved the children almost as much as Michael and Abigail did.

"You said not to run in the *hall*," Lily corrected. "It wasn't the hall. It was the kitchen."

Michael exchanged a glance with Abigail. "This is all on you, love. She inherited your love of the particular."

"You correct a man once on the time of day, and you go down in infamy as meticulous," Abigail complained good-naturedly. She stooped down, sliding the shoe back onto Lily's foot, much to her daughter's chagrin. "Don't you want to look nice for your aunt?"

Michael readjusted the collar of Hugh's shirt. "Even Hugh looks dashing."

Hugh gurgled an incoherent response to that, waving his chubby little hand at his sister.

"Fine, I'll wear shoes," Lily grumbled with as much consternation as if they'd asked her to wear a hair shirt. After putting her shoe back on, she wove her way around the furniture, coming to stand at the window. Reaching up, she tickled her brother's foot.

Hugh laughed again. Though it had been only five years since they married, Michael had a hard time remembering what life had been like before. When he wasn't at the Met, he was home with his family.

Abigail lifted Hugh from his arms. Michael knelt down next to Lily, scooping her up in his arms. Soon she'd be too big for him to pick up—but for now, he'd relish the sound of her laughter as he held her up in the air, moving her around as though she were flying.

The doorknocker sounded through the house, interrupting their tableau. Smithers dashed to go answer the door, but in a few seconds, a welcome voice echoed through the house. "Is anyone home?"

"Auntie Bess!" Lily cried, running out into the hall.

"At least this time she kept on both shoes," Abigail murmured, as they followed Lily out into the hall. They stood back from the gathering for a minute, letting Lily embrace her aunt.

Bess had come home for the holiday break from Miss Huntingdon's Finishing School. Clothed in a turquoise traveling dress and a jaunty hat, he would barely have recognized the stylish adolescent as the little girl who'd worked in the factories. Bess had blossomed at school, exhibiting quite a talent for drawing.

"You know what your sister's return means," he whispered in Abigail's ear, sliding his palm around to cup her arse while no one was looking.

She shifted closer to him. "We'll have someone to watch the children."

He gave her rear a firm squeeze. "And I intend to use that time to make sure you're *thoroughly* pleasured."

She shushed him as Bess approached, but her grin told him she'd appreciated the flirtation. The years together hadn't decreased their love—or their lust—for each other. Being with Abigail was still the best damn experience he'd ever had. As he looked around the room at their little family, he couldn't imagine a better life than this one.

He was the luckiest of men.

* * *

Did you miss Poppy and Thaddeus's love story? You'll want to read SECRETS IN SCARLET!

And next up in the Rookery Rogues, meet star-crossed lovers Mina Mason and Charlie Thatcher as their passion ignites a gang war reaching across all of East London.

Author's Note

The story of Beauty and her Beast has appealed to me ever since childhood. As an awkward, bookish girl, I wondered when someone would truly appreciate the real me. I must have watched the Disney movie a hundred times. At the very core of Beauty and the Beast is the friendship that builds between the two protagonists. Though Beauty is initially hesitant to spend time at the castle—unsurprising, given the circumstances of her arrival—she starts to see the Beast in a different light the more time she spends with him. After a while, he is no longer this scary creature, but instead a man she's come to love.

While the central focus of most of the folk iterations of Beauty and the Beast is on the Beast's transformation, the stories tend not to characterize Beauty beyond her obvious aesthetic appeal. I think that's why I've always loved the Disney version the best: it shows that both Belle and Beast are affected by their newfound relationship. Beast is no longer trapped in his past pain, and Belle has finally found someone who thinks she's incredible just the way she is.

I find this is a central theme in every romance I write. To me, true love is about acceptance. It's about seeing the complete beauty of a person. That's why Beauty and the Beast has always been my favorite: their love becomes something more. It is not based solely on visual appreciation, but instead a bond between two souls.

There are several commonalities in the iterations that I chose to incorporate into writing this book. The basic premise that Beauty must enter this deal with Beast because of something her father has done. The presence of siblings: though in most texts, only Beauty has two sisters, I chose instead to give both Strickland and Abigail sisters. Beauty returns home and then realizes she loves the Beast. And of course, there are a few scenes I snuck in as direct homages to the movie version.

When Abigail Vautille popped onto the page in *Secrets in Scarlet,* I knew that she needed a happily ever after. Her scars made her believe she's the Beast, and she must learn to love herself again. Michael Strickland, who also debuted in *Secrets in Scarlet,* captivated me from the beginning with his devil-may-care attitude. While Michael is physically attractive, he has a lot to learn about life and love. In this sense, then Abigail and Michael are both the Beast, and at times they're both Beauty. This dichotomy interested me. I think we all go through moments where we are either beastly or beautiful; we are never just one thing. It is our flaws that make us beautiful, as much as our strengths.

This novel contains my first depiction of a real-life person in the scene with Superintendent Thomas Bicknell, who really did lead the H-Division of the Metropolitan Police at this time. All characterizations of Bicknell as a bumbling egotist are mine and mine alone, bearing no historical relevance and added simply for story enrichment.

Beauty and the Rake also draws on historical setting details from the East London areas of Cheapside, Whitechapel, and Spitalfields. Between the repeal of the Spitalfields Weaving

Acts in the 1820s and the advent of the Industrial Revolution, many Huguenot weavers like Abigail's family found themselves without work, for there was no longer any need for the hand-weaving techniques they'd perfected over many decades. For Abigail and Bess's work in the factories, I tried to stay as histori-cally accurate as possible—though I know I took liberties with how the jacquard loom could be used as a torture device.

Today, Spitalfields still remains a vibrant community rich in culture. I have tried to stick as close to the actual street layout and locations of shops, etc. that was relevant in 1832—though of course, some errors may occur in my placement, for many streets have changed names throughout the years. The Ten Bells public house still exists at the corner between Fournier Street and Commercial Street in Spitalfields, and it is most remembered in history for being across the street from Jack the Ripper's murder of Mary Kelly (found in Miller's Corner, Dorset Street). And while still the Crispin Street Market is still active today, the clothing markets in Petticoat Lane are sadly no longer in exis-tence. The Chelsea Bun-House mentioned by Abigail was indeed a real shop that closed in 1839. According to a late nine-teenth century map of London, there really was a factory located on White Lion Street, though whether or not it was a weaving factory is anyone's guess.

I greatly enjoyed doing the research for this book, and I hope that it adds a feeling of authenticity to your reading.

Acknowledgments

This book could not have been published without the assistance of the following individuals, for whom I am exorbitantly grateful.

Many thanks go to Emma Locke and Kristine Wyllys for their intensive edits on multiple drafts of this book. Also to Erica Ridley, Emma Barry, and Tracey Devlyn for reading early drafts of this book and offering up their critiques. Eileen Richards, Gaylin Walli, and Lori Macc also assisted with plot elements. I am so thankful for your wisdom.

To my editor, Meghan Hogue, who always squeezes me in on a tight deadline and never seems to mind when my books end up being way over my estimated word count.

To my husband, Kevin, for tirelessly supporting me through all my "author moments," like when I rapid-fire alternate between declaring that this book will devour my soul, and I'm the most brilliant woman alive. Your belief in my ability to move mountains sustains me.

To my mother, for demanding Abigail's story, and to Amy Jo Cousins and Rebecca Paula for insisting Strickland's needed to be written as well. Your wish is my command.

To the family and friends I cancelled upon because I was up against the wire with this deadline, I'm sorry and thanks for still loving me.

And lastly, to my readers—I am so very, very blessed to have you. I appreciate your kind messages, e-mails, and tweets. It still astounds me that you actually *want* to read my words. Thanks to you, I have the job I've dreamed of since my childhood.

The Rookery Rogues

Beauty and the Rake is the third book in The Rookery Rogues. While each book reads as a stand-alone, the series is best enjoyed in chronological order. Joined by the poorest neighborhoods in London, called rookeries, the heroes and heroines in this series defy social expectations and find love in the darkest of circumstances.

A Dangerous Invitation (Kate and Daniel)
Secrets in Scarlet (Poppy and Thaddeus)
Beauty and the Rake (Abigail and Michael)
Stealing the Rogue's Heart (Mina and Charlie)

Read on for an excerpt from *Stealing the Rogue's Heart*

An Excerpt from Stealing the Rogue's Heart

Where *West Side Story* meets East End London with star-crossed lovers Mina Mason and Charlie Thatcher

Ratcliffe Rookery, London, England
     1833

Mina Mason perched on a barstool in the Three Boars public house. Every Friday night for the past four years, she'd sat on this seat, her slipper-clad feet barely reaching the bottom rung. For Mina, this stool—a dilapidated oak with three legs that had long ago seen better days—was more welcoming than any of the plush, absurdly expensive armchairs in her brother's sprawling townhouse. Here, deep in the heart of the Ratcliffe rookery, she wasn't a princess locked in a tower.

She was simply Mina, a woman with her own desires and life.

And so, every week, for three hours, Mina would come here and escape from her sheltered existence. She'd pretend she was like everyone else here, even if one of Joaquin's men sat across the room, watching her every move. His gang, the Kings, was such a constant presence in her life that most of the time, she ignored them. It was easier than arguing with her brothers.

She darted a glance toward Joaquin's man, Isaac, in the back of the room. He'd been her guard for the last year, though his presence was largely unnecessary. The guard before him had insisted on sitting next to her. Isaac, however, agreed she didn't need such close observance.

She liked Isaac for that reason.

She'd never run into trouble here. While the Three Boars was considered a meeting house of the rival Chapman Street Gang, she didn't have anything to do with her brother's organization. Surely, there'd be no reason for the men to think she was a threat. According to them, she was a mere chit who did not need to know the business of important men.

But she did understand enough of the world for a slow smile to form on her lips when a strumpet sidled up to Isaac, whispering something in his ear. In a flash, Isaac pulled the strumpet onto his knee, where she balanced with practiced ease. Mina's smile turned into a full-fledged grin.

That was the beauty of Isaac—he was easily distracted.

Maybe she'd get some time away from Joaquin's control, after all.

"Evening, Mina." Coming to her side of the counter, Jane Putnam greeted her with a smile. "You want something to eat?"

"No, but thank you." Mina returned Jane's smile.

The petite barmaid was one of the few true friends she had. Most people viewed Mina as an opportunity to curry favor with either one of her brothers: Joaquin managed several gaming hells, and Cyrus was a renowned pugilist. But Jane didn't care about that. Even after she'd broken up with Cyrus, she'd kept in contact with Mina.

Jane had said no one could pick their family. Mina

shouldn't be held accountable for the sins of her brother. If only Jane believed that about herself—an air of sadness clung to her since her brother had been imprisoned in Newgate. He'd been caught trying to break into a house by a Metropolitan Police officer.

"Have you heard from Penn recently?" Mina asked.

"Went to see him last week." Jane turned around, pouring an ale for another customer. She slid the tankard to him across the bar and then returned her attention to their conversation. "Nothing much ever changes. I suppose that's good. Zacharias keeps telling me to have patience. Says that when the time is right, Penn will be freed."

"I'm so sorry." Mina reached for Jane's hand, squeezing it. "I know how hard this has been for you both."

"Another day in Ratcliffe." Jane sighed, her eyes narrowing as another customer waved her down. "I wish I had more time to stay and talk, but the drink orders are never-ending tonight. I'll send Charlie over."

Mina tried to keep the excitement out of her voice as she thanked Jane. Though it was well-known she'd been friends with Charlie Thatcher since they were children, she didn't want anyone to know how much she truly cared for him.

For the next few minutes, she watched the crowd. She recognized a few of Charlie's friends, but mostly the gang was unknown to her. Over in the corner of the room were Kate and Daniel O'Reilly, laughing as Jane stopped by with their plates of mutton. Mina knew them by reputation only. Kate had been one of Chapman's best fences before marrying O'Reilly, and she was good friends with Jane.

"Minnie!" Charlie called, hurrying over to the bar. He slid behind the counter, smiling at her and making her stomach flip precariously.

He'd changed so much over the years, transforming from a

lanky boy to a tall Corinthian, all lean muscle and strength. But the one thing that remained the same was that boyish smile.

"Six and tips, right?" He waited for her to nod, though he knew her drink better than she did. After all, he'd been the one to introduce her to the whisky cut with small beer.

She loved that about him.

He was the only man who ever bothered to ask what *she* wanted.

He filled a tankard and passed it to her. "So, I see you've got Isaac guardin' you again tonight. He's back there pawin' at Becks."

"Thank you." She accepted the drink, wrapping her fingers around the tankard's handle and taking a small sip. The whisky glided down her throat with the dangerous slink of irresistible temptation, slow and steady. She allowed herself one more sip before setting the tankard back onto the countertop. "Is Becks all right? Should I go over there?"

Charlie shook his head. "Saw him pay. Becks will be furious if you interrupt her while she's workin'. Once I asked her if she wanted another drink, and she threw a bloody plate at my head."

"Did it hit you?" Mina raised the tankard to her lips, drinking.

Charlie tapped the left side of his head, right above his ear. "Damned if it didn't bleed, too. Thought I was gonna need a loblolley boy."

Mina shuddered. "Don't you dare go to the 'doctors' in Ratcliffe. If you need medical attention, Cyrus knows a man."

In the rookeries, any man could trawl the streets with a cart claiming to be a surgeon. The idea of Charlie being operated on by any of those quack doctors terrified her.

Charlie flashed her another grin. "Look at you, worryin' about me. Makes a man feel wanted."

She swallowed, his words setting tremors off in her belly. She did want him—more than he knew—and in ways that she wasn't supposed to know about as an innocent maid.

But they could never be.

She did the only thing possible: she changed the subject. She looked back from Charlie to Isaac, who had his hand halfway down the prostitute's shirt. "At least *somebody* enjoys Isaac being here."

"Don't know why Joaquin keeps sendin' him." Charlie frowned. "You're safe here. I'll protect you. Always."

Mina pursed her lips, staring into the six and tips as though it could provide all the answers. "Even with the peace between the gangs, he says he doesn't trust anyone but a King to watch over me."

"Because *his* men are so much better than us." Charlie's frown deepened, becoming that scowl she knew all too well— the one he wore any time they talked about her brother's rival gang.

A precarious truce had held for the last two decades between the three East End gangs: the Chapman Street Gang of Ratcliffe and Wapping; Joaquin's Kings of Whitechapel, Bethnal Green, and Stepney Green; and Jasper Finn's Tanners of Jacob's Island and Bermondsey. Members could travel throughout London without fear of attack, as long as they refrained from doing business in rival territories. But the execution of resurrectionist Finn a few months prior had upset the balance of power—without a clear leader to take his place, both Chapman and the Kings were chomping at the bit to seize his holdings. From the snippets of conversations that she'd overheard at home the last few weeks, she guessed the Kings were going to make a move soon for Finn's most profitable enterprises.

She was *supposed* to care about the Kings. Supposed to believe that they were the best, always justified in their actions, because a member of the Mason family had led the gang for the last forty years.

Yet Mina had never felt at home among Joaquin's men, and she certainly didn't find any of them appealing. How could she when she'd grown up with Charlie by her side? From the night they'd first met thirteen years ago, he'd been there by her side through every trial and triumph of her life. Her father's death. When she'd fallen climbing the big oak tree outside her bedroom window and broken her arm. When Cyrus was unfaithful to Jane, ending their engagement and any hope she had of having a sister.

So, while she didn't care about the gangs, she cared about Charlie. She wanted to run her thumb across his lips, smooth away those frown lines until the boy she'd known reappeared. That boy could always make her laugh, even when the situation was dire.

Maybe that boy had died long ago, and the man left in his stead was Chapman through and through, loyal to his thief brothers.

They meant more than she did.

Chapman had taken Charlie in, given him a home when his father passed. Mina was tolerated here because of Charlie, but she never, ever forgot where Charlie belonged.

At the opposite end of the bar, a patron waved at him, trying to get his attention. Charlie nodded swiftly, but instead of helping the man, he grabbed a threadbare towel from behind the counter. He swiped at the surface, even though it already gleamed from his earlier efforts. He continued cleaning as the patron made a rude gesture and stood up, leaving the bar area.

"You can take care of the other customers," she told him, her voice soft yet firm. "I don't need to be watched."

"Wouldn't dream of it." The flush on his cheeks belied his

protest—she'd caught him red-handed, and he knew it. "Jane can see to the other customers. The boys like her better."

Mina shook her head, wishing her damnable heart wouldn't squeeze so at Charlie's guardian act. She ought to be irritated with him—he was one more man trying to shelter her from the realities of life. Yet his watchfulness never felt like a gilded cage; it filled her with a hazy warmth, like being snuggled in a fluffy blanket with a steaming cup of tea between her hands. Underneath Charlie's observant gaze, she always felt special. Worthy.

Appreciated for who she was, instead of a prize to be auctioned off to the highest bidder.

Yet that was her reality. The men in her life *ought* to be sheltering her from that—instead of nonexistent danger—but they never did.

Two nights ago, she'd overheard Joaquin discussing her engagement with a wealthy, far older business associate, as though it was already done and negotiated. Despite the fact that she'd never once been consulted. Despite the fact that she barely knew Nigel Donaldson. He'd been a friend of her father's. But Papa had died years ago, and Donaldson hadn't been as close with her brothers.

Until now, when he'd appeared from the shadows of the past because apparently at nineteen, she was an appropriate bride for a man who had known her when she was but a child.

The very idea made her stomach roil. She gripped the tankard in her hand again, but this time, she took a long drag from it. The whisky flooded her throat, no longer the sweet taste of victory over her bodyguard. Now it tasted stale, like sweat and punishment, so vile upon her tongue that she sputtered and coughed as it sloshed down her throat.

"Easy there," Charlie cautioned. "I've never seen you drink like that. What's botherin' you?"

Her grip tightened against the mug. No use telling Charlie

her problems. He'd want to try and fix them, and there wasn't a damn thing he could do to get her out of this. No, she'd have to convince Joaquin herself that Donaldson wasn't a proper match for her.

"I thought Isaac might be finished with the woman soon." It was a lie, of course, but she was proud of herself for how smoothly she delivered the line. "I don't want him to tell Joaquin I've been drinking, as it'll get me another lecture on propriety."

Charlie raised a disbelieving brow. "Minnie, I'll serve you in a cup and tell him it's tea if that's what you're worried about."

"Thank you," she said for the second time that night. It still didn't feel like enough, for all the times that Charlie had shown her kindness throughout the years. Him and his quiet acceptance, never once asking more of her than she could give. While the rest of the world treated her like a fragile doll, Charlie allowed her to be a real woman.

A woman with feelings and a bleeding, broken heart, mourning what she could never have.

"I'm fine, really," she assured him, breathing a sigh of relief as another patron tried to flag him down. "But look, somebody else is trying to get your attention."

He followed her gaze, grimacing as he recognized the two men on the other side of the bar. "That's Jason Baines and Matthew Harper."

Baines was the son of Chapman's leader and a veritable hothead. She didn't recognize the other man, who was all lofty leanness and sinews, while Baines was short, arrogant stockiness.

"Then you'd better go."

Charlie hesitated, but when she shooed him with a wave of her hand, he gave in. "I'll be back later. You stay here. If you need anythin', tell Jane, and she'll get it for you."

She nodded, watching him as he headed down the bar, his fit form as familiar to her as her own silhouette. At the motion of Baines, Charlie untied his apron, coming out from the bar. He ran a hand through his short brown locks as Harper spoke, nodding in agreement. Then he was gone, following them, his quick, fluid stride separating him from her as he headed toward the back. She lost sight of the trio in the dense crowd that filled almost every table.

Mina cupped her hands around the tankard, wishing she could stay in this spot where she was safe and didn't have to face her future. Where she could pretend, for a few minutes at least, that Charlie was hers to claim.

She looked about the room, trying to locate him. Her gaze came to rest on Kate and Daniel O'Reilly again. Kate leaned forward, placing a kiss on Daniel's cheek. His entire face seemed to light up, his green eyes twinkling with such joy that Mina's heart tightened.

God, how she wanted that life. The doting husband. A child on her knee. The love, real, impossible love, blossoming from a true connection versus a business merger and an impressive dowry.

She frowned into her half-empty tankard, silently cursing her decision to go to the Three Boars. How could she have thought that it'd be a good idea to be near Charlie tonight, so close she could reach out and touch him? It was torture. Had been torture for years.

Before, she'd at least had the *hope* of a good future.

"What's a pretty gel like ye doin', frownin' like tha'?" A man's voice, coarse like sandpaper and thick with the slur of drink, cut into her reverie.

Bloody, bloody hell.

She'd been so caught up in her own predicament that she hadn't noticed him approach. As she lifted her head to meet his gaze, he smiled at her, his bloodshot eyes focusing in on her lips.

"I'm Al McNair. And ye are?" He sidled closer, looming above her stool. He smelled of stale ale and backwater sewage as if he'd dunked himself in the Thames and then decided to upend a keg atop his greasy, dirty straw-colored locks.

Before she could stop herself, she'd wrinkled her nose and drawn back from him.

His expression transformed instantly from leering to vengeful. "Ay, bitch, ye think ye're too good fer me?"

He leaned closer, his breath stiflingly hot on her neck, the noxious scent of him clouding her nostrils. He was too close.

"No," she gasped out, her eyes scanning the room for Charlie. He would make everything right. He always did.

But she couldn't find him. Her heartbeat sounded in her ears, swift and hectic, echoing her desire to flee.

"Good," the man said, but he didn't appear pleased. His eyes had darkened. Before he had met her gaze—now he stared solely at her bodice, making her skin feel as though a thousand ants crawled upon her.

Mina knew his intentions. She spoke the language of pain and power, of men who derived pleasure from hurting others. Men like that only respected those with *more* power.

But devil take her, she was a Mason. Her name carried weight, and she needed no one's help. Whether or not her brothers believed it, she could fight her own battles.

"Mina Mason," she said, her voice so loud, so clear that several tables' worth turned around to stare at her with rapt attention. "My name is Mina Mason, and you need to leave me be."

A group of sailors by the door let out a hoot of approval, whilst another table of Chapman members that she recognized vaguely sat up straighter, their hands automatically dropping to the knives sheathed at their sides.

I'm a Mason.

She needed to remember that power did not always mean knives and bullets. If she had learned anything from Joaquin over the years, it was that power could also be a well-placed word, a cut direct that stripped a business associate of his funds.

Raising herself up to her full—albeit still quite short—height, she assumed the cold, distant mien that had led to her being christened the Ice Princess of the Kings. They didn't need to know it was all a lie, and that the ice within her veins was nothing more than frozen dreams.

"That's right," she said, with a nod at McNair. "You know my brothers, Joaquin and Cyrus. You know what they'll do to you if you so much as utter another foul word to me."

"They's got no 'old 'ere," McNair said. "Ye're in Chapman territory, lass. Ain't nobody gonna save ye 'ere."

She swallowed down the bile that rose in her throat, her fist wrapping tight against the fabric of her gown. Her brothers weren't here—what good was the threat of vengeance if she was dead?

She searched the crowd again, eyes wide. No sign of Charlie. Where was Isaac? Wasn't it his job to protect her? The one time she needed him, he'd disappeared. God, she regretted telling him that since he had to accompany her, he might as well enjoy himself.

She'd been so *sure* she'd be safe.

But there was no one to rescue her.

She'd have to save herself.

So, when McNair took his eyes off her to reach for his drink, she slipped off the stool faster than she ever had. She dodged to the left when he grabbed for her. He was drunk already, so his fingers touched air instead of the sleeve of her muslin gown.

She'd gone from the pot to the waiting fire, for as she flung herself away from McNair, she slammed into the path of another man making his way to a nearby table. She caught sight of big, wide shoulders and a scruffy chin before her face met his burly chest head-on. Strong, calloused hands gripped her shoulders, righting her before releasing her.

"I didn't mean to—" she stammered as she stepped back from him. In Kings's territory, she wouldn't have had to apologize. The man would have bowed before her, simply to avoid retaliation from her brothers.

"'Tis my mistake, lass," he said, his deep voice containing no traces of resentment.

She had no time to thank him. McNair lumbered toward them, his ham-fists clenched at his sides. Mina gulped, wishing she'd taken the dirk Cyrus had tried to hand her that night. They'd passed the point where she could bluster her way out of this.

Perhaps Joaquin had been wrong. Perhaps power really was only weapons and blood.

"There ye are, Jones," McNair said. "'Arper's been lookin' for ye. Run off now. I got this 'ere bunter."

Her breath sucked in at such harsh language. She was no man's whore, and certainly not a diseased one. McNair tracked her startled inhale with a sick grin.

The man she'd run into—Jones—looked from McNair to her, his eyes narrowing beneath his bushy brows. He was a mammoth of a man, all muscle and strength, yet somehow, he didn't intimidate her.

"Don't know 'bout that," Jones pronounced after a long moment of silence, each word slow and clear, as he'd sounded when addressing her a second before. She got the impression he rarely spoke—and when he did, most people listened.

Except for McNair, who apparently had enough blue ruin

in him to make him unwisely bold. "Back off, Jones. She's mine for th' takin', ye 'ear? Me blunt's as good as any man's. Ye can 'ave 'er when I'm done."

Jones contemplated this with a frown. Mina stepped closer to him. Yet as Jones stood there, engaging in a noiseless battle of egos with McNair, the two men from before approached. Harper and Baines, followed by—bless the good Lord, Charlie.

Fueled by spirits and perhaps a good dose of self-aggrandizing delusion, McNair viewed their approach as a stroke of good fate for him. "'Ey, mates!" He waved them over. "Look 'ere wha' Mason sent us for dinner—'is little sister. Shall we show 'im what we do to Kings's cun—"

Before he could finish the sentence, Charlie hauled off and slugged him. A sickeningly wet snap echoed through the room, as the bone in McNair's nose broke. He staggered back, one hand grabbing wildly for the table behind him to steady his caving knees and the other pressed to his nose in a futile attempt to staunch the streaming blood.

But it kept coming, that red, red, red shiny slickness, coating his lips. He let out a muffled gurgle as he sucked in one breath, then another, his gasps coming out in garbled wheezes.

She couldn't move. She kept staring at McNair, fixed to that point. Even as the men at the table McNair leaned on for support pushed him back up and rooted him on. Even as Isaac skidded out from the back closet, doing up the flap of his breeches as he ran. He made it halfway to her, pushing through the crowd. So intent was Isaac on approaching her, he didn't see the Chapman man sneak up behind him and cold cock him with a broken bottle.

Unconscious, Isaac fell to the ground with a sickening thud. The crowd cheered wildly, while panic clutched at Mina's throat.

The chant of "Fight! Fight!" rang out throughout the public

house, and every person seemed to swivel in their seat toward them.

Because there was Charlie, standing with his fists raised at the ready, his toned legs spread apart in a fighter's stance, his broad shoulders back and his jaw locked. His brown eyes were narrowed. Yet the darkness, the unbridled rage she saw in those eyes sent a frisson of eager heat through her, belaying her cloying fear.

She had never seen Charlie like this. So masculine.

So protective.

Of her reputation. Her honor.

Of *her*.

These thoughts flashed through her mind with alarming alacrity, in the space of no more than three seconds, though time seemed to slow around her. Awareness skittered down her spine, and that new, enticing warmth lapped at her core. She hated when Cyrus and Joaquin defended her, but Charlie's protectiveness felt different. A show of support without an expectation that she'd fall in line with his demands.

She couldn't stop to analyze these unfamiliar sensations, for McNair was hacking and spitting out blood onto the floor. His mouth open wide, his teeth as red as the fluid pouring down his face. She was too slow, too dulled by the shock and awe that echoed through her in competing waves. Time started to speed up, so quickly, her gasp was swallowed by the noise that was no longer a muted roar but instead an untenable din.

And again, there was Charlie, darting to the right as McNair surged forward, swinging his fists at the air. Charlie delivered a hook to McNair's ear. The blow wasn't hard enough to distract the man from pursuing him further. Then another hard slap by McNair, a grappling of bodies, and a surge of excitement from the crowd, as Charlie's wild haymaker slammed into McNair's chest.

For a second—one precious second—it seemed as though the fight was over, and Charlie had won. Mina took a step forward. McNair had fallen back against the table, the breath knocked out of him. He spat out more blood and snot, the vile combination landing with a plop. Yet he did not stay away. The men at the table urged him on, shoving him at Charlie, giving him encouragement to continue the attack.

McNair came at him, pounding a ham fist into Charlie's jaw. When he reeled back, McNair slammed the full weight of his big, bulky body into his opponent's shoulder.

Charlie went down, impacting the ground with a hard crunch.

"Charlie! God, no, Charlie!" She heard her scream before she realized the words had left her mouth. Before she could rush forward and try to block him—before she could do anything at all besides shriek helplessly—she felt a hand on her arm, pulling her away. She tilted her head to the side, one eye on the person behind her, while still trying to keep watch over Charlie.

Jane's fingers dug into the lavender fabric of her sleeve. "You need to leave."

When Mina tried to slap her hand away, tried to move forward again, Jane's grip tightened. She was strong for such a small woman. "*Now*." Jane hauled her away with such firmness and speed Mina stumbled. Jane righted her but kept on tugging.

"Let go of me," Mina demanded, planting her feet on the floor.

"You think you'll save him? Wrong. They'll eat you alive," Jane hissed. "You, a *Mason*, were the cause of this, and Chapman won't forget. Come on."

Mina barely heard her. How could she leave Charlie there? The hollers of the crowd were like knives to her heart, as they berated Charlie for not getting up and fighting. "I have to help him."

325

"He's up," Jane said, pointing as Charlie accepted a hand up from Jones. "Now move your bloody arse. Charlie did this so you'd be safe. Don't make it worthless."

She started to protest, but Kate and Daniel O'Reilly sidled up to them. Daniel slid to the other side of Mina, grabbing hold of her. She could have resisted Jane, but three people? Mina was surrounded.

The lull in the fight had made the audience thirstier for blood. Altercations—first verbal, soon to become physical—popped up around the room. A jagged bottle whizzed past Mina's ear, almost nicking her face before shattering upon the ground. All around her, men were beginning to choose sides, needing little reason to draw blood. They were poor and hungry and tired, and the fight made them feel alive for a few minutes.

"Go or die," Jane snarled, yanking her arm.

So, Mina fled, a coward in chaos, allowing them to lead her around sailing tankards and men engaged in fisticuffs. When they reached Isaac's prone body, she attempted to help him, but Jane urged her onwards.

They navigated a circuitous path, seemingly two steps forward and one step back, the straight route to the back entrance blocked by fighting men. And as she ran, the cheers of the intoxicated onlookers rose in her ears, and she hoped to God that Charlie would survive this fight.

Books by Erica Monroe

I Spy a Duke

The Rookery Rogues

A Dangerous Invitation

Secrets in Scarlet

Beauty and the Rake

Stealing the Rogue's Heart

Gothic Brides

The Mad Countess

The Determined Duchess

The Scandalous Widow

Sign up for Erica's newsletter at ericamonroe.com and receive a free, exclusive short story!

About the Author

USA Today Bestselling Author Erica Monroe writes dark, gritty historical romance. Her current series include Gothic Brides (Regency Gothic romances) and The Rookery Rogues (pre-Victorian gritty working-class romance). She was a finalist in the published historical category for the prestigious Daphne du Maurier Award for Excellence in Romantic Suspense, and her books have been recommended reads at Fresh Fiction, Smexy Books, SBTB, and All About Romance. When not writing, she drinks too much coffee, listens to a lot of true crime podcasts, and reads a ton of books. She lives in the suburbs of North Carolina with her husband, daughter, and many rescue pets.

Erica loves to hear from readers, so please feel free to visit her website at ericamonroe.com.